Praise for dating is murder

"Wollie Shelly is big-chested, big-hearted, and just as big a smash here as in her debut . . . Lively prose, seamless plotting—and, good golly, there's Wollie."

—*Kirkus* (starred review)

"Wollie . . . is spot-on perfect, humorous, and poignant enough by turns to win the series new fans and make Kozak a contender in the never-ending quest for the perfect quirky mystery."

—*Los Angeles Times Book Review*

"Kozak has a breezy style and delightful wit that leave us with just one question: Where's book 3?"

—*Entertainment Weekly* (A-)

"Rates right up there with Janet Evanovich . . . The characters are zany; the prose is witty in this whodunit."

—*Green Bay Press-Gazette*

"Featuring wonderful characters . . . Kozak's smart whodunit is as fresh and funny as her first 'dating' mystery."

—*Library Journal* (starred review)

"Kozak's novel is bright, breezy and full of chick-lit cheek—an ideal companion for a long, relaxing weekend."

—*The Orlando Sentinel*

"Kozak's writing is to die for."

—*Lincoln Journal Star*

"Combining lighthearted humor and romance with a suspenseful plot, [Kozak] has created a compelling story."

—*Chicago Sun-Times*

"This delightful follow-up to Kozak's first outing surpasses its predecessor and will have readers anticipating Wollie's third adventure."

—*Booklist*

"I can only hope that [DATING IS MURDER] will be just the second in a long series of Wollie books because it's rare to find a novel that's funnier than most sitcoms or films. Plus, I've just got to spend more time with that luscious Simon."

—*Edge Boston*

dating
is
murder

Also by Harley Jane Kozak

Dating Dead Men

dating is murder

a novel

Harley Jane Kozak

Broadway Books *New York*

Visit our Web site at www.broadwaybooks.com

First Broadway Books trade paperback edition published 2006

Book design by Chris Welch

The Library of Congress has cataloged the hardcover as:
Kozak, Harley Jane, 1957–
Dating is murder / Harley Jane Kozak.—1st ed.
    p.   cm.
1. Women detectives—California—Los Angeles—Fiction.
2. Reality television programs—Fiction. 3. Dating (Social
customs)—Fiction. 4. Los Angeles (Calif.)—Fiction. 5. Missing
persons—Fiction. 6. Mate selection—Fiction. I. Title.

PS3611.O75D38 2005
813'.6—dc22
2004050225

ISBN 0-7679-2124-0

1 3 5 7 9 10 8 6 4 2

For my mother,
Dorothy Taraldsen Kozak,
who would've gone to the ends of the earth
for us . . . and no doubt still does.

1

"**M**oth harmonica."

That's what it sounded like, the guttural, heavy-accented syllables coming through my answering machine. A piece of haiku, until the woman rattled off an almost unintelligible series of digits that went on and on, like a credit card number or the miles from earth to Jupiter. I picked up the telephone.

"Hi, this is Wollie," I said. "Who's this?"

"California? America? *Ja?*"

"Yes, California, America. Who's this?"

"Encino?"

"No, not Encino, West Hollywood. Forty minutes away, traffic permitting. Who's this?"

"*Ja, ja,* who this?" she asked.

"That's what I'm asking," I said. "Who are *you?*"

"I am Moth Harmonica."

Okay, I've heard worse. My own name, Wollstonecraft Shelley, is no picnic, especially for a girl. Or woman, as my friend Fredreeq insists I refer to myself. "Who are you trying to call, Moth?" I asked.

"Who are you?"

"No, who are—" I stopped. This could take a while, and I didn't have a while. "I think you have the wrong number," I said, and this brought forth a flurry of words that started with *"Nein! Nein!"* and ended with "Annika."

"Annika?" I said. "Wait. Not moth—you're—mother. Of Annika. You're Mrs. Glück?"

There was an excited assent, lots of *Ja! Ja!*s, and another flurry of words. I closed my eyes and took a deep breath, trying to dispel a sudden bad feeling.

"*Meine* Annika," Mrs. Glück said, "called not tomorrow—no, no, yesterday—and yesterday is Sunday, we call every week Sunday. So I leave message for host family, but called me not back. I feel for Annika *Gefahr*, um, danger, *sie ist in* big danger, as *sie* call not Sunday."

I was nodding now. My friend Annika had called her mother from my apartment the previous week. "She would freak out if I did not call each Sunday," Annika had said. "But she will call me back so it will not be on your bill." Which was why Mrs. Glück had my number.

I said, "I'd really like to help you, but I have no idea where Annika is. She's tutoring me in math, and we were supposed to meet last night"—I hesitated, not wanting to admit how I'd worried, thinking, *Annika's never even late*—"and she didn't show."

"Ah, *Gott im Himmel*, *sie* is dead."

"No, I'm sure she's not dead, I'm sure she's—" The doorbell rang. "Can you hold on?"

I zipped through the kitchen and living room and opened the door to Fredreeq, told her to give me two minutes, and zipped back to the kitchen. "Mrs. Glück?" I said. "I'm sure Annika will turn up, and if I hear from her first—"

"*Nein, nein*, for me you must to find her. The host family call me not back, and the agency call me not back, no one in United States of America to—"

"But if she's really missing, I'm sure her host family will contact the police—"

"*Nein*, no *Polizei*, no trouble—you are friend, *ja*? So you are to ask host family what is happen. For my daughter. *Mein Kind.*"

Fredreeq, having followed me into the kitchen, pointed to her watch and mouthed the words "Joey" and "double-parked." I nodded and waved her off. "Okay," I said. "Do you have the host family's number? All I have is Annika's line, with her machine." On which I'd already left two messages.

Minutes later I hung up and turned to Fredreeq, who was studying the contents of my refrigerator. It was early evening in late November, dark in my kitchen, but my friend was illuminated by the utility bulb. It was enough. She wore a tight, fringed jumpsuit in hot pink, low-cut with a big plastic zipper running the length of it. She had the kind of va-va-va-boom body that could pull this off, and the kind of temperament that would want to. Her hair this week was as blond as mine, not unusual in Los Angeles, but whereas I had pale skin to go with it, Fredreeq was black, a less common combination. "Where's your water?" she asked.

"In the sink."

"You don't have bottled water? What do you take on the road?"

"I don't take water on the road."

"Sister, you have got to change your ways," she said, herding me into the living room. "You have cosmetic responsibilities now. Who is this Monica person?"

"Annika, not Monica. Our Annika, from the show. Her mother in Germany says she's—disappeared." I grabbed my keys and backpack, alarmed at the word I'd just said.

"And who does the mother think you are, the FBI?"

"She doesn't know who I am, she just happened to have my phone number. She can't reach the host family—Annika's an au pair, did you know that?"

Fredreeq handed me my jean jacket. "What are you doing answering your own phone? We gotta get you thinking like a celebrity."

The word "celebrity" made me want to hide under the bed with a bag of Oreos. But Fredreeq had overstated it. I was only a celebrity to those rare people who watched a TV reality show called *Biological Clock*—too few in number, according to the Nielsen ratings, to materially affect my life. I reminded myself of this as I followed Fredreeq out of the apartment, down the stairs, and out to the street.

Rush-hour noise from Santa Monica Boulevard accosted us. There was pedestrian traffic too as we walked down Larrabee, mostly male, as befits a neighborhood known as Boystown. Fredreeq attracted her share of attention, her skintight jumpsuit an object of desire. West Hollywood is a bastion of gay and lesbian culture, which I, as a heterosexual female, found comforting in ways I didn't exactly understand.

I caught myself really looking at people, on the street, in cars. Looking, illogically, maybe, for someone considerably shorter than I, brown-haired, apple-cheeked, pretty. A girl in the last days of her teens. Annika.

"There's Joey," Fredreeq said, waving to a green Mercedes stuck in slow traffic on Santa Monica, a mass of red hair visible in the driver's seat. "What's she doing circling the block? I told her to stay put. C'mon, let's catch up." She grabbed my hand and we ran as fast as her three-inch heels allowed, click-click-clicking our way to Joey.

My friends were driving me to the night's location of *Biological Clock.* The reality show featured three women *d'un certain âge,* as Joey put it, dating in rotation three men of various ages, so the TV audience could ultimately vote on which combination of genes should produce a child, with or without romantic involvement on the part of the chosen couple. I was one of the women.

It hadn't been my idea.

Here's how it happened. I'd been—okay, still was—recovering from a broken engagement to a guy named Doc. Doc had some issues that stood between him and marriage, namely, a wife and the certainty of an ugly custody battle for their daughter, Ruby, once the wife became an ex-wife. The wife was keeping Ruby in Japan, so Doc had taken a job in Taiwan to be nearby, production work on an American film called *Mao, the Movie,* which threatened to go on as long as the Cultural Revolution. Custody would be a problem for six years, until Ruby turned eighteen, and Doc felt I shouldn't wait for him. Joey and Fredreeq agreed. I felt otherwise, but nobody seemed to care about my opinions any more than Chairman Mao had cared about the opinions of the bourgeoisie.

Joey's husband, meanwhile, had invested money in this reality show, *Biological Clock,* which had inspired Joey and Fredreeq to send my audition video to the casting director. I hadn't known I'd made an audition video. I'd thought I was being interviewed for Fredreeq's niece's sociology project. Apparently, though, me talking about my dating history was compelling stuff. Also, I was the right age and had attributes—big chest, long legs, and height, six feet of it—that made a nice visual contrast to the other two front-runner women contestants, and I'd thus beaten out several hundred hopefuls for the job. Not that I'd wanted the job. I'd turned it down flat once it was explained to me. I found the premise of the show cheesy, despite the disclaimer at the end of each episode that no couple would be required to have sex or bear children. As for fame, I'd have been happy to fork over my fifteen minutes to someone else, the way senators give away their floor time in debates to fellow senators.

But then *Biological Clock* had mentioned money. Despite the low budget, I'd be paid five hundred dollars a week for two nights' work, unusual for reality TV. And that wasn't all. The producers had invested in a number of other businesses, including a health maintenance organization offering benefits to the winning contestants and their dependents, current and future. Some people say insurance isn't sexy, but for those with dependent paranoid schizophrenic brothers on pricey antipsychotic medication, it's sexy enough.

A horn honked.

"Girl, you got some kind of bad gene that makes you change lanes every twenty seconds?" Fredreeq asked Joey.

"Yeah, it's called effective driving."

"Well, maybe they do that in Nebraska to get around the cows, but here people get shot for those maneuvers." Fredreeq and Joey had an ongoing city mouse, country mouse routine, although Joey was no more country than any other ex-model/actress who'd lived in L.A., New York, and Paris for the last fifteen years. "And can we turn down this twangy banjo stuff? You want people to think you're a hick?"

"I am a hick. Hey, Wollie," Joey threw over her shoulder, "why so quiet?"

"Cell phone." I'd dialed the number Mrs. Glück had given me for Annika's host family. In Encino, a machine answered. The voice was warm, chatty, female. "Hi there. You've reached the Quinns. Gene, Maizie, Emma, Annika, and Mr. Snuggles can't come to the phone right now. But leave us a message and we'll call you back. Bye-bye. Woof."

"Hi," I said, envisioning the people Annika had described. "I'm trying to reach Annika, your au pair. If she's not around, I'd appreciate a call from any of the Quinns. Preferably one of the humans." I spelled out my name and repeated my home and cell-phone numbers.

"Is that our Annika? From the show?" Joey asked. "How's she doing?"

"I'm not sure," I said. "She seems to be sort of . . . missing."

Joey turned to me. Traffic was at another dead stop as we neared Beverly Hills. Fredreeq had switched on the interior car light to rummage through her purse, and the glow made Joey's eyes very green and her face very white against her auburn hair. She was more than beautiful; she was intriguing, with a subtle scar running from temple to chin, white on white, a half-moon. "What do you mean, missing?" she said.

"She didn't show up for my math tutorial last night. And she didn't call her mom in Germany, which is her Sunday night ritual, so her mom is seriously upset, and she doesn't know a soul in America. Except me. And the host family, who's not returning her calls."

"Interesting."

"What is?"

Traffic moved. Joey faced forward. The Mercedes inched ahead. Our eyes met in the rearview mirror. "Annika," she said. "On the set last week, she was asking people where she could get hold of a gun."

2

"**T**he set" is one of those show biz terms that always makes me think of dancing girls in the forties doing the cancan on a stage at the MGM studio, or maybe a street in the Old West, the saloon and general store and jail all false fronts with nothing but fields behind. The set of *Biological Clock*, however, was whatever bar, bowling alley, or bistro Bing Wooster and the producers could persuade to let us film in. It wasn't filming but taping, as Joey pointed out, but Bing, who had filmmaking aspirations, had us all using movie lingo.

It was going on nine P.M. The set du jour was a restaurant called Pine on Beverly Boulevard, on a site that had seen a lot of restaurants come and go over the years. The fact that Pine was the kind that let a show like *B.C.* shoot there did not bode well for its longevity.

"Keep it moving, folks," Bing Wooster said to the onlookers gathered with us on the sidewalk in front of Pine. "Come on, it's L.A. You never saw a film shoot before? Never saw a gorgeous six-foot blonde? Go watch her on TV. Eleven P.M. weeknights, ZPX."

I stopped scanning the crowd for teenage German girls and tried to look unconcerned, as if Bing's speech had nothing to do with me, as if the sidewalk were full of six-foot blondes wearing too much makeup. Bing was our big kahuna. Joey had explained that most shows have producers and directors and cameramen, but *Biological Clock*, being low budget, had Bing. Bing made creative decisions, operated the camera, and generally played God, six nights a week. Bing had an assistant, Paul, who did everything else: lighting, heavy lifting, crowd dispersal, and sending out for pizza. There was also Isaac, the sound guy, but he was so quiet that, despite his being the size of a grizzly bear, we tended to forget he was there. At the moment, Paul was changing tape, which was why Bing and I were stuck on the sidewalk, waiting to videotape me walking into Pine.

"Bing?" I said. "When did you last see Annika?"

Bing frowned at a figure halfway down the street, a bulked-up guy with a goatee. "Who? Annika? Saturday, maybe. I don't know. Paul, let's go, let's go, let's go."

Paul nodded, his baseball cap bent over the Betacam, a twenty-five-pound video camera the size of a small dog, something I was trying to make friends with.

I tried again. "Because Joey says—"

"Oh, well, if *Joey* says, let's all pause to listen to *Joey*, our instant *producer*..." Animosity curdled his voice. Since Joey's husband was the new investor in Bad Seed Productions, Bing was convinced that Joey was there to spy on and eventually wrest power from him. "What does our esteemed Mrs. Rafferty-Horowitz say?"

"That Annika talked to you about buying a gun," I said.

Bing stared at me for a moment, then glanced at the goateed guy down the street. "What am I, the NRA? Paul, thirty seconds to reload that camera or you're fired."

"I can't be fired, I'm not paid enough."

I said, "Because she's disappeared, Bing. Annika. Have you noticed?"

Bing looked at me again. "What do you mean, disappeared?"

"I mean that nobody's been able to reach her for—well, I don't know how long, exactly, but at least twenty-four hours. Which is scary. It's not like her."

Bing's eyes grew wide, stricken. "She's not here? I have a call in to the German guys tonight, I need her to translate."

Paul's baseball cap tilted up, revealing an acne-scarred face. "She hasn't been around all weekend."

"Christ. And you didn't think to tell me?"

"She's not on the call sheet," Paul said.

"She's not on the payroll, idiot, but we have a deal—she talks to Munich for me every time we—. Christ, get that camera loaded, then see if Sharon's still in the office, tell her to find someone who speaks German. What time's it in Munich?"

"Nine hours ahead," Paul said.

"Tell Sharon she's got till midnight." Bing ran both hands through his preternaturally thick black hair and groaned.

Paul's eyes met mine, mirroring my concern, then went back to his camera.

Fredreeq approached with a handful of makeup tools, from which she selected a lip pencil. "Don't think about this now," she said. "I've got so much base on you, if you frown, you'll crack. Open your mouth and hold still. I think Mac's drying out your lips, I'm gonna try Clinique. You're not licking them, are you? Don't answer. Hold still."

Fredreeq was not a professional makeup artist, but she'd worked as a facialist for years and was grabbing this chance to break into show business. She'd hung out on the set during my first episodes, wormed her way into Bing's affections, bad-mouthed Venus, the original hair-and-makeup person, saying she made everyone look like drag queens, then offered her own services at bargain-basement prices. Bing gave her Mondays and Thursdays on a trial basis. Mondays and Thursdays were my work nights, so Fredreeq got to work on me and all three men, but not the other two women contestants. Venus, not happy about having her hours cut by a third, was now committed to one of "her" girls getting the audience vote, and had declared all-out war. Fredreeq was therefore heavily invested in me winning the *B.C.* contest. I myself wouldn't have cared, if not for the health-care plan.

"Fredreeq," I said, when my lips were my own again. "Annika

hasn't been around the set. That's very weird. She considers this her second job, because Munich's planning a German version of the show and Bing promised to recommend her as a coproducer when she goes home. It's called *Biologische Uhr*, she talks about it all the time. Paul says—"

"I don't care what Paul says." Fredreeq waved a rabbit-hair makeup brush in my face. "I don't know where this girl is and you don't either. But we know where she isn't, which is inside that restaurant, hiding in a basket of chicken fingers. So you put her out of your mind and get some heat going between you and Carlito. I know it's not easy, with that piece of hair he's got sticking up in front like a unicorn, but there's a lot at stake here."

Fredreeq's worries were twofold: me winning the *Biological Clock* contest and the show finishing out the season. Our ratings were paltry, even for ZPX, where a 1.4 household rating was a big deal. We struggled for the million or so viewers reported to be watching us, and listened to rumors that ZPX planned to replace us with *Nearly Nude News*.

Twenty minutes later, I sat alongside Carlito Gibbons in a Naugahyde booth, watching him pick at his cowlick, as Paul-the-assistant placed a bottle of sake between us, the label prominently displayed. Takei Sake was the show's sponsor, and all six contestants drank sake, or tap water in sake cups, in every episode. Finally, Bing mounted the Betacam on his shoulder, hung over an adjoining booth like a toddler on an airplane, and started shooting.

Carlito, the youngest of the show's contestants, was handsome in a class-president way. He came to life when he'd had some sake or when the camera was on him, speaking without hesitation on any topic, a talent that fascinated me. "I'm a paralegal," he said, responding to the evening's Biographical Question. "People don't know the difference between a paralegal and a legal secretary. I'm more than a glorified file clerk. I draft the bones of the complaint, the lion's share, only a few critical details of which are filled in by the attorney."

"Hey, what's the difference between an attorney and a lawyer?" I asked. Bing had given me strict orders not to let Carlito go more than three sentences without interrupting him.

Carlito brightened. "Good question. I like to say, Every law school graduate is an attorney, but it takes an outstanding attorney to be a *lawyer*. People don't realize——"

"Cut!" Bing said. "Fine. Carlito, ask Wollie what she does for a living. Wollie, don't mumble. Sparkle. Be sexy. Head up. And don't look at the camera."

I nodded, feeling awkward, and tried to smile at Carlito. "Well, Carlito, I design greeting cards. I have my own line, the Good Golly Miss Wollies——they're alternative greetings, not the standard Happy Birthday to a Wonderful Nephew genre. Not that there's anything wrong with those. Nephews need birthday cards. I just don't do them. To supplement my income I'm painting a mural of frogs in the kitchen of a house in Sherman Oaks. Oh, and I'm working on getting a bachelor's degree in graphic arts. I'm finding math a little challenging."

Carlito had stopped listening and was checking out the menu.

"Cut," Bing said. "Okay, I've got some usable stuff. Let's bring in the doctor."

Following the Biographical Question, each *Biological Clock* episode featured an expert in the parenting field who raised hot-button issues that helped the viewing audience assess our parenting potential. The show wasn't big with the eighteen- to twenty-four-year-old demographic, but it had once won its time slot with whatever twenty-five- to forty-nine-year-old women were awake at that hour, which Bing liked to point out, in case this was as compelling to anyone else as it was to him.

Paul escorted to our table a fiftyish man in a good suit, who smiled broadly and shook hands all around. "Daniel Exeter. Hi. Sorry I'm late, I had an ectopic pregnancy to deal with."

"Where's your lab coat?" Bing asked. "Paul, didn't you tell him to bring a lab coat?"

Daniel Exeter looked taken aback. "It's in the car, but as I told Paul, it's not something I wear outside the clinic and——"

"It's all about visuals, Dan. Raises your IQ thirty points and establishes credibility, which is what TV is all about. Get it for him, Paul."

The doctor fished a valet-parking stub out of his pocket. "Porsche Carrera."

Paul took off at a trot. Bing eased himself out of the booth and said, "Right in here, Dan, opposite our stars. What are you drinking? Sake?"

"It's Daniel, actually. A glass of white wine will be fine."

"Too gay; let's go with Scotch rocks. And forget first names. To us, you're 'Doctor.' "

Bing got us situated. Paul came back with Dr. Exeter's lab coat, its Westside Fertility logo visible on the breast pocket. Joey, helping out, adjusted a light on a tripod and nodded to Fredreeq, standing by with a compact of pressed powder. As a former actress, Joey always knew what was going on ten minutes before Fredreeq and I did. Isaac, his ears covered with headphones, moved in with his boom, a large, fur-covered microphone on a broomstick.

Bing had Carlito ask the doctor which was better, sex or artificial insemination.

"Is anything better than sex?" Dr. Exeter asked. "Sorry, little joke. For the average couple trying to conceive, sex works just fine. However"—here he glanced at me—"when a woman enters the winter of her reproductive life, that fact becomes a fertility issue."

"Go ahead, Dan, ask her how old she is," Bing said. "No, don't look at me—never look at the camera. Look at Wollie. The girl."

Dr. Exeter turned back to me. "How old are you, Wollie?"

"I'm—"

"No, don't tell him, Wollie," Bing said. "Say something coy."

Behind him, Joey rolled her eyes. I said, "Actually, I don't mind telling—"

"Wollie! Just say, 'I'd rather not say.' "

"I—I'd rather not say," I said, hating myself for not being able to come up with something snappier. Also for setting feminism back a few years.

"All right," Dr. Exeter said, "let's assume you're a senior citizen, in ovarian terms. Late thirties, early forties." He leaned back and took a sip of his Scotch, then made a face. "Adoption, surrogacy, donor eggs, surrogacy *and* donor eggs, these are all options for late-in-life mothers. Trying to do it yourself at that point is a long, heartbreaking proposition. A thirty-five-year-old woman is fifty percent less likely than a twenty-year-old to conceive unassisted. A forty-year-old has a one in fifteen chance each month. At forty-five, you're like a vegan trying to contract mad cow disease."

"But what about——" I said.

"Yes, we all know exceptions—the Irish Catholic neighbor who keeps churning them out, the grandmother who gets knocked up—but those are anomalies. And the movie stars you hear about? Probably not using their own eggs, not if they're over forty, but who's going to cop to that in Hollywood?" He picked up a breadstick and began to butter it. The butter was ice-cold and uncooperative. "Nature didn't intend for you to need bifocals to see the baby you're breast-feeding. Fortunately for you, God created fertility doctors." He took a bite of the breadstick, producing an audible crunch. Isaac moved the boom in close, to pick up the sound. The doctor pointed the breadstick's jagged end at Carlito. "You have it relatively easy. Given a normal rate of motility——"

"What's motility?" Carlito asked.

"How many sperm are swimming. Assuming yours are plentiful, with sufficient forward progression, go easy on the marijuana, keep your underwear loose, and you can do this when you're as old as Larry King."

The thought of Carlito's swimming sperm made me think not of sex but of tadpoles, and I wondered, not for the first time, if I was cut out for this work. Even though no *B.C.* participants would be required to actually procreate, the audience would expect to see us kiss. I prayed that my warm feelings for my fellow contestants would heat up.

Dr. Exeter finished off the breadstick. "So what was the question? Oh, yes, sex. Go at it like rabbits, and don't waste any time. Every menstrual cycle counts."

"What about freezing her eggs right now?" Fredreeq asked. "In case Prince Charming is running late?"

The entire room, it seemed, turned to look at her, sitting in the booth behind us.

"Cut! Hey, Miss Dumb," Bing yelled. "You are the makeup artist. You do not speak."

"Yeah, sorry, forgot," Fredreeq said.

"Good question, though," the doctor said, turning back to the camera. "You can freeze anything, but what survives the thaw? Sperm. Also embryos—fertilized eggs, that's egg plus sperm— which requires both Prince and Princess Charming. Eggs alone? Not so great. The technology's improving, but even when it happens, the time for freezing is in your prime. Early twenties, in a perfect world. In your case, uh, Willie, I'm afraid that boat has sailed."

"Great, beautiful," Bing said. "Let's move in on our dream couple. Dr. Dan, do that whole speech again, so we can get Wollie and Carlito's reaction to it."

My reaction was simple. How many menstrual cycles had I squandered on my former fiancé? Five. Not that I blamed Doc for moving to Taiwan, but the devotion that made him a good father to his child meant he'd never father mine. He couldn't abandon Ruby to her wacky mother, and by the time he was free to divorce and remarry, my eggs would be in a retirement home.

"I need a bathroom break before my close-up," Carlito said.

This was a chance for the rest of us to take five. Out came cell phones as people took care of whatever business needed taking care of at 10:57 P.M., mostly checking in with significant others. As I had no significant other, I kicked off my shoes and took a walk around the restaurant. The other diners were gone, and the waiters sat at a table near the kitchen, counting tips and eating a meal of their own by candlelight, roast chicken with all the fixings. Their camaraderie was evident.

Melancholy engulfed me. I wanted to mother a child almost

more than I could say. If I won the *B.C.* audience vote, one prize would be six months of fertility services at Dr. Exeter's clinic, either with my fellow winning contestant or with a man of my choice. I was keeping an open mind about the contestants, but the man of my choice was in Taiwan and although he'd come back one day, he wasn't coming back to me, not for six years. I looked at my watch. How long before another man would look sexy to me, not merely appealing? What was the statute of limitations on true love? Longer than the working life of my ovaries?

A greeting card began to take shape in my head, featuring hens. It would be a combination birthday and condolence, something along the lines of "Happy 40th, Sorry About Those Eggs."

A voice whispered in my ear, startling me. It was Paul, the production assistant.

"Wollie," he said. "I've been, like, flipped out all weekend. About Annika. Something's not right. She wouldn't just not show, because every Monday she's at the production office like an hour before call. Saturdays too. And Sundays, she always wants to watch editing, or just hang." He looked miserable, his face tense with anxiety. Poor guy. For someone like Paul, Annika would've been an angel of mercy, a girl that pretty wanting to "just hang." She'd probably adopted him as she'd adopted me, not caring that to American girls her age, he was a geek. Annika was an egalitarian. Plants, children, homeless pets, math-challenged adults—there seemed no end to the things she cared about.

"When did you last see her?" I asked.

"Friday. But we talked on Saturday. I called to see if she wanted to come on a location scout Sunday. She said she couldn't get the car, but it sounded not right to me."

"Not right how?"

"Just . . . you know when someone's, like, blowing you off? Like that. Only she wasn't ever like that."

"Did she ask you about a gun?"

Paul took off his baseball cap and scratched his unwashed-looking hair. "She asked if I had one, and I was like, Get real, why would you even want one, and she said, Tell you later. Then she asked Bing, and Joey, and Joey was saying about the waiting periods, and Annika was like, You're kidding, so Joey said, Talk to Henry. Henry was the contestant that night, him and Kimberly, the miniature-golf-date episode. And Henry says, Find a gun show, you can buy one on the spot, and everyone's like, No way, you can do that? And Annika says, Okay, Paul, if I find a gun show and give you money, can you buy me one? And I go, Not this weekend, I got the location scout, and she seemed kind of bummed by that and said she'd get back to me."

"Why would she need you to buy the gun for her?" I asked.

He shrugged. "Maybe you have to be twenty-one or a U.S. citizen or something."

Maybe. But why would a math-whiz au pair who phoned home every Sunday want a gun? I started feeling sick again. "Have you called her today?"

He nodded. "Today, yesterday, but I just get her machine. I don't have the number for the people she lives with."

"Paul! Are we lined up with Munich yet?" Bing's voice boomed from across the restaurant. "And hey, bartender! You get ZPX? I got an episode airing."

The bartender aimed a remote at the TV screen suspended above the bar, catching our opening sequence. A ticking clock grew bigger and bigger, then metamorphosed into an hourglass, which in turn became a test tube and, finally, a baby. Disco music pulsed in the background. The faces of the six contestants came into focus, each with a big question mark like a halo suspended overhead. The girls were first: coquettish Kimberly, with perfectly ironed straight black hair. Savannah, the dazzling redhead. And me.

I looked away. If there's anything worse than hearing my voice on tape, it's seeing myself on television. The opening sequence was bad, the actual episodes worse. Towering over my dates even when seated, breasts too big, hair too wispy, weird facial expressions that reminded me of my mother—it was more torturous than a bad photograph. Carlito, coming from the bathroom, was drawn to the small screen like a cat to canned tuna. Fredreeq, too, although her VCR would be recording the episode, came to watch. They stood together in perfect harmony for once, like the theme music, joined in mutual adoration of their work.

I thought of Annika, who never tired of watching the show, *her* show as much as anyone's, even though she never turned up onscreen, in the credits, or on the payroll. She was so often on the set, *Biological Clock*'s biggest fan. I could picture her here, one eye on the television as she called Munich for Bing and negotiated on his behalf in German.

It was on the set that I'd last seen her. Four nights ago, at a bad Chinese restaurant in North Hollywood. Long past midnight Bing had yelled, "That's a wrap!" and Annika had followed me to the bathroom.

"I have a problem, Wollie," she'd said. "I am in some trouble and I do not know who to tell who will not think badly of me. Could we talk for ten minutes? No more."

I'd said yes, of course, knowing it would be far more than ten minutes, knowing Annika and I had never talked on any subject for less than an hour. But then Paul needed me to sign for a paycheck and Fredreeq needed to pull off the false eyelashes she'd been trying out on me, and Bing needed to discuss with us the bags under my eyes, and by the time I was alone and ready to go, Annika wasn't around. I didn't really look for her. I didn't check the bathroom. I didn't ask if anyone noticed where she'd gone. I was tired. I went home.

I hadn't seen her since.

She was my friend, and I hadn't even given her ten minutes.

3

I woke up Tuesday thinking about Carlito. We'd stopped filming a mere five hours earlier, after an on-camera discussion about Carlito's desire to have children. His was a patriotic view of procreation, a commitment to keep America's gene pool strong in the face of unattractive, evil, and just plain stupid people out there multiplying like rabbits. This, for me, was not Carlito's finest hour.

Biological Clock taped six nights a week, with a different couple combination each night, and a new expert and restaurant every three days. Bing handed off this footage to a stressed-out editor, who turned it into a week's worth of episodes, each episode featuring all the contestants. This gave viewers the impression that the six of us partied together Monday through Friday, when in fact each contestant worked two long nights per week, never encountering their same-sex competition. We did get to know our dates. After nine or ten hours together, bonds form—the kind, I suspect, that are experienced by victims of natural disasters.

How, I wondered, had Annika stayed on the set with us all those times and got up the next morning to take care of a toddler, her real job, her job job? After four hours of sleep, I felt like mice had been chewing on my esophagus.

I made my way to the navy blue kitchen, considered coffee,

opted for apple juice, and headed for the shower before the kitchen walls made me nauseous. The apartment belonged to Hubie, a friend who needed someone to water his plants while he followed the rock group Supertramp around Europe. Hubie's offer came just as my former fiancé, Doc, left for Taiwan. The house I'd shared with Doc was expensive, the thought of acquiring a room-mate depressing, so I'd moved my stuff into storage and myself into Hubie's until I could figure out what to do with the rest of my life. I hadn't figured it out yet, but I still had five weeks. Hubie would be home by Christmas, and it was now a week be-fore Thanksgiving.

I left another message on the phone machine of Annika's host family, the Quinns. Then I got dressed and hit the road.

The weather was gorgeous, the air clear and smogless in a Disney-blue sky. Halfway to the 405, the every-hour-is-rush-hour freeway, I decided instead to take Beverly Glen Boulevard to the San Fernando Valley. I was passing De Neve Square, a tiny park above Sunset, when I remembered to turn on my cell phone. There was one message, from the friend whose frog mural I was painting. His Texas twang precluded the need to identify him-self. "Darlin', take the day off. My floor guy called to say he var-nished them and they're still wet. Check in tomorrow."

Darn. I missed my frogs. And now I was halfway to Ventura Boulevard. Disinclined to make a U-turn, I checked my mental lists to see if I had any Valley errands.

Uh-oh. The Quinns—Annika's host family—lived in the Valley. Encino.

Forget it. I could turn around. I was smack in the middle of the low-rent section of Beverly Glen, just past Fernbush, with old, yardless houses practically falling onto the street. I could take a right on a little road called Crater and turn around, no problem.

Yes, problem, said a voice in my head. Ruta. My childhood babysitter, dead for years, still talking to me. *They don't answer their phone, these people, you should go visit them.*

"In L.A. you don't just drop in on people," I said. "It's not done. I don't know how they do things in Germany, but I don't think Mrs. Glück expects me to run all over the San Fernando Valley, bothering everyone."

Of course she expects it, Ruta said. *She is a mother. This is her little girl.*

"Plus, they have a dog. A guard dog, probably. A pit bull. Mr. Snuggles."

Not to mention the fact that I didn't know where in Encino they lived. I could go home, get Mrs. Glück's number, call her in Germany, get the address, and visit the Quinns some other time. Immediately I felt better.

Until I remembered directory assistance. To my annoyance, 411 gave me an address on a street called Moon Canyon Road. What kind of people, I wondered, are listed in directory assistance? I tried to recall what Annika had said about them. A mom with some home-based business, a doctor or lawyer dad, a child Annika adored. I did not want to barge in on them.

None of this would've happened if you had taken more math in high school, Ruta said. *Or finished college when you were supposed to, instead of futzing around, in and out, in and out all these years. Then you wouldn't have need for a math tutor. Then you wouldn't care so much about this girl. But you didn't, so you did, and you do, so now you must.*

I wished I were someone else: the kind of person who can be rude to telemarketers, who doesn't recycle, someone who'd simply get herself another math tutor and to heck with somebody's mother in Germany. I wished I'd given Annika ten minutes last week.

I was nearing Mulholland now, the summit of Beverly Glen, where the road was wider, the real estate costlier, and the view spectacular. I pulled over and searched my trunk for the Thomas Guide, a book of maps as common to Southern California cars as Gideon Bibles are to hotel-room drawers.

Fifteen minutes later I was in the wilds of Encino. I hadn't even known Encino had wilds. I thought of Encino, when I thought about it at all, as suburbia, inhabited by women with standing appointments to "get their hair done" and men who maintained the lawn. Or hired immigrant workers to maintain the lawn. This Encino, however, was enchantingly rural, marred only by distinctive white trucks at the end of the street indicating a film shoot. Film shoots, around L.A., are as common as surfboards.

I drove slowly down Moon Canyon Road, enjoying the multicultural architecture: a Spanish hacienda next to an Italian villa opposite a Tudor manor. I came to the number I was looking for, which was painted on a rock, and parked on the street. An electronic gate stood wide open—a sign from the universe, if you believe in such things. The gate was wood and managed to look quaint rather than high security. I walked through it and followed a flagstone path through a yard that was half garden, half forest, complete with a pond inhabited by koi. The house was traditional American, butter-yellow clapboard with white trim on the shuttered windows. I looked up. A balcony extended from a second-story room. Wind chimes tinkled on a porch, and when I rang the doorbell harmonizing chimes sounded somewhere in the house.

The response was immediate. Set in the front door was a small window at face level, and through the glass I could see a small furious canine head—not a pit bull's—appear and disappear, appear and disappear, as if the animal was jumping up and down repeatedly on the other side of the door, although how this was achieved without a ladder I couldn't understand. The yapping would drive a reasonable person to drink. "Hi, Mr. Snuggles," I said, and awaited the appearance of a human or the sound of a voice telling Mr. Snuggles to shut the heck up.

None came. I rang the doorbell again, which brought on another of Mr. Snuggles's jumping fits. Was anyone home? I looked around for cars, but the driveway was some distance from the house, presumably leading to a garage or carport in the back. Maybe the family was simply out of town, and Annika with them, in a place without telephone access. A canoe trip, for instance. An impulsive, spur-of-the-moment canoe trip. Perfectly good explanation, I decided, and I descended the porch steps, preparing to leave.

A big white bird waddled up the flagstone path to meet me. Too fat for a swan, too white for a turkey, it was, I deduced, a goose.

"Hello, Goose," I said, walking toward it.

The goose took exception to this, flapped its wings violently, and honked. I backed up.

This was a mistake. The goose lunged at me, enraged, honking and hissing. I turned to get out of its way and stumbled over a rosebush, and the goose was on me, pecking my calf through my painter's pants. This hurt a lot more than one would think. I became a little enraged myself, and more than a little scared, and tried to kick the bird. As I was wearing Keds, the damage would've been minimal, but in any case, I missed. The goose came at me again. I swung at it with my backpack, missed again, and with my right hand slapped at it, connecting slightly. Then I turned and ran.

The goose, affronted by the slap, intensified its demented honking and came after me. We ran around to the back of the house, and I spotted the garage. It was a six-car garage, with five cars in residence. I jumped into the back of a pickup truck, a Toyota Tundra, and ducked.

I've been in some undignified situations in my life, but hiding from poultry was a low watermark. It worked, though. The goose gave a few more honks, but they lacked conviction. It must have seen me jump into the truck, but either geese have short memories or it felt I'd conceded the fight, because it waddled off toward the house. I know this because I peeked.

Suddenly I heard the song "Anatevka," from *Fiddler on the Roof,* coming from somewhere behind the house. I climbed out of the pickup and saw drops of blood; the palm of my hand was wounded. Happily, the Toyota was red. There was also a minivan, a bright green Volkswagen bug I'd seen Annika drive, and a white Lexus inhabiting the garage. In the driveway was a Range Rover. All the vehicles looked freshly washed.

"Anatevka" grew louder. I followed the sound across the lawn and came to a structure that appeared to be some sort of guest-house or artist's studio. The door was open. I looked in.

The structure was a high-ceilinged, skylit room. Along one wall was a kitchen, dominated by a granite island work surface. The rest of the space was a hobbyist's dream: power tools, gardening supplies, sawhorse, sewing machine, kiln, easel, loom, and computer artfully arranged, a masterpiece of organization and aesthetics. A working fireplace occupied the wall opposite the kitchen. Autumn leaves and pomegranates covered the granite work surface, a wreath-making project in progress.

Across the room, a woman with her back to me stood on a ladder. She wore heels. She was stacking glass bottles in compartments on floor-to-ceiling shelves. Dozens of bottles filled the shelves, the kind used for lotion or bath oil, Art Deco–looking things in amber, violet, and moss green. A subtle scent, spice or oil or potpourri, permeated the room. It reminded me of Annika. Near the loom sat a little girl, playing with the volume on a CD player. The mournful "Anatevka" zoomed in and out.

"You are making Mommy a little crazy," the woman said, without pausing in her jar arranging. "Please stop."

"Dora the explorer, Dora the explorer, Dora the explorer," the little girl chanted.

"If you watch *Dora the Explorer* now, you can't watch *Sesame Street* in half an hour."

"Dora the explorer. Dora the explorer. Dora the exp—"

"Okay, okay, okay. But no more TV till bedtime, when Mommy's at pastry class. Run into the house and tell Lupe you can watch Dora."

The little girl jumped up, then caught sight of me and stopped. I smiled. She didn't smile back, but when I gave her a little wave, she raised a hand in response, opening and closing her fist in a toddlerlike gesture. The woman saw it and turned.

"Hi." I sneezed. "Sorry to barge in. I tried the house, and nobody answered, so . . ."

An overfed yellow cat jumped with a thump onto the granite

work surface and sniffed at the leaves. The woman on the ladder and the child looked at it, then turned back to me, as if it was still my turn to speak. They were both blond, with wide faces and peaches-and-cream complexions. They wore light blue work shirts and white jeans. I tried to recall if I'd ever seen a mother and daughter wearing matching outfits outside of a catalog.

"Mommy, that lady has blood."

I looked down. Three drops of blood lay on the white tile floor, from my hand. It didn't seem polite to say their bird had assaulted me, so I closed my fist over the bleeding palm and said, "My name is Wollie. I called yesterday and left a message. I'm a friend of Annika's . . ."

"Of course." The woman climbed nimbly down the ladder, someone who obviously lived in high heels. "I'm Maizie. I'm so sorry, I was writing down your number last night and little monkey here hit the delete button. Emma, love——" She frowned at the girl, now chanting something that sounded like *alla myna engine*. "Emma, why don't you run in and watch *Dora*?"

"Emma want to stay with Mommy."

Maizie looked like she might argue the point, then turned to me. She had an attractive face, with good bones. "So. Annika. It's all so—disturbing."

"Yes." I sneezed again.

"Allergic to cats?" she said. "Sorry. This guy wandered in and adopted us. Adopted Annika, actually. Are you a close friend?"

My stomach clenched, thinking of the last time I'd seen her. I nodded. "She's like a little sister. A smarter sister. She's been tutoring me in math. We met on the set of a TV show."

"She is smart." Maizie smiled, dimples softening her face. "It sold my husband on her. He respects intelligence." She ruffled her hair. It was thick hair, well cut. "We've been out of town; Annika had the weekend off and I've been telling myself she misunderstood, thought we were coming back later. But now it's Tuesday. I hate to say this, but I think she's—taken off."

"Where?" I said.

"I can think of a few places." Maizie glanced down at her

daughter, who followed the conversation with the intensity of a cub reporter. "But there's a lot in her life I'm not privy to. A boy she's quite taken with; I've been trying to remember his last name. And there's—well, she's on duty with Emma from six A.M. until four in the afternoon, eleven on Fridays, which leaves a lot of free time. And she fills up those hours. It's one of the things we love about her, her independence, but it makes it hard to—narrow it down."

Emma spoke up. "Annika not here, Mommy."

"No, she's not, bunny."

"Where is Annika?"

"We don't know. That's what we're trying to figure out."

"We better go find her, Mommy."

My sentiments exactly. "Is her stuff still here?" I asked.

Maizie took a moment, then nodded. "Come see for yourself," she said.

4

We entered the house through the back door. There was no sign of the killer goose, but Mr. Snuggles approached in a frenzy, the kind small terriers excel at. Maizie gave me a treat for him, a miniature faux T-bone steak. Mr. Snuggles ate it and accepted me into the pack.

"Emma feed him," Emma said. "One scoop. His bowl is yellow."

"Oh," I said. "How old are you, Emma?"

"Two and three-quarters."

"Two and eleven-twelfths, if you want to get technical," Maizie said. "Santa brought you to me." We trooped single-file through a laundry room and hallway to a staircase. I wanted to study details, but with Mr. Snuggles setting the pace and the two blond Quinns flanking me, there was no dawdling. I had an impression of mahogany, Oriental rugs, and lemon oil.

"Beautiful house," I said, on the landing.

"Thanks," Maizie said. "We love it. Bought at the bottom of the market, and we've put a lot into it over the years. Horrible commute, but I tell my husband he'll have better luck moving his office building than moving me. One more flight up," she said, as Mr. Snuggles raced down the second-floor hallway. Emma barreled after him, calling, "Loo-pay, Loo-pay, alla myna engine!" From a distant room, a vacuum cleaner switched off. Maizie led me to what looked like a closet, closed with a hook-and-eye latch up high, out of reach of small fingers. This turned out to be the door to another stairway.

The third floor was an attic room, wallpapered and wood floored and charming.

Annika wasn't a slob, but she was no neatnik either. Under the multicolored quilt, the bed was made, but it was the work of an amateur. Books filled the bookshelves, in English and German, along with a collection of videos and DVDs—every genre from *Blade Runner* to *The Parent Trap*. Framed pictures covered a dresser and snapshots overlapped each other on a bulletin board. On the walls were posters: Albert Einstein, Eminem, Keanu Reeves. Maizie opened the door to a cedar-paneled walk-in closet filled with clothes, shoes, suitcases, and the miscellany of a young woman's life. The suitcases were old and somber, with the look of hand-me-downs, the clothes bright and cheap, built to disintegrate in a year or two.

"We stayed out of here, except for Lupe, once a week for cleaning, so I can't say if anything's missing." Maizie raised shades and cranked open windows. "I came in last night. I didn't see a passport, but she always carried that in her purse. Which isn't here, of course."

She seemed to assume that no female would leave the house without a purse. I remembered Annika's suddenly, a red patent leather shoulder bag.

"What about that?" I pointed to a computer, hooked up to a small printer. "She wouldn't leave that behind."

Maizie squinted at it. "You don't think so?"

"No. She'd been saving up for it forever."

"It does look brand-new." Maizie switched on a Tiffany lamp to get a better look. "I'm afraid my husband is the computer person here. And Emma. It's scary how quickly children pick up technology. Are these expensive?"

"Expensive enough."

"I guess anything's expensive on a hundred forty a week. It's a selling point, how cheap au pairs are, but it's embarrassing to pay someone so little." Maizie perched on the edge of the bed, as if afraid to get comfortable, not having been invited. "You know, she's due to go home next month, so I can't understand why she'd leave early. The agency imposes a financial penalty if they don't finish out the year, and she's very frugal."

"It's true," I said, still startled by the small salary. "Have you called her mother?"

"Oh, God." Maizie looked at me and glanced away. "I don't have the heart for it. What do I say? I spoke to her once last summer; it's painful. Her English is bad and my toddler knows more German than I do." What she'd done, she said, was call the au pair liaison, a woman named Glenda, who'd notified the agency. They, in turn, would contact Mrs. Glück, using someone who spoke German. "I'm sure she's heard from Annika by now. They're very close."

"You don't think something happened to Annika?" I asked.

"Such as—?"

"I don't know, whatever happens to people who disappear. Kidnapping, or . . ." I hesitated to say anything worse out loud.

"You know, I really don't." Maizie pressed her lips together, then shook her head. "Two months ago, I might've thought so, but now . . ."

I waited for her to finish her sentence, but she seemed to be struggling with a decision. Then she stood, grasped the footboard of the mahogany bed, and moved it out from the wall.

There were dust bunnies on the floor where the bed had been—Lupe must've cut a few corners here—and a dime, a small amber bottle, and a stray pill. Maizie picked up the bottle, set it in the palm of her hand, and held it out. "Do you know what this is?"

It was a tiny jar with a screw-on top and a miniature spoon attached by a chain. Memories of an old boyfriend came flooding back, not pleasant ones. An old boyfriend with bad habits, one of which had killed him. "Is it for cocaine?" I asked.

"That's my guess. There's white residue inside. I haven't seen one of these since college. And how about this?" She bent down and plucked the pill from the floor and handed it to me. She had a craftsman's hands: short nails, no polish. Like mine.

The size of a vitamin, it was round and blue, with a marking pressed into it. ℞. A kind of symbol, or maybe a short word, with letters so stylized I couldn't recognize them. I shook my head and handed it back. She set the pill and vial on the floor and pushed the bed against the wall once more.

"I don't know what to do," she said. "Or why I'm leaving them there. I found them last night. Should I get the pill analyzed somehow? Obviously, if she has a drug habit, I can't have her around Emma, but I hate to think this of her. She's so not the type."

"No, she's not. Did you tell the agency?"

"God, no. They'd have her on the next plane to Germany. My husband too, he'd just——. I can't tell him this. I can't just ruin her life without talking to her first. What would you do?"

It was my turn to look away. I didn't want her to see in my face that I was holding back, that I had my own secret knowledge of Annika. Guns. And now drugs. And whatever "big problem" she'd wanted to talk about. "I guess I wouldn't tell anyone either," I said. "Are you sure those are hers? Has anyone else stayed in this room?"

"No. We have two guest rooms. And we bought the bed the week she came, so no one else has even slept in it. Of course, she has friends over occasionally. And Lupe——" Maizie gave a short laugh. "Well, let's just say if Lupe had a cocaine habit, I expect she'd clean a lot faster. God. I've been trying to figure this out. Annika *has* been distracted recently. Erratic behavior. Keeping to her room instead of hanging out in the kitchen. Cooking. She loves cooking, but I can't remember the last time . . . but it's a tough age. It was for me. It never crossed my mind that this—moodiness—could be a drug thing."

All I knew about drugs was that unless the person was pretty far gone, it was hard to tell who did them and who didn't do them, especially if you're someone who doesn't do them. Joey was good at drug detection. I wasn't.

"What about her boyfriend?" I said. "Have you heard from him?"

"No. So maybe she's with him, maybe they took off together. I wish I could remember his last name. Rico—but whether that was a nickname, or short for Richard . . ."

Richard. I remembered a tutoring session I'd had with Annika at one of our hangouts, a coffee bar. When we finished, Annika stayed, saying she had a date. With—Richard? Maybe. Richard Something. "But if she didn't take off with him," I said, "if something bad happened, shouldn't you tell the police? Before the trail gets cold."

Maizie opened a door to a bathroom. "The agency's doing that, they have procedures for when girls take off. Apparently it happens enough. I don't mean to sound uncaring, but for a seven-thousand-dollar fee, these are the problems you hand over. Or so my husband says."

I nearly choked. "Seven thousand—and Annika makes a hundred forty a week?"

Maizie explained that the fee covered interviews, psychological evaluation, translating references, airfare, and training in child care, CPR, and first aid. The host family was interviewed too, their house inspected and their references checked. An au pair was less an employee than an instant teenage daughter, and the girls weren't in it for the money but for a year in America. "Otherwise," Maizie said, "you may as well hire a nanny. Which my husband now says we should have done. But I feel like she's coming back. I just do." She straightened a yellow bath towel embroidered with "Annika," then pulled it off the rack, saying, "She should at least come home to clean towels."

It still seemed there was something missing here, something we should be doing. "If she's not in trouble, why hasn't she called anyone?" I said, thinking about the gun. "Her mother, for instance. Why not leave a note for you?"

"What if she's doing something she thinks we'd disapprove of?" Maizie switched off the bathroom light and leaned against the wall, cuddling the bath towel. "I don't know what's happened to her. But I know what I wish, and that's that she comes walking in the back door at dinnertime, asking what smells so good." Her voice trembled a little. "Emma keeps asking about her." She looked at me and cleared her throat. "You might want to check with Glenda, the au pair counselor. Come, I'll get you her number."

Glenda Nacy worked at Williams-Sonoma, a housewares store in the Westfield Shoppingtown Promenade, farther into the Valley. I decided to go there rather than wait for a return phone call, which Maizie warned me could take a while. Glenda was a volunteer, she explained, although why anyone would volunteer to supervise foreign teenage babysitters was something Maizie had wondered about all year.

I found my way to the mall and to Glenda Nacy, a sixtyish woman in orthopedic shoes with lipstick on her front teeth. As I explained my mission, she stocked packs of potpourri on a display table alongside boxes marked "Snowflake Spice Balls," spreading the scent of ginger, cloves, and nutmeg. This was the kind of store I avoided these days, a sensory reminder that I had no husband, no children, and no cooking skills. Glenda offered me a cup of hot apple cider and said, "I can't give you much time. My boss puts the kibosh on personal business during shifts. She's off-site, but if she comes back, ask me about crockery."

"I won't take long," I said. "I'm just wondering if you filed a police report on Annika."

"Oh, that's not for me to do. I'm the community counselor. That would be up to the agency, Au Pairs par Excellence." She pronounced it "Ah Pairs per *Ex*cellence" as though there were nothing French about it. "The moms—the host moms, I should say—they'll call me instead of the agency, because I have a personal relationship with them and the girls. Then I contact the agency, so that's how that works." She was, to hear her describe it, a combination mediator, interpreter, tour guide, and spiritual adviser.

"So you really got to know Annika," I said. "Any idea where she might've gone?"

"Well, golly." Glenda reached up for a silver cheese grater from a well-stocked wall display, and began to rub the handle with her apron. "I'm not sure I'm supposed to discuss this or anything, being a volunteer."

"Discuss what?"

"You probably should just talk to the agency."

"Glenda," I said, "I'm not anyone. I'm not an investigator or the police or—. I design greeting cards. Annika's my friend, and I just want to make sure—"

Glenda glanced over my shoulder and, with a forced cough, handed me the cheese grater, then handed me two more. I turned. Coming through the door was a woman considerably younger than Glenda and much better dressed.

"I think three should do you," Glenda said, in a bright, salesperson voice. "Fine, coarse, and ribbon. And what else do you need for your dinner party?"

"Uh—" Deception came as easily to me as sheep shearing. "Oh. Crockery?"

"Right this way." Her voice dropped to a whisper. "Now listen. Why don't you just give a call to Martin, he's Southern California regional director—"

"I promise I won't quote you or anything," I whispered back. "I'm just curious about what you thought of Annika. I mean, she's been here almost a year now, and as the den mother—. I'm sorry, what did you say your title is?"

"Community counselor."

"As community counselor, you must know her better than Martin, unless—. How big's the community?"

Glenda perked up at this. Big, she said. She was responsible for L.A. and Orange County. However, only three au pairs currently inhabited the community: Annika in Encino, Britta in San Marino, and Hitomi in Palos Verdes. Hitomi had a nice setup, a whole guesthouse, which she deserved, Glenda felt, for caring for two sets of twins. Each month, Glenda organized a Sunday excursion. "Like picnics or Magic Mountain, and we have all sorts of fun and the girls tell me how things are going."

"And how were things going with Annika?"

"Well, she never complained. This is Wedgwood transferware, called Highgrove, after Prince Charles's country estate," Glenda said, picking up a plate. "Dishwasher safe."

"Oh . . . good."

"Too ritzy? The Emile Henry, then." She pronounced Emile "E-meal," like something you'd eat online, and spoke loudly. "The Auberge collection, inspired by the simple, warm restaurants found in French country inns. Feel that roaster. Go ahead, handle it."

I picked up the roaster, big enough to house a turkey, as the well-dressed woman moved past us through a door marked "Employees Only." Glenda replaced the plate and took the roaster out of my hands. "If anyone had cause for complaint, it was me, not that young lady."

"Annika?" I said. "You had problems with her?"

"The excursions. She was late to Cinco de Mayo because of working at some food bank. She skipped Knott's Berry Farm due to a TV program she got involved in. So I sat her down and I said, Look, this is not optional, the excursions are mandatory, you're here to have cultural experiences. Next thing you know, she's volunteering at a pet shelter. The girls are not supposed to work themselves to the bone. They put in forty-five hours a week with child care, and their studies on top of that. But that wasn't the worst."

"What was the worst?"

Glenda raised her voice. "It's the latest, a nonstick tapas pan, eight and a half inches. Once you get it home, you'll wonder how you ever got along without it."

The well-dressed woman had emerged from the Employees Only door and was checking merchandise fifteen feet away.

"I don't actually cook a lot of tapas." This was an understatement. I used my oven for storing paper grocery bags. The pilot light was out. "So what was the worst?" I whispered.

"That young lady was boy crazy. I see it all the time, the girls want Disneyland and Starbucks and American boyfriends. You can't blame them, but you have to be strict."

"Gosh," I said. "How many boyfriends did she have?"

"Well, just the one, that I know of. But she talked about him to the others all through the Lotus Festival. Didn't think I was listening, but I keep tabs, because whatever one girl is up to, the others think they need to be doing it too."

"Did the Quinns complain about the boyfriend?"

"No." Glenda pursed her lips. "We discourage letting the girls have a boy up in their room, but if the host family allows it, our hands are tied. They're lovely people, the Quinns, but they don't keep tabs. Mrs. Quinn especially, she thinks Annika is just perfect, but teens need tough love, is what I tell my moms and dads."

"Sounds like you know what you're talking about. So did she meet this guy at school?"

"Now, that's another thing. The girls need six units of college-level coursework, not aerobics or commercial auditions or what-not but things pertaining to our culture. Annika wanted physics. I told her no, physics has nothing to do with America, so she went ahead and took it on her own, in *addition* to ESL. She wanted to do everything. I don't know when that girl ever slept. She was a bad example for Britta and Hitomi, with her extracurriculars. I tell them, Do your job, help out with the dishes and such, but then enjoy yourself. You're here to experience the American way of life, not run yourself ragged."

For some of us, running ourselves ragged was the American way of life. "So what do you think happened?" I asked, hesitant now to mention drugs. An aproned woman headed our way and I grabbed a gadget from a rack. "Say, these are awfully cute. Like a little mallet. For meat, I suppose. What do you call these?"

"Meat mallets." Glenda glanced at her fellow salesperson, then rubbed her eyes, leaving little dots of cakey mascara on the delicate skin underneath. "I couldn't say where she is, with all her goings-on. I better ring you up."

I started to tell her I don't cook, but her boss was approaching, so I let her sell me three cheese graters and the meat mallet. "After all, everyone eats cheese," she said.

"But you don't think Annika met with foul play?" I asked, glancing out into the mall.

"Well, dear, with what you hear on the news these days, I'm surprised we all haven't met with foul play."

The Au Pairs par Excellence agency answered with a machine, a woman's voice promising an end to my child-care problems once I made the decision to bring an au pair into my life. She urged me to check out their Web site and leave a message after the beep.

I left a message every half hour up until six o'clock.

The next morning, I started in again at nine A.M. Then I went down to San Pedro to find them.

5

Wednesday was another unseasonably gorgeous day. Joey and I could fully appreciate this along with everyone else on the 405 South because the San Diego Freeway was moving us along at the speed of barges. Which gave me time to wrestle with the idea of Annika being a druggie.

"I wouldn't say an unidentified pill and an empty coke vial constitute a druggie," Joey said. "Not where I come from."

"You come from Nebraska."

"Exactly. The decadent Corn Belt. Hey, you're getting a little obsessive, aren't you, going to San Pedro at this hour? What happened to your day job, your mural deadline?"

"Their floors are still wet. And I wouldn't have to go to San Pedro if people would answer their phones. Thanks for the ride, by the way."

Joey opened a window. Her Irish setter hair whirled around the front seat, a victim of the Santa Ana winds. "Thanks for qualifying me for the carpool lane." She was on a mission to sell her husband's year-old BMW. "Not one person answered Elliot's newspaper ad," she said, "so now we deal with the dealers. Today, Long Beach. Tomorrow, City of Industry. Don't marry a man who needs a new car every year; life's too short."

"Why doesn't he just trade it in?" I asked.

"He says it's worth more than they offered. We went through the same thing last year."

"Why doesn't he just lease?" I asked.

"Who can say? Why does he do anything? Why invest in a reality TV show?"

"Okay, why?"

Joey changed lanes. "I like to think *Biological Clock* is a money-laundering scheme and my husband is stowing large amounts of cash in a Swiss bank, preparing to buy me a small village in Italy for our third anniversary. Elliot says it's a case of Larry, his old fraternity brother, needing a partner in his production company. Swears it'll pay off." She changed lanes again. "That's what he said about the race horse. And then it died."

"And does this actually make you a producer, being married to an investor, or is that something Bing made up?"

"Both," Joey said. "In one sense, there's no limit to the number of producers on a show—it's like ants at a picnic. You invest money or head the production company, you're a producer; you find the writer or star or idea, you're a producer; if you're a big enough writer or star or director, you're a producer, and maybe your agent and manager are too, along with your husband, girlfriend, maybe your mom. In the glory days, they all got screen credits. Now they have to fight each other for them." Joey honked at a Ryder truck one lane over making a preliminary move to cut her off. "Anyhow, the real producer, in this case Bing, who hires the crew, does the budget, shows up on the set, that's the lowest form of producer, which is why he resents me. I'm a producer-by-marriage, and also because I once made a lot of money by modeling and doing schlock TV, enabling my husband, who knows zip about show business, to invest that money in schlock TV. There's a symmetry to all this."

Eventually we found the car dealer, who made a lowball offer on Joey's husband's BMW, citing a scratch on the front fender the depth of a strand of hair. Joey argued that a jeweler's loupe was required to see this, and heated words were exchanged before I dragged her away, to the western regional offices of Au Pairs par Excellence.

If there was a high-end section of San Pedro, this wasn't it, a mile or two inland from the harbor. The storefront office was wedged between a Laundromat and a shoe-repair shop called the Leather Goddess. The office staff was a young woman behind a gray metal desk reading a copy of *In Style* magazine.

"Hi," she said. "Are you guys the exterminator?"

My guess was, they didn't get a lot of walk-in business. Desks, floor, and the top of the gray metal filing cabinet overflowed with boxes and stray papers. Novel filing system.

"No, we're not exterminators," I said. "I've called four or five times, but no one called back, so I came in person. I'm worried about one of your au pairs, Annika Glück, who's been missing since Sunday. I want to know if you've contacted her mother or filed a police report."

"Um, want to come back this afternoon?" the receptionist asked. "Marty'll be in then."

"No," Joey said with a big smile. "We want you to call Marty and ask him to come in now. Unless you'd like to be the agency spokesperson. I write for the *L.A. Times,* and by this afternoon my article will be on its way to tomorrow's edition."

"Wow." Her eyes sparkled and she sat up straighter. "You sure you want us? We're just a branch office. Maybe you want to call main headquarters in New York—"

"No," I said. "We don't want to call anyone. We want Marty."

She nodded. "Okay, I'll do an SOS on his pager."

I marveled at Joey's improvisational ability. Joey calls it lying, but that's because she's modest. We sat on folding chairs along the wall, watching the receptionist page Marty, then return to her magazine. After a moment, she got up and looked through the glass door, staring at something. "I have a new car," she said.

"Congratulations," I said. Joey asked what kind it was.

"Honda Element. Orange. I hate parking it here. Those Laundromat people next door are really careless, they park too close and they bang it with their laundry baskets."

The phone rang. Oddly enough, she didn't answer it. The three of us stared at the message machine as a nasal voice expressed in-

terest in an unspecified position and informed us she'd just had
her teeth done and needed the extra money, which was the reason she'd decided to call. The receptionist replayed it several
times, jotting notes on a "While You Were Out" notepad. Ten
minutes later, a dirty white Mustang with a bad paint job pulled
up. A man got out and peered at us through the glass doorway. He
checked the soles of his shoes, the way you do when you suspect
bubblegum or something worse, then walked in. The receptionist jumped up and handed him the "While You Were Out" message. He glanced at it and told her to take an early lunch. He was
thirty or thirty-five, slim, in khakis and a button-down shirt, with
slicked-back hair. A prominent Adam's apple reminded me of
the marbled reed frog, *Hyperolius marmoratus*. Because of my
mural, most things these days reminded me of frogs.

When the receptionist was gone, he smiled at us. "Temp," he
said. "My girl's out on maternity leave. I'm Marty Otis. How can
I help you ladies?"

I didn't have to look at Joey to know her reaction to "my girl"
and "you ladies," but Marty seemed oblivious, so I went through
my "worried about Annika" spiel. Marty gestured toward a desk
across the room. We moved our folding chairs to it. Marty took a
seat and smiled some more. "Let me start by telling you a little
about us. We're a licensed agency participating in a cultural ex-
change program established by the Department of State in 1986.
Young people from around the world come to live with host families in America, to provide child care and further their education. By the way, which of you is with the *L.A. Times*?"

I started to speak, but Joey jumped in. "We work together."

"Marty," I said, "we're wondering if you've filed a police report on Annika."

He leaned back, folding his hands. "Let's put this in context,
shall we?"

"So that's a no?" I asked.

"You need to understand teenage girls. Off the record? Oppor-
tunists. They come here with some kind of work ethic, because
that's how it is for them back home. Then they see their American

counterparts, and in three months, they're as reliable as rock stars."

"They don't come from Mars," I said. "It's not like there's no sex, drugs, rock and roll in Europe."

Marty shook his head. "These are working-class types, slated for factory jobs until they get married and produce kids of their own. They're from backwater towns. If they were more sophisticated, they'd be in college, not coming to change diapers for minimum wage."

"What's that got to do with—" I said, but he cut me off, sitting forward.

"What do you think happens when these sheltered young things get turned loose in L.A.?"

"I imagine that depends on the sheltered young thing in question."

"Right. Type One gets homesick, fat, runs up the phone bill. Type Two? She gets drunk, she gets a tattoo, she gets knocked up. That's the type to take off and leave us holding the bag, finding a replacement for the host family."

"And what if Annika wasn't a One or a Two?" I said. "Have you met her?"

"I don't have to." He patted a stack of documents. "We've had complaints. Discrepancies on her application, for starters. Go to the police? Police aren't going to care about some German girl skipping out on her job a month early."

I had an urge to reach out and grab the papers off his desk. "Can I see the application?"

"Our files are confidential."

"Isn't that handy?" Joey said. She'd been leaning so far back in her folding chair, I worried she'd tip over. Now she straightened up, the front of her chair hitting the floor sharply. She smiled. "Smart guy, Marty. Why search for a girl who could turn up dead, which would be bad for business, when with no effort she can stay missing and no one will care?"

Marty walked to the door and held it open. "Excuse me, ladies. I have work to do."

"Nice business license." I went to inspect the document on the wall behind his desk. "Cheap frame. Is this something you're fond of? Because I wouldn't take it for granted."

Marty left his post at the doorway to join me behind the desk, perhaps feeling he'd made a tactical error in leaving it. He was shorter than me, and there was a subtle smell emanating from his shirt, the kind that comes from ironing clothes that aren't quite clean, trying to get another day's wear out of them.

"Get out of here," he said. "This is private property and you're trespassing."

"Okay," I said. "Call 911."

Joey strolled to Marty's other side, so that he was now pinned between desk and wall, Joey and me. "Go for it, Marty. Tell them you're being menaced by two tall girls." Joey *was* tall, and as menacing as a stalk of celery. Still, Marty could not physically remove us without resorting to violence and considerable loss of dignity.

"You media people are sick," he said. "What do you want from me?"

"What's the discrepancy on her application you referred to?" I said.

"This isn't for publication. I'm not giving you permission to print this."

"I guarantee it won't make it into print."

"There was an incident with the police back in Germany that she didn't tell us about."

"What kind of incident?"

"All I know is, she lied about it. You want specifics, ask the German police."

"Marty," Joey said. "We came to San Pedro. That's our limit. Why not just tell us?"

"I'm telling you. There's a police report on her. Unspecified."

"How'd you find out about it?" I asked.

"I got a phone call, I don't know who from. They said, Take a closer look at her application. I put in a call overseas, and sure enough, they got something on her."

"But it could be something minor?" I said. "Unpaid parking tickets?"

"Doesn't matter. Any run-in with the law is a no-no. She lied about it, that's fraud, that gets her deported."

"So you were getting ready to deport her?" I asked.

I saw his mind working, trying to figure out which answer would sound best. "We were considering our options."

"Let me get this straight," I said. "Annika had a police record, but you didn't bother to find out what it was, or tell her host family?"

A mulish look came over his face. "We had the matter under investigation. Things of this nature take time."

"Yes, we can certainly see how swamped you are," Joey said.

"Go to hell."

We'd pushed him into a corner. I took a conciliatory tone. "What else? You said there were complaints, plural."

"I don't have another word to say to any goddamn reporters," he said. "And I'm calling the *Times*."

I smiled. "Oh, did you think we work for the *L.A. Times*? I'm sorry, you misunderstood. We read the *L.A. Times*. Joey even subscribes. Me too, but only on Sundays."

"Sometimes we write letters to the editor," Joey added.

Marty turned red, then pushed past me with some force and marched over to the receptionist's station. "Get out."

"Gladly," I said, moving to the door. "By the way, Annika is not fat, drunk, stupid, lazy, irresponsible, or blinded by the American way of life. Happy Thanksgiving."

"Bye, Marty," Joey said. "Enjoy the job while you have it." She joined me out in the sunshine and aimed her keys at the BMW, which beeped in response. "Just when you think a used car salesman is as bad as it's going to get," she said, "you meet Marty. Where to now?"

"Where nobody else wants to go," I said. "To the cops."

6

The West Valley Community Police Station was on Vanowen Street just west of Wilbur, in a neighborhood that hadn't changed its socks since the 1950s. Cramped bungalows occupied tiny lots, tract houses in need of paint jobs, the kind I might one day afford. Yards were area rugs of patchy grass, a far cry from the lawns of the Quinn estate in Encino. Probably the only thing these people had in common with the Quinns, in fact, was this branch of the LAPD.

If I hadn't been obsessed heading to San Pedro, I was edging toward it now. The encounter with Marty Otis had intrigued Joey, but it disturbed me; I hoped that laying it out for the police would quiet my anxiety.

The cops were housed in a series of trailers behind a green public library. Next to the library was the future police station, surrounded by a construction fence, a municipal project that might or might not reach completion during anyone's lifetime. Joey and I circled the block twice before we found the interim parking lot, on a side street called Vanalden.

The main trailer was packed, which was to say there were six other citizens in there. At the head of the line, a woman wept as an officer across the counter took notes. Across the room another officer struggled to find English simple enough to be understood by the carjack victim she was interviewing. Near some vending

machines a third officer advised a middle-aged couple in matching leather jackets about their elderly parent who liked to help
herself to periodicals at a newsstand. A fourth officer canvassed
the line, directing people the way they do at LAX, expediting
things on a busy day.

"We're here to file a missing person's report," I said when he
reached us.

"For a child?" he asked.

"No, she's nineteen. No one's seen her for several days."

The officer looked up at me. "Mentally ill?"

"No."

"Any indication she was the victim of a crime?"

Thoughts of blackmail crossed my mind, anonymous calls to
her au pair agency, threats of deportation. "Not yet," I said. "But
she wouldn't just walk away from her job and her friends." And
her computer.

"Not much we can do. People do wander off. With nothing to
go on . . . got a photo?"

"We can get one," I said.

"Well, bring it in," the officer said, "but it may not help
much."

"Can we file a report?" Joey asked.

"Yes, you could do that." His tone indicated that this would be
a waste of everyone's time, but he pointed us to the officer across
the room.

This woman was crisp but friendly, probably happy to be hearing her native tongue. She asked questions and wrote down
answers on the requisite form, a single sheet of white paper. It
depressed me, the things we didn't know about Annika. We put
her at five foot three, 115 pounds, but her birth date, identifying
marks and characteristics, even jewelry were trickier. I recalled a
red watch and silver hoop earrings. Joey thought she had a birth-
mark on a forearm. Neither of us knew the name of her dentist.

"So what happens now?" I asked as the officer finished
writing.

"We send it next door to a detective."

"Can we talk to him? Her?"

"I'm not sure who'll be assigned, and if they're in right now. Anyhow, there's nothing they can tell you."

"But if we were really horrible people," Joey said, "and made a big scene and started yelling and demanded to see a detective, what would happen then?"

The officer looked up. "Then you'd get to see a detective." She stood and called to her colleague manning the counter, "Who's around next door? Anyone?"

"Cziemanski," an officer called back, without looking up.

"Cziemanski," she said, and pointed to the exit.

Detective Cziemanski worked in a trailer marked "Detectives," at one of twenty or so desks crammed into a small area. The carpet was the same teal blue as the one next door, but less worn and dirty. Both trailers gave the appearance of having outlasted their intended lifespan and maximum occupancy by 25 percent.

"Shum," Detective Cziemanski said. "Shum-*man*-ski. Not Chum or Zum or Sum or Chime or Zime. Here's what happens: I take this report, I see there's no clear indication of a crime, so I send it to Missing Persons."

"Where's that?" I asked.

"Parker Center. Downtown." He ran a hand through his hair, or what would have been his hair had he had any, which he didn't. His skull glowed as if oiled, reminding me of the White's tree frog, *Litoria caerulea*, which I'd been researching for the mural. "They put it in the computer. I never see it again. Your friend turns up in a week or a month, and—. Okay, are you the type, when you can't make a dinner reservation, you call the restaurant to cancel?"

"Absolutely."

"Okay, so you call me up to say she's back, or she's living in Bali with her boyfriend, and I say thanks for letting me know." He smiled. His smile made him look younger, too guileless for a detective. His baldness made him look older but made his ears more prominent, which made him look younger again. I put him between twenty-nine and sixty.

"So you don't investigate anything, and you're just talking to us now to humor us?" Joey said.

"Yeah, pretty much. Next door sends people here, we send them back. Which is okay, I like talking to you. You seem rational, you're clean, you're worried about your friend. You're also good looking, both of you, but I'm not supposed to say that. I think you can sue."

Joey smiled. "That's why you're working in a trailer. All those sexual harassment lawsuits." Joey had family in law enforcement. She was right at home here, even drinking the coffee, which smelled like it had been brewing as long as Cziemanski had been on the force.

"And if Annika doesn't turn up?" I said. "Same scenario, except we don't call to cancel the dinner reservation? We just wait around, year after year?"

"Unless she's a juvenile, a criminal, or very elderly," he said, "I'm limited. There's no law against disappearing. As long as you're not wanted for a crime, it is, as they say, a free country. Now, you report a lost kid, or a mentally handicapped person, we're out there in numbers and we stay out till we find them. Or let's say your friend's a victim of domestic violence, her husband threatened to kill her last week—I take it that's not the case?"

Joey and I looked at each other and shook our heads.

"Does she have a drug problem?"

"Maybe," I said, at the same time that Joey said, "No."

He looked back and forth at us. "What'd you have in mind for me to investigate?"

"I guess I figured you'd check out her known associates," I said. "On the other hand, we're her known associates." There was also Maizie Quinn, who might feel compelled to show the police the drugs under Annika's bed, and Marty Otis, who'd describe her as a liar and a felon. What if Annika showed up tomorrow and found herself, thanks to me, facing criminal charges and deportation? Maybe I hadn't thought this through.

"We have to look at the odds," Cziemanski said. "This kind of thing, she's off in some time-share she forgot to tell you about. That's how it pans out, usually."

"Unless you're Chandra Levy," Joey said.

"Who?" Cziemanski and I said it at the same time.

"A few years back. She slept with a congressman and disappeared, and it was all over the news for weeks. And she turned up dead."

"Did your friend sleep with a congressman?" Cziemanski asked.

"No," I said, at the same time that Joey said, "Maybe."

He looked back and forth between us.

Joey said, "Would it help if she did?"

"Sure," Cziemanski said. "It'd help more if she *were* a congressman. Anything to set her apart from the other forty or fifty thousand missing Americans. Not including kids."

"Forty or fifty thousand?" I said. "And she's not even an American."

"Well, then. Unless she's wanted for war crimes, it'll be tough getting anyone interested. You two the only ones worried about"—he looked at his report—"Annika Glück?"

My heart sank. "Except for some odd people on an odd TV show. And her mother."

Detective Cziemanski folded the report in half, then unfolded it and added it to the mess on his desk. "I've got your numbers. Let me know if anything else turns up on your end. Meanwhile, I'll look into it. But don't get your hopes up."

We walked out of the trailer to Joey's husband's BMW, shiny and sleek, a standout in a parking lot full of trucks, minivans, and nonluxury vehicles. "Amazing," Joey said. "You go in expecting to hear 'Let us handle this' and instead, they all but deputize you. What fun."

"I hate when people say 'Don't get your hopes up,' " I said. "It's as bad as saying, 'Don't give up hope.' You either hope or you don't, but you don't adjust yourself like a toaster oven."

Joey clicked her key at the BMW. "I'll tell you what he hopes.

Cziemanski's hoping for a reason to call you, because that cop likes you."

"No, he doesn't."

"His name's Peter. I read his reports upside down. He'll ask you to call him Pete."

"I'm not calling him Pete. I'm immune to—I'm still recovering from—"

"Doc. I know. But consider this: all we need for Cziemanski to work Annika's case is one or two suspects. So first we hand him the boyfriend—cops always suspect the spouse or the lover. Then we offer an alternate: Marty Au Pair. Give me a minute, I'll make up something incriminating about him."

"I'm all for finding the boyfriend," I said. "But you're wrong, Joey. It's not suspects Cziemanski wants, it's a crime. Dollars to doughnuts, nobody's going to care about Annika Glück until we come up with a dead body."

7

If there's anything trickier than finding a missing person, it's finding the boyfriend of the missing person when all you have to go on is "Rico."

We called Annika's mother from Joey's car, on the 101 freeway. It was three P.M. in L.A., midnight in Germany, but I figured Mrs. Glück wouldn't be sleeping well, and I was right. All she could tell us about Rico, though, whose last name she didn't know, was that he was a "goat boy." There aren't a lot of goats that need tending in Southern California, so I decided she meant "good boy." I told her I'd call when I had news, and hung up before her lamentations could put me over the edge. I was worrying quite well on my own.

I tried Maizie Quinn, on the chance that she'd recalled Rico's last name. A human answered—Lupe, the housekeeper, who said Mrs. Quinn was at her sushi class. When I hung up, my phone rang. I answered it and was met with silence, the kind that signals a telemarketer about to take a stab at your name. Did telemarketers call cell phones? *Hello,* I repeated.

"Wollie Shelley?"

"Yes."

"Just checking."

That was the whole conversation. I said hello again, then did something I must've picked up from the movies: I pulled the phone away from my ear and stared at it.

"What?" Joey said. "Who was it?"

"No idea." I shook my head, disoriented. An electrical current of sorts was running through me, shaking me up despite the prosaic nature of the words. It jogged my memory. "Wait, I've got it. His last name. It's Feynman."

"Annika's boyfriend?" Joey said. "Rico Feynman?"

"Well, she called him Richard. It was after one of our tutorials. We were at the coffee bar, and I was going to walk her to her car, but she was going to wait around, she had a date. I said, 'A nice guy, I hope?' Because we'd been talking about our tendency to fall for the wrong kind of guy, and she told me not to worry, this one was a fine man. Literally. That was his last name. Feynman. She spelled it out."

"Did you meet him?"

"No," I said. "I walked by the coffee bar an hour later and looked in the window. She was reading a book. I wondered if he'd stood her up. Did Annika ever talk about this guy to you?"

Joey took the Laurel Canyon exit south, toward L.A. "No, but I know she brought him to the set to visit. I heard Savannah talk about him. Did I tell you, Elliot and Larry want me on the set every night from now on? Like my presence will improve ratings. The only thing that will improve our ratings is Elvis showing up as a guest expert. Sorry. Is Elvis a sensitive topic? I saw you crying in the grocery store when 'Suspicious Minds' was on the Muzak."

"No. That was just—Fritos. I used to buy them for Ruby; they're hard to get in Japan."

I missed twelve-year-old Ruby with a persistence that surprised me. I wondered if that's why I was reacting so strongly to Annika's disappearance—she'd filled that place left empty by Ruby. I missed Doc, too, but in a different way. It was no longer like an ice pick through my heart to think about the hundred or so sexual encounters with my ex-fiancé. Sometimes I had to work to recall the sound of his laugh, the way his hands looked on a steering wheel, the feel of his beard stubble against my face. I had no erotic stirrings for anyone else, though, let alone that rampant libidinous hunger, where you fantasize about the NBA, or random heads of state on the front page of the paper, or the checkout clerks at Costco.

Yet. Fredreeq said it would happen again. Joey too. That's what friends do, they keep a grasp on reality when you're stuck down some emotional rabbit hole . . .

"Joey," I said. "Annika might not've talked to us about Rico, but she talked to friends her own age. The other au pairs. Glenda, the counselor, even complained about it."

"Do you know their names?"

I racked my brain. Berta? "One took care of twins," I said. "That's all I remember. And I can't ask Glenda—she was very nervous talking to me at all. She kept saying she was a volunteer, as if that were some neurological problem."

"I'll get her talking," Joey said. "Tell me about her."

Minutes later Joey was calling Williams-Sonoma, doing what she called gagging, impersonating someone on the phone. She adopted a British accent. "Ms. Nacy? I'm Caroline Maxwell-Grace, with the Department of State in Washington. Your name was mentioned by Martin Otis of Au Pairs par Excellence as an Outstanding Community Counselor. . . . Yes. . . . So we're adding you to our list of national finalists, one of whom we'll honor with a—an honorarium." Joey slammed on the brakes, honking at a car coming to a sudden stop at Mulholland. "At a banquet. Attended by the secretary of state. . . . Pardon? . . . Funny how many Americans don't know the secretary of state." Joey turned to me, her face a plea.

I went blank. The secretary of state? I shook my head at her.

"As Henry Kissinger used to say, Beg pardon?" Joey looked at me again, eyebrows raised. "Cappuccino machine? I'm sorry, I already—ah. Aha . . ." Glenda's voice could be heard chirping away. The car ahead of us inched forward. We inched too. Joey said, "Safe to talk now? Right-oh. I do apologize for calling your work. Now: we're sending a field agent to California to gather testimonials, so which of your host families would you prefer us to interview? I understand there are three assigned to you . . ."

Horns honked on Laurel Canyon, angered by the standstill. "Mr. Otis *does* authorize you to make this decision, or he would not have had us—" Outside my window, a convertible was creating a new lane on the shoulder of the road. "By all means, confer with him, but my problem is, further delay may prevent my field agent reaching your people. You know what let's do? I'll order a cappuccino machine for my office staff. As you write up the order, think about which of your host families we should speak with. How does that sound?"

I rummaged through Joey's bag for a credit card, and handed it over as Joey made up an address for the State Department. She repeated names and neighborhoods and thanked Glenda, ending the call. "She doesn't have the numbers on her," Joey told me. "We'll try information. If they're not listed, we'll just have to bludgeon Marty Otis for them."

In San Marino there was a listing for R. Dobbler. After a fast phone call and an illegal U-turn, we were headed back to the Ventura Freeway.

San Marino street sweepers run a tight ship: no fallen leaf was allowed to loiter in the stately, silent residential neighborhood. "Is the whole town like this?" I asked.

"Smug wealth?" Joey nodded. "What do these people do? That's what I want to know. Back in Nebraska, there's money, but everyone knows where it comes from. You drive down a street like this, you say, That guy's chief of staff at Saint Elizabeth's, that family owns five car dealerships. . . . Even Beverly Hills, you can point to a house and say *Lethal Weapons Seven, Eight* and *Nine* bought that. Here, who knows? They must commute to L.A., right? There can't be enough business here to support this."

"The really rich don't go to work," I said.

"But these aren't even the really rich, these are the medium rich. The really rich don't have houses you can see from the street." Joey shook her head. "I lead a life my family back home can't comprehend, but next to this, I'm the working poor."

The Dobbler family's was a Spanish-style mansion. We parked in the driveway under a basketball hoop and stepped around bicycles and skateboards to the entrance. I was glad there were no signs of smaller offspring, being acutely baby-sensitive these days. Joey knocked on the rustic wooden double front doors with iron door knockers. The girl who answered verged on womanhood, in low-slung blue jeans and a peasant shirt. Her white-blond hair was a perfect match for her porcelain skin and pale eyebrows.

"I am Britta," she said. "You are the friends of Annika?" Her accent was so like Annika's it unnerved me.

We followed her to a large, antiseptic kitchen. We sat in a breakfast nook around an octagonal table set with five woven placemats. Britta didn't offer us refreshments. She said she had only twenty minutes before the two Dobbler boys returned from swim practice.

"You've heard that Annika is gone?" I said.

"No, I didn't hear this." She seemed almost excited by the news. "She is sent back?"

"To Germany? No," I said. "Why would you think that?"

A look of doubt crossed her face. "*Ja*, okay. I don't know. I just thought."

"That she was sent away? You don't think she'd leave on her own?"

"No, of course not." Britta opened her eyes wide. They were blue-green, too close together for beauty, but in combination with her white-blond hair, striking. "Her situation is very good, just one girl to care for, and the host family very nice. She can drive the car everywhere, whenever she likes." This seemed to be a thorn in Britta's side.

"You don't get to drive?" Joey asked.

"The insurance is very expensive. So for some host families it is not expected that the au pair will drive. For example, here the housekeeper will drive the children to school and activities. Also, the housekeeper will drive me, for example to English class."

I could see what a tragedy that could be, stuck without wheels in a neighborhood with all the excitement of a golf course. "So Annika was happy in the U.S.?" I said.

"Yes, why not? Everything was very lucky for her. She drove a car just for her, not even to share with the family. She never had to ask—if she had free time, she could just drive it."

"And then there was Annika's boyfriend," I said, to distract her from her automobile envy. "She wouldn't want to leave him, I suppose?"

"Rico." She cheered up instantly. "Of course she would not leave Rico Rodriguez."

"Rodriguez?" I said. "That was his name?"

"Yes."

"Not—Feynman?"

"Who?"

I looked at Joey. "Another man she—was friends with. Also named Richard."

"Rico's forename is Richard." Britta laughed. "But he calls himself Rico, to annoy his father. He says that Rico is the only Spanish word his father knows. He is so funny."

"Is he a student?" I asked.

"Yes, at Pepperdine. He is very smart, but he has little time for studies, because he is popular and goes to many parties and has many interests as well."

"Like Annika," Joey said. Britta looked blank. "She had many outside interests too."

"*Ja*, okay," Britta said. "She has a car, you see."

"So," I said, "Rico has a lot of friends? Girls as well as boys?"

Britta nodded and smiled. "Everyone loves Rico. He is completely great."

"Do you think Annika might be staying with him?" Joey asked.

Britta stopped smiling and considered this. Then she shook

her head. "The university, it is strict Christian. The mans and the womans, it is not permitted that they are in the same room, for example, after midnight or perhaps one o'clock. So Annika would not be there. Also, Rico has roommates. There is no space." The thought seemed to bring relief, and she looked at us again, awaiting the next question. She was an accommodating interviewee, I thought, and a remarkably incurious one. And one who knew a lot about her girlfriend's boyfriend.

"Do you think Annika did drugs?" Joey said.

She found this startling. "Oh, no. Annika? She is very . . . I do not know in English. *Vernünftig*. You could say, rational. . . . But in any case, no drugs." A troubled look came over her face. She nibbled on a nail.

"Would you happen to have Rico's telephone number?" I asked.

Britta looked at her watch, a large-dial pink plastic job, as easy to read as she was. "*Ja*, okay. I be right back." She took off at a jog, the sound of footsteps receding quickly.

"Well, there's another neighborhood heard from," Joey said. "She doesn't think Annika's a druggie any more than we do. And I wonder who this Feynman guy is. I don't really see Annika playing the field." She jumped up and opened a kitchen cupboard, revealing glassware. She closed that and tried another, a pantry jammed with enough food to keep a family of four snacking for a month. "Just curious," she said. "Don't you love how people eat?" She was headed for the refrigerator when we heard the footsteps returning. She took her seat.

"So where do you think Annika might have gone?" I asked Britta as she bounded in, a daisy-motif address book in hand. "We've talked to her mother. She's not in Germany."

"I do not know. Perhaps San Francisco. Or Disney World. Look, we made this picture only one month ago." She handed us a snapshot of three people, arms around each other. I recognized Annika, her face turned away. The boy in the middle towered over the girls, smiling at a glowing Britta. He was out of focus but clearly tall and dark, and possibly handsome. I handed the photo to Joey. She took a look and handed it to Britta, who smiled and traced over it with one finger before placing it carefully back in the address book. I asked Britta if she had another photo of Annika; she didn't.

She copied Rico's number in loopy, back-slanted handwriting, and asked that we send him her love, and tell him he should call her. She also gave us the number for Hitomi, the au pair in Palos Verdes, but saw little point in us contacting her. "She is not social," Britta said. "Also, she is Japanese."

She did not seem especially worried about her friend and compatriot. She was, as Joey observed walking out to the car, considerably interested in the sudden availability of Rico Rodriguez.

The next day I would find out why.

8

I started Thursday the way I started most Thursdays, picking up my Uncle Theo in Glendale and driving up the coast to Rio Pescado, the state mental hospital that my brother, P.B., called home. "Breakfast with the troops," Uncle Theo called it, referring to the fact that while we were technically visiting P.B., in fact we were joined by several more patients desperate for visitors of their own. The faces changed regularly and so did the mental disorders, which made for a lively ninety minutes. P.B., with adult-onset paranoid schizophrenia, was one of the longest-term residents because of his participation in UCLA-sponsored drug trials. The drug trials were coming to an end, though, and he was scheduled to graduate soon to an outpatient program, a halfway house in Santa Barbara his doctor had pulled strings to get him into. Even with the added expenses, I was excited by the prospect. P.B., however, was anxious.

"What about the trees?" he said, staring skyward, squinting. We were finishing breakfast at a picnic table, enjoying the sunny November morning. A couple of birds had their eyes on our trays. I was trying not to think about Annika. Or Rico Rodriguez, for whom I'd left several messages.

"They have trees in Santa Barbara," I said, nibbling on a piece of toast.

"Fifty-foot *Quercus agrifolia*? I'm worried about these. They're not well."

"Change is good, P.B.," I said. "I know you'll miss people here, but everyone moves on eventually. It's a hospital; that's the nature of it. And now it's your turn. Do you know how much better you are? I almost never worry about you anymore." I reached over and pulled a leaf from his hair. We had the same hair, blond and fine. I was rarely happy with my own, but for some reason I loved it on my little brother.

P.B. continued squinting skyward. "I was of no use to these trees," he said.

Uncle Theo said, "When I'm concerned about you or Wollie, I take comfort in the Heisenberg uncertainty principle. If the act of observation changes that which is observed, then witnessing itself has value. You've participated in the life of these trees."

P.B. shook his head. "Except it's the particle interaction, not the conscious observer that matters."

I listened to my brother and uncle discuss concepts completely foreign to me, wondering what it meant that I was the odd duck in a family like ours. A patient at a nearby table, disturbed by a squirrel she found threatening, let out a scream, stopping all conversation. By the time a psych tech led her indoors, trees were forgotten, visiting hours were up, and good-byes were said.

"It's a longer drive to Santa Barbara," I said to Uncle Theo, on the ride home, "but it's beautiful. Dr. Charlie showed me photos of the halfway house, and it's nicer than my apartment. Any of my apartments."

"I shall miss Rio Pescado," Uncle Theo said. He plucked something from his hand-knit cardigan, a garment he'd worn since the sixties. He unrolled the passenger side window and flapped his hand in the wind. "Good-bye, little bug. Safe home."

This was where Rico Rodriguez found me, via cell phone, on the 101 South, approaching Oxnard. He apologized for taking so long to return my call. "Roommates," he said. "Not great at messages. Totally lame, in fact."

No problem, I said, and explained why I wanted to see him.

"I'm off campus today," he said. "My campus, anyway. I'm in Santa Monica now, but if you want to do Malibu, I'll be at Murph's in an hour. I could give you fifteen minutes there. Otherwise, I'm booked through the weekend."

Booked. That sounded more like a caterer than a student. I glanced at my uncle in the passenger seat, singing, "Where Have All the Flowers Gone?" I couldn't drop him in Glendale and make it to Malibu in an hour, so he'd have to come with me.

"We'll be there," I said to Rico. "What and where is Murph's?"

Murph's was on the inland side of Pacific Coast Highway, just off Cross Creek Road. It was small, smelled of frying bacon and brewing coffee, and was packed, a hangout for the Pepperdine crowd. Uncle Theo and I grabbed a newly vacated table and settled in. We didn't have long to wait.

I could tell by the way Rico Rodriguez entered the room that it was him. He paused in the doorway, stopped by the crush of bodies. Easy to see why he was loved by two German girls, and probably hundreds of American ones. He was over six feet, slim and muscular, with a swimmer's body, in black denim jeans and black T-shirt. To me, he looked a little like Doc. A taller, younger, handsomer version, but to me, all sexy men looked a little like Doc.

He spotted us and approached like someone confident of his welcome. He shook hands, then conferred with the waitress who'd materialized, sucked into his magnetic field. Uncle Theo asked for hot water and produced from his cardigan a crumpled tea bag. We'd had the car windows open since Oxnard, and his white hair stuck straight out in every direction, producing a halo-like effect. For an instant I was back in high school, suffering from the strain of trying to appear hip for some boy while simultaneously being related to Uncle Theo.

Rico took a cell phone from his jeans pocket, placed it on the table, and leaned back. "So, okay," he said. "Annika. Yeah, she hasn't been around. What's up with her?"

"I was hoping you could tell me," I said.

"Why would you think that?"

"Well, I was under the impression—aren't you her boy-friend?"

He gave a rueful smile, one corner of his mouth turned up. "That depends on who you're asking."

"Let's say I'm asking you."

"Look. Annie's great. Got a lot going for her. We hooked up. Fun girl. But if she told you it was, like, serious—" Our waitress set down an ice tea and tried to weave around a cluster of bodies. A man entered the restaurant carrying a baby in a car seat. The car seat got caught in the screen door, requiring people near the door to move and, in a domino effect, the rest of us move accordingly, chairs scooting toward tables.

"Actually," I said, "she didn't talk about you at all. When did you last see her?"

He shrugged. "Week or so ago. We'd hook up after my chem class, that's Tuesdays, so . . . Tuesday. Last week."

"Not this week?"

"No. I kind of expected her to call, but . . ." He stirred his ice tea, then looked up through long black lashes. Another half smile. "She didn't talk about me at all?"

I smiled back. "Not to me. But to other people, her friend Britta—"

"Britta." His smile expanded. "Now there's a—"

The baby in the car seat screeched, awakened by a collision with the waitress. I half-stood, propelled by something other than my conscious mind, then sat again. The man put the car seat on the floor and crouched down to unbuckle the screaming baby. I turned to Rico. "So you weren't serious about Annika?"

"I don't want to sound like a jerk, but we weren't getting married or anything. Come on, I'm twenty-one. Who needs that?" He laughed. "I'd like to catch my dad's face, seeing her at the dinner table. Yeah, Dad, she's a professional babysitter. Doesn't go to college. Oh, and by the way, she's German. Yeah, like that's gonna go over."

He looked a little less attractive to me. "Did Annika know you didn't consider her . . . relationship material?"

"I guess. I mean, her visa's up next month, what's she expect?" His eyes dropped. "I try not to lead them on, but girls seem to . . . I don't know . . ."

The baby continued to cry, sounding like a cat. "Rico," I said, "was Annika into drugs?"

He looked at me quickly, then away. "No. Not Annie."

"Sex?" The word just popped out of me.

He looked at me again, and smiled. "You mean did she like it? Uh, yeah. As far as I could tell." There was a moment of actual heat between us. Good heavens.

"Sorry," I said. "I don't mean to get personal, I'm just trying to figure out what happened to her. Actually, I'm trying to figure out who she was. I get a different picture from everyone I talk to." Math whiz, gunrunner, drug user, sex fiend. Babysitter.

He chugged his ice tea, then set down the empty glass. "It's the accent. I thought it was hot at first, but my roommate says accents are totally Third World."

"It seems to me," Uncle Theo said, "that the more foreign the person, the easier it is to project onto them our fantasies and prejudices, the most extreme example being extraterrestrials. Rico, I'm admiring your earring. Is it a sociopolitical statement?"

Rico looked surprised. His hand went to his ear, to the small gold stud embedded with a red gem. "No, just something a bunch of us did in high school, my buddies. The earring was my mom's. She lost the other one. I think it's a ruby."

Ruby. The word gave me a pang, reminding me of my almost-stepdaughter. I mentally shook myself. "Do you remember a specific piece of jewelry Annika wore? Or did she have any distinguishing features?"

"You mean, like a scar or something?" He looked down at his hands. "She had really smooth skin. That's the main thing I remember."

"And didn't she wear a watch?"

"Yeah, a Fossil. I gave her a hard time about it, because it was like, cheap, but she never took it off. Well, except in the shower."

"Yo! Dude!"

Rico's head turned with a snap. He held up his index finger, signaling to two college-age guys in Murph's doorway. He stood, took out his wallet, slapped a ten-dollar bill on the table, refused change, and apologized for having to leave abruptly.

I followed him toward the door. "One more thing," I said. "Did she ever mention a Richard Feynman?"

He turned, frowning. "I think I know the name. Maybe not."

"Did you know she wanted a gun?"

Rico froze. His hand, in the act of returning his wallet to his back pocket, stopped in midair. "Annika? No, I . . . Jesus. You serious?"

If I'd wanted a show of concern, I was getting it now. His friends called to him again, but Rico kept staring at me. Then he mumbled a good-bye and turned to go, so distracted he bumped into people on his way out. I returned to the table.

Murph's was quieter with the lunch rush over. Uncle Theo and I went to the counter to pay the check and got into conversation with the father of the baby.

The baby's name was Annabelle. I got to hold her while the father went to the men's room. She spit up all over the front of my white shirt, then rewarded me with a big gummy smile. For some reason, this made me want to cry.

9

Thursday night on the set of *Biological Clock* I talked about Annika with Henry Fisher, my date and fellow contestant of the evening.

"Yeah, she brought her boyfriend around a couple times." Henry Fisher scratched his beard. "He's got no idea where she is?"

"No," I said. "And there's a guy named Feynman—did she ever mention him to you?"

"No, we mostly talked the Bible. Football. Guns." Henry pulled at his collar. Tonight's location was Hot Aloo, an Indian restaurant in west L.A., small, redolent of body heat and curry, doing a brisk business. Henry was built for a Barcalounger, not Hot Aloo's flimsy furniture. And beer. Hot Aloo didn't have a liquor license, so the ubiquitous Takei Sake bottle would hold water. Henry was now drinking *nimbu ka pani*, a sort of lemonade. He was as handsome as Carlito, in a very different style, with lots of facial hair, a respectable amount of head hair, and a predilection for jeans and flannel shirts. A guy you'd want if you went white-water rafting and ran into bad rapids. Not that that happens a lot in L.A. "I did tell Annika to go to a gun show," he said. "You heard that right."

"What kind of fool thing is that to tell a teenage girl?"

Fredreeq said, approaching with a compact of translucent face powder.

"She's here to see America," Henry said. "What's more American than gun shows?"

"Jell-O. Pez. *The Brady Bunch.*" Fredreeq brushed flecks of powder from his beard.

"Henry, did you tell Annika to buy a gun?" I asked.

"Nope. Told her to educate herself. Talk to people. Find a class. Gun safety. Practice regime. No point owning a piece of equipment you can't use. Too many ignorant people think buying a gun makes them safe. It doesn't."

"Did she mention wanting one right away?"

"Yup. Wanted to know if I had one I could lend her. Told her that's not how we do things. Regardless of what they say about us over in Europe. Or what Bing Wooster says."

"Bing?" I looked through the plate-glass window at our director, pacing outside the restaurant, cell phone to his ear. I was about to ask what Bing had had to say about guns when Isaac, the sound guy, approached. He handed me a small bullet-shaped thing attached to a wire and pointed to my cleavage.

"Body mike. Ambient noise," he said. I told him this meant nothing to me. With a sigh, he reached inside my silk blouse and attached the bullet thing near a buttonhole with a piece of electrician's tape. I have large breasts, so we couldn't avoid physical contact, but I feel safe in saying it was not an erotic experience for either of us.

I now had a microphone between my breasts and a wire running down my rib cage and circling my waist, ending in a black box the size of a deck of cards that Isaac stuck in the pocket of my linen pants. As he went to work on Henry, I imagined us plugged into an electrical outlet and lit up like Christmas trees. The image began to turn into a greeting card, but it was a little suggestive of electrocution, not a very Christmassy concept, so I let it go.

Bing came into the restaurant and picked up the Betacam.

Fredreeq retreated. I joined Henry on his side of the table. Paul set up a cheap light on a tripod, augmenting Hot Aloo's votive candles. A burst of laughter across the room punctuated a foreign-language discussion.

"Paul, what's with the crowd?" Bing asked. "You said the place was empty when you did the scout."

"That was lunchtime," Paul said.

"So?"

"It's Ramadan. They have a big Muslim clientele."

"So? Okay, whatever. Wollie," Bing said. "Same drill as the other night. Ask Henry what he does for a living. Action!"

It always startled me, Bing yelling "Action!," since he seemed to do it only when everyone was within whispering distance. Joey said it was also inappropriate to a videotape format, but this was a distinction only she and Isaac would understand.

"Henry," I said, trying to sound spontaneous, "what do you do for a living?"

Henry was a Christmas-tree farmer, something we all knew. "Monterey pines," he said, warming to his subject. "A long-needle tree. Not as classy as your noble; more like a good Douglas fir. Your four-year-olds will run eight to ten feet. I do a four-year rotation on fifty acres, fifteen hundred trees per acre, one-fifth lying dormant."

"Uh . . . huh."

Bing, his camera running, waved his free hand at me in a "Go on, keep talking" gesture.

"What else?" I said. This was not inspired repartee, but all those numbers had frozen my thinking process.

"Lot of farmers do seventeen hundred per acre, but I don't like to squeeze my trees."

"Okay. Good," I said.

Henry perked up suddenly. "Funny thing. I get thirty-five, forty bucks per tree, cut and carry. Little Annika, I tell her this, she calculates on the spot how much I lose annually doing fifteen hundred instead of seventeen, then compounds the interest—"

"Cut," Bing yelled. "Hey, guy, none of our viewers knows who Annika is. And nobody cares. So don't talk about her."

"Oh. Okay." Henry deflated a little. The camera started rolling and I quickly asked him what he did when it wasn't Christmas-tree season.

"Pull stumps," he said. "Plant. Irrigate. Irrigate more. Prune, spray for mites and pine-tip moths, weed control. You can't slack off, you start right in after Christmas. Santa Ana winds come before the baby trees have time to manufacture root hairs, you're sunk."

I loved that he called them baby trees. I hoped that moment would make it onto the TV screen, because I thought it showed Henry in his best light, strong yet vulnerable. I was fond of Henry. I was fond of Carlito too, but Henry Fisher didn't have a self-promoting bone in his body, and that was an endearing quality.

Then it was my turn. Bing had me describe my home, something Savannah and Kimberly, the other female contestants, would also be discussing. This was a bad moment. A one-bedroom sublet in West Hollywood, a.k.a. Boystown, does not suggest a woman ready to mother a child, but I told myself it was better than being homeless, which was what I'd be soon unless I mustered energy for apartment hunting. After that we took a bathroom break.

Two women in saris came out of the ladies' room as I went in. I wondered what to do about the sound system I was wearing. Would Isaac listen to me pee? No, Isaac was a professional. He could've listened to bodily functions of people far more famous than I, if he were so inclined. Nevertheless, I covered the microphone between my breasts in toilet paper and squeezed my fist over it. It was so tiny, a microphone for a mouse. Or a frog. This brought on a greeting card idea, karaoke for frogs. I began to develop it as I exited the ladies' room.

Isaac, in headphones, came out of the men's room at the same time. He avoided me.

Henry sat at the table reading a magazine while Paul sat opposite, working on a laptop. I squeezed in next to Paul and glanced at the folded-over page Henry held in front of him, an opinion piece. "If our allies harbor drug lords like Joseph Juarez and Vladimir Tcheiko," it read, "are they deserving of the term 'ally'? Why not make trade agreements contingent upon extradition treaties—" The rest of the sentence was hidden beneath Henry's index finger.

Vladimir Tcheiko. I'd heard of him, but I couldn't recall the context. He sounded less like a drug lord than a drug count, I decided. Count Tcheiko. A vampire. I tried that on, seeing if there was a greeting card in it, a vampire awaiting extradition. As with frog karaoke, no occasion immediately presented itself. Some images you have to live with for a while.

"Hey, Henry," I said. "You think Annika ever did drugs?"

He lowered the magazine, shocked. "That little girl? Not likely."

Paul looked up from his computer and stared at me.

"What, Paul?" I said.

He looked over his shoulder, then leaned in. "This one time, she asks me, 'Paul, where does one buy drugs? At university?' which was so funny, how she'd talk formal sometimes, not like, 'Where do I score some blow,' or whatever. Like some English teacher probably told her, 'When you go to America, here is how to ask for ketchup—' "

"Paul!" Bing yelled, gesturing with his cell phone. "The chick can't find a parking place. Go out there, drive her car around, and send her in. Let's go."

"What chick?" Paul asked.

"Whatsername. The expert."

Paul nodded, closed his laptop, and took off. Henry and I looked at each other. What did it mean, what Paul had just said? Henry frowned and returned to his paper.

I checked my watch. In Germany, it was Friday, and Mrs. Glück would be waking up. She'd left another message on my machine, begging me to call before she left for work. Maizie

Quinn had called too, wondering what I'd found out and how Mrs. Glück was doing. I pulled out my cell phone and turned it on. Could I possibly discuss drugs with Annika's mother? Maybe. The signal was lousy, though, so I left Henry to his reading and went outside.

Hot Aloo was on the upper level of a minimall. I found I got a good signal by hanging over the balcony. Traffic sounds from Wilshire Boulevard wafted up, and from somewhere, the smell of a cigarette. The November night air was a welcome change from the stifling restaurant, even for me, who cranks up the heat when the temperature drops below seventy. Sweater Girl, Doc used to call me. I smiled, remembering, then felt my smile deflate. How long until I could think of him without melancholy, without wondering what my life would've been had he stuck around? How long until I'd look at a man without measuring him against Doc?

My call to Germany didn't go through. The computer operator suggested I check the number and try the call again. I did this.

The minimall was deserted, its only movement an up escalator, a waste of electricity, since Hot Aloo had closed its kitchen to the general public. The shops were dark. I thought about when I'd managed a minimall shop and had come close to owning it. I missed my shop. I missed my ex-fiancé. I missed his daughter. I missed Annika.

A lone figure stepped onto the escalator. I watched the escalator rise as my call went through and Mrs. Glück answered. She and I struggled through pleasantries, then I explained I was working and couldn't talk long.

"*Ja*," she said. "You have find host family?"

"The Quinns. Yes." The person on the escalator was quite tall. Male. Not, then, our evening's expert, the "chick." I asked Mrs. Glück if the agency had called her.

"How?"

"Au Pairs par Excellence." No response. The escalator man reached the second level. "The agency," I repeated. "In San Pedro. Marty, uh—Otis. Marty Otis?"

"Ah, *ja, ja,* San Pedro. Au pair."

"Have they called you?" I asked. The tall man was coming toward Hot Aloo. Beautiful gait: long stride, hands in pockets, relaxed. Funny thing to notice, a gait.

"*Nein.*"

"He didn't call? No one's called you?"

"Where?"

Here we go again, I thought. No wonder Maizie had opted out of calling Mrs. Glück. "Okay," I said. "I met Mrs. Quinn. She's nice, she's worried about Annika, but thinks she's safe." It would've been more accurate to say that Maizie thought Annika had run off with Rico, the Goat Boy, or was holed up somewhere doing drugs, but I didn't have the heart for that.

"*Nein,* you to me must to listen," Mrs. Glück said. "*Sie* is *brav, meine* Annika. *Brav.*"

"Blov?"

"*Brav.* Brav. *Verantwortlich!*"

Her English deteriorated as her anxiety level rose. I revised my plan to question her about guns or drugs. "Listen, did she talk to you about Richard Feynman—"

"*Nein,* you must to listen. *Sie* is not safe, or *sie* must to call me."

He was very close now. Four feet away. Well within my personal space. How odd. He leaned on the railing, the same way I leaned on it, and looked down over the minimall.

"Yes," I said. "I agree it's strange, but what can we do?"

Mrs. Glück had apparently given this some thought, but only in German. Annika did the same when excited, abandoning English. As the language of Goethe and Rilke sounded in my ear, I stared at the tall man. He had a tough profile. Hard angles. There was a bump on the bridge of his nose, as if it had been broken. Not a face you'd want to meet in a dark alley. Or even a dimly lit minimall.

I reminded myself that twenty feet away was a restaurant full of people.

Mrs. Glück abruptly returned to English. "—peoples to look for her? California? Marty Otis, the family Kvin?"

Lying is so hard for me, I couldn't say yes. But I knew a little of what this woman was going through, knew what she was doing up at six A.M., talking to me, a stranger. What I said would matter, so I couldn't tell her that in fact, no, not one of these people was looking for her daughter. "I wish I had something concrete—"

"*Bitte, bitte, du bist die einzigste*—you must to *versprechen*— promise to me. Promise to me, you. They must her look. They must her find."

I looked at the man again. He wore a suit. A beautiful one. I had a bizarre urge to touch it, to see what the fabric felt like. What a strange place the world was, people standing within touching distance of each other, not relating. "You know what?" I said. "*I* am looking. I'll keep looking. I won't give up."

Mrs. Glück thanked me and blessed me in two languages, then hung up.

I was about to go back into the restaurant, but I'd just made a promise and it could be hours before the next break. I punched in Maizie Quinn's number. It was easy to remember, only one digit different from Annika's. I got the machine. "Hi, Maizie," I said, self-conscious now because of the man next to me, but too stubborn to walk away. I'd gotten here first. "It's Wollie. Calling about the—au pair situation. I went to the agency. You have my numbers." I ended the call, wondering why I was hesitant to say Annika's name aloud.

The man turned to me. His eyes were blue. It must have been a trick of the moonlight, because they looked transparent. This intrigued me. "Something I can help you with?" I said.

"Yeah."

I expected him to elaborate, but he didn't. He seemed to be studying me, and I felt myself blush. I turned to go. Again.

"Wait," he said. "Do me a favor. Walk away from this."

"Well, which is it?" I said. "Wait or walk away?"

"I think you understand me."

Perhaps he was mentally ill. I often attract mentally ill people, feel an affinity for them, probably from years of dealing with my brother's schizophrenia. Also, the mentally ill can have the most beautiful eyes; why is that?

"This thing you're walking into," he continued. "Get out."

I said the first thing that occurred to me. "Get out of—*Biological Clock*?"

"What?"

"I think you understand me," I said. Two could play this enigmatic game.

"You think you can't get hurt?"

What a strange thing to say. I'd been hurt quite a lot, I could've told him. Who in life had not? But his face was so hard, except for those eyes, that I was not tempted to bare my soul to it.

He'd been leaning on the railing, but now he straightened up and I was aware of how very tall he was. And I'm six feet myself. He looked down at me. "Think you're that pretty?"

I stared at him. If only I had a clue what he was talking about.

He leaned in close. He smelled clean. "You are that pretty. But you'll go down, just the same."

The words paralyzed me. Then Bing's voice broke the spell. "Our expert's coming," he yelled from the doorway of Hot Aloo. "Let's go, folks."

The tall man walked away. He didn't look back, just headed for the stairs, not even acknowledging he'd heard me when I called after him, "But what is it I've done?"

I didn't know how I would concentrate on anything after that, but then I met Dr. Theodora Zagan.

Dr. Theodora Zagan looked about eighteen; apparently she'd begun her postgraduate work at puberty. She asked the waiter for the beef vindaloo Henry was eating, but spicier. She asked Fredreeq for a mirror, checked her lip line and fluffed her bangs, then told Bing to start rolling tape anytime. At his "Action!" she turned to me.

"Are you ready," she said, "for the financial burden you assume with your first child? The answer," she said, as I opened my mouth, "is no. Because you have no idea what that burden is." She took a sip of water and turned to Henry. "Statistically, *you* will spend more time with your child than your father spent with you. But you'll put in nowhere near the eighty-hour week this woman will, between her job and her mothering. You'll pick up a fraction of the child-care duties, regardless of which of you is the household's primary breadwinner."

"Henry and I don't live together," I said.

"Then the gap widens. Child support won't begin to address the cost of parenting. Unless you, sir, are extremely wealthy and, more to the point, generous. Oil magnate, record-industry executive?"

"Christmas-tree farmer," Henry said.

Theodora turned back to me. "In lost wages alone, from the overtime hours you will refuse, the minimal maternity leave you will take, the absentee days you will accrue in order to tend to your child when he or she is ill, and, most debilitatingly, the promotions you will not obtain or even seek due to the fact that work is no longer your life, as it is to your male or childless female colleagues—this will add up to an average of one million dollars in the course of your lifetime. This does not include the actual cost of raising the child, the food, clothing, shelter, medical, education, and miscellaneous costs."

"I'm sorry," I said. "Did you say one million dollars?"

"Per child. More if you're a trained professional. Less if you're an unskilled laborer."

"I don't have a college degree."

"Then you'll be at the lower end of the scale," Theodora said.

Thank God. I couldn't afford a million dollars. "Do you have children?" I asked.

"No, I'm the childless colleague I just referred to, the one angling for the promotion. But I'm quite young. I have a rigorous investment program, in case I fall prey to the biological imperative you're experiencing."

I managed a vague smile. "So I'm—doomed? To penury?"

"Poverty." Theodora nodded. "The single biggest predictor of a woman growing old in poverty is having children. In America. Most developed countries subsidize the caregivers of their future taxpayers. Here we recognize human capital as our most valuable resource and the early years as the most developmentally crucial, yet the lion's share of investment in this resource comes from family, not government—"

"Says who?" Henry asked.

"Gary Becker, Nobel Prize, 1992. If children were acres of corn, we'd subsidize them. They're not. We don't. A day-care worker makes peanuts, but she does accrue social security; take care of your own kids and you're a fiscal deadbeat. You're better off as a single parent, forced to work outside the home. A stay-at-home mom falls off the map entirely. Disappears."

Disappears. Funny to hear the word used in that context. Maybe that's what happened to Annika: she became a stay-at-home mom.

"Are you a feminist?" Henry asked.

"God no. I'm an economist," Theodora said.

I raised my hand. "I'm a feminist." No one paid any attention.

"My politics are irrelevant, in any case," Theodora said. "There's no lobbying group for caregivers as there is for senior citizens, for instance, even though as a group, caregivers—mothers, let's be frank—outnumber every other demographic you can think of."

"I plan to help out," Henry said.

"Good." Theodora turned to me. "Get it in writing."

"Cut!" Bing cried. "Print! Perfect!"

Our food came. Our expert dug in, Henry sniffed everything with an air of suspicion, and I just nibbled on *naan,* wondering if I should start my life over as Theodora Zagan.

We progressed to on-camera dessert and discussions of living trusts for the baby that none of us had. The one I'd neglected to save up for. It was a long night, and I had a headache at the end. The only bright spot was Paul telling me he left messages every day on Annika's machine, with the shooting schedule. Just in case. It made me feel less alone.

It was long after midnight before I walked down Wilshire with Joey and Fredreeq to our cars. My friends were discussing whether my longed-for college diploma would be worth the paper it would be printed on, given what Dr. Theodora Zagan had just told us. Joey said it wouldn't. Fredreeq vehemently disagreed, quoting wage-earning statistics for holders of bachelor degrees. That's when I told them about my encounter with the man outside Hot Aloo. I did not mention his eyes.

My friends came to a dead halt on the sidewalk, staring at me.

"Now, that is creepy," Fredreeq said. "So, along with everything else, I got your physical safety to worry about now."

"I'll follow you home," Joey said. "And I'll keep my phone on."

"I hate to say this," Fredreeq said, "but I wish Doc was here. He was short, but he was scrappy. How am I gonna be able to sleep nights, knowing about this?"

Doc. How extraordinary. I hadn't thought about Doc for hours.

10

Fredreeq wasn't kidding. Worrying about me had disrupted her sleep, she said, calling at seven A.M. "Let's shop," she suggested.

"I can't," I said. "One, I can't afford to, and two, I have to be at SMC at nine-thirty."

"That's fine. I gotta get the kids to school and, anyway, nothing opens till ten. Westside Pavilion. Eleven. Be there."

SMC, or Santa Monica College, was one of those places that did for me what shopping malls did for Fredreeq. When I was young and impressionable, I saw the film *Love Story* and developed a yearning not just for Ali MacGraw's glossy black hair and pea coats but for college campuses. Circumstances like money and family issues diverted me from getting a degree in the normal fashion, but did not keep me from enrolling in classes in various odd learning institutions. Part of this was longing for a legitimacy I felt belonged to the college-educated. Part of it was that I aspired to an actual career, like a teacher, not a series of jobs I'd invented or fallen into or the kind that could be done by a really gifted chimpanzee. Mostly, though, I took classes for the thrill of being on a campus. Even at Santa Monica College. There was little ivy, the grass was patchy, and the bathrooms utterly frightening, but Friday morning as I strolled to the counseling office, I could, without too much trouble, hear piano music in my head and picture autumn leaves swirling around me.

This semester, in lieu of an actual class, I was developing a strategy to get a degree. To that end, I'd acquired a counselor, Mr. Pinneo. Although it was our third appointment, Mr. Pinneo had not invited me to address him on a first-name basis. Probably this was a sound tactic with normal college freshmen, as Mr. Pinneo, like Dr. Theodora Zagan, looked about twenty.

"More transcripts, Wollie?" he asked, scratching his nose ring. We were in a tiny cubicle he shared with several people.

"Yeah." I handed him the envelope. "I remembered an astronomy course I took eight years ago through DuMetz Community College. We met in the desert in the middle of the night to watch meteor showers. As you see, I got an A."

Mr. Pinneo studied the document. "I'll run it by my supervisor. I'm not sure it meets the Intersegmental General Education Transfer Curriculum requirement for your physical science. It might. Then again, it might not. Best thing to do meanwhile is sign up for a math class. Any of those in your past you might've forgotten?"

"No," I said. "I barely took any in high school. But I've been studying the course-sequence chart in the catalog, in itself pretty challenging, as some course numbers go backward, meaning that Math 81 precedes Math 20—but anyway. Correct me if I'm wrong, Mr. Pinneo, and I hope I am, because by my calculations, I need to take Math 81 or 81T, then Math 84, then Math 31 or 31T, then Math 20 and 21 or 41 and 52, at which point I'll be caught up with normal college juniors."

Mr. Pinneo took from me the weighty catalog and peered at it. "You're right."

My heart sank. "And I have to take these courses one at a time, in sequence."

"Unless you test out."

"You mean the math-assessment test. I did that, remember? You have the results."

Mr. Pinneo shuffled through a file that was extensive, considering I had not yet registered for classes. He withdrew a sheet of paper. "Yeah. Not real good at math, are you?"

"No. But after that test, I got a math tutor."

"Good. How's that going?"

A vision popped into my head of Annika, with her mechanical pencil, drawing for me Galileo, Newton, and Einstein as happy faces: Quantification, Gravitation, and Relativity. "It's—it was going well," I said. "So how long before I should take the assessment test again?"

Mr. Pinneo glanced at my test scores. "Maybe you just sign up for Math 81. Basic Arithmetic. That's for people who haven't—"

"—done long division since the Reagan administration. I know. But I can't afford to stay here taking math, one class at a time, for the rest of my natural life. I'm hoping to transfer to UCLA." UCLA had a beautiful campus. Equally important, it offered the graphic arts degree I was seeking. It would not admit me, though, until Santa Monica College had certified me, according to the terms of the Intersegmental General Education Transfer Curriculum.

"Okay," he said. "Take the assessment test anytime before your registration date, which is"—he typed into his computer—"two weeks. You get one more shot, then you have to wait three months to retest. Meanwhile, might as well do the math. Without math, you won't do squat in science. Good luck, Wollie."

I walked out into the sunshine, squinting. The campus no longer seemed the symbol of possibility it had been a half hour earlier. I felt old, stupid, and poor. But I had to make this work, because my other dreams weren't panning out. Marriage and children were remote possibilities, people were fleeing my life with alarming frequency—college was the one thing under my conscious control. It wasn't cheap, but instead of three or four classes at a time, I'd take one. One per semester. But not if it was math. Not for the next seventy years. I'd had a better attitude when it looked like Doc would be around to help with homework. Maths 21 through 82 wouldn't have fazed him; he'd gone to MIT.

They hadn't fazed Annika either. "You are missing out on this fun!" she'd said, hearing of my math phobia. "Did you play with puzzles when you were small? This is geometry. In school, did you have code words with your girlfriends? This is algebra. Music, language, baking cookies, stars in the sky, everything is mathematics. It is just that no one has shown this to you, but I will show it to you and then everything will connect to every- thing else and you will be so happy."

She'd done this. Annika had opened a window onto a world, just a crack. Enough to peek through. But now she was gone.

I missed her.

An hour later I was at Westside Pavilion, replaying my con- versation with the blue-eyed guy. "The more I think about it," I said to Fredreeq, "the more I'm sure he was talking about Annika."

"No," she said, leading me past the food court. "I've been thinking too, and I'm thinking industrial sabotage."

"Industrial—? What industry?"

"How many industries are you involved in?" She took a left, heading to a boutique called Plastique, which was having a going-out-of-business sale. "Television, you nut. This isn't just a show we're doing, it's a contest. People bet money on contests, which means other people are making money on the people bet- ting money on this contest. Vegas people."

"What people? Fredreeq, I'm not going to find anything in here." I stopped in front of a Plastique Boutique mannequin. She looked like a heroin addict, her face featureless except for deep pink eye sockets, her emaciated torso wearing a shirt made of shoelaces.

"Never mind that. It's a big bad world out there, with scams going down you've never even— Hello," she said to a girl at a sale table, stacking sweaters in a desultory manner. "Can you tell me if Kim Karmer's working?"

The girl didn't look up from her sweaters. "No."

"No, you can't tell me, or no, she's not working?" Fredreeq

asked. A salesclerk at the register, I noticed, stared at us as she picked up a phone.

"I don't know her schedule," the sweater stacker said.

"Well, who might know her schedule?" Fredreeq asked. When the girl gave a world-weary sigh, Fredreeq grew frighteningly polite. "I'm sorry, am I bothering you? I'm not asking you to go out on a limb here and make eye contact—"

"What am I, a Web site?" The girl blinked spiderlike eyelashes. "You people come in wanting to know all this stuff, you could at least buy some clothes."

Fredreeq put her hand on her heart. "Oh, are these *clothes?* I thought they were something that fell off the space shuttle. You know, sweetie, frown lines are not as sexy as you probably think. Another ten years and a laser's going to have to remove those."

I pulled Fredreeq to the door. "Why do you want to meet Kim Karmer?" I asked. "Is it even kosher for me to talk to another contestant?"

Fredreeq pointed at Robinson-May and made a beeline for the cosmetic counter. "The question is, Who else wants to know about Kim Karmer? What did that twit mean by 'you people'? This fits my saboteur theory. Vegas is backing Savannah Brook to win the vote, and they're nosing around you and Kim to come up with some dirt. It's exactly like politics."

I pondered this at the Clinique counter, while Fredreeq tried out lip crayons. It seemed so unlikely that the tall enigmatic man from Hot Aloo was haunting the mall, questioning surly salespeople. He was too . . . what?

What was it about him that so intrigued me? Aside from our odd conversation.

I was still pondering this when Fredreeq, now trying out powder blush on my face, looked back out at the mall. "Let's go," she said, eyes wide. I turned to see two men in leather jackets walking purposefully toward us from Plastique Boutique. They were not smiling.

"Come on." Fredreeq took my arm and led me farther into Robinson-May, steering us behind a clothes rack. We watched

the men go past, then we doubled back and out into the mall.
Fredreeq's fear was infectious, and I was tempted to break into a
run.

We hurried past the movie theater and a seemingly endless
number of stores devoted to children and babies, looking over
our shoulders every fifteen seconds. We were nearing Nordstrom's
when I saw them, gaining on us. We did run then. Fredreeq, who
does in heels things I couldn't do barefoot, set a good pace. We
flew through Nordstrom's and down a passageway that overlooked
Pico Boulevard. I was utterly lost now, but Fredreeq knows her
malls. Eventually we were in a bookstore, racing down an escalator. A café within the bookstore was to our right, and on impulse
I took Fredreeq's hand and led her through the waist-high gate
that separated customers from café workers.

We crouched behind a glass bakery case, face to face with soft
pretzels, cheesecake, and Rice Krispies Treats. A green-aproned
man came through a swinging door from the back room, but we
were more concerned with our pursuers, rushing down the escalator. When they reached our level, they paused. Then, with
teamlike precision, one took off into the book aisles, the other
circling to another down escalator.

"May I help you?" the café man asked.

"No, just hiding, thanks," I said.

And then we were out of there, back up the escalator to the
third floor, retracing our steps back to Robinson-May. To the
parking structure. Freedom.

"So who were they?" I asked, sitting in Fredreeq's Volvo,
with the doors locked. She started up her car, preparing to drive
me to mine. The good news was that Westside Pavilion parking
is so labyrinthine, you can barely find your own car without a
map, let alone someone else's. Still, we were scared.

"Goons," Fredreeq said. "Thugs. I didn't want them messing
up your face; that's all I care about." She dabbed her own forehead with a tissue. "Maybe they work for Kim Karmer or maybe
Kim's boutique homies are in league with the Savannah Brook

campaign, but either way . . . I went there to do an info share with Kim Karmer, but forget that now. Now she's on her own. She might be the enemy or she might be the friend of the enemy, but either way, this is war and she's going to go down."

Go down. It was a phrase I'd heard twice in twelve hours. It didn't sound good.

11

Sherman Oaks is an appealing 'hood, not as buff as Encino to the west, but a whole mountain range away from Westside Pavilion. An hour after my mall adventure, this mattered.

My friend Rex Stetson had bought a lot, gutted the tired two-bedroom occupying it, and put up a stark five-bedroom, eight-bathroom structure Joey and Fredreeq called the Mansion. I believed it would warm up when furnished, but right now the Mansion's sole link to humanity was a pizza box left behind by the paint crew. Its link to the greater animal kingdom was all over the kitchen walls. Rex, honeymooning in Maui, had hired me to paint a mural as a surprise for his bride, Tricia. A frog mural. Tricia was mad for frogs. All kinds of frogs.

I'm not a trained muralist. Many children feel a compulsion to draw on walls, and I just never outgrew mine. My mother had turned a tolerant eye to my creations, and no subsequent landlord had cared what I did as long as I repainted before moving on, but the Mansion was my first commissioned work. I'd taken it on with trepidation.

The problem was not the work, which I loved, nor the money, which was generous. It was not the subject; to my surprise, within days of my starting, frogs and toads had seduced me with their habits, their lore, their protruding eyes. My previous relationship to amphibians had been marked by indifference, but for three weeks now they'd hopped their way into my dreams, daydreams, and greeting cards. The problem was, mansions are not greeting cards. If you don't like a greeting card, you don't buy it. A wall is different. I'd never met Tricia, but the Tricia in my head was assuming popelike proportions, her kitchen turning into the Sistine Chapel, which made me the Michelangelo of Sherman Oaks. It was no use telling myself she could paint over what she didn't like, because now her frogs were my frogs. I had a personal as well as professional stake in them.

I unlocked the Mansion, happy to return after a five-day break. In the kitchen I turned on the boom box I'd brought from home with a croaking-frog CD Annika had given me. The kitchen, Fredreeq estimated, had set Rex back nearly two hundred grand, with stainless steel backsplashes, black granite countertops, and flush-mounted telescopic vent systems. Nothing in the room suggested a family breaking bread together. Performing autopsies, maybe. But right in the midst of all this high-rent austerity, shoulder-high on one Blush White wall, gazing glumly down the hallway, was the West African goliath frog, *Conraua (Gigantorana) goliath.*

I gazed back into his lovely red golfball-sized eyes, then turned my attention to his buddies on the adjoining wall—Darwin's frog, Smith frog, pickerel frog, pig frog. The spring peeper. There was a spot near the Gaggenau cooktop where I was putting a neotropical Surinam toad, *Pipa pipa.* I'd just started painting when my brother called.

"I can't leave the hospital," P.B. said. "I can't live in Santa Barbara."

"Why, what did you do?" My stomach tightened in alarm. There were countless ways my brother could get in trouble, and I saw the coveted halfway house sprout wings and fly off.

"It's Christmas next month."

"Yes. So? Santa Barbara has Christmas."

"Do you know this personally? Have you been there during Christmas?"

"No," I said. "But I think we'd have heard something if they weren't—"

"I have heard something." P.B.'s voice dropped. "Ramon says it's a town ordinance."

I didn't address Ramon or town ordinances. My brother, even at his most lucid, operates from a belief system independent of logic, conventional wisdom, or even empirical knowledge. Direct argument is futile. "Is Christmas that important to you?" I asked, trying to recall if he'd ever given me a present.

"It's not for me, it's for . . ."

"Yes?"

"People are listening. You'll have to guess."

I groaned. Making phone calls in the common room of a mental hospital, with all your friends and enemies eavesdropping, can't be easy. But I didn't want to play the game of going through the alphabet to guess the name of a person I'd never heard of for whom Christmas was important. "Can this wait till Thursday, P.B.? Because I'm having a frog issue."

"In Germany, people used to put frogs in jars with little ladders and if the frog climbed the ladder to the top of the jar, they thought the weather would change."

"Really?" I said, interested. Nearly everyone had a frog story, I'd discovered.

"But weather changes. Frogs want to get out of jars. No correlation. Didn't anyone notice this? Tell me your issue."

I put down my paintbrush. It's rare for my brother to ask about my problems. Not that he doesn't care; it just doesn't occur to him. So I explained how my West African goliath started as a Fowler's toad that I couldn't get right, how the more I "corrected" him, the bigger he got, until I had the inspiration to turn him into a South African pyxie. It felt like cheating, like Monet using Wite-Out, but what are you going to do? People make mistakes. But when I kept on making them, the South African pyxie became a West African goliath, which was his final incarnation, as there is no known frog larger than *Conraua (Gigantorana) goliath*. And still, he kept growing. I'd fix one part of him, and then the proportion would be off somewhere else, and I'd enlarge that. Annika had used him to illustrate the concept of transcendental numbers, going on and on.

"Aren't you using a grid?" P.B. asked. "Drawing it first, then enlarging it for the wall?"

I sighed. He wasn't the first to ask me this question. "No. I'm doing it freehand. It takes math skills to use a grid. I'm just . . . making it up as I go along. It's more organic anyway."

"Okay, then. The frog's big because he has to be. In order for you to hear."

"Hear what?"

"What he's saying. Most people are visual—they don't hear what they can't see. Not blind people, but most other people. Someone here has to use the phone. Good-bye."

I stood for a moment, phone to my ear, staring down the hallway into the Mansion's whiteness. I hadn't solved P.B.'s Christmas problem, and he hadn't solved my frog problem, but he'd said something important. People don't hear what they can't see. I dialed Maizie Quinn, and after work I headed to Encino.

The electric gate leading to the Quinn house was closed. The whole street was less appealing in the dark, and I was glad to be in my car. I reached for the gate's call box, pressed a button, and talked to an electronically filtered voice. The gate opened. I drove through.

Emma, the two-and-three-quarters-year-old, stood on the porch, holding the hand of a short woman. I parked in the driveway and walked up the flagstone path toward them.

"Lupe," Emma said, pointing to me, "is that cousin Mandy?"

"No, I'm Wollie," I said. "I met you a few days ago. Where's your goose?"

"Goosie asleep."

Thank God. I introduced myself to Lupe, the housekeeper. Mr. Snuggles raced down the hall to protest my entry. Lupe picked him up and shushed him with a treat pulled from an apron pocket.

"Do you want to play alla myna engine?" Emma said.

"She does not know, *m'hija*," Lupe said, bending down to kiss the top of her head. "Only Annika play this game, *porque* it's German. That's the reason."

Emma, suddenly shy, stuck her hand in her mouth, all four fingers up to the first knuckle. Lupe reached down and pulled the hand back out, murmuring in Spanish. Emma turned and raced down the hallway, Mr. Snuggles close behind. Lupe followed him. I followed her.

We passed two darkened rooms and a third lit with a crackling fire and the flashing images of a wide-screen TV. Emma shouted "Hello, Grammy Quinn!" without breaking stride and was hailed in return, and then the smell of firewood gave way to an odor of baking bread and we were in the kitchen.

It was huge, bigger even than Rex and Tricia's, a kitchen worthy of a castle. Overhead lights hit every work surface. Strains of Chopin were piped in from somewhere. Maizie stood behind a butcher block, oven-mitted hands on hips as she consulted a cookbook.

Emma ran to the butcher block and climbed onto a stool. Maizie looked up at me.

"Hi, there," she said, with a smile. "Give me a second. This bread is baking too slowly, and I'm trying to figure out what I did wrong. It better not be my oven." Behind her was the biggest gas range I'd ever seen outside a restaurant, black enamel with red trim. She turned to it and lifted the lid on a saucepan. Steam rose in a cloud around her.

"It smells great in here," I said. It actually smelled like Williams-Sonoma.

"Cranberry-ginger chutney. Thanksgiving advance work."

"And bread?"

"Yes. Corn bread and sourdough." She wiped flour from her chin with her oven mitt. Her cheeks were flushed, as if she'd been physically exerting herself. "I'm trying two new stuffings this year. You have to let the bread go stale before it's cubed."

Cubed. I grew disoriented, hearing in my head, "Cubed: raised to the third power." Annika's voice. But Maizie was talking baking, not algebra. The idea that people make bread from scratch only to let it go stale amazed me.

"I may do two birds, a smoked and a classic. I haven't decided yet. Lupe——" Maizie spoke briefly in Spanish, which jogged my memory.

"Maizie, I found Annika's boyfriend," I said. "Rico Rodriguez."

"Rodriguez. Of course. How'd I manage to forget that? And how'd you find him?"

"Circuitously, and he wasn't much help, but he remembered Annika's watch. A Fossil."

"Annika have a watch," Emma said. "Mommy have a watch. Grammy Quinn have a watch. Daddy have a watch. Lupe no have a watch. Emma no have a watch. Mr. Snuggles——"

Maizie plucked her daughter from the bar stool, interrupting the inventory. "That's right, a Fossil. Wollie, it's so kind of you to do this. I can't understand why the agency isn't——. Okay, don't get me started on them. Emma, let's show our guest the photo album."

Emma took my hand. It surprised me, the tiny fingers, unexpectedly cold, finding their way into my palm. With her mother following, she led me back down the hallway, to the room we'd passed. On a far wall was a built-in TV screen, but the rest of the room was devoted to books on floor-to-ceiling shelves. Hardcover. Lower shelves held children's books, oversized and skinny, alive with color. A miniature wooden rocking chair stood by, occupied by a large plush bear. The fire glowed in a stone fireplace, heavy scarlet drapes shrouded the windows, and a Persian rug covered the floor.

"Grammy Quinn!"

A woman at the far end of the room turned, then rose from a sofa, a soft afghan falling to the floor as she did. The TV screen went dark. Emma let go of my hand to run over and wrap herself around her grandmother's thigh. Thus hampered, the woman advanced with a smile and a limp. "Hello. I'm Grammy Quinn. Sometimes known as Polly."

Maizie introduced me and continued to call the woman Grammy Quinn, which amused me, as Grammy's body, in a bright red jogging suit, gave no indication of advanced age. Her hair was gray but cut short and shaggy, and she wore makeup and some serious-looking jewelry. A very hip Grammy. Emma was persuaded to release her leg only when Maizie repeated the magic words "photo album," at which point we adjourned to an enormous coffee table surrounded by overstuffed chairs. Emma then climbed onto her grandmother's lap in a chair alongside Maizie's. I sat opposite.

Maizie flipped through the pages of a large leather album. Emma pointed at pictures, shouting out names, until Maizie found what she was looking for. She turned the book around to face me.

The photos showed an expedition to the Santa Monica Pier, a Ferris wheel visible in the background. There was Emma, Emma and Grammy Quinn, and Annika holding Emma. Maizie indicated a close-up of Annika alone. "I thought this would be good," she said. It was a clear shot, but uncharacteristically solemn. I imagined it stapled to a missing person's report.

I pointed to the one next to it. "This one's better. It's more like her." Grammy Quinn nodded. Maizie liberated the photograph from its plastic sleeve and handed it to me.

Annika was looking into the camera. She had on her brown leather jacket, with a white T-shirt. Her apple-cheeked face was creased in a smile; her hair, brown and straight, was blown back by a breeze. Her lipstick was bright. She exuded affection. She was not quite beautiful, but she was pretty and happy and so animated you couldn't look at the picture without recalling her laugh and hearing her voice, her English fearless and charming.

"That's Annika," Emma said, leaning forward. "Mommy, where is Annika?"

"Bunny, we talked about this, remember? Annika went home to her own house."

"Annika go home to Annika's own house," Emma said to me.

Grammy Quinn gave her daughter-in-law a quizzical look, but

Maizie shook her head at her, reaching over to stroke Emma's hair. She encountered a tangle in the blond locks and attempted to unknot it.

The girl wiggled out of her mother's reach with a laugh. Then she grew serious. "But Annika forgot to give Emma kiss good-bye."

12

It was dark when Detective Cziemanski found me at Grounds, a coffee shop in West Hollywood. Meeting on my side of the hill was his idea; Grounds was mine. Annika and I had met here for so many of our tutorials it seemed some part of her might linger. I was doing pencil drawings while I waited, but when I saw Cziemanski in the doorway I closed my portfolio and smiled. He smiled back, oblivious to the attention he was getting from the mostly male clientele. He stopped at the counter to order a drink, then joined me.

"Nice shirt," I said.

He nodded. "Glad you like it. Nice decor."

I looked around at the putty-colored walls, floors, and ceiling, devoid of decoration, and wondered if he was being sarcastic. "Glad *you* like it," I said. "Here's the photo. Will it help, Detective Zhe—Che—"

"If you can't say Cziemanski—Shum, not Chum—you'll have to call me Pete. Photos always help." He studied the picture. I wanted him to comment on Annika's prettiness, but he didn't. "Especially when you have a sketch you're trying to match to—"

"What kind of sketch?"

He pulled on an ear. A greeting card began to take shape, a little boy pulling on his ear at school, then going home to a long-eared family, all pulling on their ears. "Sometimes the coroner will come up with a drawing," he said, "reconstructing a face from bones. Or we get a witness, we put them together with a sketch artist."

"You're saying you'll only find her if she's dead?"

"Or robs a bank." He paused. "Having second thoughts? You only want the happy ending?"

I saw myself telling Mrs. Glück to come collect her kid in the county morgue. Or in twenty years, after her release from prison. I gazed at my decaf cappuccino. "No. Yes, I want the happy ending, but mostly I want to know. I just—I'm not sleeping well."

"I don't suppose you have money to hire a private investigator?"

I smiled. "If I scrimp, I can just about cover the double espresso you ordered."

"You're not paying for my espresso. I'm paying for your—whatever that is."

"That's not how it works, Detective. I was the one who asked to meet."

"At the station. Where the coffee would've been on me."

"Well, anyway," I said. "Your paying would make it like a date."

"No, when it's a date, you'll know it."

I studied my hands. They had paint on them around my nails. Green. I was experiencing a combination of pleasure and alarm. "Actually, I don't. Date." Except on national TV.

"Everybody dates. You're not married, right? Not that that's always a deterrent, but some people are put off by it. I'm not married either, in case you're interested."

I was interested. How interesting. "The thing is, I'm behind on a job I'm doing involving amphibians, I'm working every other spare minute on my greeting cards—"

"You don't date public servants."

"No, I like public servants." I looked at him. "Okay, the real thing is, I was engaged. Recently. Well, three months ago. So I've been—depressed and I need to—"

"Eat bad food, rent videos. I can help you with that—what'd you think I had in mind? The philharmonic?"

"Well, yeah," I said, laughing. "You've got to impress girls. At least at first."

"For how long?"

"Depends on the girl. Anywhere from an hour, hour and a half, to seven years."

Cziemanski cleared his throat. "I was counting on wowing you with my police scanner and portable siren."

"Okay, fine," I said. "We'll meet late at night and drive around looking for criminals. Meanwhile, though, I found Annika's boyfriend. Rico. He doesn't know where she is, which means they're not off for a weekend in Bali. Which is what you said probably happened." I paused. Cziemanski did not look excited. "And he remembered her watch was a Fossil."

Finally. He went for a pen. "A what? Fossil?"

"It's a brand. Fun. Affordable." I finished my cappuccino as he wrote on the back of Annika's photo, in small letters. "I know it's not feasible for you to get hysterical over each case, but something's weird here, not—evidence of a crime, just a feeling of—"

"What?"

"Doom." I looked down, ill at ease. Cops, with their civil codes and case numbers, probably didn't deal much in doom. I studied the sticky white residue in my mug. I recalled how Ruta, my childhood babysitter, would read the future in her coffee cup. She'd used an old tin pot that left grounds everywhere. "Anyway, I just want you to know."

Cziemanski's cell phone rang, giving me the chance to go to the counter and pay our tab. He gave me a hard time about that a minute later, but I told him to consider it a bribe. "I'm grateful for whatever effort you put into this," I said, and pulled a business card out of my portfolio. "Call me anytime, day or night, I'm always up. These days."

"I am calling you. You owe me a date." He looked at my card, then slid it into the inside pocket of his beige windbreaker with

Annika's photo. I had the whimsical thought that Annika was warm in there, next to his chest.

Cziemanski and I parted ways in front of Grounds, he heading to his car, me turning left, toward Larrabee Street. He apologized for not walking me to my door, being in a hurry to get to some top secret detective-type meeting, but I told him the chances of me being accosted in the six and a half minutes it would take me to get home were slim to none.

I was wrong.

13

As soon as I turned up Larrabee, I became aware of him, the sound of his shoes on the sidewalk. The back of my neck tingled. My shoulders tensed. I speeded up. This made my own footsteps louder, so I focused on walking softly. Yes, there they were. Shoes. Hard soles on concrete.

I dropped my backpack, then crouched to pick it up.

His footsteps stopped. I turned.

He was ten yards behind me.

Waiting.

I froze.

What to do? My apartment was blocks away. My fingers unfroze, working the clasp on my backpack, searching for keys, feeling for the roundish one that unlocked the building—

Don't go home. Then he'll know where you live.

Ruta's voice. It was the kind of thing she would think of, having spent World War II in Poland, hiding. Okay, Ruta, so what should I do?

Be still, like a little mouse.

I felt like a mouse, crouched on the sidewalk. Breathing fast, panting, trying to be still. What did he imagine I was doing, crouched like this? Could he tell I was watching, or was it too dark? Maybe he thought I was tying my shoe.

Why didn't he approach me?

Was it the man from Hot Aloo? The blue-eyed man?

Or one of the men from Westside Pavilion? No, I didn't want it to be them. And how many stalkers does one person need, anyway?

But was he stalking? He could be some guy with a perfectly good reason for lurking on Larrabee, wondering why a woman was crouched like a mouse on the sidewalk ahead.

Maybe the thing to do was walk over and say, "Hello, can I help you?" Joey would do that. Fredreeq would stand up and yell, "What the hell are you looking at, freak?" and have the whole neighborhood waiting for the answer.

I tried a whisper, to see if I could pull it off. "Hello." It was a tiny, wispy sound. I cleared my throat and tried again. "Hello." Not much better.

He was looking at me. My eyes were adjusting to the dark. He wore a hat.

To confront, or not to confront? What were the guidelines? You didn't confront an alpha male gorilla. Same with grizzly bears. I knew from experience not to confront a mentally disturbed person, or a violent drunk, usually. But with thieves, certain rapists, and serial killers, I'd read, you stand tall, look aggressive, and at the slightest provocation scream, "I have Mace!"

But he wasn't provoking. He was standing, and if I screamed, "I have Mace!" I risked death by embarrassment. How could fear of making a scene rival fear of being murdered?

We were close to Santa Monica Boulevard, enough that people would hear if we struggled. But would they rescue me? And that meant going toward him. Sunset was where I wanted to go, the other way, north. But Sunset was far. I was in okay shape, but running is not my gait of choice, especially with a backpack and a portfolio. Unless he was elderly, he'd catch me. Or would he? Do stalkers catch, or just stalk? I looked north. Darkness. Why was Larrabee so dark, and why hadn't I ever noticed this? What had possessed me to move here, anyway? Free rent. You get what you pay for.

A couple emerged from the darkness, probably from Betty Way. I'd always liked Betty Way.

I stood. I walked toward them. Their faces registered suspicion. They were women, each nearly a foot shorter than me. "Can I walk with you guys?" I said. "There's a man following me."

Suspicion disappeared. With words of reassurance, each woman took an arm, and we set off, toward Santa Monica Boulevard.

Something flashed as we passed. A gun, a knife, catching the light?

He called to me. A single word. It was just about the last word I wanted to hear from a stranger in the dark, and I kept walking, even when he said it again.

"Wollie."

Book 'Em, D'Agneau was what its owner, Lucien D'Agneau, subtitled "A Literary Emporium" on the sign. Like many of the neighboring establishments, it kept odd hours. My rescuers left me at the door, inviting me to join them at Girl Bar should I need an escort home.

I found Lucien in a corner of the store, advising a customer on contemporary lesbian poets. Lucien was a burly man in draw-string pants and Birkenstocks. His brick-walled room was stocked with avante-garde books, magazine, CDs, and greeting cards. There was a small bar in the back, but it had an exclusionary feel; no one worked it, and I'd never ask Lucien to pour me a drink unless I were a personal friend or making a hefty purchase, Lucien being a known despot.

"You," he rasped, turning on me. "Yes?"

"I'm looking for a German-English dictionary. And anything you have on frogs." When he beckoned me to follow, I added, "I'm Wollie Shelley. You carry my greeting cards, the—"

He turned. "The Good Golly Miss Wollies. You dropped by in September, didn't you? With your uncle. When you moved to the neighborhood."

"Yes. I'm actually seeking asylum tonight." I told him about the stalker. "I mean, I do need a dictionary, but if I could also hang out awhile . . ."

An hour later we were still talking. Customers came and went and Lucien waited on them as if it were a big favor. They seemed to like this. Lucien, in turn, seemed to like me. He brewed me decaf and brought out liqueurs. We sat on vinyl-covered bar stools in the back of the shop, where I was able to see the door while staying hidden by a display rack.

"Your cop friend is correct," Lucien said. "People disappear all the time. But you are also correct—the compulsion to look for our fellow man is primal. Those lost to us call with a mythic power. Think of Anastasia Romanov. Whatever happened to Sean Flynn?"

"Who's Sean Flynn?"

"Sean 'son of Errol' Flynn, when I was young, was on the inside of cheap matchbook covers. You'd go for a match and read, 'Whatever Happened to Sean Flynn?' He was a photojournalist working for *Time* in Vietnam. The last we know is that he made his way from Phnom Penh into the Cambodian countryside. He and a friend rode motorcycles to a roadblock and vanished."

"What do you mean, vanished?"

"Taken prisoner by the Vietcong. And, later, the Khmer Rouge, who presumably executed them. At the time, I knew none of this. Only his picture, black and white in those matchbooks. Gorgeous man. Well, consider his father. Also died too young, and what a waste, both of them. Sean was a Gemini, born on Memorial Day. Beautiful people, Geminis."

"What did the matchbooks want you to do?" I asked. "Look for him?"

"I don't recall. But people do look for him. Still. Sean Flynn was more famous in his absence than if he'd come home and carried on another fifty years. Now he lives on, eternally twenty-nine, a symbol of possibility."

"Except to his mother. I expect she'd prefer fifty years of her actual son to a symbol."

"I expect. In my fantasy he returned and fell for me." Lucian sighed. "But realistically, he would then contract AIDS, another dead boyfriend to bury. Which raises another possibility. In my world, people disappear to die alone, spare their loved ones the hell of terminal illness. Could this apply to your little Teutonic friend?"

"Illness? I can't imagine why she'd keep that a secret."

"Pregnancy?" Lucien lumbered over to the front door and turned the Open/Closed sign over, so that Open faced us.

"Same story. We'd all have helped her, whatever it was. Why would she run?"

"My dear, what are you doing right now?" Lucien returned to toss off his Sambuca, the liqueur glass tiny in his giant hand. He disappeared through a door to a back room, still talking. "Running from some nameless person, who may not even wish you ill, but who nevertheless has the power to keep you away from your home and bed. In your imagination, a monster. And so you seek refuge with a stranger." He returned with a coat, turning off lights. "Who shall now walk you home. You'll wear my coat and we'll find you a scarf and I'll have my police flashlight and we shall encounter no one more startling than a cat."

I stood, staring out the picture window. It was late. My mind was fuzzy with Sambuca.

"Children at play, birds of prey," Lucien said, closing out his register, "and dogs may chase anything that moves. But in general, we are not pursued because we run; we run because we are pursued. Someone wanted something from this girl—love, money, her body, her mind. Find out what pursued your friend, and you find your friend."

I couldn't sleep. I was no longer scared of the stalker—in a building full of people I felt safe, however illogically—but sleep eluded me, as it had done every night for the past week. I got out of bed and turned on the TV and bumped into the drafting table crowding the bedroom. I opened my portfolio and pulled out the sketch I'd been doing earlier. The karaoke frog.

I didn't know yet where the greeting card was going—sometimes the caption comes first, sometimes the image—but I thought of Annika as I sketched. She'd loved looking at my frog books. It was she who'd pointed out that the male of the species is the one with the voice. Girl frogs don't sing at all, at least at mating time. My karaoke frog should be male, then. What species?

The TV distracted me with a documentary on liposuction. I watched in mild horror until I realized that if I was going to watch bad TV, it should be my own bad TV. I popped in one of the *Biological Clock* tapes Fredreeq had given me with instructions to study the competition the way professional boxers do.

The tape wasn't rewound, so I watched the closing sequence, a couple in silhouette on a beach at sunset. There was the same pulsing disco music the opening credits used, but with an announcer's voice saying at auctioneer speed that no contestants would be forced to have sex or procreate as a result of participation in the show, that no opinions expressed or services described were endorsed by ZPX network or Bad Seed Productions, and that the voting process would occur on the *Biological Clock* Web site at the conclusion of the series.

I rewound to mid-show and watched Henry Fisher talk about his belief in the biblical injunction to be fruitful and multiply. I rewound further and saw the episode's expert, an adoption attorney, in conversation with Savannah Brook, the radiant redhead.

What, I wondered, was I supposed to gain by watching an inexpressibly lovely and effortlessly charming woman be lovely and charming? "I really want to adopt," Savannah was saying, with just a hint of a southern accent, "particularly a special-needs child. But I also want to experience the miracle of pregnancy and childbirth. No matter what you accomplish professionally, for a woman, is there any force stronger than a baby?"

I shook my head. I couldn't speak for other women, but I was right there with Savannah. The longing for a child was an ache in my stomach, a pain that woke me in the middle of the night and terrorized me, like sudden knowledge of my own mortality.

I didn't require a biological baby; Doc's daughter, Ruby, would have done just fine. But Ruby had never been mine, as I was now finding out, which left me feeling fractured and empty.

No more dating men with children. No more near-stepchildren velcroed to my heart.

The phone rang. I stared, frightened. I didn't want to answer, but I thought of P.B., Annika, even Ruby—anyone who might need me in the wee hours of the morning. I went to the night-stand.

"Hello," I said. *Click.* A hang-up.

Heart beating faster, I replaced the receiver. After staring blankly at the TV, I went back to my greeting card. And discovered I'd abandoned the karaoke frog.

Looking up from my sketchbook was Annika's face.

14

The ringing phone woke me. "Wollie. I may have a match to the photo."

I sat up in bed, disoriented. I had no idea who this was. "Okay. What time is it?" I said. And who was I saying it to?

"Eleven. Can you get downtown?" Cziemanski. It was Detective Cziemanski.

"Where downtown?" I went over and pulled back the drapes. Sunlight assaulted me.

A pause. Then, "The morgue."

Downtown L.A. was a place I rarely went. Not that there was nothing happening there. There was the Convention Center, some major conventioneer hotels, quite a few law firms and banks and museums and hospitals, Staples Center for sports fans, the Mark Taper Forum for theatergoers, the Dorothy Chandler Pavilion and Disney Concert Hall for music lovers, the fashion district, jewelry district, flower market, Little Tokyo, and Chinatown. There were government buildings: City Hall, the Civic Center, courthouses, the LAPD at Parker Center. And east of all that, at Mission and Marengo, there was the Los Angeles County Department of Coroner. The morgue.

Two buildings shared the parking lot. Following instructions on a sign, I parked, got a parking permit from one building, then returned to place it on the dashboard of my Integra, which was when I noticed Joey's car parked next to a Department of Coroner's vehicle. Thank God. I'd had the shakes since Detective Cziemanski's call awakened me. He'd suggested having a friend go through this with me, since he couldn't get downtown himself, and I was grateful for it now, entering the other building, white stone with the look of an old penitentiary.

Joey met me in the lobby with a smile. I tried to smile back. "Fifty-four minutes," I said. "That's how long it took. I hate how downtown streets are one-way—you're supposed to somehow know that Flower runs south and Temple dead-ends—"

"Flower? What were you doing on Flower Street?" Joey asked.

"I got sucked onto the 110 freeway from the 101, I couldn't get over in time and nobody would let me out of the exit lane and—"

"Never mind. You're here. She's here," she said louder, to a woman in a reception cubicle. "My friend. She's come to ID the body."

The woman spoke into a headset and told us to have a seat. Neither of us did.

The lobby did not exceed my expectations. Pea-soup linoleum, a plastic coffee table simulating wood, a vase of artificial flowers. Joey studied photos of the Board of Supervisors in a glass trophy case. I wandered across the room, to a poster of a baby in the arms of a doctor. "Pregnant?" it read. "Confused?"

I moved closer. The baby looked new, too little for its diaper, but with a full head of velvety black hair. The poster was not, as I expected, endorsing prenatal care but urging readers to leave newborns (seventy-two hours or younger) with an emergency room employee rather than abandon them, since "A trash can or Dumpster is never a choice." I studied the infant. He looked startled. He's a model, I told myself, he wasn't found in a trash can. But I noticed myself clutching my backpack, digging my nails into it—

"Wollie . . . Shelley?"

A young man with a clipboard introduced himself as Kent

Something and asked us to follow him. He led us through a locked door to an elevator, another floor, and a long hallway, the linoleum changing color from pea soup to mustard to avocado.

We came to a room crowded with desks, files, and the detritus of an office that housed a staff of dozens in an area built to accommodate five or six, or perhaps a staff of five or six doing the work of dozens. Weekend stillness hovered like a fog layer. Kent took us to a room within the room, carpeted in the same dark teal the West Valley LAPD used. Was there a municipal contract with the Teal Blue Carpet Company? Kent asked me for identification. He had me sign my name, took my thumbprint with an ink pad, and then, satisfied that I was who I purported to be, told me that Mrs. Heike Glück of Moosburg, Germany, had, via phone and translator, named me her proxy, authorizing me to identify the body of her daughter, Annika. Then he walked out.

The room was very hot.

"When do we see the body?" I asked Joey. My mouth was dry.

"We don't. I asked. It's all done by photo."

"Oh. Okay." I studied my ink-smudged thumb. "That doesn't sound so bad." Except that I wasn't ready. Is this where the staff ate lunch, on this old, beat-up table? Strange to think of people taking coffee breaks here, eating tuna salad, having an office romance in a place where other people faced the worst moment of their lives. Thank God it was me doing this and not Annika's mother. Thank God she was too far away.

The door opened. Kent walked in with a file. An image of a greeting card started to form, one of my good-luck cards, but I pushed it aside.

Joey took my hand, gave it a squeeze, then let go.

Kent took a seat, opened the file, and picked up a single sheet of paper, to which was stapled a Polaroid. He kept it facing away from us. His facial expression was professionally neutral, signaling that this was not the aspect of his job he most enjoyed. "You understand," he said, "this is a crime-scene photo. We don't clean things up for the family, much as we'd like to."

"Okay," I said.

He put the report in front of me, the Polaroid in the upper left-hand corner.

She lay on grass, her dark hair fanned out from her face. She wore a white T-shirt. Her eyes were open. Her mouth was slack. Her skin was white-yellow, or maybe that was the quality of the photo. She had been lovely once.

Maybe. Hard to say, really.

My nose burned, then my eyes, and my vision blurred.

"It's—" I cleared my throat. "It's not her."

Her name was Jane Doe 132. They'd done tests, an autopsy, fingerprints. Now they'd leave her file open and periodically check the missing-persons database for women like her. They'd keep her until someone came looking, someone like us, worried about their friend, daughter, sister. If no one came, in a few years they'd burn her body and bury her remains in a common ground in a Boyle Heights cemetery.

Kent answered our questions, relaxed now, interested to hear that Joey had once worked in a morgue. Jane Doe, he said, wore a red watch, was in her teens or early twenties, and had dark hair, which was why the computer had alerted Cziemanski.

"She's a head trauma," Kent said. "Fell off a bike near UCLA. Bad year for coeds. Raves, suicides, drownings, cars wrapped around trees..."

"How do people die at raves?" I said.

"Ecstasy, usually. This year we've seen fentanyl. It's an analgesic, highly toxic. Had a kid last summer try to get high drinking Goo Gone, a cleaning solvent. Mind gone."

After a while we thanked him and walked out to the parking lot, into a Saturday afternoon full of traffic and sunshine and the noises of life.

I felt giddy with relief, but Joey was uncharacteristically morose. "What's that expression about someone walking on your grave?" she asked. "Anyhow, I have to get home, I'm driving the

BMW to Oxnard, but I want you to know—" She paused, looking toward the freeway. "I'll help. With Annika. I want to find
her."

She'd been helping all week, I was about to point out, but she
was already heading to her car.

I called Germany from my own car while still in the parking
lot. It crossed my mind that my cellular bill was going to equal
the gross national product of a small country, but when I told
Mrs. Glück that it was not her daughter lying dead in the morgue
and heard the ecstatic weeping that ensued, I decided it was a
Christmas present to myself, a month early.

15

I spent Saturday afternoon in the Valley with my mural, resisting the urge to enlarge the West African goliath by keeping my focus near a wall-mounted microwave, where I painted a small Central American red-eyed leaf frog, *Agalychnis callidryas*.

On my way home I stopped at a Ventura Boulevard newsstand. Fredreeq had insisted I check out the winter issue of *International Celeb*, featuring a story on Savannah Brook that, while fiction, was the kind of press she felt I needed. I flipped through the magazine until the clerk barked at me, pointing to a sign that said "No Free Reads."

Half annoyed, half embarrassed, I took my place in line. If I walked away in a huff, I'd have wasted time, a great parking place, and a quarter for the meter, but if I paid six ninety-nine for what turned out to be a one-paragraph article, I'd feel like a loser. I resumed my page flipping, determined to read and run. What could the clerk do, shoot me?

It was a three-page article. I forked over seven dollars to learn from my *Biological Clock* competition that beauty and brains were not incompatible, nor were a successful business and budding television career impediments to romance, cocooning, and baby making. Having lived in five countries in her nearly three decades, Savannah said, she was now eager to put down roots. An accompanying full-page photo showed her in a bikini, a faraway look in her eye, and was captioned with a quote: "Whether traveling the world or in my own backyard, I live life to the fullest, in every way."

And just how, I wondered, did Fredreeq expect me to be an International Celeb, I, who'd barely been north of Highway 118? I sat in my car, using up my meter minutes, feeling desperately provincial. Obviously I now had to read the damn magazine cover to cover, having invested so much money in it, having looked at nothing but books on frogs for weeks. No wonder I had no repartee. Grimly, I caught up on Britain's royal family, an Iraqi boy band, and unexpected volcanic activity in Hawaii, then came to a dead stop on a page called "Hard News." A grainy photo caught my attention, a man with a look so salacious I blushed. Bedroom eyes. So I was not, after all, dead to sexual feeling. I should move to whatever country he was from. I read the caption under the photo. Vladimir Tcheiko, fugitive, murderer, head of a notorious eastern European drug cartel. Well. Nice to know that crime was no impediment to international celebrity. At least I'd heard of this guy, which was more than I could say about trends in Muslim head scarves, the news that only 9 percent of Vancouverites were obese, and the sudden celebrity of political wives in France.

I went back to Savannah's article and a detail I'd missed on the first reading, because, of course, it had to do with math. Her "almost three decades"? Savannah was well into her thirties, unless she'd lied on her *B.C.* application. Talk about a discrepancy. I looked up from *International Celeb* and remembered another application, another discrepancy, then realized I was on Ventura Boulevard, just east of Encino. I picked up my cell phone.

Maizie Quinn met me in her driveway, talking before I was out of the car. "God, you're a trouper, doing this. Have you found out anything?" She was wearing jeans tonight, tight ones, with a pink spandex turtleneck and her usual heels. Maizie had curves I'd never guessed at, hidden as they'd been before under work shirts and aprons.

"Not much," I said. "And I'm sorry to bother you on a Saturday night, but I just now thought of it."

"I should've thought of it the other day when you stopped by." She led me down the path to the artist's studio. "Gene, my husband, says I'm always out to lunch." She laughed. "In my dreams. With Alain Ducasse, discussing chiffonade versus julienne." I was about to ask who that was and what that meant, but Maizie was already far ahead, surefooted on the flagstone pathway, even in the dark, in high heels.

The studio was warm and well lit. Gone were the leaves and wires from the center worktable, replaced by a turkey on a cutting board. It seemed early to be doing a turkey, five days before Thanksgiving, but maybe this was a rehearsal bird.

"I'm trying to think what else might help us." Maizie crossed to a distressed-wood file cabinet. "This sounds awful, but Gene checked Annika's computer, to see if we could find . . . well, anything. About where she might've gone. Gene says a stranger could re-create his whole life from what he downloads from the Internet." She pulled from a drawer a pink file. "But no luck. Gene says it would take a hacker to get in there."

I was barely functional on my own computer, but maybe Cziemanski had access to hackers. I'd ask him.

Maizie held the pink file in both hands, as if picking up vibrations. "Here it is. Letters and cards she sent us, little mementos. I'd like it back eventually—there are things I want to keep for Emma." She opened the file and took out some stapled pages. "I found her au pair application in her room. As soon as she came, she wanted to see it, to read her letters of recommendation, and how she did on her interview—" She turned the pages over and frowned, then smiled. "There's another girl's application on the back. We download them from the Internet, and Gene uses both sides of every sheet of paper in the house. Annika too, but she was a recycler. Gene's just cheap."

"Maizie, did you ever notice discrepancies in the application?"

"Discrepancies?"

"Things that turned out not to be accurate, or . . ." I couldn't repeat what I'd heard at the au pair agency. Why make her worry in retrospect about the girl she'd entrusted her child to for a year?

She moved to the worktable. "Only in the positive sense. Her grades were average, except for math, but she turned out to be so intelligent in person. Always reading. What are you hoping to find?"

"Personal data, mostly. Height and weight, medical records, for the police report. I don't suppose they've been in touch?"

"No. Not yet." She glanced at her watch, then grabbed an apron from a wall peg and put it on. It was stained, like my paint clothes, with the evidence of countless projects. "Will they, do you think? I'd really like to be more proactive in all this—"

"Don't hold your breath," I said. "But at least they'll have accurate information for the database. I've been trying to learn about Annika through other people, but everyone I talk to has a different story. She was into drugs, she wasn't into drugs, she was boy crazy, she wasn't boy crazy . . . maybe I haven't talked to the right people. Do you know any of her friends, besides the au pairs?"

"Everyone was her friend." Maizie rolled up the sleeves of her sweater, gazing at the turkey. I noticed she wore makeup and that her chin-length hair had been blown dry. All dressed up for Saturday night but unable to stop cooking. "Monday I took Emma to her music class and half the moms and nannies asked about Annika. God. Not even a week ago. When I still thought she was coming back . . ."

"Maybe I could talk to some of them."

Maizie went to the sink and washed her hands. "The music moms? I have to confess, I don't know anyone's last names. There's Rachel, Brandon's mom, and Georgine, Hallie's mom, and I'm Maizie, Emma's mom. . . . I'll try to find a class roster." She dried her hands. "Wollie, mind if I work while we talk? I'm so behind, with Thanksgiving coming up, and Grammy Quinn's invited half of Palm Springs for dinner..." She took a small knife and made a slit between the turkey's legs, a deft movement, drawing the knife neatly up to its abdomen.

"Is this what you do professionally?" I asked. "Annika said you had a business."

She laughed. "Cooking? No, cooking's my passion. My business is aromatherapy." She nodded to the shelves across the room, filled with the Art Deco glass bottles. "Bath, body, and hair products. No preservatives or carriers, just pure ingredients, beautiful packaging, and beautiful markup. I keep it small, high-end boutiques and some mail order, so I can work from home. I'm not very ambitious. I like my freedom, my hobbies. My family. I like cooking." She made another incision in the turkey, this one horizontal. I was fascinated. No one in my house had cooked much. I should start watching cooking shows. Maizie looked up. "Can I ask—don't misunderstand, I think it's wonderful of you to take this on—but it's a lot of trouble, isn't it?"

"Have you ever not taken the time to listen when someone needed you to?"

Maizie's eyes grew soft. "Every single day. I'm a mother. There's never enough time. Maybe when you're a grandmother..." She took a breath and went back to work.

"That's the reason I came here, that first day," I said. "Guilt. And her mother had called, and I felt sorry for her because I've been in that position." I gazed at the turkey. I'd never seen one still wearing feathers, tiny ones all over its body. I said, "I have a brother who's had some problems, he used to wander off, and trying to find him—you're dependent on people's goodwill, asking favors of total strangers. It can be awful. And people have been kind to me, too many times to count, and to him. . . . So it started like an errand, the sort of thing anyone would do, except that I'm not anyone, I'm her friend, and even though in the back of my mind I thought I'd hand it off to someone, someone would say, 'Okay, we'll take it from here,' that never happened. And now I can't hand it off, it's a mission. I have to see it through."

"The curse of the volunteer." The cat came through the open

door, the fat yellow guy I'd seen the first day. Maizie looked up. "You sign on for table decorations and end up doing puff pastry for two hundred. Because you're the only one who can do it right."

I sneezed. "Believe me, anyone could do this better than I can."

Maizie moved to the sink and washed her hands again. "You know what I think about? How young Annika is, for all her independence. Smart, but not sophisticated. I should've been a better mom to her." Maizie grabbed the fat yellow cat and deposited him on a chair, away from the bird. He immediately jumped down. "And how will you know when it's long enough, when you've done enough? That's what Gene keeps asking, how long we have to wait before we close the book on this."

I shrugged. "I just keep doing the next thing that occurs to me. Until there's nothing left to do."

Maizie picked up the cat again and went outside. I followed.

"There's always something left to do," she said, and pointed to the house. "See the lights?" The wraparound porch was trimmed in tiny icicle lights, hundreds of them, giving the house a welcoming look. "I put them up that day you came for the photo. My husband thinks I'm crazy, but I can't turn them off, night or day. It's just a little thing, but it's what I do. Gene says I'm leaving the porch lights on for Amelia Earhart."

17 January. Dear Emma, Thanks for the present and the super photo. I am so surprise that you remember my birthday! And Mr. Snuggles must wear a birthday hat. I have only 1 week with you, but you are my family. Good night and sleep tight.
    Annika

There were other letters like this, plus cards for holidays, the English improving as the year went on.

I'd parked just south of Ventura Boulevard, back near the newsstand, unable to wait until I got home. The au pair application was exhaustive, eighteen pages long. There were photos, a medical history, letters of recommendation in German and English. Annika had two hundred hours of child-care experience, worked in a kindergarten, and had studied French and Latin as well as English. She had no siblings. She did not attend church or temple. She'd had chicken pox as a child. Her blood pressure was 120/80. Her grades fluctuated—she was great at *Mathematik* and *Biologie*, okay at *Englisch* and *Musik*, not great at *Geschichte* and *Sozialwissenschaften*, whatever those were.

The photo collage didn't display much artistic talent. The captions were sloppy, but the energy and joie de vivre were unmistakeable. There was Annika with friends, cat, dog, horse, goats, and dozens of children, all of them smiling. There she was with her mother—"Mutti"—an older, rounder version of Annika, same brown hair, same apple cheeks, same incandescent smile. Glasses. There was no mention of a father.

There was an essay, eager, sincere. "I wish to be a gift in the life of children."

One thing caught my attention. Although the application was in black and white, a page near the end had a date circled in red, and a question mark next to the circle. The page was in German, official and terse: Name, address, birth date, and place of birth translated easily enough, but not the word in the middle of the page: *Führungszeugnis.*

The date circled was February, two years earlier. I checked the date on the first page. Last October. I counted it out on my fingers. Twenty months between the time of the *Führungszeugnis* and the day Annika applied to be an au pair. Was that significant? It seemed that someone thought so.

My gazed drifted. What Maizie had said about Amelia Earhart rang a bell. Why?

A man stood at the newsstand, holding a newspaper but looking my way.

I remembered. Annika had talked about a scientist who, using fuel levels and wind velocity, had determined where Amelia Earhart's plane had gone down. "Physics," Annika had said.

"People think, 'This is a mystery' or 'That cannot be known' but if we have facts, we can make an equation. With equations, we understand the world. I may not be smart enough to make equations, but someone is. Is this not reassuring?"

It hadn't reassured me then, but it reassured me now. Wherever she was, whatever trouble she was in, Annika wouldn't panic. She'd do the math. I stared at Ventura Boulevard, as though I might see her walking, pocket calculator in hand.

The discrepancy between the dates on the *Führungszeugnis* and the application—was there an equation to be made there?

The man at the newsstand was still looking, pointing me out to another man.

Except they weren't pointing at me, but at something behind me. I turned and saw a sports car. Parked. Occupied.

The man in the driver's seat was looking at me.

The car door opened and he started to get out. I locked my doors, turned the ignition key, and stepped on the gas, harder than my Integra liked. It made a groaning sound. Annika's file slipped off my lap onto the floor as I sped away.

16

"**W**hat's he driving?" Joey asked, her voice scratchy over the cell phone.

"Some sports car." I glanced in the rearview mirror. "I don't know if he's following me. All headlights look the same."

"Okay, get off Ventura Boulevard—that's a circus, you'll never be able to spot a tail. Try one of the canyons. Coldwater—that shouldn't be too bad on a Saturday night."

"I passed it—no, there it is." I zoomed into the right lane, an act of courage that would normally take me blocks to work up to, and swerved onto Coldwater Canyon. "Now what?"

"Now you coast awhile, give him a chance to follow, assuming he's going to—"

"What do you mean? I thought I was losing him."

"You probably did, but here's how to find out. Harvard-Westlake is coming up on your left, it's a high school. Pull in, signal first, and see if anyone follows. No, don't signal. Too obvious. I wish I knew his skill level. Tailing is tougher than you'd think."

"I'd think it's plenty tough," I said. "Joey, there was a guy on my street last night. Not this guy, someone shorter. Maybe one of the guys Fredreeq and I saw."

"Doing what?"

"Standing. Lurking. Hovering."

"They probably work together. Surveillance is a team sport. This guy tonight, he's the one from Hot Aloo?"

"I think so." Coldwater Canyon was nearly deserted, but I caught up to another southbound car, the red taillights like a friendly animal leading me down the mountain road. "He's tall, anyway. I looked at him, he looked at me, I panicked. I'm still panicky."

"No, you're not, you're fine. Your cell phone may cut out, but you're in civilization, it's Saturday night. Harvard-Westlake probably has some play or game going on, so you'll feel safe."

"What about you, Joey, how are you doing? Recovered from the morgue thing?"

"I'm good. I'm having a margarita, and my neighbor just brought over a joint. I didn't think anyone in Pasadena got high, but it turns out—"

My cell phone cut out before Joey could enlighten me about drug habits in the San Gabriel Valley. How long until she realized I'd turned into dead space? How much information went unreceived every day, people talking to themselves on cell phones? Pondering these metaphysical questions, I drove past Harvard-Westlake. Damn.

I checked the rearview mirror. There was a car behind me now; at least one, maybe more. Coldwater veered to the left, then right and soon would start the nausea-inducing curves that gave the canyon roads character.

Should I keep going? Could I live without knowing if he was following me?

Yes.

Could I sleep tonight?

Well, sleep. Who needed sleep?

You, Ruta said. *You aren't getting nearly enough. And you can't lead him to your doorstep. We talked about this.*

Why was I listening to a dead babysitter? What kind of way was that to live a life? What would Fredreeq do in this situation? What would Joey do?

I took a right on Mulholland, a turn so sharp it was nearly a U-turn.

In the rearview mirror, nothing. Good. I'd drive to some observation point and turn around. Mulholland Drive was littered with observation points.

I looked again. Headlights appeared, twin full moons in the blackness.

I panicked. I stepped on the gas.

What a stupid idea, trying to think like Joey. Joey loved driving. I didn't. Teeth clenched, shoulders scrunched up around my ears, I negotiated the horrible turns. If Coldwater was curvy, it was nothing compared to Mulholland, the road through the mountains running to the sea. What was I doing, I who hadn't bothered getting a driver's license until my twenties? Why did I live in L.A.? I should've moved to New York long ago, or Boston, Chicago, Paris, Rome, Buenos Aires, anywhere with functioning public transportation. Failing that, I should never, ever go near Mulholland Drive, the road that killed James Dean, or was it Montgomery Clift? One of those sports car—mad movie stars and who knows how many other people over the years, crashing into the mountain on one side, driving off the cliff on the other, coyotes eating them, joggers finding what's left of their bodies . . .

The headlights were still behind me, closer now. Tailgating.

How far to the next outpost of civilization? Beverly Glen? Yes, the Glen Center, with that Italian place, a video shop, sushi . . . could I make it that far?

He was right on top of me. Not just scary, but rude.

What to do? Slow down and he'd plow into me. Speed up and I'd drive off the road. There were places to pull over, but I couldn't see them until I was passing them.

I turned on my brights. There—on the right. I pulled over.

He passed me.

He slowed. The taillights went from red to redder.

He went onto the shoulder, then into reverse, the red orbs

coming toward me. Who backs up on Mulholland? Was he wearing a parachute?

I did a fast and awkward series of moves to get my car facing the other way, achieving it as his taillights grew close. I drove back toward Coldwater Canyon. How far was it? One mile? Six?

And then his headlights were behind me again. He'd made a U-turn. Did he have a death wish? And where could I go now?

TreePeople. Yes! At the corner of Mulholland and Coldwater, TreePeople, a nonprofit organization that planted trees, studied trees, lobbied for trees, gave tree tutorials, trees as Christmas presents. . . . They'd help me. That's what nonprofits do. And I'd made a donation—this year? Last year? Whenever. I was a donor, I was one of them. They'd rush to my defense, armed with— clubs. Tree stumps. Like medieval villagers.

He flashed his lights. What was that supposed to mean?

Would anyone be at TreePeople? They often had hikes during full moons, rustic fund-raisers, the well-heeled paying top dollar to roast marshmallows among the conifers. Was it a full moon? I glanced skyward. A moon, yes, but not—

HONK!

The rearview mirror showed more flashing lights, veering to the right. He was trying to pass me. What kind of demented—?

Fine. I veered to the left, across the center line. If he wanted to risk a thousand-foot drop down the cliff, who was I to stop him?

He did. He passed me easily, thanks to a turnout on the right, then did a near-fishtail spin of his car, so that it came to rest on the center line, in profile, blocking the road completely. I slowed, then stopped.

We stared at each other.

It was him. The guy. The one from Hot Aloo. All I could see were eye sockets, but I knew the rest. Hard face. Blue eyes.

Here we go again, I thought. A strange sensation began sneaking up on me, a feeling that all the fluids in my body were draining downward, down my arms and legs. Soon they'd pool in my feet and my hands, swelling them all out of proportion, so that I wouldn't be able to drive, my hands too heavy to raise to the steering wheel, my foot stuck on the brake. And where was there to go? To my left was a ditch. To my right the sheer drop. Behind me were darkness and death-defying curves.

I could ram my car into his. The problem was that people, particularly Los Angelenos, grow displeased when their cars are damaged. This man, already on emotional thin ice, judging by his driving habits, could crack. Why were we staring like this, in the dark? There was a hypnotic quality to it . . .

His car door opened. Okay, he wasn't hypnotized. He came toward me, long stride, maximum ground covered with each step. Tall. A tall guy. Six foot five or six.

I slammed my Integra into reverse and hit the gas pedal. The engine roared and the car, inexplicably, went nowhere.

He reached my car.

My hand moved of its own volition to lock my doors. They were already locked.

He was at my window. He wore dark pants. A dark polo shirt. A belt. His crotch was at my eye level. I stared at it. My cell phone was in reach, but I knew it was worthless. Doc had talked me into it, for emergencies. He must've meant emergencies in neighborhoods with better cell signals.

I can't stand to be afraid. When I'm cornered, my fear aversion is stronger than my fear, so strong that I experience a kind of denial and act as if what's happening is not happening, as if I'm in a parallel universe where everyone is my friend and everything is fine. Joey calls it playing dumb. Fredreeq calls it dumb.

He was leaning down now, his face level with mine, elbows resting on the car door. With a flick of the hand, a snap of fingers against the glass, he motioned me to roll down my window.

The advantage of playing dumb is that it postpones the moment of confrontation, when you acknowledge you're on opposite sides, when someone fires the first shot. If you're already at a disadvantage—like, for instance, if your car's in neutral when you thought it was in reverse—it gives you a chance to reach for a weapon. I slid my hand to the passenger seat, distracting him by rolling my window down an inch.

"Hi, there," I said, and cleared my throat. "What's up?"

He flicked his finger against the window again, motioning. "Come on. Open."

"No, it's chilly. Out there. There's a chill in the air. I'm—"

"Chilled. Yeah. Open." He didn't look threatening, merely annoyed. "I'm not going to hurt you."

"Then quit it!" Fear moved over, making room for anger. "If you're not going to hurt me, quit scaring me, quit following me, quit driving me off the road—"

"I was trying to get you to pull over. Why didn't you stop?"

"I did stop. I—" I rolled down the window, tired of talking through it. "I'm stopped. I stopped last night, too, I was cowering on the sidewalk forever, so why—"

"Last night?"

"Larrabee. Outside my—" *Don't say "apartment," dummy. Maybe he doesn't realize you live there.* "—friend Hubie's apartment."

He said nothing.

"So," I said. "What do you want from me?"

Mulholland was quiet. Then an owl hooted. He spoke. His voice was conversational. "I'd like to think I made an impression on you the last time we met."

"You did."

"Yet here we are."

He had nice breath. That's unusual, when someone's very close to you and you don't know them and you find their breath appealing. It happens with babies, of course, but not often with people over the age of four. "Okay," I said, "I have a question. When you told me to back off, did you—"

"I said 'back off'?"

I thought about it. "Or 'buzz off.' "

"I wouldn't have said 'buzz off.' "

No, he wasn't the type. He was the type who dresses up for an airplane flight. "Back off, buzz off, words to that effect," I said. "You didn't say what from."

The blue of his eyes was purple in the dark. He smelled like soap, like he'd just showered. For Saturday night. Such an intimate smell. "From what," I amended. Maybe if I could keep my prepositions in their proper places, my thoughts would follow.

"What is that you're holding?" he asked. "Price tag's still on it."

I looked down at my hand. "This is a meat mallet. I've been meaning to return it." I put the silver gadget back in the Williams-Sonoma bag.

"What were you doing downtown this morning near Temple Street?"

"Looking for the morgue."

That surprised him. After a moment he nodded. "I want you to rewind a week," he said. "Go back to Sunday."

"Okay." Sunday: paying bills, clipping coupons, researching frogs, that leftover piece of quiche, so disappointing because of the soggy crust . . .

"Now stay there."

I stared. "What the heck does that mean? Stay in Sunday?"

He turned to check out the traffic, which did not exist, or maybe to check out the owl. The owl quieted. He turned back. "Monday you showed up on my radar. I want you to drop off again."

"Why don't you just turn off the radar?"

"You don't turn off radar."

"Fine. I'm not a radiologist—"

"Physicist."

"—but you'll have to get more explicit about this problem you're having."

He leaned in very close. "You're the problem I'm having. Think about the bad things you do. Then stop doing them."

I blushed. I didn't even know what I was blushing about. "I . . . um."

His eyes were looking at my mouth. Was there food on it? When had I last eaten? No, there was nothing on my mouth but a pair of lips. Could it be he was going to kiss me? Was there something I'd said that made him think I wanted him to?

Did I want him to?

And then he was gone, a shadow in the moonlight, heading back to his car. But there was an echo of the thing he'd said so softly I wasn't sure if he'd said it or if I'd just thought it. Five words.

"Forget you ever met her."

17

I drove toward West Hollywood in a daze. "Forget you ever met her," he'd said.

Forget her? I couldn't forget him, and I didn't even know him.

I replayed our conversations. For some reason this man wanted me to give up looking for Annika but wouldn't come out and say so. What kind of enforcer, or whatever he was, followed someone only to play twenty questions? Maybe he was just a bad bad guy. A novice. A bad guy with scruples. A big, blue-eyed bad guy who looked like he was in good shape, judging by the close-up I'd had of his waist, which suggested abdominal exercises, because a lot of guys get a little cuddly right there once they hit forty, which the lines on his face suggested to me he had. I liked the lines on his face. The hardness of his face. I like a face that's been around.

Okay, he was on my radar now.

The question was, Why was I on his? Why bother with me? It's not like I was doing such a bang-up job of finding Annika.

Unless I was closer than I knew. Maybe I'd ruffled someone's feathers asking about her. Not Marty Otis: I couldn't imagine this man, this blue-eyed force of nature, in the employ of rabbity little Marty.

But I didn't have to worry about it tonight. He was done for the night, unless he suddenly remembered another cryptic utterance he had to make. I should give him my phone number, save

him some gas. Maybe he had it, I thought, remembering the recent hang-ups.

Waitaminute.

The guy lurking last night on Larrabee—when I'd alluded to
the incident, Mr. Tall had said, "Last night?" like he didn't know
what I was talking about.

He didn't know what I was talking about. They weren't part-
ners.

Someone else was following me too.

The thought made me swerve. Get a grip, I told myself,
clutching the wheel. I hated this Integra, Doc's hand-me-down.
It swerved too easily. I checked the rearview mirror. Yes, there
was a car behind me. Two cars, four, endless cars, hundreds of
people following me, a nocturnal procession. When we got out of
the canyon into the flat part of Beverly Hills, my cell phone rang,
alerting me to missed calls. Three. All from Fredreeq. I called her
back, with compulsive glances into the rearview mirror.

"Joey told me we have another stalker situation," she said.
"She waited for you to call back and now she's having sex with
her husband, so I'm taking over. You home?"

"No. Car. Sunset. Beverly Hills. Fredreeq, I'm scared to go home.
There was someone outside the apartment last night and—"

"I'll talk you through this. Francis and I are at a bowling alley
with Franceen's sixth-grade class. We got eight more frames.
That should get you parked and inside the apartment and you
can check all your closets."

"What if I don't make it, what if—"

"I hear any screaming, I put you on hold and call 911."

"That's ridiculous, it'll be too late—"

"It won't be too late, because it won't happen. I'm not saying
you're not being followed, but I know nothing bad will happen
this week. I just did your chart. Nobody gets hurt with the two
major trines you got going."

Astrology. I have no firm opinion on its merits, but Fredreeq
was willing to put my life on the line for it. She talked trines and
sextiles and a bunch of other mathematical-sounding jargon

while I made random turns on the sleepy blocks of Elevado, Linden, and Carmelita. Then I was back on Sunset, heading west, reasonably sure I'd lost anyone who wasn't following me from a hot-air balloon.

I was still on the phone an hour later. I was in bed, holding a package of Pepperidge Farm cookies and dressed in my signs-of-the-zodiac flannel pajamas, a gift from Fredreeq four Christmases ago, so fragile now I wore them only in times of stress.

"Pick you up at ten-thirty tomorrow," Fredreeq said. "Lights out now. No math, no frogs. You need your beauty sleep."

I may have needed it, but not even the threat of waking up as Tammy Faye Bakker could get me to sleep at that moment. I said good-bye, the face of the blue-eyed man rising in front of me, as if he'd been lounging on the edge of my consciousness, eavesdropping, waiting to take center stage and obsess me some more.

I saw him in his polo shirt, and then in his suit. I saw him in the fluorescence of the minimall and the moonlight of Mulholland. I thought of all the ways I'd seen him and expanded on that, imagining him in a grocery store picking out produce, in a movie theater eating popcorn, in my kitchen.

I saw him in boxer shorts, kicking back on the sofa, watching CNN.

My God. I opened my package of cookies. What was happening to me?

My eyes wandered to a bookcase across the room, to a photo of Doc and Ruby. Black Irish, dark hair, infectious smiles, both. *This is your fault*, I told them. *I wouldn't be having these kinds of thoughts if you guys hadn't left me.*

My ex-fiancé looked back at me with lovely, normal brown eyes. *Don't eat all of those Mint Milanos in one sitting*, they seemed to say.

I awoke with a start, amid cookie crumbs and with *Amphibians and You: A Layman's Guide to Creatures of the Air and Water* facedown on my stomach. I jumped up, driven by the idea that had wakened me.

Annika, like Maizie's husband, Gene, used both sides of sheets of paper.

All the stray paper in my life was stuffed into file boxes on the floor of Hubie's bedroom closet. I switched on the light and rummaged through sketches, greeting card ideas, tax receipts, and photocopied frogs, searching for math homework.

Annika didn't like textbooks. "These books are stupid, Wollie. They tell you facts or equations that connect to nothing. We will make our own equations." She'd done these on her computer, decorating them with flowers and frogs, bringing them to our tutorials each week to illustrate the philosophies, practical applications, and mathematicians she loved to talk about. The equations themselves were of no interest to me now, of course. What I cared about were the backs of my math work sheets.

I found them. Half of the flip sides were printed-out e-mails, the end pages with all the incomprehensible—to me, anyway—data. I set these aside. Maybe there was a way to e-mail these people, but the data looked German, and wouldn't her mother have contacted Annika's German friends already?

There were pages that weren't e-mail: four in German, a recipe in English, a sheet with the words "Emma, EMMA, emma, **Emma**, *Emma*, EmmMzzzapso," Annika's work schedule, forty-five hours over the course of a five-day week, and a downloaded bank statement showing $165.38 for the month of September.

And there was a fragment of an e-mail. In English.

"because this is life in Hollywood. So my host father says. But me, I think it is not fair your life is horrible because of one person! It is better you quit, but then, no Biological Uhr (sorry! spell?) in Munich? So I think you will stay. BE CAREFUL. Can R.R. not help, if it is dangerous? Okay, we are Friday in Tahiti on holiday, so no e-mail but good news, no snow! (I share room with the baby but at least, maid service!) Ciao! Marie-Thérèse

I read it again. I ate four Mint Milano cookies and kept reading. Marie-Thérèse must be another au pair. The job in Munich would be *Biologische Uhr*, which Annika planned to coproduce. Despite *Biological Clock*'s dismal ratings in America, a German company wanted to try their own version. A nineteen-year-old girl without connections or education getting to coproduce would be a small miracle, but that's what Bing had promised. His sponsorship and her experience on our show would put it within reach.

"How lucky am I?" she'd said just weeks ago. "To work in TV! In Munich. My mother will move, to be near me. This job is the best of anything I can imagine."

So what had happened? The Annika I'd known until that last, disturbing night on the set had been incorrigibly cheerful. Maizie, though, had noticed a change, and so had Paul. Marie-Thérèse implied that the problem lay in the show itself, a problem serious enough to warrant quitting. But to suggest that R.R. help? That must be Rico Rodriguez, but the Rico I'd met was not likely to drive four miles out of his way to help Annika Glück.

Except that Rico had been disturbed to hear she wanted a gun.

The return-path line at the bottom of the page, I realized, would be the e-mail address for Marie-Thérèse. The whole thing could be cleared up in a few short sentences.

I danced out to the kitchen to start up my computer. This was it. I knew the key was finding Annika's friends. Girlfriends. Rico might be cavalier about her fate. Marie-Thérèse was clearly not.

I carefully composed the e-mail, explaining my relationship to Annika and the situation. I encouraged Marie-Thérèse to call me anytime, collect, or to e-mail me. I sent it off, ate six more Mint Milanos, and went to bed.

I didn't sleep well, tossing on Hubie's California king–sized feather-top mattress, kicking at the sheets assaulting me. In my dreams I fled from a man, my feet turning to concrete as I ran. When I turned to him he smiled from behind the wheel of his big car, one eye brown and one blue. "Are you Richard Feynman?" I asked.

"Forget her," he said.

"Ruby?" I said. "How can I forget Ruby? She's just a little girl."

But he drove away, and I saw a face in the back of his car, its nose pressed against the window. A little blond girl. Not even three. Two and three-quarters.

When I woke the next morning, my computer informed me that my e-mail to Marie-Thérèse had been returned, undeliverable.

18

Sunday morning found Fredreeq and me at the Beverly Center.

"Shouldn't you be with your family today?" I asked. "Or church?"

"The mall is my church, and Francis took the kids to paintball. Now listen," she said, pulling me along level six, past the frogs in Pet Love. "This Marie changed her e-mail—maybe she got DSL or switched ISPs, people do it all the time. None of this matters. Go back to Mulholland Man. The radar part. You showed up Monday on his radar, he said?"

"Yes. And it was Monday I got the call from Mrs. Glück and started asking questions around the set. Tuesday I met everyone else, Maizie Quinn and Glenda, the au pair volunteer, and then on Wednesday creepy Marty at the agency, so this isn't about them, it's about the show. Someone on the show doesn't want me looking for Annika."

Fredreeq steered me past Bloomingdale's. "No, no, no, forget Annika. It's Savannah. Savannah's now the odds-on favorite in Vegas. I saw this on the Internet. My theory is, Kim's getting stalked too, but she mistook us for the enemy, which explains the thugs at Westside Pavilion. That part we're going to take care of today."

I followed Fredreeq through the busy mall, searching the crowd. I wasn't even sure who I was searching for. "Why is Savannah the favorite?"

"The crowd loves her," Fredreeq said. "She's got that perky Paula Abdul thing going, and she's into some kind of boxing, she's got style. You were a stiff the first two weeks. But you're coming to life now, and that's a threat to Savannah's people."

"I gotta tell you, I don't think this tall guy is some *Biological Clock* fan."

"Not a fan," Fredreeq said, "a professional saboteur. Big difference. But he watches the show, and I can prove it. When did his radar kick in? Monday. Monday was the episode where you wore Joey's peasant blouse that was a little small and you talked about wanting your baby to have a father in its life because your own father walked out when you were six. The waitress in the background actually cried."

"My God, how embarrassing—Bing was filming that? I didn't realize we—"

"That was your finest moment. You left Savannah in the dust. Get it? Monday night." Fredreeq took a good look at me. "Let's hit Bebe."

"Oh, please God, not Bebe, Fredreeq. It's been a bad week, but I'd rather go back to the *morgue* than stuff myself into—"

"A celebrity dresses like a celebrity. You dress like a Home Depot clerk. Look at yourself. Here's your New Year's resolution a month early: No more fleece."

"This is my good fleece—"

"Ever since Doc dumped you, you're as sexy as cold oatmeal. Come to the party, girl. Who got press this week? Savannah Brook. You know who else? Raquel Welch. Yes, it's a tacky story, it's tabloid fodder, they went through her garbage. The point is, she's older than God but she stays in the news because she is a star down to her toenails. She works it. She dresses up for 7-Eleven. She's your role model from now on. No one's going through your garbage, and doesn't that bother you?"

"Look," I said, "even if you're right about the tall-guy stalker watching *B.C.*—"

"Hold Everything." Fredreeq came to a dead stop.

"Okay, maybe 'stalker' is too strong a word—"

"Where is it?"

"What?"

"Hold Everything. It used to be right there." She pointed to Bikini Bazaar. "They sold shoe trees. Man, I hate to lose a store." Fredreeq strode ahead once more, me trotting to keep up. "Restoration Hardware, that's our only hope. The day they fold is the day I start shopping online."

Inside Restoration Hardware, Fredreeq got into deep conversation with the greeter and I pulled out my cell phone and called Maizie Quinn. I was explaining Marie-Thérèse to her machine when she picked up.

"Hi," Maizie said, breathless. "Just getting a brioche out of the oven. Marie who?"

"Marie-Thérèse. I came across an e-mail—I think Annika confided in her."

"About what?"

"Problems on *Biological Clock*. Annika was a sort of an unpaid production assistant, you probably know, and I think something there led to her disappearance."

"Good Lord." An audible sigh. "I should've kept a closer eye on her, but— Okay, let me think. She met so many au pairs in New York—all the girls start there for a week of orientation and training, a sort of boot camp before they meet their host families. Marie-Thérèse was probably one of those, the other January arrivals."

"Did all these girls come from the same agency? Au Pairs par Excellence?"

There was a pause. "I'm not sure. I can— Yes, Emma, what?" Maizie's voice went into another mode, pronounced patience. "No, Mommy's on the phone. You need to wait one minute and I'll do it for you. If you need it right now, you have to ask Lupe or Grammy Quinn." Maizie returned to conversational mode. "Sorry, you were saying?"

"I have another thought. Emma's music class—you said Annika made friends there? If I could visit the class—"

"The problem is, Music with Miss Grusha has a 'no observers' policy. She says visitors create performance anxiety. She was not very gracious to Grammy Quinn last month. You have to be enrolled in class and participating. Gene's mom doesn't do participation. If it involves hopping."

"Oh," I said.

"And I can't alienate Miss Grusha; she's my ticket into preschool. But I'll ask the moms—oh, not tomorrow, I'm interviewing nannies. But next week, definitely."

Next week? A week was a lifetime, I thought, hanging up. I joined Fredreeq at the register and told her about Miss Grusha's antivisitor injunction. "What can I do?" I said. "I've got to talk to these women."

"Why?"

"Because I've gone through everyone else who knows Annika— the Quinns, the agency, Glenda, Britta, cops, boyfriend, mother. If I can't find Marie-Thérèse or Richard Feynman, these music moms are my only hope." I took the au pair application from my purse, but Fredreeq grabbed it.

"Here's an idea. Give it a rest. You're like a crazy person—"

"I'll meet you up on seven," I said, grabbing back the application. "I need a better German dictionary, and maybe a how-to book for finding missing persons—"

"Level eight," the salesclerk said, scanning with a wand what appeared to be a butterfly net. "The bookstore's on eight. Brentano's. Down from the food court—"

"Thank you," Fredreeq said, glaring at him. "We know all about level eight." She turned to me. "That's the most ridiculous thing I've heard this week. A how-to book on missing persons. No. We are not going on a wild book chase. There is no such book, because there is no market for—"

"But there is, there are forty thousand missing Americans—"

"This is a missing *German,* who's gone back to *Germany* and hasn't told her fruitcakey *mother,* because she's probably sick and tired of talking to her on the phone every damn Sunday. The cops told you that, the agency told you that, the Mother Goose mom told you that, how many votes have to be in—"

"No. There's no consensus on what happened to her, everyone's got different theories, and mine is, something happened on the show—"

"So someone hit on her. Welcome to show biz. Is that my total? Did you take off the extra ten percent on the fly gun and the card shuffler?" Fredreeq studied her receipt, then turned to me. "Look. We have two objectives today: destroy the competition and work on your wardrobe. No Soviet kindergartens, no German dictionaries..."

We argued about it all the way to a clothing store called Parsley Sage Rosemary, where Fredreeq's voice dropped to a whisper. "No one shops here except people trying out for *Hamlet.* Okay, bury your face in brocade and stay low until I give the word. Here, hold my butterfly net. Excuse me," she called, walking away before I could ask questions. "Is Kimberly working today?"

I realized this was the second day job for Kimberly Karmer. So I wasn't the only *Biological Clock* contestant with multiple odd jobs. And Parsley Sage Rosemary was odd, as odd as Plastique, the velvets and ruffled blouses suitable for fairy tales, for maidens who hang out with unicorns. Greeting cards took shape: Hamlet at the mall, fencing across level six, up the escalator... My thoughts drifted for ten minutes or more until Fredreeq tapped my shoulder.

"Let's go," she said. "We got what we needed."

Fredreeq couldn't see why gathering dirt on Kim did not sit well with me.

"I came here to create an alliance with her," she said, leading me past Baby Gap, "but she called in sick today, so I chatted up her coworkers. Is that a crime?"

"Fraud?" I said. "Yes, that's a crime. Slander, libel, defamation of character, telling people you're with the *National Enquirer*, that you'll pay—"

"I never used the word 'dirt' and I only implied I'd pay *if* a story checked out. Lighten up. It worked. Kim has been followed; she's called mall security twice in two weeks. Which confirms it's Savannah who's in league with the saboteurs. And Kim's had breast implants, which I suspected, and enough botox to kill a cow. They hate her there—they're on commission and she poaches customers."

I gazed at a pregnant woman walking past us. "But how could anyone but *B.C.*'s editor influence how people vote? And if he did that, featured one contestant over another, wouldn't we notice? Wouldn't the producers?"

"Yes." Fredreeq stopped, eyes wide. "Who's to say the producers aren't in on it? Maybe they kidnapped Annika, to create some buzz. Or—wait, wait! The saboteurs could be holding her hostage; they'll release her after the producers do their bidding."

I just stared.

"Yes!" she said excitedly. "The producers, in cahoots with bookies in Vegas. Not Joey, of course, but Elliot's always been a little shady." She took out her phone. "You go buy that dictionary. If this Music with Mrs. Khrushchev class is our only lead, I'll get you in there. If someone's kidnapped Annika and we expose it, we're home free, because I don't care what our ratings are, that story is headline news. So deal me in."

In the bookstore I stood holding a German-English dictionary and staring at one page of Annika's au pair application, the *Führungszeugnis*.

No single English word expressed it. *Führungszeugnis* needed its own sentence: "document issued by police certifying the holder has no criminal record."

This sounded like good news except that the date circled in red pointed to the fact that Annika's *Führungszeugnis* was several years old. And obsolete.

Someone else had figured this out too, someone who'd circled the date in red. And then what? Blackmailed her with the information? Who? To what end?

And for what crime?

19

"**S**azheeq, this is Wollie," Fredreeq said. "Auntie Freddie's friend."

I squinted through the window at the child in the car seat that took up half of Fredreeq's Volvo. We were in front of Wee Willie Winkies Preschool, on a quiet block of Moorpark in Studio City, in time for Music with Miss Grusha. "Hello, Sazheeq," I said.

Sazheeq said nothing. She was two and a half, younger than Emma Quinn but as tall, I could tell—all skinny arms and legs and pigtails.

"Come say hello to Aunt Wollie." Fredreeq hauled her niece out of the car and deposited her in my arms. Sazheeq climbed out of my arms. "Remember: french fries afterward if you're good. We'll rendezvous at Mickey D's."

Miss Grusha's was crowded. Two- and three-year-olds with attendant adults sat on the floor of the small room amid toys. A thin woman in red overalls and implausibly blond hair jumped up from the piano to greet us. "I am Grusha. You are Wollie? This is Sazheeq?" She was no spring chicken, but she looked like she could give toddlers a run for their money in the energy department. "Come," she said, taking Sazheeq's hand. "Tell us your favorite song so Miss Grusha may play it for you on the piano. If I sound funny it is because I have an accent. Miss Grusha is Russian."

Sazheeq, finding this acceptable, walked off with Miss Grusha. I joined the group of moms and mom substitutes on the floor.

"Adorable girl," one said. "Adopted?"

"Uh, no," I said, then realized that this was the most reasonable explanation for a pale white adult with a very black-skinned child. "I'm taking care of her."

This did not dispel curiosity; a black child with an Anglo-Saxon nanny would be sociologically odd. I was about to say I'd borrowed her but then I'd have to explain that, and what was the point of a cover story if you spilled the beans at the outset?

The woman introduced herself as Rachel. She pointed out her son, Brandon, and recited the names of the eight other children, all of which I immediately forgot. Rachel then rejoined her conversational pod, discussing someone's pediatrician's divorce. Two other women chatted in Spanish. An Asian girl stared out the door, clearly bored, the only adult young enough to be Annika's peer. I crawled over to her under the pretext of recovering a Nerf ball. "Hi," I whispered. "Do you know Annika Glück?" She looked at me as if I'd suggested something distasteful and moved away.

I'd crawled back to Rachel to ask her the same question when a musical triangle sounded. On cue, the children tossed toys into a wicker basket. Miss Grusha went to shut the door, just as Maizie Quinn and little Emma squeaked through.

Maizie scanned the room and saw me. A look of surprise replaced her smile, then curiosity as Sazheeq sat next to me. Emma waved in a matter-of-fact way, as though seeing me in her music class were an everyday occurrence.

The next hour we danced with scarves, hopped like bunnies, rode hobbyhorses, sang songs involving hand puppets on a shopping spree, and acted out a condensed version of *The Nutcracker Suite* with me assigned the role of someone's uncle. Sazheeq spent part of the time watching, part of the time trying to open the door and make a break, and part of the time lying spread-eagled on the floor, barking like a dog. I attempted talking to her during a dog episode, but this brought forth a scream of such epic proportions that I backed off. Other children hugged, climbed on, and clung to their attendants, but at no time did Sazheeq treat me as anything but a chance-met stranger of dubious character. This caregiver business wasn't as easy as it looked.

Others seemed to enjoy themselves, and Maizie had particular success as a sugarplum fairy, suggesting ballet in her past. Class was still in progress when she and Emma took off. "Nanny interviews," she said, and left behind homemade pumpkin cupcakes in honor of Thanksgiving week. Miss Grusha handed out napkins and sent us outside to plastic tables. This was my opportunity.

I told Rachel that Annika had disappeared, that I was looking for anyone who'd been a friend of hers, and that Maizie had recommended this class as a place to start. Rachel was astonished, concerned, and delighted to be drafted. "Georgine! Michelle!" She hailed moms from the cupcake tables. "Come!"

I recounted to them the events of the past week.

"I'm shocked." Georgine, in workout clothes and full makeup, looked less shocked than titillated. "She was the übernanny. I tried to hire her. Offered her a real salary, but she wouldn't leave that family. I bet they have a seriously nice house. Seen it?"

"Yes. Very nice," I said. "So Annika didn't seem depressed to you, or—"

"No," Georgine and Rachel said together. The other mom, Michelle, was silent.

"Did she ever talk about a Marie-Thérèse? Richard Feynman?" I asked.

More head shaking.

"I'll tell you one thing," Georgine said. "Maizie, Emma's mom? Not that she's unattractive, but come on. She's not twenty. I don't care how good her cupcakes are, she's nuts to have a girl as pretty as Annika live in."

"Maybe she's divorced," Rachel said.

"No, there's a husband," I said. "I've never met him, but she talks about him."

"I've met him," Georgine said. "An HMO doc, so I bet she has to work. And those guys don't keep super-long hours, not like real doctors, so there you go."

"What are you saying, the husband had an affair with Annika?" Rachel asked.

Georgine glanced at the picnic table. "Hallie, no more cupcakes, you'll get carsick," she called, then turned back to us. "It happens. Ever read *Jane Eyre?*"

Good God. This was something I'd never considered.

Michelle, an athletic brunette, smiled. "So why would you hire her, Georgine?"

"I was separated. Last summer, before Allen came crawling back. Now I've got Maria, two hundred pounds and gray hair. Hallie loves her, Allen doesn't. Hallie! Two more minutes, then we have to go shoe shopping!"

Belatedly, I remembered my own charge. Sazheeq, now in the sandbox, was bathed in orange frosting. How many of those damn cupcakes had she eaten? Stricken, I went to collect her. The party broke up as bigger children and their keepers filtered in for the next class. I separated Sazheeq from the sandbox and Miss Grusha separated twenty-five dollars from me, saying she hoped to see us again.

Rachel wished me luck. "Georgine might be right, but I'll tell you, I never saw a kid and a nanny crazy about each other like Emma and Annika. I hope for Emma's sake that you find her. And that it's nothing—you know. Icky."

When we got out to the parking lot, Michelle was squatting in front of a Jeep Cherokee, brushing crumbs from her son's overalls. She stood when she saw Sazheeq and me and flagged us down.

"I didn't want to say anything in front of Georgine," she said, "but two weeks ago—well, the last time I saw her—Annika asked me how to find a lawyer. I told her I'm a lawyer. I don't practice, but I'm a member of the bar. She got a little flustered and said no, she needs the kind who finds lost people, an immigration lawyer. I said that's not what lawyers do, but she said she'd heard of ones who find people who disappear."

My heart was beating a little faster. "Disappear."

Michelle looked down at her son and Sazheeq, staring at each other the way children do before manners set in and force them to either converse or feign disinterest. "Disappear into the judicial system. Noncitizens, held without charges, who don't get a phone call. She heard about it on National Public Radio." She rubbed her forehead. "I was in a hurry. I said, Don't worry, you're not a terrorist, this wouldn't happen to you. But she wasn't the worrying type. She was in trouble, I'm thinking now. Damn it. I should've asked more questions."

"Damn it," the little boy repeated.

"Okay, you, jump in your car seat," Michelle said. She opened the Jeep and her son climbed in the back. She reached into her glove compartment, withdrew a business card, and handed it to me. "In case you find her and she's in trouble. I did estate planning, so as a lawyer, I may not be much help. But as a mother I may be."

Michelle's words rang in my ears. I dialed Annika's mother, as I'd been doing periodically since waking up. I'd done the same the day before, Sunday, until ten P.M. German time. The response was the same now as it had been the last eight tries.

No one picked up the phone.

The answering machine wasn't on.

Mrs. Glück seemed, in fact, to have disappeared.

There were no horned frogs on my mural. I realized this as I changed into an old pair of Doc's sweatpants at the Mansion. I was not fond of the grumpy, cannibalistic ceratophrines and had let personal taste outweigh artistic considerations, but really, is eating one's own species worse than eating "prekilled" pinkie mice or the vitamin-dusted crickets that other pet frogs call lunch? And while I found horned frogs homely, Tricia might thrill to them. People did.

I found a place over the vegetable sink for a Chaco horned frog,

Ceratophrys cranwelli, and set to work. To achieve the mottled effect of the Chaco's brown-on-beige markings, I needed a daub cloth, and I was searching the Mansion for a rag when I recalled something else about the Chaco. And about Annika.

It was nearly the last time I'd seen her. She'd been looking through one of my frog books, lying on the floor of my apartment. "How do you call this one?" she'd asked. "*Chay-ko*, like the drug lord?"

I'd told her my guess was *Chock-o*, more Spanish-sounding, since the frogs were South American. And then, wondering why a drug lord would be a point of reference, I'd asked what her interest in Tcheiko was.

"He grew up in East Berlin," she'd said. "We hear of him, even before—but he is so evil, this man, and scary—" And then she'd changed the subject, visibly disturbed. I'd wanted to tell her she wasn't responsible for every bad egg who ever lived in Berlin.

I wondered about this now, thinking about the bedroom eyes I'd seen in *International Celeb*, but the thoughts troubled me, and I tried to focus on work. I tore off one leg of Doc's sweatpants below the knee, creating a daub cloth. If I'd had a degree in graphic arts, maybe I'd be better equipped for this kind of work, instead of making up tools as I went along. Not that it was a big sacrifice; the sweatpants were spattered with saffron-colored paint and destined for the ragbag anyway. Which would please Fredreeq.

What wouldn't please Fredreeq was me stopping for gas on the way home, in full view of Ventura Boulevard at rush hour, without changing back into my "good" sweats. While the gas pumped, I went for the squeegee. A dirty car is a moral issue in L.A., making my Integra a degenerate. A sports car pulled up behind me— strange, considering there were four empty self-serve islands at the station. I turned toward it.

The car was clean. Metallic. A grille like a flyswatter.

A man got out of the car. Tall. Very tall.

The Guy. The Mulholland menace. My heart started *thump thump thump*ing away, the blood sprinting through my veins.

If I dove into my car and drove off, would the pump go with me or would the hose disengage, spraying gas all over Ventura Boulevard? What about my gas cap?

The man walked toward me. Long strides. Relaxed.

What should've concerned me was that we were the only ones here at the gas station—not counting the clerk inside, who wasn't paid enough to intervene, should this encounter turn dangerous. What did concern me, of course, was how I looked.

He stopped in front of me, inches away, and settled against my extremely dirty car, hands in pockets. A beautifully casual pose, like a clothing ad.

"Hello," I said. It came out crackly. I cleared my throat. "Hello. Again."

"Hello."

I could sense his body temperature. Standing this close to someone signaled impending contact: Teeth cleaning. An eye exam. Assault.

A kiss.

This preoccupation with kissing: could I be coming down with a psychiatric disorder, some late-onset obsessive-compulsive stress-induced—

"You're dripping."

"I beg your pardon?" I looked down to see the windshield squeegee raining soapy water onto my pants, my saffron-spotted sweatpants, cut off below the knee on the left side, as if I'd borrowed them from a peg-leg pirate.

He reached out and took the squeegee and set to work on my windshield.

I stood, lumplike. Another person would've asked what kind of stalker cleans his victim's windshield, but not me because I was too busy watching his forearms flex. He wore a pale yellow dress shirt with the sleeves rolled up. His arms were muscular, tanned, with fine blond hair glinting under the gas station lights and a silver watch going back and forth, back and forth with the squeegee, his moves displaying the grace of an athlete or a professional gas station attendant.

Why on earth was he doing this? Why wasn't I asking?

He finished, returned the squeegee to its water pail, and instead of using the paper-towel dispenser, wiped his hand on the back of his pants, which made me like him more. They were beautiful pants, charcoal, well-fitting, knife-creased, worn with a belt I recognized as a Cartier. Not that I was staring, I told myself. It's just sad, having a stalker so much better dressed than oneself.

"Shall I check the oil?"

I dragged my eyes from his lower anatomy to his face. "No, thanks. I already did that this year."

He smiled. His face wasn't hard after all. How had this happened? "I was wrong about you," he said. "You're a very good girl, aren't you?"

I winced. Guys did not, in general, fall for very good girls, any more than girls went for very nice guys. I tried to keep the defensive note out of my voice. "Sometimes I leave shopping carts in the parking lot instead of returning them to their racks."

An eyebrow went up.

"Sometimes I eat grapes in the produce section. I tell myself it's to make sure they're not sour, but after the first eight or ten, I lose credibility. Also, I read magazines I don't buy."

"Is all your bad behavior grocery based?"

"I don't rotate my tires."

We were flirting. How could we be flirting?

He disengaged the gas nozzle from the Integra with a little flip, sending drops of gasoline flying. It struck me how masculine a gas nozzle is, how feminine a gas tank—how had this escaped my attention my whole life, the sexual nature of pumping gas? He pressed a button on the credit card pad, screwed on my gas cap, then took the receipt that popped out of the machine and handed it to me. "Going home?"

"What?" I was completely distracted by the sex act I'd just witnessed.

"Go home. Take Sepulveda; Coldwater's bad right now, Beverly Glen too. Freeway's worse." He went to the driver's door and opened it.

I just stood, staring.

"Unless," he said, "you need to stop at the store for a quick crime spree?"

I shook my head, less in response than to disperse the fog of bewilderment. I felt a horizontal gravitational pull toward him. I resisted it.

"Come," he said.

I stopped resisting. I can't say why. I got into the car, and he shut the door after me, gently, then leaned down and in.

"Who are you?" I said.

He smiled. That was it. It changed his whole face. "I'll call you when you're home," he said. "Shouldn't take more than an hour."

I did not go home. I might've had a mental disorder, I might've been under the effect of toxic gas fumes, but I'm not a lemming; I don't just go home because tall, well-dressed strangers with strong opinions about routes tell me to. I went west on Ventura, because that's the direction my car was facing, coming out of the gas station. When he passed me and speeded up, that metallic sports car weaving in and out of traffic like a movie stunt car, I did a clumsy U-turn and went on with my life.

20

It had been a week since Mrs. Glück's initial phone call, the one that changed my life. If not for that call, my frog mural would be finished, I'd have studied for my math-assessment test, I'd certainly have had more rest. But Monday night found me fidgety, distracted, and sleep deprived, facing work on *Biological Clock*, a show that had once seemed merely seedy and now looked sinister.

The setting didn't help. RockiSushi was on south La Brea, a block where you took everything of value out of your car after parking it, then considered removing your tires. Fredreeq and I arrived an hour before the *B.C.* shoot to do hair and makeup, and Joey, as producer, came to ensure that the restaurant was open for us. On a real TV show, Joey said, there would be a makeup trailer at the location, a generator to power it, transportation people to help you park, and a catering truck with coffee and food for everyone. Low-budget reality TV was a lonelier affair. "Paul said they were expecting us," she said, peering through a window, "but is this place even in business?"

The door was unlocked. We walked into a room empty of people and smelling of fish. Through a curtain a man moved toward us as if through a fog, intoning, "Table for three?" Joey introduced us as *B.C.* people. He sighed and showed us to the restroom.

Fredreeq stuffed Kleenex around the neckline of my raw-silk blouse while we filled Joey in on the day's events. I did not, however, mention the tall man. "This *Führungszeugnis*—" I said. "I think someone discovered that Annika had a police record and threatened her with deportation, which is maybe why she needed a lawyer. And Marie-Thérèse's e-mail implies that someone on the show was making her life hell, enough to make her quit, and even disappear. I don't want to offend you, Joey—obviously I don't suspect Elliot, but since he and his partner hired everyone—"

"Listen, if it's good for business, Elliot and Larry would make their own mothers disappear. If they weren't already dead."

Fredreeq sponged foundation on my face. "Could they make mine disappear?"

"Speaking of mothers," I said. "First Mrs. Glück calls me every day, twice a day, and now—nothing. Your child's missing, what's the first thing you do when you walk in the house? Check your messages. You'd never leave your phone machine off. So why can't I reach her? Speaking of phones, would you go in my backpack and make sure mine's on? P.B.'s been trying to reach me."

Joey emptied out my backpack. "What's *Algebra, Geometry, and Beyond*?"

"Seventh-grade honors math." Ruby, my almost-stepdaughter, had sent it to me from Japan a month earlier, with instructions to skip the boring parts and go right to the "and Beyond." Her confidence in my ability was touching, albeit misplaced. "I thought I'd take another stab at that math placement test next week."

"Next week's the eclipse," Fredreeq said, powdering me. "You can't pass a test in the shadow of the eclipse."

"I have to. There's a registration deadline. What's a shadow of an eclipse?"

"Astrology. Take the test tomorrow, before the eclipse effect kicks in. I happen to know, because I'm comparing your chart and Savannah's, that you have Mercury trine Saturn tomorrow. A one-day-only transit. A trine like this, you can ace any test."

"I can't take it tomorrow," I said. "I'm not nearly ready."

Joey flipped through the book. "You can be. I'll coach you: what's an integer?"

"I can't focus on math tonight. Someone on this show was tormenting Annika. Bing, Paul, Isaac, any of us contestants—"

"I think you can leave yourself out of the lineup," Joey said.

"Hold the phone." Fredreeq stepped back, hands on hips. "You know my theory on this: I wouldn't put anything past the saboteurs, but you can't go acting like you're on *America's Most Wanted*. Savannah and Kim come on like sex kittens, with their capped teeth and collagen lips, and here's you making citizen's arrests—"

"Okay, but—"

"No. Joe Friday is not attractive. Hold still while I tweeze your eyebrows."

"So let's get back to integers," Joey said.

"I have no idea what an integer is," I said.

"A number without a decimal or fractional part," Fredreeq said.

"If a vertical line can be drawn through a graph that intersects that graph more than once, can the graph in question be a function?" Joey asked.

"No," said Fredreeq.

"Correct."

I let my friends talk math in the small bathroom, wondering how so many people in the world understood something so foreign to me. I needed Annika. She had a gift bigger than Isaac Newton's: she could explain Isaac Newton. She coaxed comprehension out of me the way you'd coax a cat out of a tree, and I doubted I could pass an assessment test without her. It bothered me that my feelings for Annika were not without self-interest. One more crummy thing I'd discovered in the past week.

Vaclav Gadosh, the third male contestant on *Biological Clock*, greeted me with a wrestling-hold embrace. He was my height and a few pounds lighter, with a model's chiseled face.

He had a scrappy attitude with men and a flirtatious one with women. I found him engaging in a dissipated sort of way.

"Vollie, how are you?" he said, pouring me sake. His accent was subtle, except for the transposition of *v*'s and *w*'s. I'd asked him, on our first date, where he was from and he'd told me Culver City. He was reticent about his past. And his present.

Vaclav worked at Rand Corporation, a think tank. For me, the term "think tank" brought to mind people sitting around in swimsuits, dangling their feet in water as they pondered grave issues of international importance. I'd been excited to meet a real tank thinker, for clarification on this, but Vaclav had declined to enlighten me. "I would tell you what we do," he'd said, "but then I'd have to kill you." He delivered this shopworn line with pride, as if he'd made it up. Fredreeq believed he worked there in a janitorial capacity.

I studied Vaclav now, chewing absently on a cuticle and sipping sake. He had callused hands, I noticed. How well had he known Annika? He was openly sexual, far more so than Carlito or Henry; did his taste run to nineteen-year-olds?

"Vaclav," I said, "are you—attracted to—teenagers?"

He looked up, a smile forming. This was his kind of conversation. "Are you?"

"Not sexually. But I know age differences can be—for some people—"

"Do not knock it. You must try it."

I had a sudden vision of Rico Rodriguez, how he'd made me blush. But then I thought of Mr. Tall, the blue-eyed man, twice Rico's age, and my whole body went weak. What was happening to me? I was interrupted from contemplation of this interesting question by the arrival of Bing.

It was clear our director-producer-cinematographer was having a bad day. The whites of his eyes were pink, indicating sleep issues I could relate to. He told us that the Biographical Question was religion, moved us to the sushi bar, and began filming.

Vaclav and I sat side by side. Bing got us in profile, then turned his camera toward the sushi chef, edging closer to me until his waist was next to my cheekbone. Something in his pants hit my breast. I hoped it was a gun, a knife, a banana—anything but an anatomical part. The fish smell was getting to me. I fought off a wave of nausea.

Isaac, the sound guy, moved in, headphones covering his ears like earmuffs. What did the customers think, a camera the size of a microwave creeping around them, another man with his long-handled boom microphone looking like he was fishing? The five actual diners seemed not to notice. This was, after all, L.A.

At Bing's signal, I posed the night's question to Vaclav, expecting him to reply that religion is the opiate of the people. Vaclav surprised me.

"It was my misfortune to be raised without religion, a sad disadvantage."

"Why?" I asked.

"A belief in God and prayer has been shown to reduce stress by a margin of some significance."

"So—you believe in God?" I asked.

"No. Only stress reduction."

"Okay, cut!" Bing said. "Paul, have the cute waitress take their order and then, Vaclav, ask Wollie the question."

Fredreeq jumped up to powder me. "Gorbachev here just lost the Bible Belt vote," she whispered. "Nobody likes an atheist. Talk Jesus."

"Okay, Round Two," Bing called. "Food, then God. Action!"

Vaclav ordered monkfish liver, *uni* with raw quail egg, and beef *sabu-sabu*, the kind of thing Doc would've ordered. I went with vegetable tempura, in honor of Ruby. Vaclav asked me my religious preferences, which reminded me that the camera was on.

"I started out Catholic," I said. "Around age ten, I turned to Judaism, but never converted because I couldn't give up Christmas; I'm not sure whether that makes me a closet Christian or just . . . sentimental. Then I read *Be Here Now* and fell in love with Buddhism, but every time I meditate I fall asleep. Same problem with Sufism, another lovely religion, headed by a very charismatic guy, and if you're into poetry, they've got Rumi, a great person to have on your team. I'm a little sketchy on Hinduism, but I have a necklace with Hanuman on it, he's a monkey demigod, and——" In my peripheral vision, Fredreeq was jumping up and down, gesticulating. "Oh! Sorry. Jesus," I said. "Jesus is great. I've always loved him. The parables and the miracles are fine, but my favorite moment is when he tells the thief on the other cross that they're headed for paradise. What a happy ending to a really bad day. Not that I'm well versed in the Bible. Protestants are much better read than the Catholics. Better singers too, *The Sound of Music* notwithstanding. A good gospel choir is a peak experience, don't you think, like sex? And if you're down South and visit a church where they do snake-handling and speak in tongues——well, wow."

Fredreeq was frantically waving her hands over her head, signaling something. It didn't appear to be unqualified approval.

Vaclav said, "So what will your children be? Catholic?"

"No, I'm a bad Catholic. Even as a child I was only in it for the stained glass. And the incense. Frankincense. Or myrrh? Very heady stuff, and would come in handy right now to obscure these fishy odors——" I remembered again I was on camera. "Oops. Oh, does it matter, Vaclav? Most people I know turn their backs on their parents' religion. I'll probably just read my kids poetry and pray they don't become Raelians."

"Cut," Bing said.

I turned to look at Fredreeq, who had dropped her head into her hands. Joey was talking on a cell phone. Paul studied a menu. Vaclav occupied himself with the Takei Sake bottle, the drink for once appropriate to the cuisine. Joey's phone reminded me to turn on mine, now that filming had temporarily stopped.

Instantly, a buzzing dentist's drill noise indicated that I'd missed a call. I pressed buttons and listened to a message from Detective Cziemanski. I called him back. "What's up?" I asked. "Is it about Annika?"

"No, it's about Wollie. What are you doing for dinner?"

I laughed. "Tonight? Eating tempura on national TV." I explained *Biological Clock*, a show that he, like most Americans, had never heard of.

"You didn't tell me you're a star," he said. He didn't sound thrilled.

I looked around. Vaclav knocked back sake. Paul leaned against a wall, dozing. A fly skimmed the surface of the sushi bar. Plastic fish adorned the walls. "It's nonstop glamour," I said. "But only Mondays and Thursdays. The rest of the week I slum."

"Okay, I don't know how to ask this, but—that name, *Biological Clock*—is there something we should talk about here? Not that I need to know your age before I buy you a burger, but I take it you're a little older than . . . twenty-eight, twenty-nine?"

"A little. Is that a problem?" I asked.

"I don't know. Is it? In terms of kids?"

"My understanding, Detective, is that if you and I had sex every half hour from now till next year, I'm more likely to get pregnant than I am to fall into an active volcano. But not by much." Silence. "I'm exaggerating."

The silence continued. Then, "The thing is, Wollie, I was hoping for—"

"Kids?"

"A bunch of them." A call-waiting click occurred, on his end. He apologized, saying he had to take the call. "Listen, I'll be in touch. I still want to be friends, but—"

I sat very still, listening to a dead phone, feeling a little sick.

"Boyfriend problems, Vollie?" Vaclav's words slurred a little.

Before I could reply, the restaurant door burst open. "Bing Wooster!" a man yelled. "Where are you, you worthless asshole?"

Bing turned toward the voice. We all did.

Then Bing pulled out a gun.

A long moment of silence followed, interrupted by Joey's gravelly voice. "Jesus."

More silence. Finally, Bing spoke. "Get off my set." His voice shook. His hand shook too, his gun hand, but still, he was showing more courage than I'd expect from Bing, a director defending his production. The Betacam was still on his shoulder, but Paul moved in behind him, ready to take the camera.

The man laughed. He was muscular, with a goatee, wearing a black T-shirt. I'd seen him before. Outside the restaurant last week, on the sidewalk. "Or what?" he said. "You blow me away?" He walked forward with a swagger, arms open, fingers spread, body language saying, "Shoot me."

Bing shook some more.

"You're holding the gun wrong, Wooster," the man said. One hand snaked out and the gun went flying across the room. The Betacam wobbled and slipped from Bing's shoulder.

The gun skidded into a wall.

The Betacam fell into Paul's waiting arms.

The gun didn't fire. The restaurant exhaled.

The goateed man had both hands on Bing's gun arm, doing something that forced Bing to his knees. When he let go, Bing bent over, holding his hand, whimpering.

"Now that I've got your attention," the man said, leaning down, "you pull a no-show again, I'll kill you. I don't need a gun to do it. Two, you don't pay, you don't play. I make her disappear, get what I'm saying? You never see her again." He spoke quietly, but because no one in the room was even breathing, we all heard.

The man walked out of RockiSushi.

We all looked at one another, the chef, the staff, the *B.C.* people, the five customers. Two or three cell phones came out. "Do we call 911?" a woman at a table asked.

"Did anyone die?" Fredreeq said.

Paul went over to Bing, who was nursing his hand. Bing told Paul to get lost.

Joey, meanwhile, had crossed the room and picked up the gun. She went to the window, gun pointing down, glanced outside, then walked out the door.

Seconds later, a man came in. Cadaverous, middle-aged, and dressed in a Nehru jacket, he looked around, smiled, and made his tentative way to the sushi bar.

"Excuse me," he said to the sushi chef. "I'm Dr. Arthur

Ostroot. I'm supposed to meet some people here with a TV show?"

"That's us, honey," Fredreeq called. "Sit down and have some edamame beans."

Vaclav offered our expert some sake while Bing hauled himself up off the floor. He wobbled, glanced around the room, and steadied himself.

"Paul, what are we waiting for?" he yelled. "Next setup. And who's got Vicodin?"

21

Despite our director's stoicism, we wrapped early Monday night. Bing's fingers swelled so badly he had trouble operating the camera, and he swilled so much sake to deal with the pain that he fell over backward into the sushi bar, enraging the chef. Joey wasn't there to do her producer thing, soothing ruffled feathers and handing out twenty-dollar bills, so we were asked to leave.

Tuesday morning, Fredreeq called to say she and Joey were en route to my apartment. "To take you to an undisclosed location, in order to save your life. Wear running shoes. Dress sporty."

These last five were words I'd never expected to hear from Fredreeq. My curiosity aroused, I was waiting on the curb when Joey's Mercedes pulled up. "Is this about the guy who broke Bing's fingers?" I said, climbing into the back seat.

"Indirectly," Joey said.

"Absolutely," Fredreeq said. "It came to us the exact same moment. Bing's gun went flying and we both thought, 'Krav Maga.' "

"Excuse me?"

Joey steered with her thigh and wrestled her red hair into a scrunchie. "I called Bing last night, but even drunk as a skunk, he wouldn't say who the goatee guy was."

"It's obvious who he is. He's blackmailing Bing." Fredreeq pulled out a cell phone. "Keep talking. I just gotta call my kids."

"Where'd you go last night?" I asked Joey.

"I tried to follow the goatee guy, just to see if I could. I couldn't. I don't even know when I lost him, because I followed what I thought was his truck all the way to Inglewood. I did get his license, though, right at the beginning."

"The goatee guy," Fredreeq said, putting away her cell phone, "works for Savannah Brook. Or organized crime in Vegas. He's our saboteur. He's the messenger, and here's the message: Make sure Savannah Brook wins this contest or we make someone disappear. Annika, Wollie, Kimberly—"

Joey said, "That is the wackiest theory I've ever heard."

"Wacky?" Fredreeq said. "You two ever hear of Nancy Kerrigan and Tonya Harding? Did I make that up? Did Pete Rose bet on baseball?"

"So what is this undisclosed location?" I asked. "We're not going to buy an attack dog or dye my hair or—"

"Dye your hair?" Fredreeq turned around in the front seat to stare at me. "Are you drunk? Women in this town run to their colorists every six weeks to get that shade of blond. We just told you. Krav Maga."

"Yes, but what is it?"

"Hebrew," she said. "Very trendy."

"A deli?" I said.

"Much more fun than that." Joey zoomed across Sepulveda. "A martial art."

Uh-oh. "Is this something we're going to watch?"

"Nope," Joey said. "It's something we're going to do."

"But I don't want to do this. This is not something I'd like doing."

"It's very hip," Fredreeq said. "It's more martial than art, so you don't have to learn calligraphy and eat seaweed and wear those white pajamas." She, I now noticed, was wearing tight, rainbow-colored workout clothes. "In less time than it takes to get your teeth capped, they turn you into a killing machine."

I didn't want to become a killing machine. I articulated this as clearly as I could, but my friends were unmoved. My life was at stake, Fredreeq said. Was I or wasn't I being stalked? Forget getting myself a gun. Had a gun helped Bing? Or Annika?

This would give me confidence, Joey said; I owed it to myself to give it a try.

I expected a low-ceilinged, mildewy room, because an old boyfriend had taken karate in a place like that, but Krav Maga shared the ground floor of the City National Bank building, and maybe the bank's decorator and cleaning service. It was an aesthetically pleasing space, with a small boutique near the front, displaying, among other things, Krav Maga baby T-shirts.

Three people worked behind the desk, one more cheerful than the next. "Excessively happy people signify cult activities," I whispered to Joey. A lovely girl introduced herself as Taffy, checked us in, had us sign a waiver in case we were maimed during the introductory class, and handed us three pairs of leather gloves.

"Not me. Sciatica," Fredreeq said, indicating her lower back. "I'm just here for moral support."

Taffy nodded and explained that the free introductory classes were usually held on Saturdays, but one had been added this week due to a sudden holiday demand.

"Are people anticipating a Thanksgiving crime wave?" I asked.

"Exactly." Taffy smiled, immune to sarcasm. "The Orange County ATM thieves."

"But this is a Jewish organization?" I asked, growing crankier by the minute. "And you work on the Sabbath?"

"Imi, our founder, was Jewish, but we're open to everyone. I'm Presbyterian. And we train seven days a week, because criminals work seven days a week. This way!" She came out from behind her desk and led us through a lobby surrounded by workout rooms. The workout rooms had windows for walls, enabling us to see the people within, red-faced, dripping with sweat, punching bags with rigorous intensity. One man had strange headgear on. A woman's knees were bandaged. No one was smiling. "Level two," Taffy said, pointing. "And over there is Fight."

And this was supposed to sell us on the program? What kind of people enjoyed watching other people suffer?

Joey. She was salivating, a diabetic looking into a bakery. Fredreeq inspected the lobby, pointing out vending machines, a TV suspended from the ceiling, and walls covered with photographs, magazine covers, and articles featuring testimonials from movie stars and cops. "Tasteful," Fredreeq said. "Like the first-class lounge at the airport."

Taffy pointed to the locker rooms and sent us on our way.

I expected our instructor to be some Special Forces type from the Israeli army, but again, they outmaneuvered me. Ten of us, all sizes, shapes, and ages, stood around, looking mostly uncomfortable, and at 8:47, a lanky guy disengaged himself from a trio of teenage girls, walked to the front of the room, popped a CD into a player, and introduced himself as Seth.

Seth had shaggy hair obscuring puppy eyes, and the energy level of someone who'd woken suddenly out of a sound sleep to find himself in the front of this room. He pressed a button and soft, alternative rock music massaged our ears. In a self-deprecating voice, Seth rattled off his résumé: a couple of black belts, in karate, Tae Kwon Do, Ho Chi Minh—I lost track. Then he pulled off his worn sweatshirt to reveal a tank top underneath, which in turn revealed a torso like the ones you see on late-night TV, belonging to guys selling exercise equipment. He told us about Imi Lichtenfeld, the guy who'd come up with Krav Maga, and demonstrated the martial art's only formality, the bow, accompanied by some word that meant, in some language or other, "bow."

"Ordinarily, we'd turn to the back of the room, to Imi's photo, but there doesn't seem to be one in this room, so, uh—" Seth smiled sheepishly. "Okay, just bow to me."

I decided this wasn't so bad after all, that it was, in fact, a cute sort of martial art, with cute bows, a cute instructor, and a founder with the cute little name of Imi.

Then the music changed.

Heavy metal took over as we jumped, jogged, kicked, punched, hopped, yelled, hammered, elbowed, kneed, ducked, and weaved ourselves into a frenzy. This explained the waivers. Seth, his sleepiness gone, egged us on. Periodically, he yelled "Time!" and let us sit, panting like dogs, as he demonstrated antimugging techniques. He attacked a punching bag with such force that the heavy bag flopped around like a balloon, decimating any doubts I'd had about his teaching credentials.

"Best targets? Crotch, neck, soft parts of the face. Knees. Eyes." He smiled apologetically. "Some people get a little squeamish about eye gouging. But look: if you see an opening, don't waste it on someone's arm or their abs—a guy's in good shape, he might not even feel it. Maybe you only get one shot. Maybe he's got a knife. Maybe there's three of them and one of you. Do the math. Make it count."

I hate it when people say "do the math." I didn't want to do math. I didn't want to do this. I wanted to go paint frogs.

I glanced in the mirror. My face was tomato red, my bangs sticking out, stiff with sweat and last night's hairspray. I'd worn two jogging bras to keep my breasts from having a life of their own. I didn't have the physique for this. I didn't have the physique for any sport except wet T-shirt contests.

Joey was another story. Built like a skinny fifteen-year-old, she was in her element. She caught my eye in the mirror and winked.

"Defense and counterattack," Seth said, "are peanut butter and jelly. Self-defense without counterattack gets you killed, if you're dealing with someone bigger, or someone with a stick, screwdriver, handgun . . ."

Screwdrivers? People were out there with screwdrivers?

"The main thing is, you don't give up," Seth said. "If you walk away with nothing else from today, take this: worst thing you can do is curl up in a ball and quit. Don't quit, don't get in their car, keep screaming, keep fighting. I don't care how scared you are or how bad you're hurt. If you're not dead, you're not done."

"Is this great?" Joey bounced past in search of a towel. "Everything he talks about makes me think of sex."

Before I could wonder about my friend's carnal habits, we

were back on the attack. Seth told me I was doing fine, I just needed to rotate my hips when I punched, but I knew what he meant was "You have no aptitude for this—I've seen houseplants in better shape." Still, I appreciated his tact and, of course, his amazing muscles.

And then it was over. We bowed to Seth, Seth bowed to us, and I staggered into the locker room while Joey went to the front desk to sign up for a lifetime membership.

Twenty minutes later I found Fredreeq in the waiting area talking to a bald man who looked like he'd just been released from the state penitentiary. I was reading a testimonial letter on the wall when I heard him say, "Here she is now. Hey, Savannah!"

I looked up to see a petite woman in a baseball cap and a T-shirt that said "Contact Combat" hurry past the front desk. Even hearing her name, I needed a moment to place her as my fellow *B.C.* contestant, because I'd never seen her in the flesh.

Fredreeq hissed, flattening herself against a vending machine. Her tie-dyed spandex did not lend itself to inconspicuousness, and I didn't understand the need for secrecy, but her paranoia was contagious. Obviously, she hadn't expected Savannah to show up here. I looked for shelter.

Too late. Savannah raced across the lobby, cell phone to ear, and reached up to flick a switch on the television mounted on the wall. She was halfway between Fredreeq and me but paid no attention to either of us, or to the man who'd called her name. She stared at the TV and I stared too, at ads for cat food, allergy medication, and dental stain removers and, then, a Channel 4 Live late-breaking-news special report.

I knew him at once, the face smiling down at us, a face made for TV. Missing for forty-eight hours, the reporter said. Student at Pepperdine. Son of a congressman.

Rico Rodriguez.

His face disappeared, replaced by a couple in their mid-forties facing a barrage of cameras. The man looked familiar. Congressman Rodriguez, a journalist called him, asking a question I didn't catch. The congressman nodded. "Richard was to drive home Sunday to join us on a family trip to Telluride for Thanksgiving. He spoke to his mother Saturday afternoon, confirming he'd be home for dinner. To our knowledge, that's the last anyone's heard from him."

Another journalist asked a question, one that Channel 4 didn't pick up, but it didn't matter. The camera tightened on Mrs. Rodriguez, lovely, blond, anxious. Her answer came out softly. "His favorite. Linguine with clam sauce."

His mother. A chill went up and down my spine, a feeling that had nothing to do with the shower I'd just taken, the wet hair dripping down my back. It was the sudden conviction I had that Mrs. Rodriguez would never make that particular meal again.

22

By eleven I'd gone home, changed, and made it to Santa Monica College. I had yet to feel the happy effects of the astrological transit Mercury trine Saturn that Fredreeq had promised.

The first thing I'd done, from Krav Maga, was call Detective Cziemanski. If the cops hadn't made a connection between the disappearance of Rico Rodriguez and the disappearance of his girlfriend Annika, I could save them time. Cziemanski didn't answer, so I explained this to his voice mail. I told myself Rico's plight could be good for Annika, focusing attention on her case, but this didn't cheer me up. Seeing Rico's mother on TV had been profoundly disturbing.

The last thing I needed was a math test, but postponing it didn't make sense, so I braved the parking facility and trudged across campus to the Liberal Arts Building, only to find the assessment-test office closed. Doughnut break?

I walked to the cafeteria for a doughnut of my own and realized that if the police were really going to focus on Annika, things could get complicated. I rummaged through my backpack and found the number for Britta, the au pair from San Marino, and left a message on her host family's machine. In the cafeteria, I tried Cziemanski again, and got lucky. He apologized for our last conversation, then got to the point. "Everyone's heard about the Rodriguez case," he said. "The senator's son."

"Congressman's son," I said. "He was dating Annika Glück."

There was a pause. "Really?"

"Yes. I talked to Rico last week. He had no idea where Annika was and now he's gone too, and that's an awfully big coincidence, don't you think?"

"It's worth looking into," he said. "I'll put in a call to the detective on the case."

"Why aren't you the detective on the case? You're Annika's detective, and if it's a—a serial disappearance, shouldn't all the cases get the same detective?"

"First, Annika's 'case' right now is a missing person's report. Second, Rodriguez goes to Sheriff's Department, not LAPD. Third, we don't know they're related; if they are, LASD may get both."

"How come Rico's is a case and Annika's isn't? Because his dad's important?"

"No. That's why it made the news. It's a case because the kid's Corvette was found at LAX twenty-four hours after he was supposed to be home for dinner."

"That doesn't sound so dire," I said. "Maybe he made a detour to Tijuana."

Another pause. "If he did, he left two grand in the glove compartment. And what looks to be his own blood all over the trunk."

Oh. I'd missed that, back in my apartment, channel surfing. The case was on the local stations, but I'd caught only snippets, most featuring Rico's father, John J. Rodriguez: John's career as congressman, John's business as an industrial developer, and John's ex-model wife, Lauren. One reporter stood outside the Rodriguez's multimillion-dollar home in Lost Hills. John and Lauren did not appear, but a Dalmatian was spotted on the front lawn, its identity confirmed as the family dog, Hero.

His own blood in the trunk of his car. I felt sick. I pushed aside my doughnut, wishing I'd eaten it before calling Cziemanski.

I was headed back to Liberal Arts when my attention was caught by a guy smiling as he walked toward me. I couldn't place him, but I smiled back anyway, on general principle.

He stopped. "Wendy," he said.

"No, uh—"

"Winnie."

"It's Wollie."

"Troy." He stuck out his hand, and we shook. "We met last month. Some coffee place in West Hollywood. I'm Annika's friend. Well, her tutoree. Tutee. Whatever. And you're her other one, right? *Alle meine Entchen?*"

"Um, I don't speak German. Sorry."

"Oh, okay, I'm a geek." He gave me a quizzical look. "She wasn't tutoring you?"

"In math, not German," I said. "What was it you just said?"

"Oh." He grinned. "This nursery-rhyme thing she made me memorize, to help with prepositions. I figured you'd know it too."

Something nibbled at my memory banks. "How does it go?"

"Well, she told me not to try picking up German girls with it, they'd laugh at me."

I smiled. "Why? What's it mean?"

"Okay." He smiled again, dimples showing. "*Alle meine Entchen*—that's, uh, all my little duckies—*Schwimmen auf dem See, schwimmen auf dem See*—swimming in the sea, swimming in the sea—*Köpfchen in das Wasser, Schwänzchen in die Höh,* heads in the water, tails in the air. Okay, the plot's weak, but you know what? It helped. I aced my German final. She'll be so jazzed. *Bin ich nicht gut?* Hey, do you know, is she out of town?"

With a shake of the head, I told him what was going on, and watched his face fall.

"Disappeared? You're kidding," he said. "That is, like, so weird."

"Yeah, it is weird."

"Yeah." He gazed off, clearly troubled. "The last time I saw her was right here. Well, there. In front of the bookstore. Man, you wanna know what's *really* weird—" He stopped, looked at me, then at his watch. "Shit, eleven fifty-two? Shit! My psych teacher said one more late, it counts against my grade. Sorry, man—" He turned and took off at a lope.

"But—!"

"Can't slow down," he yelled over his shoulder.

I loped after him. I hate loping. It attracts stares. "Troy! Wait up!" I yelled. Also, I wasn't in loping shape. Especially after Krav Maga.

Happily, Troy wasn't in shape either. He slowed, I caught up with him, and we switched to racewalking. "Jeez," he said. "Gotta get to . . . the gym . . . more."

"Me too," I said. "So what's 'really weird' about Annika disappearing?"

He held up a hand, battling for breath. "Confidential."

I said, "I already know she was looking for a lawyer, and a gun, that she worried about disappearing into the criminal justice system—"

He stopped. "No shit?"

I stopped too. Nodded.

"Okay, shit." He was panting heavily. "Not good. I was the one who told her this could happen. This means—what? It means she did what I told her not to. Unless she'd done it already. You know, I'm pretty sure I shouldn't talk about this."

"Troy." I fought for breath and patience. "I have no idea what you're not talking about, but as I seem to be the only person in North America looking for her, anything you know—please. Please, please, please."

Troy veered to the right, and I veered with him, still racewalking. We passed the facilities maintenance building. "Okay," he said. "I told her about how my roommate's brother in Chicago got in trouble with the Feds because he lent his cell phone to someone who was part of a drug deal that was going down. He disappeared—"

"The drug dealer?"

"No, my roommate's brother. The Feds arrested him on conspiracy, and he didn't get a phone call, so no one knew where he was. For, like, two weeks. Of course, he's Iranian."

"Your roommate's brother?"

"My roommate too. Second generation. No accent whatsoever, and not even Moslem or Muslim or whatever, but they busted him anyway. He's doing time now."

"For conspiracy." I was struggling to follow the story. "How's this tie in to Annika?"

"Man, she's German. The Feds totally have it in for Germans. And the French."

"Why would she even come to their attention? She's an au pair in Encino."

Troy looked at me, then away. We'd reached an old, fairly ugly brick building. He took the stairs two at a time, and at the top grasped a railing to recover, breathing hard. Apparently he wasn't here on an athletic scholarship. "She wouldn't," he said, "come to their attention. If she was smart. That's what I told her."

The conversation couldn't have been less clear if it were in German. "Does this have to do with guns? Or drugs? Or a guy named Feynman?"

Troy said nothing. My heartbeat, already in the anaerobic range, beat faster. I could see him teetering on the fence: to tell or not to tell. He glanced inside the glass door of the building.

"Please, Troy," I said. "I'm not the Feds, I'd never talk to the Feds, I'm practically a Socialist; heck, I'm a Communist. Well, in the area of universal health care."

He looked at the people hurrying into the building, then back at me. "She wanted to know about—the drug scene on campus, how you'd score stuff. So I told her the thing with my roommate's brother. I told her, Don't even go there. Keep your nose clean."

"What kind of drugs was she interested in scoring?"

"She said she was just asking, but why do you ask about them unless you want them, know what I mean?"

"Troy, what kind of drugs?"

He closed his eyes and sighed. "Euphoria."

It was a sister drug to Ecstasy, only a warmer, fuzzier trip, he said, a way more happy trip. As my knowledge of Ecstasy was limited, this was not really helpful. I remembered when you got ecstasy through transcendental meditation, when a rave was a good review, when euphoria was a guy you liked liking you back. How innocent I was. How ancient.

Troy hadn't done Euphoria himself, he assured me, but it was the Next Big Thing. Very hard to get. U4. He drew the nickname in the air with his finger. And then he went to class.

And I went to my assessment test. The office was open. I put drug thoughts aside long enough to state my intention to a girl in capri pants and an SMC sweatshirt, who led me into a small room and set me up at a computer terminal.

Fredreeq believed my stars were so aligned today as to make a multiple-choice test impossible to fail. I considered what Vaclav had suggested about religion, that mere belief conferred an advantage. Why not try to believe in astrology? I cleared my mind of its kaleidoscope of concerns and focused on the computer screen. Amazingly, I sailed through the first two levels of questions. Annika's tutoring worked. I was exhilarated. Then came question thirteen.

13. Which of the following is equivalent to $\dfrac{1 - \cos^2 \varnothing}{\cos^2 \varnothing}$?

What? I didn't even understand the question. A buzzing sounded in my brain, a phenomenon that occurs when people talk to me about auto mechanics, computer programming, or compound interest rates. Next would come singing fairy voices and hummingbirds and bunnies cavorting in a meadow. My hand, taking on a life of its own, doodled on my notepad, copying the equation or whatever it was. I attached long sticky fingers to it, bulging eyes, some spots, and watched it turn into a greeting card: My Frog Ate My Brain.

Concentrate, Wollie, I told myself. You're a grown woman, you once operated a small business, you can set your VCR to record. How hard can this be, really?

I decided to pick the answer that looked prettiest: D. ($\csc^2 \emptyset$) - 1

The next problem, number 14, asked, "From a point on the ground the angle of elevation to a ledge on a building is 27 degrees, and the distance to the base of the building is 45 meters, blah, blah, blah" and had a diagram next to it that looked like either a treehouse or a club sandwich. I chose answer B, for Believe in the Stars. After that, I didn't bother reading questions; I just went straight for the answers. This astrology thing either worked or it didn't.

In this case, it didn't.

I headed to Rex and Tricia's Mansion, fully depressed. Having flunked the assessment test, I was now doomed to take Maths 81 through 21, a course at a time, followed by endless science classes, which would keep me on SMC's grubby campus until menopause set in.

At a standstill on the 405 North, I dialed Britta again, and this time she answered the phone. She couldn't see me after three P.M., as personal visitors were forbidden when she was working. With difficulty, I persuaded her to see me in the next hour, while her charges were still in school. Tricia's frogs would have to wait.

Britta once again showed me to the kitchen, same table, same seat, same place mat. I was hoping she'd offer coffee or tea, after the hour-and-a-half drive I'd survived, but none was forthcoming. She sat opposite me, displaying the hospitality of someone facing a tax audit. I handed her the application page I'd been puzzling over, the one marked *Führungszeugnis.*

Before I could ask, her face told me she knew what it was. She looked happy.

"You recognize this?" I asked.

"*Ja.* The *Führungszeugnis.* It is the paper that states you are not in trouble with police."

"Is there anything strange about it?"

Her finger went to the date, prominently circled in red. "It is old."

"Did you have to get the same document for your application?"

"*Ja*, but mine is new, not even one year past."

"So what do you think of that?" I asked. "Why would Annika's be so old?"

"Perhaps, if Annika has some trouble with the police in Germany, and she knows the agency will not take her, and she wants to be an au pair in United States, and she has a *Führungszeugnis* from a different year, before she was in trouble, this is what she uses to make the application. And no one has noticed this, so she is allowed to come, and find a good family and has a car for her own use, because she is so lucky."

I stared. "Annika told you all this?"

Now Britta looked confused, her eyes darting to the left as a hand went to her throat, to play with her necklace. "Told me?"

"That this happened."

"I am just—okay, it is just—for example, it could be like this."

I thought of myself as a bad liar, but Britta was much worse. "Oh, I see," I said. "Does everyone in Germany have one of these?"

"No. Only, for example, in a job where one must be trusted. A bank. Or au pairs."

"Why would Annika have one from two years earlier, I wonder?"

Britta looked at her shirt, plucking something from the sleeve. It was the same shirt she'd worn the first time I'd met her. "Perhaps Annika made an application a year before as well, to be an au pair, but for some reason she did not come then."

That's exactly what had happened. Annika had told me that she'd wanted to come to America a year sooner, but her mother had had a medical problem that delayed her.

"And why do you suppose the date is circled there?" I asked, pointing.

"Someone finds she is lying. And so they look at the *Führungszeugnis.*"

A woman came into the kitchen, large and brooding, in stretch pants and a "Billy Joel Live" T-shirt. She carried a broom. I introduced myself, but she just glanced at Britta and left.

"The housekeeper," Britta said. "She does not like people to mess the house."

"Oh. Okay." I removed my hands from the table, worried I'd left prints.

"Now she will tell them I had a guest. Even though you are a girl, so I am allowed."

"Sorry. Didn't mean to get you in trouble," I said.

Britta made a face. "She is jealous because she thinks I do not work hard. Also because I am not so fat like her. Also I have blond hairs. But this is not my fault. Germans have the blond hairs. Annika, no, but many others."

"So anyway," I said. "You think maybe Annika lied to come to America, and someone discovered this, and perhaps reported her? Do you suppose that's why she disappeared?"

"Yes, why not? If she lied to come here, she should go home."

It seemed that Britta had sold out her friend. To whom? The agency? Marty Otis had alluded to a complaint call. "Do you know another au pair, Marie-Thérèse?"

"No, I don't know."

"If Annika met her in New York," I said, "if they were in the same orientation session, does that mean she'd be from your agency?"

"Yes, we are all Au Pairs par Excellence, but all from different countries, and we are all going to different places in America. The other girls are jealous to come to California. They don't even know of San Marino, they think everybody is in Hollywood at Starbucks with Matt Damon and Josh Hartnett." She was sinking into bitterness.

I took a deep breath and asked if she'd ever heard of something called Euphoria. Her eyes widened. She glanced at the doorway through which the housekeeper had gone, then looked back at me. "No, I never hear of this," she said. "Did you meet Rico? Is he not cute?"

Uh-oh.

I spoke carefully. "Have you watched the news today?"

"No, I don't like news."

"Rico is missing. No one's seen him since Saturday night. The police are investigating."

Britta's jaw went slack, her mouth opening as if to say "Uh." Her brow furrowed. Then, to my surprise, her facial muscles contracted and she began to weep, mewing sobs like a distressed kitten, not attempting to cover her face. I reached out to touch her shoulder, but she pulled back, then got up from the table and left the room.

I waited for several minutes. When she didn't return, I stood, straightened the place mats on the table, walked outside, and drove away.

23

I didn't expect a call from Detective Cziemanski anytime soon, but he found me and my cell phone stuck in stop-and-go traffic on the 134 West, just past the 5.

"Guy named Yellin," he said. "Sheriff's Department in Lost Hills, he's working the Rodriguez case. I gave him your number and he'll get in touch. When did you say you met the Rodriguez kid?"

"Thursday, lunchtime."

"So it's not like you're the last one to have seen him."

"I don't know much about Rico," I said. "It's Annika I know about, and her connection to Rico. Speaking of which, I have the license number of a guy that's threatening this other guy, Bing, who knew Annika and possibly Rico, who—"

"All right, tell it to me, but it's Yellin's case now. I meant what I said, though, last night. About being friends. I'm feeling like a jerk about this whole thing."

"No, it's my fault. I should've met you a decade earlier." Or had kids of my own that he could fall in love with. I should've gotten pregnant before Doc left. And gotten a college degree. Yes, it's a lot to squeeze into a five-month relationship, but the race, as they say, is to the swift. "But it's okay," I said. "I'm always up for another friend."

Generally, I see stopped traffic as an opportunity for manicure touch-ups, eyebrow tweezing, and the cleaning out of glove compartments and purses. Today I was preoccupied with failed math tests, missing boyfriends, jealous German girls, and blue-eyed men. If Britta had sold out Annika, reported her outdated *Führungszeugnis* to the agency, why hadn't the agency reported it to the Quinns? Had Marty Otis blackmailed Annika? I pictured him calling her, scaring her, saying, "We're on to you," and Annika in her attic room, circling the date on her *Führungszeugnis*, thinking, *I have to run*. But why? How bad had it been, her trouble with the German police? And what could Marty Otis want from her? It's not like she had money. And what did any of it have to do with *Biological Clock*? Or Rico's disappearance?

Traffic inched toward Forest Lawn, whose inhabitants moved more slowly than we on the freeway only because they were dead. I noticed my mail scattered on the seat next to me, retrieved from my box on my way to the math test. I picked it up, sorted through bills and catalogs, then tossed it aside and picked up Annika's pink file. On the back of her application, as Maizie had noticed, was another girl's, this one from Thailand. Nootjaree "Noot" Chanaboon. She was adorable. I imagined Gene Quinn happily downloading au pairs from the Internet . . .

Uh-oh.

It was the woman at Miss Grusha's music class who'd put this in my head. I didn't want to be thinking this, about someone cheating on Maizie, a mom who made her own bread. And I didn't want to think of Annika in an adulterous relationship. With her employer. The HMO doc. A man twice her age.

Grown men lusting after nubile babysitters is a cliché, but clichés are clichés because they happen so often. Gene Quinn could've had the hots for Annika without her encouragement. In fact, this scenario might have given her another reason to disappear.

I pulled the *Führungszeugnis* out of the pink file, stuffed it in my backpack, and called the Quinn house.

In some cultures—Japanese, for instance—frogs presage good fortune. In others, they're a symbol of the devil. I assumed that Rex and Tricia took the benign view, since they'd commissioned the mural, but there's a difference between tree toads hopping about and the visual assault of a West African goliath of biblical proportions.

I stood in the foyer of the Mansion and peered down the long hallway at my amphibian. It's not like Rex wouldn't pay me if he and Tricia hated the mural. Rex was a good egg. I'd dated him briefly, so I knew this. He'd pay me, then pay the painters to paint over the kitchen, then spend the rest of his life never inviting me for dinner, to spare my feelings. I'd be the object of pity and ridicule.

I couldn't look at the West African goliath. Looking at him made me want to futz with him. I turned my back on him and set to work on my horned frog, the Chaco. My cell phone rang.

"Hi," a voice said. "We met last night at the gas station. I take it you got home?"

My pulse rate increased. Standing still, I could feel it. "Is this the first time you've called me, or have you called before and hung up?" I asked.

There was a pause. "First time. What's that in the background?"

"Croaking frogs." I considered turning down the CD player, and decided not to.

"Would you mind telling me where you are right now?"

"You're slipping," I said. "Yes, I would mind. A good stalker shouldn't have to ask."

"And if I were to ask you to go straight home when you're finished there?"

"Then I'd assume you know where I live, and since you've misplaced me, you want me to return to 'Go,' " I said. "Look, if it's this tough for you to keep track of me, maybe you should try a different line of work. Or practice on something simple, like a city bus. They're harder to lose."

"I'm not going to lose you," the tall man said.

Slowly, I hung up. I stared at my frogs for a long time. Then I put away my paints, cleaned up the kitchen, cleaned up myself, and drove to Encino.

"Miss Maizie no home." Lupe, the housekeeper, held an apoplectic Mr. Snuggles in her arms. She stood in the doorway of the big house, feeding the dog a steady stream of treats from her apron pocket. "You want talk to Mrs. Grammy?"

"No, that's okay," I said. "Is Mr. Quinn home?"

"Lupe!" called a high-pitched voice. "Where my ice cream?"

"Coming, *m'hija!*" She threw a look over her shoulder, then turned back to me. "Mr. Gene in the studio. You know where is it?"

"Yes, I know. Thanks." What luck.

I skipped down the porch steps, icicle lights twinkling at me, and followed the flagstone path to the back of the house. I kept an anxious eye on the grounds, but no crazed goose appeared to torment me. When I reached the studio, I knocked. Twice. After a moment, I went in.

A man sat at the worktable, his back to me, stuffing envelopes. AM talk radio played loudly, which was probably why he hadn't heard my knock. I cleared my throat.

"Gene?" I said. "I'm Wollie Shelley. I dropped by to return a file to Maizie."

He turned, lowered his reading glasses, and reached for a re-mote. "Who?"

"Wollie. Shelley." I moved farther into the room. "Maizie lent me this file on Annika." I held out the pink file, unsure where to go from here. "Sorry I missed her."

"She's at one of her classes. Sushi or sausage or something."

Pastry, I could've told him, but he was already back to his en-velopes. Gene Quinn wasn't the world's most polite guy, or the most curious. I walked around the worktable to stay in his field of vision. He looked fiftyish, with a receding hairline, ruddy complexion, and sand-colored eyebrows that made his dark eyes appear beady. I sneezed, and as he couldn't be bothered to say "Gesundheit," excused myself. "I'm nuts about this room," I said. "It makes me feel creative, just being in it. Did you design it?"

"No. Maizie."

"It's so quiet."

"Sound-studio insulation. Blocks out the kid and the dog. Goddamn racket."

But not the cat. The big tabby sat on top of the refrigerator, looking down on us. He was silent, which was perhaps why he was tolerated. "Doing a mailing?" I said.

"Valley secession."

This took a minute to process. What election was it, when the San Fernando Valley voted against splitting off from Los Angeles to become its own city? It had not been a close vote. "Is it—back? The secession issue?"

"It will be. Were you for it?"

Gene didn't ask me to have a seat, but I took one. "I didn't formulate an opinion. I'm sorry. I don't live in the Valley, so it wasn't on my ballot." I saw Gene's glimmer of interest fade, and added quickly, "What an art form, staging a comeback."

"It's a march. I'm a foot soldier."

"Like a second job, a project like this. You must be passionate about it."

Gene licked an envelope. "The Valley's a bastard child, sucked dry to pay for every spendthrift social program L.A. comes up with."

I'd probably voted for every spendthrift social program he had in mind. "You know what I liked?" I said. "The proposed names, if secession had won. My favorite was Valley City. There's a city in North Dakota named Valley City."

Gene licked another envelope. "I liked Camelot."

"Camelot, California," I said, envisioning a change-of-name greeting card. "Yes, that was . . . alliterative."

Gene kept licking. Another minute and he'd turn up the radio and I'd have to leave, or come up with a darn good reason for staying.

"Gene, any ideas what happened to Annika?"

"Who?"

"Annika Glück. Your au pair."

"Oh, Jesus." He tossed a stuffed envelope onto a pile. "Don't get me started."

"Why?"

"Look at this. Think I like doing it? This was one of her jobs, ungrateful bitch."

I nearly gasped. I could think of no one less bitchy than Annika. Could this animosity spring from love gone bad? "Ungrateful?" I said. "How so?"

"These babysitters have you by the short hairs. Oh, excuse me. *Nannies.*" His disgust was palpable. "Interviews, references, background checks, agency fees, temp fees, bonuses for the goddamn housekeeper to work overtime, because you know who wants to start a job Thanksgiving week? Nobody."

I made a vague noise of sympathy, which spurred him onward.

"You've got to budget time for that," he said. "We did not budget time. Or money. She should've helped herself to a few thousand bucks on her way out, that's what we shelled out this week, hemorrhaging money, and for what? Someone to serve peanut butter and jelly to a two-year-old."

"Oh."

This aria had made Gene red-faced. He went back to licking envelopes with a vengeance, having worked up a good supply of saliva. I thought about the gadget that wets envelopes and stamps, but maybe it was too pricey for his budget. I mumbled good-bye and let myself out. Gene was already reaching for the stereo remote.

Not only could I not imagine Annika sleeping with this guy, I couldn't imagine anyone sleeping with him. He had offspring—Emma looked enough like him that sex had probably occurred at some point, but it was depressing to think about. I'd rather watch people pump gas.

I was walking past the main house toward my car when the back door opened. Grammy Quinn appeared. "Hello, there—was Gene out in the studio?"

"Yes." I stiffened, seeing the unpleasant man's mother. But she was dressed in purple leggings and a pink Donald Duck sweatshirt, which discouraged harsh judgment.

She came closer, then smiled. "Oh, it *is* you—I wasn't sure. I've misplaced my glasses again. Have you found our little Annika?"

"No."

"Oh, thank God. I thought it might be bad news, for you to go out and talk to Gene first. I was just coming to get him for dinner—" A voice inside the house made her turn. "What is it, sweet pea? . . . Well, you need shoes on, don't you? Hurry. Chop-chop." She turned back to me. "Lupe and I talk and talk about this. What would make that girl walk away without a word to Emma is something we don't want to think about. But that's not helping anyone, is it? I'm supposed to keep those thoughts to myself."

She walked me to my car, pointing with interest to the film shooting down the street, which made me think she wasn't from L.A., film shoots being as common as sunscreen to us natives. I drove away from Encino, wondering about Annika's life there. Now that I'd met Gene, I had a better sense of why a teenage girl might go elsewhere for emotional support.

Like Marie-Thérèse. She and Annika would have compared notes on host families, cities, classes. Boys. There had to be some way of getting Marie-Thérèse's address, of forcing or tricking Au Pairs par Excellence to fork it over.

An hour later I got home. I was glad to see a fair amount of activity on my block, a deterrent to stalkers. I waved to a neighbor, then saw a woman sitting on my building's steps rise as I approached. She was small, she wore a baseball cap, but she was a dish.

"Wollie," she said, offering her hand. "Savannah Brook."

I shook it. "Of course. I know. I'm—I admire your work."

What was I saying? How ridiculous, to be starstruck by a fellow contestant. Also, I felt huge next to her; she couldn't have been more than five foot two.

She smiled. "Thanks. Got a minute?"

"Sure." I invited her up to my apartment, but she was due on the *Biological Clock* set in twenty minutes, so we sat on the steps.

"I'll cut to the chase," she said. "I want to do a deal."

"What kind of deal?"

She looked right at me, with perfect, doll-like features. "I'm going to win *B.C.*"

"R-really?" How remarkable. Where do people get that kind of confidence?

"Yes. The question is, by how much. I want a landslide. Kim Karmer's a lightweight, but you've got a small following."

"Do I?"

"Come on. The blonde with the boobs—it's a type, it never goes out of style. You'll pull in votes on looks alone. Kim too, but you'll get more. I can live with that, but the swing vote's up for grabs. The undecideds. I want them."

I was losing that starstruck feeling. "Why do you need a land-slide?"

"Okay. The producers are talking a sequel, *Morning Sickness*, if I get pregnant, and I have a firm offer from ZPX to host a mir-acle show, but they're lowballing me on money. That'll change if I can book mainstream network talk shows. But I can't just win, I have to take every market, because my publicist can't deliver the morning shows unless I'm a cultural phenomenon." She stood, stretched, then sat back down.

"And what do you have in mind for me to do?" I asked.

"Tone down the warmth. I'm not asking you to act; we know that's not your strong suit. Just do your awkward thing, that slouch. The worry lines so you look older. You know what I'm talking about. The wallflower. Bore the guys. Bing. Carlito."

I felt a weird smile take over my face. "And what's in it for me?"

"Five percent of my first paycheck from the next gig, if it

comes as a result of *Biological Clock,* if I win by more than seventy-five percent of the final vote. A three-hundred-dollar bonus for each network talk show I book, one fifty if it's cable."

I stood. Smiled for real. Looked down on her from my height of six feet. "You know, Savannah, even if I had no ethics or self-esteem, I do have bills. Talk about lowball offers." I unlocked the door of my building and enjoyed the look on her lovely, upturned face. "See you on the small screen."

I called Joey to tell her about the day's encounters.

"So much for Mercury trine Saturn," she said.

24

He woke me out of a dead sleep.

"I can see you're going to be a problem," he said. "What would it take to make you stay home for the next month or so?"

I sat up. I was on my living room floor, on a deep pile carpet in a shade of violet at war with the lavender walls my friend Hubie considered the last word in decorating. The voice on the phone belonged to the man with blue eyes. The tall man. I recognized it easily now. "No power on earth," I said. "Why? What's it to you? And—"

"Then how about taking a vacation?" he said. "You don't have to leave the continent; the East Coast, maybe. Or Canada. Thanksgiving and Christmas in the snow. Consider it."

I considered it. I thought about Doc wanting to take me to Boston for the winter holidays, this year or one of the next fifty years we'd planned on being together. I'd never go to Boston now. These thoughts made me cranky.

"There are so many things," I said, fully awake, "that I wonder about, like who are you and how'd you get my phone number and how do you know the routes I take and why are you following me and are your eyes really that blue or do you wear contacts—all these questions burning a hole in my brain, yet you don't hear me waking you in the middle of the night"—I looked at my watch—"or, okay, eight-thirty at night and harassing you."

"I don't see how you could, since you don't know my name or number."

Funny how easy it was to talk when he wasn't in front of me, that clean, well-dressed, six-and-a-half-foot body, the eyes. "Well," I said, settling back against a sofa leg, "I could just randomly—"

"Hold on," he said, "there's my other line—"

Surrounding me on the floor were frog photos, color plates in books, photocopies from the library, one of which was crumpled, having been used as a pillow. I straightened it out. An oak toad. *Bufo quercicus.* He looked lonely. Frogs and toads nearly always live alone, dating only when forced to by the imperative to procreate.

"What I want," he said suddenly, "is for you to live a long life. I want you to stop looking for Annika Glück."

My heart started racing. "Do you know where she is?"

"No."

My heart slowed back down. "See, that's my problem. Have you ever thought you were going to die?"

"Everyone dies."

"Yes. But what if you thought no one would miss you, no one would look for you, no one would ever know what became of you? What if you were dying, and that's what was going through your head? And what if you were right?"

There was silence at the other end.

"Her mother," I said. "Annika's mother, Mrs. Glück—at first, I was doing this for her, a . . . proxy. Now she's stopped calling. I'm not saying she doesn't care anymore, but she's not returning my calls. Her mother. You see?" I didn't know where I was going with this, what I needed him to understand about it. "And now her boyfriend."

"Damn. My other line again. Hold on, Wollie."

At mating time, male frogs may sing out all at once, a cacophony of bleeps, chirps, croaks, hiccups. I wondered what it was that called to a female frog, which particular sound reached her heart and made her leap up and take notice. Her name, maybe?

"I have to go," he said, coming back on the line. "I'll answer any questions you have, but not now."

"Answer one." I was standing, looking out the apartment window, down onto the street, a new habit.

"Go ahead."

"What's your name?"

"Simon." I pictured him smiling. "That was quick; I'll give you another one."

I thought of all the mystery surrounding this man, the myriad questions running through my mind, but only one popped out. "Are you married?"

25

"**C**all him back." Joey, in my passenger seat, was unnecessarily cheerful. "He's not married. Call him."

I glanced at the ocean, the midday surfers, then back at the highway. I thought of my cell phone in my purse, holding on to a message left that morning: "It's Simon. Call me." Four words, one phone number. It's a bad sign, memorizing messages, then saving them.

"I can't," I told Joey. "Not with you listening. I'm self-conscious enough."

"I'll call him. I'm not self-conscious—" She reached over and honked my horn. "Okay, so I haven't tried U4, Euphoria, but I'll tell you what Ecstasy would do for you right now, besides raise your body temperature and make your teeth clench. It would override the conditioning that tells you you can't fall in love with one man if you're still— What the heck is with the traffic? It's two in the afternoon."

"Day before Thanksgiving," I said, happy to change the subject. "People fleeing L.A. in search of autumn leaves and a little nip in the air. Wow. Look at that campus."

Pepperdine University burst into view on a Malibu hill. Cantaloupe-colored buildings with terra-cotta roofs dotted an expanse of green lawn. A crucifix etched into a slab of cement greeted northbound traffic on Pacific Coast Highway, proclaiming the school's religious affiliation. Joey pointed to John Tyler Drive, a back entrance tended by a small gate. "Is Ecstasy addictive?" I said, pulling up to a security kiosk.

"Debatable. I didn't get addicted, anyway. My former shrink used to recommend it, back in its golden age. Hi there," she said, leaning across me to talk to the guard. "We're here to see Lyle Ayres, he lives in Lovernich. By the way," she continued, to me, "Ecstasy's always big with students. I bet Euphoria is too. I'm dying to know what it is."

I'd spoken that morning to Detective Yellin, the guy working on the Rico Rodriguez disappearance. He had not sounded impressed by the Rico-Annika connection, so Joey had suggested we check out Rico's college roommates, who were all over the TV news, talking to anyone with a microphone.

Finding them was easy, once Joey remembered that her brother's wife's sister's daughter was a law student at Pepperdine. This girl was happy to perform introductions; along with the rest of the campus, she seemed to know all about the Rodriguez case.

Lovernich Residential Complex up close was charmless concrete with a cottage-cheese texture that discouraged graffiti. Joey knocked on a painted steel door, which was opened by a stocky kid wearing a pair of red-and-purple boxer shorts. He held a phone and a crumb-filled plate. He managed a "Come on in" gesture without interrupting his phone conversation. "Cop's like, No cell phone, no Palm Pilot, no-brainer: guy took off for Vegas. I'm like, *Dude*, who leaves three hundred bucks on his desk and goes to Vegas? Who leaves his laptop? Cop's like, Guy's rich, right? So he buys himself a new laptop wherever he is. I'm like, He's rich, he's not stupid, *you're* stupid . . . Then, like an hour later they find his car!" He paced as he talked, circling the living room—kitchen—dining area, perhaps seeking a surface on which to set his dirty dish. Plates, glasses, and utensils were everywhere, and empty soda cans overflowed from brown shopping bags, evidence of recycling.

"Okay, gotta go, some people here to interview me and Kev. . . . Yeah, and they're talking maybe *Dateline* or something, next week. . . . 'Kay. Later." He turned to us and held out a hand. "I'm Lyle. You're the private eyes. Cool."

Joey had suggested that I wear something nicer than paint clothes, which made us rather formal next to Lyle and his expansive stomach. We took seats on two dormitory-issue, sheet-covered sofas with a view of a swimsuit calendar, a particularly violent poster from one of the hobbit movies, and some framed autographed sports jerseys.

The front door opened. A wiry, fresh-faced kid with an over-bite introduced himself as Kevin. He stared at Joey with a trance-like gaze I knew. "Hey," he said. "You look just like—is it you? Gun Girl?"

Joey smiled. *Gun Girl*, her old action series, had enjoyed mod-est success and a small cult following until a random act of vio-lence committed against its star had caused its demise. The scar resulting from that act of violence was covered at the moment with makeup, and virtually invisible. I felt the scar didn't so much diminish Joey's beauty as add to her mystique, but this was not a view universally held in Hollywood, and Joey's reluctance to undergo plastic surgery was considered eccentric to the point of madness.

Kevin was wide-eyed. "My dad and I are, like, your biggest fans. My dad says you're totally hot. My mom hates you. Did you really do your own stunts?"

"Only after my stunt double was killed. Kidding." Joey punched him in the arm, which visibly delighted him. "So, Kevin, Wollie and I are here to ask a few questions about Rico. You guys must be sick of this by now, but would you mind—?"

"Gosh, no." Kevin didn't seem to find it odd that a former TV crime fighter should metamorphose into a real-life one. Nor did Lyle, launching into the story of the last time he'd seen Rico.

"Saturday. I was heading out to the movies—Vin Diesel. Rico was like, Man, it sucks, don't go. I didn't listen. You know, you never think, 'This is the last time I'll ever see you, man.' You never think that. And then they're gone."

"So you think Rico's—" I hesitated. "Dead?"

"I don't know. He's a survivor. But major crime for sure. The cops, they're like, Maybe, maybe not. But hey, do the math."

There it was again, that phrase. "Do it for me, would you, Lyle?" I said.

"Okay. He had tickets for hockey next weekend. Killer seats. He's going to blow that off? I don't think so. And: Thursday night he *studied.* You don't spend an hour on chem if you're not going to be around for finals. Who would do that?"

"Kevin, when did you last see Rico?" Joey asked.

"Saturday. Seven, seven-thirty. Dressed for a date. I don't know who with."

"Did he say it was a date?" I asked.

"No, but that was the Saturday drill. Sleep in, lunch, work out, shower, shave, aftershave, real clothes, date."

"Same girl every week?"

"Not necessarily."

"Not usually," Lyle said, and grinned.

"Did you know Annika Glück?" I asked.

They looked at each other. "She hasn't been around for a while," Kevin said.

"He dumped her," Lyle said.

Kevin said, "You don't know that for sure."

"Oh, like she'd dump him? I don't think so." He looked at us. "Kev dated her."

"I didn't date her," Kevin said. "We were friends."

Lyle laughed. "Friends. That just means you didn't get any."

"We weren't like that."

"Yeah, but you wanted to be like that. Rico snaked her from you."

"No, he didn't. I introduced them."

"First mistake, dude."

Kevin flushed. I said, "What did you think of Annika?"

"Loser," Lyle said. "No money, average in the looks depart-ment—"

"C'mon, Lyle. She was totally pretty," Kevin said. "You'd go out with her in a minute."

"So? I'm not saying she's a dog. Maybe in Hicksville, Germany, she was a ten, but she wasn't in Rico's league."

"Did you know she's missing?" I said. This got their attention. "Nobody's seen Annika for over a week. Think it could be related to Rico?"

Kevin looked stunned. Lyle said, "I don't—see how. He hasn't hooked up with her in a while. He's into someone else now."

"Who?" Joey asked.

Lyle threw a sideways look at Kevin and smiled. "He wouldn't say. But if he got a new shirt, he'd go, Does this make me look older? Is this cool? so we figured she was off-campus. Pepperdine girls, his attitude was like, They should be so lucky."

"What do you think, Kevin?" I asked. "Any ideas about Annika?"

"No, it's just—" Kevin glanced at Lyle, then looked down. "No."

Joey said, "If you had to guess, what do you think happened to Rico?"

"He had some business deal going," Lyle said. "Like a stock market thing."

"What kind of stock market thing?"

"Well, I don't know that's what it was, but there's this old movie *Wall Street*. It was on TV. Then Rico bought the DVD and studied it, and now he's all portfolios this and that, reading the paper, the business section. I'm like, Dude, to have a portfolio you gotta have something to put *in* the portfolio, but he said he had it handled."

"So he did have money or he didn't?" I asked, confused.

"Okay, gargantuan allowance, but one time we were watching TV, I'm going, What would you do for a million dollars, would you eat a live rodent? and Rico goes, A million's pocket change. By the time I'm twenty-five I'm gonna buy and sell my dad."

"That was a career goal?" I said. "To buy and sell his dad?"

"You ever meet his dad?" Lyle looked at us, then shook his head. "Hard-core."

Kevin stood. "Hey, I gotta get to Union Station, catch a train."

"Yeah, I gotta pack too," Lyle said, not moving from the sofa. "Driving up to Lake Arrowhead for Thanksgiving."

Joey asked to use the bathroom, and on impulse, I asked to see Rico's room. Kevin led me down the narrow hallway. "Cops took his computer and his mom and dad took things, but there's still stuff left."

If the room was picked over, it was hard to imagine what it had looked like before. Bunk beds, desks, and chairs overflowed with sheets, blankets, clothes, running shoes, weights, under-wear, fast-food wrappers, dishes, coffee mugs, textbooks, note-books, and backpacks. A teenage-boy smell filled the room, sweat and hormones and deodorant and dirty socks. "We shared. It's a little—we haven't cleaned in a while," Kevin said, dragging a duffel bag from a closet. He cleared off a chair for me, throwing a wet towel on the floor, along with some jeans. Coins rained onto the dirty carpet. I looked out the window. Either the glass was gray with dirt or the sky had darkened in the time we'd been in here. I'd rarely seen such a mess, from floor to—

Ceiling.

"Was Rico the top bunk?" I asked.

"Yeah. Check it out if you want."

I eased out of my slingback pumps and climbed the ladder. The male-animal smell intensified up here. I moved aside a pil-low, soft and doughy in its red flannel pillowcase. There were matching red sheets and a plaid blanket, all bunched up and per-sonal. I tried to imagine the girls he'd brought up here, but the strongest impression was of a child sleeping soundly in sheets his mother had sent him off to school with. My sense of trespassing nearly sent me back down the ladder.

But the wall was information central. Phone numbers doodled in blue and black ink. Appointment times. Address-book graffiti. I pictured Rico, a kid in his treehouse, talking on his phone, drawing on the wall. "Kevin, did the cops look up here?"

"Maybe. They were in here a while. Hey, um . . ."

"Yeah?"

"Do you—is Annika okay, do you think?"

I leaned over the bed to look at him. He sat on the floor, selecting dirty clothes to throw into the duffel. I said, "I'm pretty worried about her, actually."

"I met her on the beach." He didn't look up. "She was reading this book, *The Naked and the Dead*, about World War II. She wanted to know what Americans thought about Germany. I thought that was so cool. I told her, Don't worry about it, nobody our age hates Germans, that's like a century ago. You finding anything up there?"

There were names on the wall and the ceiling. Boys' names. Girls. Nikki. Jillian. Heather. Courtney. Emily. Initials: L.B., R.A., J.B. "Maybe."

"I heard them one time. Up there."

"Rico and Annika? You're kidding."

"No, not—I mean, they were arguing. They probably thought I was asleep. They were whispering."

"Yeah?"

"She said something like 'It's not a problem for you; if we get caught, you'll get out of it.' She said for her it was a big deal, because she's German, the rules are different for foreigners. Stuff like that. Okay, it wasn't as clear as I just said it, but I was thinking, He's pressuring her into something."

"What do you think it was?"

"I don't know. Rico was like, C'mon, no big deal. That's how he was. Nothing was a big deal for him. I think when you have a dad like his, and money, you don't think about how it is for other people."

I leaned down again, watching him pack. "What about drugs?"

"You mean, did he do them?" Kevin looked up at me. "No more than anybody. Why would he? If you're into drugs, you don't go to Pepperdine. It's not the biggest party school on the planet."

"Ever hear of something called Euphoria?" I asked, but he shook his head. "And Annika? You think she did drugs?"

He looked at me steadily. "Not with me . . ."

"But?"

"She was—you know how she was. But he'd walk in and she'd turn into . . ."

"What?" I was leaning down now, straining to catch his words.

Kevin sighed. "Like Lyle said. A loser. Sort of. So I don't know what she'd do to be with him. We call it the Rico Effect."

Glenda Nacy, the au pair volunteer, had called it "boy crazy." I leaned back against the wall. I wanted to think Annika was more than that, smarter about men, but I'd been that girl too, the one with the head on her shoulders until the right guy waltzed in and rendered her mindless. . . . I could imagine Rico talking straight-arrow Annika into things she wouldn't otherwise consider. And if he'd talked her into something illegal, drugs or otherwise, if the two of them had, as Glenda might say, fallen in with a bad crowd, then the reasons for disappearing multiplied.

As if to confirm this, her number appeared on Rico's wall, the 818 area code and Encino prefix I'd dialed so often in the last ten days it was committed to memory.

How much evidence did I need? Annika wanted a gun, wanted a lawyer, asked where to find drugs, had drugs under her bed, acted depressed and distant, had trouble with the German police . . . and had contemplated quitting *Biological Clock*, a job she'd once loved. If I couldn't reconcile smart, smiling, happy Annika with the one I kept hearing about, maybe I was in denial. I sat up. I should be copying down these numbers. "Kevin," I said, "ever hear Annika talk about someone named Richard Feynman? Or Marie-Thérèse? Britta?"

"Britta, yeah. She's been over here a couple times. I never really talked to her. And who's the guy you just said?"

"Richard Feynman?"

"Sounds familiar. Is he an astronaut or something?"

I tried to imagine Annika dating an astronaut. I thought she would've mentioned it. I said, "Did you tell the police about the argument you overheard?"

"No," Kevin said. "They didn't ask."

He gave me a pen and paper and went on talking, about the

girls who'd show up at Lovernich at all hours, girls Rico had invited over and forgotten about. I listened with half an ear, then no ear at all, because I found something on the wall, something I knew. Something I'd seen before. A squiggle. ᛘ It was the logo on the pill that had been under Annika's bed.

26

"I've seen this before." Joey, in the passenger seat, studied the squiggle. "Somewhere. Not on a pill, either."

We were still at Pepperdine, in a parking lot. The weather had changed dramatically in the last hour, from balmy breezes to cold rain, and I'd discovered something about the car I'd inherited from Doc: the defroster didn't work. My windshield was fogged up, as transparent as an igloo.

"Could I take that to the cops?" I asked, checking the owner's manual. "It links Annika and Rico. And this argument they had about getting in trouble—"

"The doodling's meaningless without the pill. And what if the pill's a No-Doz?"

"It's gotta be Euphoria. The guy I met at Santa Monica College, Annika's other tutoree, he said she was looking for Euphoria. If I had the pill, could we get it analyzed?" I thought of Joey's brother, the cop. "Could Patrick help us?"

Joey snorted. "He'd yell at me for sending it through the mail, he'd say, 'I don't know how they do things out in La-La Land, but here in New York rules rules rules . . .' I could swallow it myself and find out."

"Detective Cziemanski," I said. "My new friend. Maybe I could—"

"Sleep with him."

"No. I'm never having sex again."

"Really? Does this Simon guy know that?"

I pushed buttons randomly. The windows remained fogged up, despite a noise suggesting a defroster struggling for life. "I hate this car. I should never have ditched my Rabbit. Listen, I've known this man seven minutes total, so quit it. And Doc—"

In fact, my mental pictures of Doc were fading like fabric left out in the sun. It was easier to conjure up Ruby: the freckled face, the frizzy hair. When I tried to envision Doc, he was in shadow, turned away.

"I happen to like Doc," Joey said, "but he'd be the first to tell you to move on. He *was* the first to tell you."

"He didn't mean move on to this guy. Simon would be the Rico Rodriguez of my life. All sexual heat and no substance. A professional stalker."

"But you haven't told the cops about him."

"Like they'd care? Annika disappears, do they care? Rico disappears, they don't even ask his roommates, 'Gee, notice anything strange lately?' Brace yourself, we're going to open windows."

A blast of cold air hit. I steered the car toward the campus exit. Joey wrapped her skinny arms around herself. "Kevin didn't know Annika was missing, so what he heard didn't seem relevant," she said. "Hey, cops aren't stupid and they're not incompetent, generally, so whatever there is to find, they'll find. Know what Lyle said while you were in the bedroom? Rico dropped out of poli sci to take chemistry, weeks into the semester. By special arrangement. And it was killing him, trying to catch up."

"Joey, there you go! Rico was making Euphoria."

"I think you need more than two months of chemistry to design trendy new drugs. And why would that make Annika disappear? Or her mother? You're right, we have to find Annika's e-mail buddy, Marie-Whatserface."

"Dead end. I leave messages at the au pair agency and no one calls back."

"What's the number?" she said.

"In my backpack." I wiped the clouded windshield with a Kleenex and took a left on Pacific Coast Highway. This wasn't how it was supposed to be, spending the day before Thanksgiving freezing in Malibu in slow traffic with Joey. Not that I didn't love Joey. But I should've been with Doc and Ruby, watching cranberries . . . bake. Broil. Whatever it is cranberries do. Doc and I hadn't even made it a year. We'd only gotten the minor holidays: Easter, Memorial Day, Fourth of July, Bastille Day—

A clipped New England accent came from Joey, startling me. "Mr. Otis, this is Elizabeth Atherton, with the Department of State. I'm here in California and I would appreciate a return call, as soon as possible, please, Thanksgiving notwithstanding." Joey gave her cell-phone number, signed off, then punched a few more numbers and changed her cell phone's outgoing message to one more suited to Elizabeth Atherton.

"What about everyone else who tries to call you and leave a message?" I asked.

"Let them wonder." She then started dialing numbers I'd found on Rico's wall. One was pizza delivery, one was cable TV, and one was no longer in service. Two were answering machines. There were four-digit numbers we thought were codes of some kind, until I realized Pepperdine used a common prefix for the whole campus. We tried preceding the numbers with 456, and it worked. Joey talked to three actual people. One guy said his ex-roommate had been buddies with Rico but had dropped out the previous semester. Another guy admitted to casual acquaintance but said he was late for class and hung up. A girl with a voice so loud Joey held the phone away from her ear said if we wanted to find Rico we should check under rocks or wherever it was snakes hung out. By now we'd progressed a few measly miles, not even to Tuna Canyon.

"Yikes," Joey said. "Suspects abound. He's a much better missing person than Annika. My favorite is Kevin, the pathologically nice roommate."

My own cell phone rang. Joey answered without asking; she

knew that driving, shivering, squinting, and cleaning the windshield while talking were beyond my capabilities. "Wollie's cell phone, Joey speaking," she said, then paused. "No. She's having an automotive crisis." Pause. "Defective defroster." Pause. "Sixty thousand or so." She leaned toward me, hair brushing my bare arm, then straightened up. "Sixty-two thousand, two hundred and thirty-four." Pause. "Wasn't her idea." Pause. "I agree. Let me ask you, what are your intentions?" Pause. "Yeah?" Long pause. "Yeah." I glanced at her. She was smiling. "Yeah." She turned off the phone and turned to me. "He says to give him a call when you're not driving."

"Who?" The hair on my arms was standing up.

"Simon."

"Okay, turn off that phone. Just turn it off."

"And by the way, he's a cop."

I choked. "A—?"

"Not a regular cop. I just figured it out. He's DEA. Your boyfriend's a narc."

The rain was having a hallucinatory effect. Headlights and taillights appearing smeared and dripping, a Dalí painting. "You mean—some kind of informant?"

"No. An agent."

"He said that?"

"No, it just came to me. The way you described him, clean, clean-cut, weird. I thought 'military,' then 'law enforcement,' but that one remark, remember when he asked what you were doing on Temple Street? Why would he ask that? He follows you all over L.A. but he gets fixated on Temple Street. Why?" Joey bounced with excitement. "Because that's where you don't belong. That's his turf, not yours—that's the building the DEA works out of and he wanted to know if you'd made him."

"If I'd what?"

"Made him. Found him out. Discovered his identity. They're paranoid, those guys. He sees you downtown within ten miles of his office, he says, Me, it's all about me, she's following me."

"That's a complete long shot, Joey, it's a huge leap of logic—"

"It's not. I'm telling you, the DEA building on Temple Street, it's—"

"Then he's an informant," I said, taking a vicious swipe at the inside windshield. "In a suit. White-collar informant, taking meetings in the building. Or a janitor. Or he works at the Music Center, the Dorothy Chandler Pavilion. He can't be *in* the DEA, he's terrible at surveillance, I always catch him—"

"Oh, for God's sake, he's not surveilling you, Wollie, he's courting you."

"Plus he drives a really nice car. Too nice for a civil servant."

"Look, it wouldn't be my first choice, to fall for a narc, but that's because I'm practically a junkie. You're another story—you don't even take aspirin."

"It upsets my stomach. That's not the point." I stopped at the light at Topanga Canyon and turned to her. "I don't know anyone like that. What would we talk about, someone who—does whatever it is he does for a living? Wiretaps and so forth."

"Honey. How many of your acquaintances share your political values?"

I shrugged. "Lots. I don't know. Most of them."

"And how many of those people do you want to get naked with?"

I thought about it. The list was not long.

Joey smiled. "I rest my case."

Three hours later I'd dropped Joey in Los Feliz, where her husband's BMW was getting detailed, and got myself back to West Hollywood. It was now fully dark and pouring rain. I was inching closer to accepting Simon's alleged profession. Since shooting up together wasn't on my romantic agenda, what did I care?

But when had I acquired a romantic agenda?

Frozen and wet, I walked up the steps to my building. My down-the-hall neighbor was struggling with the front door, armed with groceries, and I ran to unlock it.

"Turkey?" I asked, nodding toward his grocery bag.

He groaned. "Darling, you don't even want to know. Seventeen for dinner tomorrow. All male. All gay. And that dreadful little efficiency kitchen of ours. If you hear screams, that will be me. Drop in, if you like. Bring estrogen."

"Thanks," I said, stopping at the mailbox alcove. "But I'm working."

I was glad *Biological Clock* was shooting. If you're not with family on major holidays, people worry, calling to see if you're being sufficiently festive, yelling at you if you eat Chee-tos for Christmas dinner. There had to be millions of others like me, orphans by circumstance, geography, or choice, but a cultural conspiracy was afoot to make us feel otherwise. Work, I decided, was the antidote.

I retrieved from my mail cubbyhole a huge assortment of holiday catalogs and some bills, and turned on my cell phone. It buzzed and pulsed, alerting me to all the unplayed messages acquired while it had been turned off. I ignored it. How had Doc talked me into a cell phone? They were more trouble than pets. My phone changed sounds, announcing an actual live call. All right. No point in putting it off any longer. "Yes. Hello," I said.

"It's Simon. Playing hard to get?"

I tried to conjure up Doc's face, but Doc-in-my-head had gone out to dinner. "No," I said. "I'm no good at that."

"Lucky me. Okay. You had questions."

"Are you a DEA agent?"

"Hell, no. Where'd you get that idea?"

I sank to my knees, picking up dropped mail. "Thank God. So what do you do for a living?" A blast of cold heralded the arrival of people dressed in pilgrim hats, doing a rock rendition of "Simple Gifts" in three-part harmony.

"Is there a church service going on there?" Simon asked.

"Of sorts. I'm in the lobby of my building."

"Go upstairs. Call me in ten minutes."

I didn't dwell on how he knew I lived on an upper floor; I was too relieved to know he was not in the Drug Enforcement

Agency. Relief is a beautiful, underrated feeling. I reached my apartment and stuck my key in the lock.

The door was already unlocked.

Uh-oh.

I hesitated, my hand on the doorknob, thinking, *Maybe I left the apartment unlocked this morning* while Ruta's voice yelled, *Run. Run while you have the chance.*

Too late.

From the other side of the door a voice called out, "Wollstonecraft? Is that you?" A voice I knew as well as my own.

"Yes, Mother," I called back, closing my eyes. "It's me."

27

"Actually, 'It is I.'"

My mother sat curled on the sofa, a theatrical piece of furniture in leopard skin. My mother wore white. Her pants and caftan, drapey as a tablecloth, pooled around her, obscuring her small frame. The arrangement was so artful it would be a pity for her to stand and spoil the effect, and my mother, in fact, did not stand.

"What?" I said.

"You don't say, 'It's me,' dear, but 'It's I.' Are you going to give me a kiss?"

I leaned over my mother, feeling graceless and large, and touched my lips to her very soft cheek. She closed the coffee-table book *Aerial Views of Los Angeles,* and smiled. "You look well. My word, have you always had those breasts?"

"Since I was twelve."

"Oh, good. I'd hate to think you had them enlarged. Mine have always been small. A more pleasing look, especially as you age. The well-endowed look matronly."

My mother was pretty much as I remembered her. Her hair was a touch more silver, the blond I'd inherited from her giving way gracefully. She wore no makeup, and I could smell the moisturizer she'd used for years.

I said, "How did you get in?"

"The plumber."

"What plumber?"

"The woman plumber, in the plumber suit. An effeminate young man let me into the building, and the plumber let me into the apartment. A little kitschy, isn't it? I would never put animal skin against these purples." She gestured to the walls and carpet. "Of course, I wouldn't use animal skin in any case. Even faux."

"It's a sublet," I said, distractedly. "Cheap. Almost a house-sit. For my friend Hubie. Was this plumber . . . plumbing?"

"I have no idea. Gay, I suppose. Your friend. They can be kitschy, can't they? Generally with more taste than this."

I perched on a chair. Maybe the building super had let the plumber in. Maybe I had a leak I didn't know about, dripping into the apartment beneath me. These things happened. I'd call the super. "How's life at the ashram, Mom? I thought you—"

"Dear, is it so difficult to use my given name? I've requested—"

"Sorry. Estelle."

"No, the new one."

"Sorry. Prana. Didn't you say only an act of God could get you back to L.A.?"

"It was an act of God that brought me." My mother set the coffee-table book on a coffee table already cluttered with books. "I am concerned for your chi."

I stood. "Okay, let me just change before we launch into . . . chi. Something to drink?" I detoured to the kitchen for a diet root beer.

My mother, galvanized, followed me. "Green tea, if you have any."

"I don't."

"Champagne, then. Or wine. Wollie, I came as soon as I heard."

"Heard what?" Being Estelle/Prana's daughter entailed feeding her cue lines to her monologues. I hadn't seen her in five years, but I could do my part in a coma.

"I have not been off-ashram since the autumnal equinox, but

this week was my turn at market, so yesterday, in the checkout lane in Solvang, I saw it. *TV Guide.*"

"Yes?" I found a bottle of wine, some cheap Chardonnay I'd gotten at Trader Joe's, and scrounged around for a corkscrew.

"Need I describe the effect it had on me? My daughter—on the cover?"

I stopped to gape at my mother. "I'm on the cover of *TV Guide?*"

My mother stared back, cheekbones high, nostrils flaring. "Your name. Your photo, the size of a tiny stamp. One among dozens, and the headline 'Who Will We Remember Six Months from Now? And Why Do We Care?' Despicable grammar. So you're on this television show, *Biology Today*—"

"*Biological Clock.*"

"—a participant in—what is it, some science program?"

"Reality TV," I said.

"What is that?"

"Television that uses real people in situations—. Never mind, you wouldn't like it. It's a job, Mother, temporary, something I fell into and—"

"My God, I used to lie awake nights, fearing my children would one day be drafted. And now my daughter, a willing tool of the patriarchy—"

"Mom. Reality TV—okay, it's morally decadent. I'm not out there curing cancer or shutting down nuclear reactors, but I'm making the rent, paying off credit cards—"

"Please elevate yourself to the level of this discussion. I speak from a spiritual plane." My mother's hands gripped the Formica counter. She was fine-boned and fragile, more delicate than I'd ever been. Her forearms brought to mind some exotic bird. "Don't you realize the danger, that your image miniaturized and multiplied millions of times over, on television screens everywhere—"

"Actually, the show's not that popular."

"—exacts a price?"

"What about actors?" I asked. "They're all in danger?"

"Actors are interpretive artists, playing parts, which minimizes the effect, but yes, they are damaged, as is obvious when you meet one. This is the cost of art. But you reveal yourself without the filter of character. Why do you suppose indigenous people shy away from cameras?"

The phone rang, and I grabbed it in irritation. "I don't know a lot of indigenous people. Yes, hello."

"There's a couple of Hopis I could introduce you to," the voice said.

"Hold on," I said to the phone, then addressed my mother. "I have a contract. I can't break it, it would be unethical. Bad karma."

My mother drew herself up to her full height. "Don't bandy about words the meaning of which you have no true understanding. This is my life's work, and I tell you that walking away is the only course of action with integrity."

"Well, I'm not gonna. Excuse me." I spoke into the phone. "Is this—Simon?"

"It is."

"I've had a fatiguing day," my mother said, oblivious to the fact I was talking to someone else. "I shall retire. Your refrigerator leaves something to be desired. Is there a place to buy tofu tomorrow?"

"Hold on, Simon." I slid the phone to my chest. "Yes, Prana. This is still L.A."

"Good. I have borrowed a pair of socks."

This could go on forever. "Simon," I said, "I'll call you in ten minutes. Someone's about to barricade herself in my bedroom and I'm desperate to get out of these pantyhose."

"You're wearing pantyhose?" he said.

"Pantyhose?" my mother said. "Good God, how Republican."

Prana had appropriated not just socks but my bed, all four pillows, the cashmere sweater Joey had given me for my birthday, and the half box of Godiva chocolates stored in my refrigerator. She'd also marked her territories with scented candles and lotions. None of this surprised me. Leopards may go to live in ashrams, but they don't change their spots.

The good news was that my mother was soon tucked away to sleep, read, meditate, or whatever it was she did in "retirement." She could do it for up to twelve hours, I knew from experience, a blessing for those who needed a half day to recharge their Prana-tolerance batteries.

I was back in the kitchen, in sweatpants, when the phone rang. "You have an elastic idea of what constitutes ten minutes," Simon said.

I poured Cocoa Puffs into a bowl. "I come by that naturally."

"Okay. So you thought I was a DEA agent—"

"No, Joey thought that." I opened the refrigerator. Instead of milk, I found a carton of something called Soy So Licious. I looked down. My milk carton was in the garbage can. "Oh—and she wondered what kind of car that is you drive."

"A Bentley."

"Is that a big deal?"

"It's a Continental GT. The cheap Bentley."

"Oh, okay." Again, I was struck by how easy it all was on the phone. "So you're not some kind of drug dealer."

"No. I'm not any kind of drug dealer."

"Good. Not that I wouldn't associate with you if you were. But we'd never have a long-term relationship. Or even dinner—" I poured Soy So Licious over my Cocoa Puffs. It looked milklike, but not white enough.

"Lunch?"

"Yeah, lunch. I'd have lunch even if you worked for the DEA. Lunch is a noncommittal meal."

"Are you asking me to lunch?"

"Well, not—"

"Yes," said a new voice. "Come tomorrow for brunch."

Silence. Then I found my voice. "Prana, what a ghastly thing to do, listening in on my phone calls. Would you hang up, please?"

"I am not eavesdropping. I picked up the phone to call Solvang."

I mentally ground my teeth. "Simon, meet my mother. Mom, tomorrow's Thanksgiving. I'm sure Simon has—"

"I'm aware of the date. I'm not a mental defective. Noon, Simon." My mother went into a purr she reserved for the male of the species. "If you care to bring something, champagne would not go amiss." There was a click.

I cleared my throat. "It would make me very happy if you'd ignore—"

"I'm very happy to come for brunch."

"—because it's news to me we're even having it, and you must have family plans. Besides—brunch: such a pretentious meal. Who has brunch on Thanksgiving?"

"I love brunch. Eggs Benedict, bloody Marys. . . . See you at noon."

"Wait, this is—awkward and—I don't know your last name, or anything about you. You can't come to brunch, you don't want to meet my mother, I don't want you to meet her, I'm not even sure—okay, you're not DEA, but who are you, what is—"

"My last name is Alexander. I'd love to meet your mother. I eat everything except beets, no allergies, and I'll try not to embarrass you in front of your family."

"Okay, but the thing is—"

"I need to talk to you in any case. In person. It's why I call. Repeatedly."

"Yes, but—"

"And I know who Richard Feynman is."

That stopped me cold. I'd forgotten for a moment, but it all came flooding back. Annika. Annika's missing mother. Annika's probably dead boyfriend Rico, his own blood in the trunk of his car. "Who is he?"

"Let's save that for brunch."

"Who is he?" I nearly screamed it.

He was silent.

I pulled myself together. "Listen, Simon Alexander, whoever you are—who are you, by the way?"

A pause. "Someone with an interest in your well-being."

"Why do I feel like I'm on a game show? Personal or professional interest?"

"Both."

Well. That was something. "And you're not in the DEA? And you weren't on Temple Street the other day?"

"I'm not in the DEA. I was on Temple Street the other day."

"Doing what?"

"We're working out some jurisdictional issues with the DEA."

"Who's—who is—" My voice shook a little. " 'We'?"

Another pause, during which my breathing stopped. Then: "The FBI."

I woke with a stiff neck, a sore back, and no immediate sense of why I was on the living room sofa with the sun assaulting my face. Slowly I remembered my mother.

And the FBI.

It was so much worse than the DEA, I'd gone into a coughing fit when I'd heard the words. I have no history with the DEA. The FBI, on the other hand, has been pissing off my family since the days of J. Edgar Hoover. And not just my biological family. Ruta had been a Communist in the Nixon years, a lonely era for Reds. She'd populated my fairy tales with witches, goblins, and G-men. I hadn't gone into this with Simon. I'd gotten off the phone as soon as I could, collapsing onto the sofa for a night of unrest and dreams populated with witches, goblins, and G-men.

The doorbell rang. My body cranked itself into a standing position. Still sore from Krav Maga—what had those people done to me?—I hobbled to the door.

Uncle Theo and P.B. stood in the hallway.

Suppressing alarm, I hugged my brother. P.B. wore a green striped shirt with khaki pants I'd given him for his last birthday, which was okay, except that he'd paired them with floral bedroom slippers he must've acquired at Rio Pescado. I was exasperated with Uncle Theo for having allowed this sartorial flub until I saw that Uncle Theo wore an orange fringed poncho suggestive of a pumpkin or a monk. "What are you guys doing here?"

"Summoned for brunch." Uncle Theo hugged me and held out a sheaf of wheat secured with a twist tie. "We caught a ride with some of P.B.'s troops, on a holiday pass. We ran into that nice bookshop man on Santa Monica, who says to stop in soon."

This was bad. P.B. was a social wild card under the best of circumstances, and brunch with the FBI was not the best of circumstances. His schizophrenia featured a preoccupation with surveillance by alien forces and government agencies. He was not currently delusional, but even asymptomatic he was intense. As for Uncle Theo, he'd actually known Ethel and Julius Rosenberg. Numbly, I accepted the sheaf of wheat, a bag of kaiser rolls, and a box of sprouts, and went into the kitchen, where P.B. tuned my radio to a show about insects they'd been listening to in the car.

I looked at my watch. Simon, if he showed, wasn't due for two hours. Plenty of time for me to run away from home.

Prana emerged from my bedroom, planted kisses on the cheeks of her brother-in-law and son, neither of whom she'd seen in five years, and announced she was off to the store. Uncle Theo went too. P.B. stayed behind. I straightened the apartment and myself, my sense of foreboding growing. An hour later, the shoppers returned to take over the kitchen. A half hour after that, Simon showed up.

Seeing him in my doorway with yellow roses in one hand and Dom Pérignon in the other nearly knocked the wind out of me. He was dressed in gray pants and a soft white shirt. I wondered about the effect he'd have on the seventeen gay men showing up for dinner down the hall later. I hadn't found him good looking that night at the minimall, but he was getting progressively more handsome, a phenomenon I didn't understand. This thought, however, was succeeded by a drone in my head: "FBI. FBI. FBI . . ."

There was that awkward—for me—hello moment where we had the option to kiss, hostess to guest, but of course I couldn't kiss an FBI agent, so I took the flowers and champagne, which acted as a barrier. I avoided looking into his eyes, as one avoids staring at the sun during a solar eclipse, and closed the door. The living room shrank. Did he have extra-high ceilings in his own house? Did the FBI live in houses, like regular people? Was he wearing a gun, by the way? Tucked into his sock? Why, why, why was he here?

He picked up a framed picture, the first greeting card I'd ever sold. He smiled.

"Okay," I said. "Who's Richard Feynman?"

"Ah, Feynman," Uncle Theo said, coming out of the bathroom. "Marvelous man."

I stared at him. "You know Richard Feynman?"

"Well, not now. He's been dead since . . . the late eighties, I believe. I heard him speak once. While he was alive. Quarks."

"But who was he, Uncle Theo?"

"The greatest physicist of the last century. Arguably. Of course, he was at Los Alamos with Oppenheimer and the others, but he was awfully young then, so we'll forgive him. Hello, I'm Theo. Are you Wollie's young man?"

Cringing, I introduced my uncle to my FBI agent, then moved into the kitchen and introduced Simon to Prana, who turned on the charm, and to P.B., who mumbled at him and returned to the radio.

"Don't mind my nephew," Uncle Theo said. "We had to leave his girlfriend at the hospital. Lovely child, severe case of body dysmorphic disorder. We invited her, but she won't eat in front of people."

Simon nodded pleasantly. I considered explaining P.B.'s living situation and then decided I needn't bother, as the FBI probably had files on all of us.

"Body dysmorphic disorder?" Prana said. "Spare me the *nouvelles* diseases."

"To quote Richard Feynman," Uncle Theo said, " 'Every woman is worried about her looks, no matter how beautiful she is.' "

I was puzzling over the connection between beautiful women and physics when Uncle Theo said, "Care for some weed, Simon?"

"Uncle Theo," I said, "I don't think—"

"Your mother felt it would be festive." He pulled a baggie out of his poncho pocket and sat at the kitchen table. "Went to some lengths to find it, but I have friends who still turn on, it turns out. Estelle and I used to do this every Thanksgiving—when did that stop, Estelle?"

"Nineteen sixty-eight." My mother popped open the champagne. "We did a blotter of acid, seven of us, and tried to contact Bobby Kennedy—"

"The séance!" Uncle Theo cried. "The one that turned you vegan. The turkey coming to life, crying out from the stuffing—"

I spoke up. "Okay, could we not—"

"The noble bird," my mother said, "exploited as we 'honor' it, just as we 'honor' the Native American. Where is the Native American at our table? Do we respect his heritage, join him in his sweat lodge, worship his gods, or just gamble at his casino? We may love peyote, we may engage in sex with—"

"Screw the government," P.B. said, surprising us all. "Feynman said that too."

"Um, everyone?" I said. "We may be giving our guest the impression— Simon, care to see the rest of the apartment?"

"No. I think we should help out here." Simon took the champagne from Prana and filled glasses. He offered one to my brother, but P.B., having made his social contribution, retreated into gloom.

"None for him," Uncle Theo said. "They interfere with his psychotropics. Drugs," he added helpfully.

The next hour brought back memories of the first half of my life. In a kitchen the size of a phone booth, Simon watched my mother and uncle get high while P.B. sat like a lump, staring at the radio as if reading lips. My brother had spent years seeing government agents everywhere, and now, faced with an actual one, he was unresponsive.

My mother was not. She was coquettish, even wrangling pots and pans. She sipped champagne, smoked grass, and played hostess. "What is your life path, Simon?"

"What do I do for a living?" He turned his stunning blue eyes on me and smiled. I stopped breathing. "I work for peace," he said. "Research, documentation, trips to bad neighborhoods—"

"Do you approve of this television program Wollie has sold herself to?"

"Prana, let's leave that for now, shall we?" I relocated the men in order to set the table. "Simon's very tall; he must be hungry. Do we have any hors d'oeuvres?"

Hors d'oeuvres. What a fantasy life I led. The entire meal consisted of sprouts, tofu-cranberry bake, undercooked yams, and Uncle Theo's day-old kaiser rolls. I found some Wheat Thins to supplement things, but my mother forbade me to bring out cheese or even butter for the kaiser rolls, citing the exploitation of cows.

"We're not meant to drink bovine milk," she said, "but human breast milk. I intended to breast-feed Wollie and P.B. until kindergarten, but I had inverted nipples."

"I never realized that, Estelle," Uncle Theo said.

"We choose our parents prior to birth. My children chose intellect, creativity, and spiritual acuity over normal nipples. For them to resent me now is pointless and—"

"Mom—I mean Estelle—I mean Prana—"

"Had you offspring of your own, Wollie, you'd empathize. At your age you'll probably stay single as well as barren. As for your brother, in that regard, the less said the better."

"Then why don't you say less?" I snapped. "Instead of talking about him as if he weren't here, especially since you haven't said one nice thing—"

Simon put a hand on my shoulder, a gesture powerful enough

to stop me. If the moment was tense for me, I seemed to be in the minority. P.B. continued to arrange Wheat Thins in a pattern on the counter. My mother looked up in bland surprise. Uncle Theo took a healthy bite of tofu-cranberry bake. "Wollie," he said, "I've given some thought to the young German girl gone missing, and I'm reminded of Joe Oklahoma."

"Who?" I said.

"My uncle. Your great-uncle. Disappeared back in the fifties, when we lived in upstate New York. We heard he was headed for Oklahoma, which is how he came to be called Joe Oklahoma. We assumed he came to a bad end, but in 1979 your great-aunt Geraldine, while attending a bagpipe convention in Buffalo, ran into him. He'd been there all along. Never left the county. Twenty-four years living up the interstate, five exits, content as a clam."

"Twenty-four years, and no one looked for him?" I asked.

"He wasn't a family favorite. There was some unpleasantness over gravestone rubbings. They were all mad for gravestone rubbings in those days. My point is, happy endings. You never know when you're in the middle of someone's."

Gravestone rubbings. The tragedy was, I couldn't even pretend to be adopted. I looked like Uncle Theo in drag, the same ungainly physique. P.B. had it too.

My uncle poured himself more champagne. "But Wollie, our little bloodhound, she's a faithful one. Keeping track of P.B. all these years, in and out of the hospital . . . and me. Always there with the car, because I don't drive. Boyfriends, too. Followed a young man to Ohio once, she was so sweet on him. She doesn't like to lose people."

What if I went to the bathroom and just never emerged?

"Ridiculous," Prana said. "Cultivate detachment. People should be free to follow their destiny."

Unless their destiny included reality TV. Simon's hand traveled from my shoulder to the back of my neck, and squeezed. My shoulders dropped twelve inches.

"What about you, Simon?" Prana asked. "In your work, I'm sure you eschew unsolicited intervention."

"That depends, Mrs. Shelley." Simon took his hand from my neck and turned to her. He was so tall, the movement seemed to rearrange the kitchen. "If I'm following the conversation, you're asking what I'd do if I lost someone I care about? I'd intervene. I'd exploit all resources available to me, and some that aren't. I'd walk away from my job, house, friends, and in the end, if necessary, I'd kill anyone who stood between me and the person in question."

My mother's eyebrows were nearly vertical with surprise. Uncle Theo regarded Simon with genial interest. P.B. stopped arranging Wheat Thins and looked up.

Simon reached for my hand. "Wollie," he said, "I think we need to walk off those sprouts. Let's go."

28

We walked side by side down Larrabee to Santa
Monica. The sun shone, unimpeded by clouds. Simon put
on sunglasses. We hadn't said a word since leaving the apartment.
The building had been full of people, the smell of roasting
turkey, a holiday mood. I couldn't identify my own mood. I felt
like someone had grabbed my remote and was channel surfing
through my psyche.

We walked close to each other, close enough to hold hands. He
wanted to hold hands, I was sure of it. No, I wasn't sure of anything. He probably just—

He reached out and took my hand. My heart started beating so
hard I thought I'd break out in a sweat. Dread and delight fought
it out. Dread of what all this might mean and how heartbroken
I would be when it ended badly, as of course it would—

"Do you cook like your mother?" he asked.

"You didn't have to have seconds," I said. "If you noticed, P.B.
and I didn't touch the food, and Uncle Theo doesn't count; he's been
known to eat raw hemp. Thanks for not arresting us, by the way."

"It's my day off." He gave my hand an admonitory shake.
"Don't worry so much. Everyone's got families, and they never
behave."

"You don't seem like an FBI agent. Are you sure you're one?"

"How many of us have you known?"

"Some. One, anyway. By the way, do you people ever dress up like plumbers?"

He turned and looked at me. "Why?"

"Nothing. So was Uncle Theo's Richard Feynman the one you're thinking of?"

"Yes. He's a hero of Annika's. She'd been reading his biography."

I stopped. Stared. "How could you possibly—what's your interest in Annika?"

"I have no interest in Annika."

"Not you personally," I said. "I mean the FBI."

"I understand. We're not interested in her. We're interested in you."

We kept staring at each other. A soft wind blew. The sun shone down on us. West Hollywood danced by. I withdrew my hand from his.

"We're investigating people you associate with," he said, "engaged in an illegal activity. Initially, we thought you worked with them, because of your proximity and a password we heard you use. Inadvertently, it turns out. We now believe you to be our best shot at intelligence gathering."

I blinked. "I'm sorry? What?"

"I want to recruit you."

"You want me to—join the FBI?"

"No. I want you to leave town. But you're stubborn, and it's illegal for me to kidnap you. So I want you working for me."

"For the FBI."

"Try to rein in your excitement."

"Me. You want me. I'm sorry, I'm having a hard time—I can't even do sit-ups. I'm afraid of guns, I don't wear suits, I—"

"You have access to an organization it would take us weeks to infiltrate."

"What organiz—?" I asked, then stopped. "*Biological Clock?*"

"I don't have weeks. I have days."

"My God. *Biological Clock*—are you serious? My cheesy TV show? You're putting me on, right? This is government humor."

"No, I'm funnier than that." He touched my elbow, indicating we should walk. He spoke casually, looking straight ahead. "It's not uncommon for us to use civilians. It's not my first choice right now, but it's necessary."

"You're saying you want me to spy? On *Biological Clock*? On my friends?"

"They're not all your friends."

A chill went through me, despite the sun beating down. It was one thing to hypothesize with Joey and Fredreeq about corruption on the show, and another to hear this from a federal agent. "What is it you think I could do?" I asked.

"Watch. Listen. Possibly wear a wire." He took my arm and we crossed Santa Monica, a boulevard so wide pedestrians were supposed to wait in the grassy median for the next light. People often jaywalked. We didn't. "Our sources indicate an imminent merger between the party you associate with and a larger organization we've been targeting for some time. This is good luck for us. We'll move in when the two parties interface. Meanwhile, we need to identify ancillary members of the smaller organization."

"Now you sound like an FBI agent." I turned to face him. "Let me get this straight. You've got a fish on the line, a fish I'm working with, and you're holding him out as bait for some bigger fish, but you want me in there swimming and spying on this *Biological Clock* fish, so you can move in and arrest the whole school of fish."

"Put like that—since you're in the water already—yes." He pointed to the walk icon. We crossed to the south side of Santa Monica and took a left. Lucien's bookstore was ahead. Open. On Thanksgiving. What a great neighborhood.

"How is this connected to Annika?" I asked.

"We approached Annika two weeks ago. The local operation tried to recruit her. Unsuccessfully. We picked this up on our surveillance and asked her to work for us, something similar to what I'm asking you. She declined."

"Why?"

"She believed her mother in Germany would be killed if she did."

I took a long, slow breath. "And then she disappeared."

"Yes."

I stopped again. He turned to face me and took off his sunglasses. A trio of men approached, arms around each other, and maneuvered around us on the sidewalk. "Kiss her, you fool!" one of them cried. I felt myself blush, but I kept eye contact. Simon didn't flinch.

I said, "Did you—the FBI—have anything to do with Annika's disappearance?"

"No."

"You don't know where she is."

His eyes glinted. "I already told you I don't."

"Rico Rodriguez tried to talk Annika into something she didn't want to do. Was it working for Little Fish?"

Simon said nothing.

I looked away. Cars passed. I pictured people driving to their grandmothers', candied yam casseroles in their laps. "If I say no, where will I end up?"

"Look at me," he said, and waited until I did. "You think we make people vanish?"

I thought of Michelle, the music mom. She'd said Annika wanted a lawyer, the kind that finds people who disappear. "Maybe."

The glint in his eye was a flash. "If Annika had chosen to work with us, she'd be here today, because we take care of our own. But we didn't arrest or deport her. She said no, she was free to walk away. Okay?"

"No, it's not okay. Because what if she was harmed or kidnapped by the bad guys—these other people she wouldn't work for?"

"That was a chance she took. I wasn't going to force her to work for us. She was scared and she was in a tough situation. But it wasn't part of my job to keep an eye on her. Had I known you cared to this extent, I might have."

"What do you care what I care?"

"Take a guess, Wollie."

I looked away again. He took my arm and we continued east on Santa Monica. "You'd sign a contract," he said. "There's some money in it, not much. You're not an employee of the FBI, you're not authorized to do anything illegal beyond what's organized or sanctioned by your handler. That's me. You're what we call a cooperating witness, a CW. If you're scared—"

"Should I be scared?"

"Yes." The word, naked and unequivocal, hung in the air between us. "But you're safer cooperating with me than not cooperating."

I caught sight of Lucien in his shop, paused in the act of stocking books in the display window. He was looking at me. "And the man following me last Friday," I said, "is that someone else I'd be 'cooperating' with? How many other goons will—"

Simon stopped, took my arm, and pulled me in close. I caught my breath. This was one big guy. This was not a guy you wanted to get physical with, unless—

"I don't like the sound of that." He spoke quietly. "You can tell me all about it in a minute, but I want to tell you something first: no one harasses you into working with us. Do it because you want to, or walk away. Your choice." He let go of my arm.

Some choice. I was about to tell him to take a hike, but a memory stopped me. Weeks ago, on this very block, Annika and I had come from the movies. She'd grabbed my arm, just as he had, her small hand pulling on my sweatshirt, giving it a shake. "We will solve your math problems, Wollie. I promise. You won't have to go through it alone." This kid, reassuring me like she was my mother.

"I'll help you catch your bad guys," I said. "If you help me find Annika."

His eyes were blue again. Not angry anymore. He let out a breath.

He said, "You're on."

29

I showed up to work at sundown, responsibility weighing heavily on my polka-dot-silk-clad shoulders.

Biological Clock had found a restaurant called Olga's Kitchen willing to accommodate us on Thanksgiving, offering a prix fixe dinner of dark-meat turkey, gravy, mashed potatoes, stuffing, and canned cranberry sauce for $9.99. A fair number of diners were taking advantage of this, including a party of fourteen, dressed for the holiday in everything from shorts and flip-flops to a T-shirt that said "I used to care but now I take a pill for that."

I regarded them all with suspicion.

Once I'd signed on to be a CW, a cooperating witness, Simon and I had walked to West Hollywood Park to discuss the details. He wouldn't identify the bad egg I was working with, referring to the malefactor as Little Fish. He admitted the illicit business was drugs only after I pointed out that an FBI-DEA joint operation was unlikely to be anything else. To tell me more, he said, lessened my value as a corroborating source and, later, a witness in front of a judge or jury. The thought of ratting out someone I knew in court was distasteful, but a bigger problem was secrecy. I couldn't tell Joey or Fredreeq what I was up to. My best friends.

The FBI, Simon explained, had no best-friends exemption.

My assignment was relatively simple. I was to listen on the set for European accents, watch for people using pay phones, and report immediately the sighting of shopping bags from Hugo Boss, Fendi, or Ermenegildo Zegna. These shopping bags were used for dead drops, exchanges of drugs or money.

Then there was the quid pro quo. Simon agreed to assign someone to track down Annika. I imagined some low-level trainee making a token call to the LAPD, then tossing Annika's file onto a "do later" pile. "Suppose I gave you a license number," I said. "You could get me an address, right? Also, could you guys trace an e-mail, even if it's no longer in service?"

"Whose?"

I told him about Marie-Thérèse, and then about the goateed man, the man who'd broken Bing Wooster's fingers and talked about making someone disappear.

"Give me the license number and the e-mail," he said, "and we'll look into it."

I shook my head. "Give me the addresses and *I'll* look into it—"

"Really? You'll find this guy and sketch him into submission?" He smiled at my reaction. "Your profession isn't classified information. Which brings up another—"

"This isn't what I agreed to, me feeding you information about Annika, and you—"

"Wollie, I don't mean this unkindly, but you paint frogs for a living. Right now my concern is you. Tell me about the man following you on Friday."

And that's how it went. I'd steer the conversation one way, and he'd grab the wheel and do a verbal U-turn. No wonder he and the DEA were having "issues"; I was developing some myself. I had a childish impulse to call the whole thing off, but Annika's fate was clearly tied to his operation, and if I was being asked to work with a paper bag over my head, at least I was on the inside. I'd just continue my own investigation parallel to his. Anyway, I'd signed a contract. He'd pulled it out of his pocket when I'd said yes.

So here I was at Olga's Kitchen, made up, coiffed, and poised for espionage. It hadn't mattered that I'd shown up a wreck.

Fredreeq could get a corpse camera-ready, and as for my state of mind, everyone around me seemed more or less unhinged. Bing Wooster was as high-strung as an Afghan hound. But Bing was working his Betacam with two taped fingers and painkillers, which might've accounted for it. I asked Joey her opinion.

"Whatever the reason, he's more peevish every day, and he's started smoking. Elliot says he's welcome to have a nervous breakdown, as long as he keeps bringing in episodes on time and under budget. He's a mess, but they'll never fire him."

"Peevish?" Fredreeq said. "He's mad as a hatter. These Vegas saboteurs have a gun to his head, making him rig the show. He's in their pocket. I'm sure as I can be about this. And *TV Guide* may be in on it too, giving Savannah an inside photo." She applied mascara to my already encrusted eyelashes. "You share the cover with thirty-two contestants from eleven other shows; she gets a quarter-page photo, two paragraphs, and they mention her horse. Her horse got more coverage than you. She's in bed with *TV Guide*. I can't prove it, but I feel it."

"You know," I said, trying to sound casual, "I'm thinking of coming in on my nights off to see how Savannah and Kimberly do things. I'd be like a customer. Sit in the back."

Fredreeq stepped away from me and stared. "The back of what?"

"Of whatever restaurant the show's shooting in."

"You want to see how they do things, why don't you just watch the show?"

"Because then I'd have to look at my own face and also, there's a big difference between what Bing shoots and what shows up on TV after it's edited."

Fredreeq turned to Joey. "You think they'll go for that, Wollie lurking?"

"I'll be in disguise," I said.

Fredreeq looked baffled. Joey said, "Working undercover, Wollie?"

I turned so fast that Fredreeq's mascara wand raked across my cheekbone. Fredreeq shrieked. In the mirror I saw black stripes adorning my face. "I can't comment on that, Joey," I said. "But if you guys were to guess what I was up to . . ."

Joey nodded. She made sure I wasn't wearing a sound mike, then told Fredreeq I was probably a rat for the DEA. While this was neither flattering nor accurate, it dovetailed closely enough with Fredreeq's Vegas theory that within minutes they'd joined forces, discussing disguises for me to wear on my night off.

"Here's mirrors," Fredreeq said. "You and Carlito check your teeth whenever Bing says 'Cut' and every hour, do lipstick. You up to it? 'Cause I can blow off Francis's family——"

"Don't be silly. It's a holiday. You have kids. I can powder my own nose. Go home."

My Thanksgiving date was Carlito Gibbons. We sat side by side in a booth, more attentive to our mirrors than each other. I wondered how actors fall in love on movie sets, given the self-absorption of this work, not to mention the crew hanging around and sound guys listening to conversations on their headsets. Which led me to wonder how actors kiss each other when they're not in the mood, which led me to wonder how Savannah, Kimberly, and I were going to kiss Carlito, Henry, and Vaclav all through Week Seven, as the show's promos indicated. Week Seven, I realized, started shooting Monday.

"Let's move to the guest expert," Bing yelled. "Paul! She here yet? Noel Whositz?"

"Not her. Him," Paul said. " 'Nole,' not 'No-Elle.' Professor Wiederhut. In the john."

"Whatever. Get him."

Carlito picked at his molars with a fork. I offered him a toothpick, but he plucked a strand of hair from his head and set about flossing. How . . . resourceful. Could Carlito be Little Fish? I couldn't see him in charge of a drug operation, but I could see how a paralegal on the team could be useful. Also, why had Annika approached Michelle, the music mom, rather than Carlito, if she was looking for a lawyer? She saw Carlito more often. And

the set, with its long hours and endless downtime, was more con-
ducive to that sort of conversation. Hmm.

"Lovely, lovely!" A gnomelike man approached, escorted by
Paul. He wore a striped turtleneck, bringing to mind a black-
and-yellow poison-arrow frog, *Dendrobates leucomelas*. "I so love
your American Thanksgiving. Cornucopia, rich in metaphor.
Vessel and phallus all at once. The fertile turkey. No coincidence
there, what?" His accent was delightful. European?

"Yo. Nole. No-elle," Bing said. "However you say it. No turkey
talk once we roll."

"Hullo, what?"

"This show isn't live. When it airs, Turkey Day's history. So
don't refer to it. Go again. Action." Dinner plates appeared before
us. Carlito and I delicately chowed down. Professor Wiederhut
held forth. Bing filmed.

"I'm a Celtic neo-Jungian," the professor said. "I applaud your
program's iconoclasm. Not easy to challenge this country's conservative culture, yet this road you travel is not without precedent.
Footprints! I speak in metaphor, the language of myth, to—"

"Don't. Speak in English," Bing cut in. "Dumb it down. Go
again."

"Hullo? Ah, yes. In a nutshell, then. Parenting as Life Path in
mandatory conjunction with Sacred Partnering is a construct im-
posed from without by a society that paradoxically—"

"English!" Bing screamed.

The little gnome face turned to me with a pained look.

"American," I said softly.

"Indeed. Some people are gifted at raising children. Others,
at sex—phenomenal, lustful, playful, erotic, adventurous, dirty,
imaginative, dangerous, mysterious, mystical sex, year after
year, decade after decade with the same partner in a long-term
intimate relationship." Noel severed off a forkful of gelatinous
cranberry sauce and tried to get it to his mouth. He was not successful. It slid onto the table with a quiet plop. "The problem is
that modern society demands that each of us be both."

Celtic. His accent was certainly Euro, but would Little Fish be one of the weekly experts? Unlikely. Joey booked the experts. Besides—

The professor was still talking, reminding me that I was on camera too. "... onerous professional responsibilities requiring total dedication," he concluded. He tried the cranberry sauce again, but it fell onto his mashed potatoes.

Carlito piped up. "So your contention is, it's okay to go have kids and not get married."

"The gods governing motherhood are not those who reign over erotic love. In ancient times, we experienced all roles through ritual and tribe, not as individuals. We paid communal tribute—*tribe*-ute—to the archetypes. Nowadays tribe is dead, ritual is reduced to greeting cards on holidays, community is television—"

"Wollie designs greeting cards," Carlito said. I was touched that he remembered.

The professor nodded. "Lovely. I am not denigrating greeting cards, I merely—"

"Denigrate," Bing said. "Go ahead. Liven things up."

"No. Design is art. Artists are sacred storytellers. They carry the psychic wound, transform it, and bring it forth as symbol. They are to be revered." He took a sip of his wine.

From inside my purse, my phone rang.

"Oh, Christ!" Bing put down his camera. "It's probably the network, canceling us. Anyone got a Xanax?" He walked off toward the back of the restaurant.

I found my phone, embarrassed that I'd neglected to turn it off. *It better not be my mother,* I thought. "Hello," I said, discouragingly.

"It's Simon. Bad time?"

"You mean you don't know? The water glasses aren't bugged?" I walked to a quiet corner of the restaurant, lowering my voice. "Tell me something. Can you figure out where I am by me using my cell phone?"

"Does the technology exist? Yes. Are we doing it to you? No."

"But other parts of my life have been bugged, right? In the last week or so?"

"I'm more concerned with who's listening to this conversation right now."

"You mean your own agency is bugging you?"

"No. I mean on your end."

I looked around. Carlito was checking his teeth. Professor Wiederhut was sniffing the stuffing. Diners were dining. Bing was sulking. Isaac was stepping out for a smoke. No one was looking at me. "I think we're safe."

"And plumbers? Anyone follow you to the set?"

"No. And Joey drove, so I'm not alone."

"What time do you get off?"

"Eleven," I said. "Bing's estimate. That's early for us, but it's a holiday."

"You busy?"

"At eleven? You overestimate my social life."

"How about if I pick you up at your apartment? You up for that? Midnight."

My heart thumped and was still. "For . . . debriefing?"

"Call it that if you like. I'm calling it a date."

We finished at nine-thirty. I called Simon, but I got voice mail, the first time I heard his recorded message. It was also the first time I left a message. My message was rambling, explaining that I could meet him earlier, unless I didn't hear from him, in which case midnight was fine. His message was two words: first and last name. It didn't seem fair.

"Bing's losing it," Joey said, gathering Fredreeq's makeup supplies. "All night, same table. No camera moves. We're not going for the Emmy, but would it kill him to do an establishing shot? And the after-hours club on the schedule—canceled. Paul doesn't know what's going on, and Paul knows where all the bodies are buried."

I looked at Paul, packing his lights into their compact cases. He was Annika's age—didn't he have a family to be with on Thanksgiving? And Isaac? I watched him wrap up his sound equipment. Isaac would be the only child of parents long ago departed to the afterlife. Isaac would go home to a squalid apartment, a hamster, a stack of *Scientific American*s. For fun he'd use his equipment to listen to his neighbors. He caught my eye. I looked away.

Or he could be a drug lord. Paul too. Paul would be a junior drug lord. A drug princeling. I wondered why the world of drugs used such aristocratic terms: drug lords, drug barons, drug czars. Other criminals didn't get that kind of respect. There were no assault earls or homicide dukes. I was pondering the possibility of a greeting card on the topic when my phone rang. It was Cziemanksi, working, as I was.

"Slow night here," he said. "Hey, I'm still feeling bad about the dinner I owe you."

"I absolve you. Listen, Pete—we're friends, I can call you Pete, right? I have kind of an odd question: why would the FBI get involved with a drug operation? Why wouldn't that be the DEA, or the police?"

"It's a question of degree. A guy shooting up on the street is LAPD. An epidemic of new crack houses around town might involve DEA. Drug traffic in and out of Asia, South America, Europe, crime syndicates—that brings in FBI and CIA, with bigger resources. In theory we all share information and work together seamlessly."

"Naturally," I said. "Any big drug lords out there right now?"

"You mean like Tcheiko? And Forio, but he's dying of cancer. Joe Juarez they'll never get—he's got his own army, never leaves the jungle."

"Tcheiko. What's his story?"

"Interesting one. Convicted last year on racketeering charges, then escaped. Left the Feds standing there with their dicks in their hands, pardon the language. Two agents died and a couple more wished they had. Careers died. Escapes are bad. No one's supposed to escape."

I said, "So catching him might involve the DEA as well as the FBI?"

"Everyone wants a piece of this guy. Someone'll get him, too, because he's cocky. By the way——" There was a pause. "Happy Thanksgiving. I did a little checking, and you still want the address of that pickup you were interested in buying, grab a pencil."

"The—what?—oh. Oh!" He'd called the DMV for me. "You're a saint, Pete."

"No, we're friends. I don't know anything about the truck, how many miles on it, so forth, so you're on your own, if you catch my drift. And you didn't hear about it from me. I have mixed feelings about this. I can't check it out myself, for . . . reasons. So you have to promise me to take along someone who knows . . . trucks."

I glanced at Joey, sitting on a table, long legs swinging, reading a copy of some glossy periodical called the *Robb Report*. I smiled. "I promise."

"Vic Mauser. That's the guy's name," I said. Joey's old Mercedes zipped west toward the Brentwood address Cziemanski had given me. "Sounds like an assault rifle. Shouldn't we wait until daylight to do this? And what is it we're doing, by the way?"

"Surprising him," Joey said. "We won't get a signed confession, but if we do this right, we'll find out if he knows about Annika."

"How?"

"By asking. He doesn't expect it, so there's this window of opportunity while he gets his story together where we'll see it in his face. We only get one shot, but it's perfect. Thanksgiving: wine, football, L-tryptophan, the stuff in turkey that makes you sleepy. He's mellow."

"He didn't look mellow three days ago," I said. "You really think he spent today giving thanks?"

"You think only nice people do holidays?"

I felt a qualm of conscience. "What about your Thanksgiving, Joey? Where's Elliot?"

She kept her eyes on the road. "Atlantic City. Elliot thinks holidays are sappy. It's okay, I got calls from four hundred family members, which more than compensated. You know, I bet Cziemanski can't check out Vic Mauser himself because it's not his case and it wouldn't be cool. I'm also guessing he asked around and found out the sheriff's guys don't think much of the Annika-Rico connection. That's why he went out on a limb and got us this address."

"What about the FBI?" I asked. "Do you think—oops."

Joey's head swiveled to me. "Your boyfriend's in the FBI? Not the DEA?"

"Oh, God. I can't believe I just said that. I promised I wouldn't—"

"Oh, boy, a Fed. A fun Fed, better than DEA. My cousin Stewart's FBI, so— Look, Chenault. What's the number?"

We parked on Barrington and walked to Chenault, a small street ending in a cul-de-sac, as Joey reassured me about my indiscretion. "It's their own fault. Anyone who's known you five minutes can see you're not wired for deception. Where's Vic's pickup?"

"They must have underground parking," I said as we reached the building. "Unless he's out assaulting someone."

"Wollie, check this out." Joey pointed to the intercom box, with its dialing instructions and list of tenants. Code 004 was Mauser/Wooster.

"Vic Mauser . . . lives with Bing Wooster?" I said, confused. We tried on the possibility of Bing being gay. It wasn't a good fit. And Vic, even on short acquaintance, suggested severe heterosexuality. "This is stupid," I said. "Sane people don't go knocking on the doors of dangerous strangers, and how do we even get into the building—"

"Look, if he's lying, we pretend to believe him and walk away. There's no reason for him to shoot us in the back. And relax. We'll get in. I have a plan."

Joey's plan involved a tenant turning up with a key or a visitor letting us in with them. When this didn't happen she began punching codes. The intercom squawked. Joey squawked back, "It's me!" On the fourth try, someone hit the buzzer.

We found 2E. We looked at each other. Joey pressed the doorbell.

A woman answered the door. She wore maroon jeans and an argyle sweater. Her hair was red, not Joey's Irish setter red, but a short, fluffy tangerine. She looked like she'd packed sixty years of living into forty years of life. "Yeah?"

"Hi," I said. "We're looking for Vic Mauser?"

She frowned. "Do I know you?"

"I don't think so," I said.

"Penny?" a male voice yelled. "What's the story?"

"Someone to see you," she yelled back, not taking her eyes from me.

"Who?!"

"I don't know!"

There was a short curse. I imagined the goateed man hauling himself out of a sofa, with unbuttoned trousers and unbuckled belt, dining recovery measures.

He appeared at Penny's side. I was wrong. He wore shorts and a yellow T-shirt. His feet were bare. His look held no recognition; then he half-smiled, half-sneered. "Well, look who it is. Did he send you?"

"Who?" Penny asked. "Who are they?"

A child appeared in the doorway, wearing pajamas with attached feet. She held a fork in her mouth. Her hair looked like a bright orange Brillo pad, inherited from her mom. Vic glanced down. "Go back and finish your pie. Go on. Penny, take her." He backed us out into the hallway and followed, shutting the door behind himself. "What do you want?"

"Annika Glück," I said.

His eyebrows drew together. "What?"

"Where is she?" Joey asked.

"Who?" Vic barked.

"Annika Glück," I said. "You don't know who she is?"

"I can't even understand what you're saying. Who buzzed you in, by the way?"

"A friend of ours is missing," I said. "We thought maybe Bing and you—maybe that's what your argument was about the other night. Annika Glück."

He looked back and forth at us. "I don't know what this is about, but you tell that slime bucket Wooster that his kid waited all day for him to show. If he can't stop reading his own fan mail long enough to pick up the phone—"

"The slime bucket," Joey said, "didn't send us. The slime bucket's not a friend of ours. We just have the misfortune to work with him. Sorry."

I was already pulling Joey down the hall. "Sorry to disturb your Thanksgiving. Really."

The elevator smelled like curry. Joey and I were melancholy with thoughts of small girls and absent fathers. There was also something about the idea of fan mail that bothered me, but I couldn't figure out what.

"So when Vic talked about making people disappear," Joey said, "I guess he meant Bing's child, taking her out of state, maybe, if Bing didn't show some interest."

"I've heard Bing mention a wife or ex-wife," I said, "so that must be her. Penny Wooster. But he never mentioned their little girl. How can someone talk about himself all the time and not talk about being a father?"

"The whole thing depresses me."

"Joey," I said. "Does the show get fan mail?"

"Well, it gets mail, and some of it's positive. Mostly on the Web site. Don't you check the Web site? No, of course not. Anyhow. I really hoped to connect Bing to Annika's disappearance, but I think he's just a garden-variety deadbeat dad."

I agreed. Much as I wanted Bing to be Little Fish, he was more of a worm. I couldn't imagine him being of interest to some Big Fish, or scaring Annika into disappearing.

Scariness, of course, is relative. For instance, in ninety minutes I had a date. It would be my first nontelevised date in four months, since the night Doc left my life and broke my heart. And I was scared stupid.

30

We got to West Hollywood an hour before I was to meet Simon. The lights were on at Book 'Em, D'Agneau, and on impulse I had Joey drop me there. I wasn't the only customer. My uncle was in the back, having decaf with Lucien.

"Waiting for my ride," Uncle Theo said. "Your brother rode back with the troops, but Prana and I took in a cabaret act. She's in deep meditation now, which requires solitude."

Lucien offered me a liquer. I declined. "Do you know a drug called Euphoria?" I asked.

"Don't you mean Ecstasy?"

"Related to it, I think. Do you know much about Ecstasy? Like, how it's made?"

"My friend Roger could tell you," Uncle Theo said. "You remember him, Wollie, the homeopath in Ojai. He'd make up batches of the stuff for Christmas presents. For close friends. It was handy because safrole, the operative ingredient, is derived from sassafras oil, which Roger had on hand for his medicines. Safrole has few other legitimate uses, you see. Unhappily, he's doing time now, although not for the Ecstasy. He didn't believe in paying taxes."

"Okay. So if Roger had gone beyond Christmas gifts," I said, "and built a thriving business, would that get the attention of a drug bigwig? Like Vladimir Tcheiko?"

"I don't believe I know him," Uncle Theo said.

Lucien shook his head. "It would take more than Ecstasy to interest Tcheiko."

"Like a new drug?" I said. "If it's a really big deal? If this Euphoria, for instance—"

"U4," Uncle Theo said. "Is that the same, do you suppose?"

I stared at my uncle and nodded.

"A young man at the hospital with P.B. described it to me," he said, "as tripping on clouds at the bottom of the ocean. 'U4 is 4U, U4 is 4U' he liked to say. He had repetition compulsion, repeating words in multiples of eight. The drug sounded quite delightful."

"Mental hospital," I said to Lucien, by way of explanation. "Okay, would that do it? Would a new drug that's big with college kids interest Tcheiko?"

"Oh, undoubtedly." Lucien refilled Uncle Theo's coffee cup. "But how far would he go for it? Actually, I'm inclined to think that if it's big enough, he would go very far. The man is a megalomaniac, a publicity slut, a player. Outsize ego made larger by his famous escape last year. He is in retreat now, on the coast of Africa, they say, but he will no more live there quietly than movie stars retire upon winning Oscars. Yes, I can imagine him needing to be associated with the next trend, whatever it is. Heroin and cocaine are the old world order and Tcheiko sees himself as the new."

He sipped his coffee and gazed at me. "Now we have questions. Yesterday a man came in asking about you. I made him buy two books and one of your greeting cards and told him nothing." He nodded at my reaction. "Receding hairline. Medium height. Unlike the well-proportioned being who walked you down the street today, who came in Sunday and bought one each of your cards, thirteen in total. I charged him for twelve. Question: why did the man yesterday leave here and drive off in a van with a plumbing logo on its side?"

"And why," Uncle Theo said, "did your building superintendent stop by to say Happy Thanksgiving and that he wasn't aware of your plumbing problem?"

I had no answers. I had no plumbing problems. I had other problems, though.

Uncle Theo and I pondered these while walking to my apartment. We arrived without incident and once I'd delivered my uncle to his friend Gordon, who was waiting in his truck on Larrabee, I headed to my own car, parked right in front of my building. I opened the trunk, removed my art portfolio, and went to wait for Simon in the lobby. While I waited, I sketched. Sketching relaxes me, occupying my hands when thoughts trouble my mind.

I'd been doing a line of condolence cards, initially inspired by my broken engagement. There is no end to things deserving of sympathy. "Sorry about that canceled wedding" led to "Sorry about your cholesterol levels," "Sorry your house has mold," and, this being Hollywood, "Sorry your series was canceled." I finished "Sorry you flunked" and was starting a new one, "Sorry about your biological father," when a knock on the building's glass door made me jump.

I slapped my sketchbook shut and went outside to meet Simon Alexander.

"Nice office," he said, indicating the lobby. He took my sketchbook. "May I?"

I nodded, watching him study my work. He'd changed clothes since this morning: different dress shirt, different dark pants, no tie. He turned the pages slowly, studying each as if it were directions to buried treasure. I realized I was holding my breath. Finally, he closed my sketchbook and handed it back. "I like your mind," he said.

I let out my breath.

He escorted me to his sports car and opened the passenger door. A first-date sort of gesture. I wondered how long he'd do that, hold the door open for me. A lot of guys never do it, which is okay. Other guys start out doing it and after a while they get in the driver's side and lean over to open the door for you, and then sometime later they dispense with opening your door at all, and the next thing you know, they're in the car and halfway down the block before they even unlock your door, leaving you to hop after them in your high heels, waving your arms. Would we last that long, Simon and me?

I wasn't in heels tonight. *B.C.* dictated flat shoes, since my feet were never seen on camera and Bing didn't want me towering over Carlito, Henry, and Vaclav. I was also in a tight black skirt that went with my tight polka-dot blouse, part of my recent Beverly Center haul. And a lot of makeup. TV makeup, as applied by Fredreeq, is just slightly more subtle than what you'd see at the circus. Would Simon think I'd worn three coats of mascara to impress him?

I snuck a look at the bump in his nose I was growing fond of, prominent in profile. He caught me looking, smiled, and went back to his driving.

"Nice wheels, your cheap Bentley," I said. "I thought Joey's husband Elliot's BMW had an impressive dashboard, but this one's downright—" I stopped before saying "sexy."

"Thank you," he said, as though I'd finished my thought. "What kind of BMW?"

"I don't know. Some convertible."

He smiled. "I thought we'd go to Falcon. Do you know it?"

"No."

"You'll like it."

"Naturally you know what I like, based on—my FBI file?"

He kept his eyes on the road. "Your favorite potatoes are french fries. You support the legalization of pet ferrets. You like watches. You hate sisal carpets, tolerate Berber, love Persian rugs, but worry about little girls in Third World countries sitting at looms making them."

Oh.

He continued. "You designed your first greeting card when you were six, you listen to Christmas carols all year, you used to think James Bond was your father."

I cleared my throat. "Okay, perhaps a government file is redundant for a contestant on *Biological Clock*. Still, you cannot predict with certainty that I'll like . . . Pheasant."

"Falcon. I've watched you eat without complaint at seedy restaurants across L.A."

"They haven't all been seedy."

"A good restaurant wouldn't allow a show that bad to be filmed on its premises."

"Is it really as bad as I think it is?"

"Biological Clock," he said, "is as bad as it gets. I'm hooked. I fell asleep in front of the TV one night and woke up to your face. Your date berated the waiter for not knowing if the beef was domestic or Argentinian, and you stood up for the waiter."

I stared. "But that was our first episode. Weeks before I appeared on your radar."

"If you're looking to keep a low profile, you might consider a different line of work."

"Okay, I'm confused. I thought I came to your attention because of this sting operation, you thinking I was in with the bad guys, Little Fish, Big Fish . . ."

"No, I've known about you for weeks." He looked at me. "Unofficially."

Something went zinging through me. "Is it common," I said, "for an FBI agent to approach someone he thinks is working with bad guys, to warn her off?"

He looked back at the road. "No. It's not common at all."

He was so relaxed. They probably taught relaxation techniques at Quantico. My heart was pump, pump, pumping away like an old washing machine with a spin cycle gone crazy. "And when," I said, "did you decide I wasn't a criminal?"

"Last week. I might have recruited you in any case, but then you'd have been a dirty source. I like it better this way."

"And you're done investigating me?" I thought about the man questioning Lucien.

"Officially, yes."

Was that a double entendre? He hadn't taken his eyes off the road. "Great," I said. "The FBI thinks I'm clean. If I want to go into crime, this is the time to do it."

The light turned green. His hand played with the gearshift. He had articulate fingers. "What makes you think I have a sense of humor?" he asked. The car shot forward, leaving my stomach half a block behind.

I said, "What makes you think I'm kidding?"

He looked at me. It was hard to hold his look, because for one thing, I was scared we were going to crash if his eyes didn't return to the road, and for another thing, eye contact like that says something after a point, something along the lines of *Yeah, I'd sleep with you.*

He looked away first. I let out a long, slow breath, as quietly as I could, focused on the appealing bump in his nose.

A smile settled in on his face. He said, "This is going to be fun."

Falcon had valet parking on Sunset Boulevard, but no obvious entrance. A gate to the right of the valet was manned by a woman: intimidating, hip, holding a clipboard. In a careful voice that could turn either respectful or discouraging, she asked if we had reservations. I wanted to say that I had some pretty serious reservations, but I let Simon answer.

"Alexander."

She thawed, smiled, and crossed the name firmly off the clipboard. "Certainly, Mr. Alexander. Straight on back, left at the arbor. Enjoy your evening."

We walked down a long path, a sort of floriferous alleyway leading to a doorway. It was an entrance ritual calculated to make us feel Chosen. Good feng shui, Fredreeq would say.

Falcon was all wood and steel and mood lighting, starkness undercut by whimsy, with fur-covered seating cubes scattered around a sophisticated bar. Booths surrounded the bar's periphery, and a lower room, actually outdoors, complete with trees and bleachers, served as a nightclub. A waiter/runway model showed us to our upper-level booth, gliding silently across a wood floor. I, in my flat size eleven shoes, galumphed along behind, making loud creaking noises.

The booths were constructed for privacy. "Bet no one in this place does drugs," I said, pulling the curtains around our table experimentally, then pushing them back.

"Think you could forget for two hours what I do for a living?"

"No. Oh, how nice. The elderly gentleman over there dining with his granddaughters. And they say no one dresses for dinner anymore. A little late for teenage girls to be out, don't you think? My, they're affectionate."

"Nervous?"

Oh, dear. We weren't in a car anymore, we were opposite each other, his blue eyes flickering in the candlelight. Candlelight fosters double entendres.

"I'm not nervous." But I was, because when the waiter came I ordered a martini with an olive, a drink I've had twice in my life and didn't enjoy, as this was a restaurant where ordering white wine by the glass could be a faux pas, which begged the question of why I cared what some waiter and bartender thought of me, for which I had no satisfactory answer.

Simon asked for something called Ketel One, and the waiter retreated. A man came by and set a small plate on our table. It held two servings of something involving phyllo dough, along with two smaller empty plates.

"*Amuse-bouche*. Veal," he said, and vanished.

Simon stabbed one of the appetizers, put it on a plate, and moved it to me. "Then let's entertain our mouths."

Not finding veal entertaining, I pushed the plate back toward him. "You speak French. Had I known of your erudition when you were stalking me, I'd have asked you to help me pass my math assessment test."

"I'd have said no." He ate his *amuse-bouche*. "Why test out if you don't know the subject?"

"Because I don't like numbers. I don't want to study them into retirement."

He pushed my *amuse-bouche* toward me. "That's because, underneath that good-girl exterior, you're your mother's daughter. You think math's not creative, it's for left-brain types. I bet you don't even like computers."

There it was again. Computers. Web site. Fan mail. There was something I needed to check out when I got home. "Math doesn't interest me," I said. "Can't I not be interested?"

"Yes. But you aspire to higher education."

"Not in math."

"Then half the world's closed to you. The language of physics. Chemistry."

"I'm not the scientific type." I pushed my plate back toward him.

"Really? Art is okay, and religion, but science, that other great mode of human inquiry, holds no appeal. Interesting. A little arrogant."

"I didn't mean—"

"I have no problem with arrogance; it can be sexy. You really think what bores you isn't worth learning? Feynman was like that. He thought literature was a waste of time."

A martini appeared in front of me. I took a long sip from the chilled glass and felt my ears twitch. Imagine getting so heated up about arithmetic. I popped the olive in my mouth and looked at him, his soft white shirt such a textural contrast to the steel booth he leaned against. What a masculine restaurant. Except for those fur-covered seating cubes. I took another sip.

"Chaco," I said. But I mispronounced it, so that it sounded like "Tcheiko."

"What?" His body tensed. I could feel it in the space between us.

"*Ceratophrys cranwelli*, predaceous South American horned frog. I'm painting it. The Chaco. Of the subfamily Ceratophryinae, within the family Leptodactylidae. See? Science."

Simon relaxed. Smiled. "That's not science, that's showing off your Latin."

The tension had been subtle, but it had been there. Simon had

Vladimir Tcheiko on the brain. And he didn't want me knowing. Tcheiko wasn't just a drug lord. He was Big Fish.

I was wondering what to do with this when Simon asked how things had gone on the set. I told him I'd followed men to the bathroom all night, lurking in the hallway in case one used the pay phone between the men's and ladies' rooms. None did. "And no one," I said, "stood up and announced, 'I am Little Fish.' One Celtic accent, no shopping bags. Nothing I did tonight couldn't be done by any first-year FBI agent, by the way."

A waiter refilled our water glasses. Simon thanked him without taking his eyes off me.

"So why me?" I said. "Why me?"

He just kept looking at me. "Stop looking for her," he said, his voice soft.

I said nothing.

It really was a great restaurant. Our waiter brought me a second martini I couldn't recall ordering, a salad I knew I hadn't ordered, and some pasta thing. Simon had a steak the size of my shoe. There were colorful sauces, kaleidoscopically arranged on the plates, and an impressive bread basket with skinny breadsticks and curly pretzelly things shooting out like earth-tone flora. The whole experience was enhanced by the fact that I was drunk.

"I've never gotten drunk with a G-man," I said, leaning over the table a little farther than the rules of good posture allowed. "I bet you have a conservative voting record. I don't often date Republicans, but Joey says they're good in bed, more so than you'd imagine."

"It's not something I've spent time imagining."

"Speaking of Joey, why didn't you recruit her? She's brave, she's intrepid, and she's a producer of sorts, so she's got a built-in excuse for hanging around the show."

"I have my reasons," he said.

"Let's hear them."

He sat back, his body languid, one hand playing idly with the espresso cup in front of him. He studied me. He studied me for so long I forgot what my question was. For a moment I sobered up. Should federal agents even be allowed to date, when the rules of conversation kept getting suspended every four minutes?

"Joey," he said, "has a lifestyle and certain . . . characteristics that make her less than desirable to work with." His hand lifted in a "Stop" gesture. "Anything I say about this is going to get you defensive. You're a little fierce about your friends."

"You mean I'm fierce about Annika but, Simon, if you knew her better, you'd like her. You'd like her better than me. She knew all this math stuff, she tutored me for free, she had no money but she volunteered at pet shelters, she was kind to plants, and so small, with those red cheeks and worried about World War II and she's not even twenty years old. If they had a reality show called *Who Should Not Disappear into Thin Air?* she'd win."

This was not, perhaps, my most lucid moment, but Simon looked at me with gentleness, a gentleness peculiar to tall men. Tall men with blue eyes. There are male frogs that turn blue in order to attract female frogs, I told myself. This got me to thinking about the most famous frog, the legendary frog turned into a prince by a kiss. I seemed to be living the legend in reverse, seeing men as princes and kissing them willingly, only to find they were in fact amphibians, leading a double life, one on land, one at sea. Perhaps this was because the woman in the legend was a princess and I was a commoner.

At some point we walked the long, long walk out of the restaurant, and when we were halfway down the flower-covered alleyway, Simon stopped. I turned to him, stood on tiptoes as if I were going to tell him a secret, which seems like something an informant might do with an FBI agent, and then I kissed him. He kissed me back. After a while, other people came down the flower-covered alleyway, and we stopped kissing and continued on our way to Sunset Boulevard, where it was the morning after Thanksgiving night.

He put his jacket on me while we waited for the valet parking guy to fetch his car. The jacket was too big. It made me feel little. When you're a girl who is six feet tall, that is nothing to sneeze at.

31

I woke up on my living room sofa, dressed. Morning. My head hurt. Memory came in slowly, like coffee through a drip machine.

Why wasn't I in my bed? Had I been so drunk last night I'd lost my way? No, my mother was occupying the bedroom. Okay. What day was it? Friday. I had to work on the frogs. I sat up. All my brains shifted to the front of my head. I lay back down. I sat up again, then stood. Okay, I was really making progress now.

Simon.

I clutched the back of the sofa and closed my eyes. Had we——? Kissed?

I sat back down. Scenes replayed like a home movie. Kisses. Outside the apartment, under a tree, in the grass, the car, the elevator. I'd found the gun he wore on his waist. He'd checked out the apartment for plumbers, but then what? Please God, tell me he hadn't stayed. Bad enough to not remember, but with Prana in the bedroom and paper-thin walls——

I got up, and this time made it all the way to the kitchen, to a quart of cold water and medication. I was able to manage the childproof cap on the Tylenol bottle, but the coffee grinder presented a problem. Would it wake my mother? Maybe. Was it worth it? No. This was why God had created instant coffee.

My eyes lit on my computer, sitting on the kitchen table.

While the kettle heated up, I logged on to the *Biological Clock* Web site. The fact that I hadn't done so until now raised an interesting question. Did I simply not enjoy computers, or was I, in fact, in denial about this show? Was I, like Prana, appalled?

The Web site was itself a little appalling, all primary colors, capital letters, and exclamation points. I felt like putting on sunglasses. There was a page called "Who's Got the Best *B.C.* Body?!" that I chose not to visit. I was drawn instead to "Biological Biographies!"

There was nothing about Carlito, Vaclav, and Henry I couldn't have written myself, because I'd been dating them, and if there's one thing I know how to be it's an attentive date. The competition was another story. I clicked on Kimberly Karmer. Kim was from a large, loving family, was a former Junior Miss, an award-winning clarinet player, and fluent in American Sign Language, thanks to a hearing-impaired mother. In the summer she taught music to underprivileged youth and she was now working in retail while pursuing a master's degree in psychology. *Dear God,* I thought, and clicked onto Savannah Brook. Worse. Laker Girl, French major. MBA from Columbia, then spent a year building houses for poor people in Guatemala, currently a systems analyst, whatever that was, for a banking consortium and an equestrienne. And, of course, a black belt in Krav Maga. The kind of date who'd fix your roof, balance your checkbook, and advise you on your groin kicks.

Then there was me. My biographical profile said I designed a line of greeting cards, painted murals, and lived in West Hollywood.

That was it? What about my failed business, my three semesters of junior college, my institutionalized brother? Or my most noteworthy accomplishment, a string of dates that, put end to end, would stretch from Beverly Hills to the Panama Canal? Oh. I recalled Sharon, the battle-weary production person in the *B.C.* office, begging me for more information.

I imagined adding "drug dealer" to either Kim or Savannah's biography, and found it plausible. Especially Savannah. Maybe she'd started this sideline in Central America, when she realized the poor of Guatemala weren't advancing her career fast enough.

I clicked on a feature called "Fan Mail" and discovered I had my own mailbox. My head throbbed wildly. This was what I'd come for, an idea sparked by Vic Mauser. A password was required for the mailbox. I tried my mother's maiden name, recalling that Sharon had once asked me for it. It worked. A daunting pile of e-mails popped up. I scrolled through, opening one at random. Someone called BarnyardAnimal wanted to know if my breasts were real.

Then a subject line made my heart beat faster: "Latte + 5 Sugars." I had a vision of Annika at Grounds, our coffee hangout, opening packet after packet of sugar. I'd told her that Doc liked sugar in his coffee too, that maybe there was a correlation between sugar, brown hair, and mathematical ability. The e-mail was two days old. Shaking, I hit "Read."

Wollie, I hope you find this, I have no other way to reach you. It is so bad, all that has happened. But you must not look for me. The danger is so great and if you die too it will be so bad. I want so much to see you and everyone, but I think I will not so always remember me with kindness. I am crying now as I write but it's OK. I did not think I believed in God, but now I find I do so everything will be all right, even if nothing turns out as I thought. I did not think my year would end like this, people so much better than I expected and also so so so much worse. It will be over soon please do not look for me PLEASE. Tell NO ONE I write to you. Do not try to write back. Worse of all would be if you die because of me. Love, Your Little Sister.

I stared at the screen, my thoughts tumbling over one another: *she's alive she's in danger she thinks she's going to die she thinks I'm going to die.* I typed back, "Are you still there? Are you all right?" and sent it. Almost instantly, a message appeared.

"Message cannot be delivered because mailbox is full."

I couldn't move. Her e-mail had come from "feynmanfan." We'd never e-mailed each other, but this had to be her account. Why hadn't she emptied her mailbox? Whose computer had she used?

What kind of danger was she talking about? Bombs? Guns? How could I guess? How did she know I was looking for her? I dialed Simon, got voice mail, and hung up. What could I say? I'm in danger. Big, general, nonspecific danger. Rescue me.

Could the e-mail be traced? I picked up the phone, and set it down again. We'd been through this, with Marie-Thérèse's mail. Yes, but it would take time. Annika's message had been waiting for two days. It could wait ten more minutes, while I calmed down. I printed it out.

In the hall closet I found some bicycle shorts and a rugby shirt. Hubie's. They didn't fit, let alone match, but they'd save me from having to sneak into my bedroom and wake Prana.

What *about* Prana?

Nothing in Annika's e-mail suggested the danger was in my apartment, and my mother wasn't one to respond to threats, in any case. She didn't believe in medical checkups, earthquake preparedness, or national security advisories, and she wouldn't believe in this. She certainly wouldn't alter her life for it.

I went outside and checked the street for female plumbers and curious men with receding hairlines. Then I said a prayer, got in my car, and headed for the Valley.

Halfway up Coldwater Canyon I started to think more clearly. Annika was alive. Or had been two days ago. If she was being held against her will, maybe she'd seen a computer, remembered the show's Web site, and typed out a fast message. But kidnappers did not typically leave computers lying around. Perhaps she was in hiding and had seen Rico's disappearance on the national news, which had so distressed her she'd written to me, frightened that what had happened to him would happen to me. But if the danger was so great, why not just tell me what it was?

And how exactly was I to stop looking for her? Should I stop thinking about her? Avoid saying her name? Not drive my car? Quit the show? Leave town? Which part of my life was the dangerous part? Being a CW, a cooperating witness for the FBI, the job she'd turned down?

Tell no one, Annika had said.

I had to tell someone. Cziemanski? Annika was still his case. No, not a case, a missing person's report. He might see this e-mail as confirmation that she'd left voluntarily.

Joey. *Tell no one* wouldn't mean Joey, because Annika, unlike the FBI, understood about best friends. When I reached Sherman Oaks, I went into Rex and Tricia's Mansion, armed myself with a gallon can of deck paint as a weapon, checked the house from top to bottom, locked the door, and left a message for Joey.

One good thing about the e-mail, beyond the fact that Annika was alive, was that it distracted me from my hangover. I don't get drunk often, being, if not a blackout drinker, a brownout one. I don't forget whom I was with, just the details of what I did with them. Which makes for some uncomfortable mornings after. This one was no exception.

"Wollie, I can't talk," Joey said on the phone, interrupting my painting. "But be home at three-thirty. I have a plan." She hung up. Immediately, my cell phone rang again.

"Joey?" I said, but it wasn't my friend's gravelly voice that responded.

"Miss Shelley?" It was a woman, soft-spoken. I thought of the female plumber and felt chills up and down my spine. "My name is Lauren Rodriguez. I'm—"

"Oh, gosh." Rico's mother. I froze. "I know who you are. How are you doing?"

"Not well." An audible breath. "Pardon the intrusion. I was given your number by Kevin Irving. Richie's roommate. I understand you met Kevin. And Lyle. At Pepperdine."

"Yes, I did."

"Kevin tells me—he's very kind, he calls the house every

day—he says you're friends with a young woman Richie dated. A girl from Germany."

"Annika. Yes."

"I've spoken to the detective in charge of my son's case. I asked about this young woman. He says the connection is tenuous. Miss Shelley—"

"Call me Wollie."

"The detective feels it best if we leave him to do his job. I am not much interested in the detective's feelings. I don't know if this will make sense to you, but I want to meet everyone my son met, go where he went; I would like to walk through his life of the past weeks. I'd like to hear about this young woman. If we could meet for a cup of coffee, lunch, anything. Anytime you like. I have nothing but time."

I felt sad down to my toes. What could I say to this woman, what could possibly help her right now?

Information. Knowledge.

"Of course I'll meet you," I said. "But there's someone else you may want to talk to. I'll make a call and get right back to you."

Maizie answered on the first ring. "Wollie! Guess what: Grammy Quinn called last night from Palm Springs, she just figured out why you looked so familiar—she's a huge fan of this show you're on. Hey, do you have an autographed photo? She'll be back for Christmas—"

"I can do better than that," I said. "She can visit the set if she wants. Listen, though—"

"Oh, my God. It would be like the Second Coming— Emma Amanda Quinn!" Maizie's voice changed drastically. "Don't you go near that ironing board. *Lupe! Dónde está?*"

I spoke quickly. "Maizie, I'm close by and I wonder if I could bring a friend to meet—"

"Yes, fine— Emma! Wollie, I'm sorry, I have to deal with this. Come on over. Bye."

I drove from Sherman Oaks and Lauren Rodriguez drove from

Lost Hills, both of us heading to Encino. As I'd expected, when she heard Annika was an au pair, Lauren wanted to meet the host family. I drove as fast as Ventura Boulevard allowed, anxious to brief Maizie on the sensitive nature of this visit. I was putting her on the spot, but I couldn't see her refusing, and I was glad not to have to meet Lauren alone. There is something scary about grief.

Lupe and Mr. Snuggles escorted me into the kitchen,

where Emma sat at the table with a plastic plate in front of her and a bib around her neck. "Emma eat lunch," the child informed me, holding up tiny silverware.

"Looks good." Turkey, stuffing, and peas sat on the plate, each food forming an island, nothing touching. A tiny, perfect wedge of apple pie occupied its own plate, just out of reach.

Maizie came through the doorway, aproned, carrying a large Tupperware bowl. "Hey, there," she said, heading for the counter. "What can I get you, Wollie? Actually, you might want to help yourself—we're doing sausage, and it's not pretty. Gene took one look and went to play golf. City boy. There's fresh-squeezed juice in the fridge."

"That's the fridge," Emma said, pointing to the paneled-front appliance. "It's a refrigerator fridge."

"I see," I said. "Maizie, you make your own sausage?"

"Yes, I'm taking a charcuterie class." She poured the contents of her Tupperware into an enormous bowl, added a measuring cupful of what appeared to be spices, and plunged her hands in. "Oh, Lupe, I have the three-eighths-inch blade chilling in the fridge, could you get it? Anyhow, Wollie, come to our Christmas Eve open house. Grammy Quinn comes in the day before—oh—" She looked up. "Did you say you were bringing a friend?"

"She's on her way," I said. "And she's not precisely a friend." Maizie looked curious but continued kneading. I said, "Her name is Lauren Rodriguez. Her son was Annika's boyfriend, Rico. He's missing. Have you heard about this? It's been on the news."

Maizie stopped working, hands suspended above the bowl. She stared at me. "His mother is coming here?"

"Yes. I think she's in bad shape, understandably, and she's trying to . . . um, retrace the steps of her son's—I'm sorry, this is very awkward. Is it a problem?"

Maizie glanced at Emma, a stricken look on her face. I felt my own face go red, as though I'd just burped loudly. I said, "I guess it is a problem. I—wasn't thinking."

A buzzer rang.

"Lupe," Maizie said, "please show our guest in." She stepped over to the sink and washed her hands. She dried them on a dish towel, removed her apron, inspected her nails, then moved to Emma's high chair. She smoothed the flyaway hair until Emma batted her away the way you'd shoo a fly. Maizie smoothed her own hair. The seconds dragged by. She gave me an uncertain smile. "It's fine, really, I just can't . . . fathom what that woman is going through. I have seen the news. It's every mother's nightmare, you know."

I didn't know. I wasn't a mother. I could only guess.

Footsteps sounded in the hallway. We all watched the doorway.

Lauren Rodriguez was medium height, shorter than Maizie and me, and ballerina slender. She preceded Lupe into the kitchen like a gazelle, long-necked and fragile. She looked nothing like Rico, her sandy hair pulled back into a ponytail and held with a tortoiseshell barrette. She wore khaki pants, a white blouse, loafers without socks, and carried a purse. Her only jewelry was a gold watch and a wedding ring. Her pierced ears were bare. She shook hands with us, with a strong grip. I remembered she was a politician's wife.

"You've both met my son." It was a voice unadorned with inflection.

Maizie asked Lupe to finish with Emma's lunch. Then she led Lauren and me into what would've been described in another era as a parlor. It was a room suited to tense conversation. The furniture was antique mahogany with needlepoint cushions, small, dark, and hard.

"I met Rico—Richard—very briefly, last Thursday," I said. "To talk about Annika."

Maizie cleared her throat. "Two or three times he came here to pick up Annika for a date, or just to visit. Once I made pizza and we all watched the World Series in the den. A charming young man. Extremely well mannered."

"Yes, he is," Lauren said. "Thank you. What can you tell me about this girl?"

"Annika?" Maizie said. "Wonderful with children, excellent English. Good personal hygiene. A little . . . withdrawn, the last month or two, but I chalked it up to hormones or homesickness. An ideal employee in every way, until she disappeared. Such a bright girl."

I nodded. "Really smart. And energy—volunteer jobs, projects, college courses . . . generous and goal-oriented."

A fleeting smile appeared on Lauren's face. "She doesn't sound like Richie's type."

"What's his type?" I asked.

"Trouble."

"Annika is very pretty," Maizie said, almost defensively.

"Yes, of course." Lauren's eyes darted around, her social mechanism breaking down. Already she looked older than she had on TV days before. A beautiful woman, affected by sleeplessness, anxiety, and heartsickness. She wore no makeup. Her pallor unsettled me.

"Lauren, I have a question—" I started, then stopped. There was really no graceful segue from teen dating to crime.

"Ask. I've been asked everything this week."

"Was your son ever involved in—or were his friends into . . . um, drugs?"

Both women looked at me with blank expressions.

"No," Lauren said. "Richie was never a problem, even as a little boy. He never liked guns or swords. Just fire engines and cars. His train set, of course. Then girls."

What a strange answer. It told me nothing about him, but something about her, what she could bear to think about.

"I have this hope," she said, "that they ran off together, Richie and this Annika. He never brought her home. His roommate, Kevin, tells me my husband might have found her . . . unacceptable. Do you think that's possible, that they eloped?" Her face was a plea.

I looked at Maizie, who studied her hands, frowning as though trying to understand the question. I swallowed. "That wasn't the impression I got from him," I said. "But of course, I'd just met him; he'd hardly confide in me."

Lauren's thin fingers worked the clasp on her bag. "It's a silly theory. Who elopes?"

"I believe Annika felt herself to be—" Maizie chose her next words carefully. "In love with your son. I can't say whether it was reciprocated. He seemed to come around less in the last few weeks." A strained silence followed. "Can I get you anything?"

Lauren appeared not to hear. "Also, he would never let me worry like this. He called Saturday from school to say he would sleep in on Sunday, but he'd be home to watch the game. Football. And dinner. He said he had a mountain of laundry. He would never lie to me, you see. He's a good boy. Not with his father, not always, but with me."

She went back to rubbing the clasp on her purse. It was Prada, I noticed. How far from these women I lived, with no children, no husband, no holiday open house. I had odd jobs. And I was dressed in orange spandex bicycle shorts and a blue, red, and yellow rugby shirt, clothes belonging to dear gay Hubie, found in the bottom of a closet. I had no costly accessory to fidget with. The only thing I owned as expensive as that Prada handbag was my car.

After an awkward conversational lull, Maizie offered to show Lauren Annika's room.

The attic bedroom was now a quilting room. Intricate quilts hung on the walls, and some sort of oversize frame was set up on the bed, holding a quilt in progress. They were gorgeous, but Lauren ignored them. She stood, breathing hard, as if she could inhale a clue. What was it she hoped to find? An emotional connection, a psychic one?

Maizie said, "There's not much here. I sent most of her things back to Germany."

"Already?" I said, wondering if anyone would be there to receive them. I hadn't told Maizie that Annika's mother was missing. Now probably wasn't the moment.

"Gene thought it was time." Maizie's lips pressed together, as though the next thought had to be held back. Then she said, "He felt a week was long enough."

Lauren's face went rigid. It was another story at her house, I guessed. Rico's bedroom would be as he'd left it to go to Pepperdine: athletic trophies, his train set, plaid blankets on bunk beds. Nothing would've changed in the last few years, and now, unless he showed up alive, nothing in that room would ever change. Lauren stared out the window, and I stared at her. Her arms were folded, her right hand gripping her left bicep. Her nails were painted a shade of pale coral, but the polish was chipped and the nails themselves ragged and uneven. This shocked me. Like spotting a cold sore on the *Mona Lisa*.

"The police," she said, as if someone had just asked a question, "think he had a date Saturday night with a girl. But they can't find the girl. So when Kevin told me about Annika disappearing . . ." Her shoulders slumped, and her head dropped to her chest.

We left the room, and then the house. Maizie walked us to the porch, and Lauren and I continued down the drive, to our cars. The film shoot that had been down the block last week was now across the street. A woman was setting up director's chairs on the front lawn. I wanted to say something personal to Lauren, but everything I thought of sounded platitudinous to my ears. Like a bad greeting card.

"Did Rico talk about Annika?" I asked.

"Not by name." A smile touched her face, making wrinkles around her eyes. This was someone who smiled a lot, in normal life. "The last time he was home——he comes home every few weekends——I said, 'Is there anyone special?' He said, 'They're all special, Mom.' "

I waited. She stayed with her memory until we reached her car, a Jaguar convertible, dark green. "He said a funny thing. He said 'Even Dad would like this one. He just wouldn't like her for me.' You see?"

"Um, no," I said.

"It's the way you described her. My husband respects a good work ethic. But whoever Richie ends up with will have to have more, and I think that's what he was acknowledging."

"What will she have to have?"

"Social prominence. Style, education. Things I assume this girl doesn't have."

I looked down at my orange bicycle shorts. "A lot of people don't."

"Something else. He said, 'Mom, she's just like you. She's beautiful and blond and she speaks three languages.' "

I stared at her, but she didn't notice.

So I just came right out and told her. Annika wasn't remotely blond.

32

Blondes. Bleach blonde, honey blonde, ash blonde, dishwater blonde. Bad blonde. Rico's last date was a bad blonde, because if she had nothing to hide, she'd go to the cops and say, "I was with him the night he disappeared. I was the last to see him." Or nearly the last. If she was truly the last, then she had reason to keep it to herself.

I was no longer thinking of Annika. Or Simon. I wasn't even hung over. Driving east to San Marino, I had a prickly feeling, like my whole body had gone to sleep and was now waking up. I hadn't called first, because I wanted to try out Joey's theory of lying, which required surprise. I had to see Britta's face.

I heard her first. Or, rather, I heard the children she took care of. Why weren't they in school, I wondered, and then realized the Friday after Thanksgiving was a holiday. I followed the sounds to the back of the house and let myself in through a gate connected to a high fence. Two skinny boys jumped off a low diving board into a black-bottomed pool in a manner calculated to create the largest possible splash. Slumped on a beach chair in a sweatshirt and tight jeans was Britta, clearly bored. Very blond.

Because of the splashing I was able to get next to her without being heard. "Hi, Britta."

She jumped to her feet. Recognition dawned, then hope. "Rico? He is found?"

"No." I hesitated, then plowed onward. "Britta, you dated him, didn't you?"

The switch to sullen was instantaneous. "It was you who have told this to police." She took in my outfit, the bicycle shorts and nonmatching shirt, and seemed to find it an affront.

"I—no, I didn't," I said. "Have they talked to you?"

"Yesterday. Joshua!" Her head snapped around. "Do not hit your brother!"

I turned to look. One skinny kid was hitting the other while the other screamed.

"*Joshua!* Stop this any minute!"

One day, some civilizing force might set in, but now the boys were monkeys. Not cute baby ones, but the hostile kind you see at the zoo, screeching when they catch you looking. Joshua paused in midattack and pointed an accusing finger. "Who's she?"

"She is—nobody."

"You're not supposed to have friends over when you're on duty."

"Anyway, she is not a friend."

Joshua's brother used this distraction to push Joshua into the pool, then took off running. Britta yelled at him not to run. He paid no attention.

"I'll leave in a minute," I said. "So the cops know you were sleeping with Rico?"

Her eyes narrowed. "I don't have to talk to you. You are not police."

"No, but—do you know what a private detective is?"

"You are a detective?"

Joey and I had already played this out with Kevin and Lyle, but it was still hard for me to lie. I sat on the chaise longue. "What's nice about private detectives," I said, "is that people tell them things, things they never have to report to the police—"

"So? This is not a crime, I think, to have sex with people." She flipped her straight blond hair with both hands.

"Of course not. And by the way, I'm sorry. I didn't know you

and Rico were in love, or I would've been more sensitive when I
told you the news the other day."

Britta nodded.

"What I care about," I said, leaning in, "is finding Rico. This
is why I ask personal questions. Forgive me. It must be painful to
talk about. I won't tell the police anything."

"This is your job? To find Rico?"

"I just met with his mother, only an hour ago."

Her sullenness dissipated. "Anyway," she said, "we didn't do
this since one week ago. The police, they are concerned with
Saturday night only. Saturday I am here."

There was no hesitation, no interest in whether I believed her
or not. She was, I believed, telling the truth. She was not the
blonde Rico had dated the night he'd disappeared.

Oh.

I thought of the names on Rico's wall, the girls he knew, the
possibilities. It was exhausting to think about. And then I remembered something else on the wall. The ß. "Britta," I said,
"I guess you didn't tell them about the—other thing."

Her head snapped around. "What?"

"The drugs Rico was involved in. It's common knowledge."

She didn't bat an eye at the mention of drugs. "What means
that, common knowledge?"

"That means a lot of people know about it."

She looked young now, like the monkey boys. "Really? I—I
didn't—"

"You're right not to tell the police. You could get deported."

Her eyes went wide. "But I did nothing. I told him no."

No to what? "Then why didn't you tell the police?" I asked.

She glanced at the boys, racing barefoot around the pool,
armed with plastic machine guns. Their swim trunks were baggy
and their ribs stuck out and they were happily blowing each
other away. I could mention the agency, Glenda, Marty Otis, the
secretary of state—

"The host family," she said abruptly, "do not like the police to
come, and park in the street where the neighbors see. But this is

not my fault. Jeremy, what do you have there?" She stood. Across the lawn, the brothers had stopped shooting and were huddled over something.

"A frog!"

"You are not to murder it. Your mother says." She settled back in her chair.

I stood. "They wouldn't really murder it, would they?" Why couldn't it be a snake or a fly? Why a frog?

"No murder!" Britta called out.

"It's already dead, stupid!" one of the boys yelled.

Forget the frog, Ruta's voice said. *Talk to this girl like you are someone clever.*

I sat. "Well, it all sounds horrible. But since you didn't do it, why not just tell them he asked you to sell drugs?" I held my breath.

"Not to sell, only to carry in the luggage. How am I to say this? Then they will return and park in the street again and the neighbors will see."

There it was: confirmation. How much further would she go? "What went through your mind when Rico asked you this?" I said.

"I said, Rico, I cannot. What if they will search my luggage, for example? At LAX. They search so many people. And also, Rico says it is not a problem to find a visa to come back once I am in Germany but it is not such an easy thing. Also, I am not living in Munich or Berlin, with university. In Wandlitz there is nothing and if I say to my father, 'Now I am to move to Berlin' just like that, what will he think?"

Not, apparently, that it was a good idea, his daughter moving to the city to enter the drug trade. Rico's judgment must have been seriously impaired. Britta as a partner in crime? It would be like doing business with Winnie-the-Pooh. "When did you and Rico discuss this?"

"You know, last week. I asked him if he asked Annika also this, and he said we should not think about Annika."

"That must have been hard for you, since she was your friend."

"Yes, it was so hard. This is what no one will understand." She sighed deeply.

"And it's not fair. What exactly—is it the Euphoria he asked you to take to Germany?"

"Yes, because U4 is to be very popular, he says."

We sat in silence, watching the boys.

"Did you ever . . . try it?" I said softly.

She chewed her lip, looking troubled. "I am frightened to. I have the asthma. But he thinks I take it, so I pretend and then he has his trip so he does not know because he is high."

"Did Rico take it often?" I asked.

"Oh, no. He was not like that. For recreational purposes only. For example, to have sex. Never during class or doing business, he said. That was his rule."

"I hear that U4 is really good. Better than Ecstasy."

"Yes, Rico says it is more mellow. So the teeth do not clench and things like this."

"Did you meet any of the others he worked with? His boss?"

"This is not a boss. Rico is to be full partner, he is to arrange it on the weekend and then we are to be rich. Only now he is disappeared."

A partner? Did this mean Rico was Little Fish? Or a partner of Little Fish? "Did he tell you who the partner is?" I asked.

"No, he does not talk in real names. It is always pretend name, I forget how you call this."

Something occurred to me. "Britta, when you didn't take the U4, when he thought you did—do you still have it?"

"Yes, in my room."

"Can I see it?"

"Why?"

"It's something detectives do. You never know what's important until you see it."

She looked unconvinced. I imagined it was the only thing he'd ever given her. "It could help find Rico," I said, then mentally crossed my fingers behind my back. "I'll return it. And I won't mention it to the police."

She turned to the pool. "Joshua! Jeremy! Time to come in. If you hurry, I will give you M&M's. But you must come right now. And leave the frog." She looked at me. "To help Rico, of course I will do anything."

Part of me wanted to tell her how misguided that was, how misplaced her devotion. But she'd learn that soon enough without me.

And anyway, I wanted that Euphoria.

33

I drove through the Valley with the Euphoria in a Tylenol bottle.

It was a twin of the pill Maizie had found under Annika's bed. Bigger than an aspirin, round, and with a logo that was both strange and strangely familiar. Stopped at a red light just before the entrance ramp to the 210, I took it out of the plastic bottle and held it between my thumb and forefinger, gazing at it. A squiggle set into its surface, a piece of calligraphy. ℞

This was the third time I'd come across it, and it gnawed at me like a song lyric gone astray: where had I seen it before? But it didn't matter. What I'd just learned connected Rico to Little Fish. Rico had asked Annika to transport drugs. According to Simon, Little Fish had also tried to recruit her. It had to be the same operation. How many drug dealers were out there signing up au pairs? And this connection might not be news to the FBI, but it might be to the police, who were on a high-profile search for Rico. If I showed them this pill, pointed out Rico's wall, and told them what Britta had told me, wouldn't they expand their search to include Annika?

Should I tell Simon I was doing this? Wouldn't he tell me to leave it to him? Yes.

My cell phone rang, startling me. I felt around on the passenger seat for it while making a left turn onto the freeway entrance ramp. In the process I dropped the pill. Damn.

Statistics on cell-phone use and traffic accidents jumped into my head. *Ring!* The car behind me honked. The entrance-ramp traffic was slow, which made people testy. I inched forward, closing the three-foot gap between me and the car in front of me. *Ring!* My hand located the phone in the Bermuda Triangle of my backpack; I found the answer button and said hello. When no one responded, I yelled, "Hello!"

"Wollie. Simon."

"H—hello."

"Everything okay?"

"Yes." I cleared my throat. The car behind me honked again, nearly sending me through the roof. Again I closed the three-foot gap between me and the car ahead. "Annika's alive," I said. "She e-mailed me. And also, Rico Rodriguez—"

"Did she say where she is?"

"No. She—" I'd had all day to plan this and still, I hesitated. *Tell no one.* Annika hadn't said, *Tell no one but the FBI.* But what counted more: whom she trusted or whom I trusted?

Whom did I trust?

"Wollie? What did she say?"

The danger is so great and if you die too it will be so bad. I had it memorized. But this was not informative, only theatrical. "The gist of it was," I said, "situation's urgent. Time's running out. Clock's ticking. But listen to this: Rico Rodriguez asked Annika and another au pair to act as couriers for him, smuggling a drug called Euphoria into Germany. Rico was working with Little Fish, he could've met Little Fish through Annika." I was now first in line to enter the freeway, waiting for the red light to turn green.

"You found out all this today, hungover?"

"Okay, I should explain that martinis—well, gin. Gin acts on me in ways that—tequila too—" The car behind me blared its horn. "Okay, it's green, I see it, I'm going!" I shouted.

"Bad time to talk?"

"No, not at all. So what do you make of all this?"

"What? You trying to pin it on the martinis?"

"Pin what on the martinis?"

"The damage to my shirt."

I searched my memory. Buttons. I remembered buttons. And cuff links. And a watch. An amazing silver— "What kind of watch do you wear?" I asked.

"A Vacheron Constantine. You liked it."

"Did we discuss why a civil servant is wearing a Vacheron Constantine?"

"Yes, I'm on the take. You really don't remember a lot, do you?"

I made a note not to take so much as a decongestant in front of this man. I was so easily disoriented by things—this freeway, for instance. Where was Lake Avenue or Orange—oh. Because I was on the 210 East, not west. Heading to Arcadia, Azusa, Nebraska. "Oh, hell," I said.

"It's okay, we left a few things in the planning stages."

I hoped he was referring to sex. "I'm sorry," I said, "I'm talking to myself. I'm one of those people who shouldn't drive and talk, drive and read, drive and trim my hair—"

"You're scaring me. Good-bye."

"No, wait. I need to ask you—"

"Call me when you get home."

I hung up and found my way off the 210 East and onto the 210 West, fighting a sensation of well-being. How could I feel this way, with the day I'd had and all that had happened? Yet the sound of his voice made investigations, drugs, blondes, veal, plumbers, frogs, math, guns, e-mails, and mothers fade into the dust, like the city of San Marino.

It wasn't until the 210 had become the 134 and then the 101 that I started to worry about what had happened to the pill.

I walked into my apartment to find Joey, Fredreeq, and my mother sitting in the kitchen. Joey was eating Sara Lee cheesecake. Prana, in a peach caftan, was laying out Tarot cards.

"Wollie," Fredreeq said, "you never told us Prana is a regressionist. She says I was a courtesan in the Manchu dynasty, and Anne Boleyn."

"Congratulations," I said, going to the window. "I raised pigs in ancient Greece. Prana, any plumbers show up today?"

"No, dear."

"Because if anyone tries to get in, if anything suspicious happens—"

"I won't be here for it. Theo and I are attending the Dances of Universal Peace."

"And we should hit the road," Joey said. "Have fun, Prana. Thanks for the reading."

"Joey, may you find peace in San Pedro." Prana looked up and removed her glasses. "Wollie," she said, "what on earth are you wearing?"

Twenty minutes later I was in black jeans, black sneakers, and a black hooded sweatshirt, in the passenger seat of Joey's husband's BMW, heading south. Fredreeq followed in her own car.

On the subject of Annika's e-mail, Joey was unequivocal. "We can't stop looking. Unless we find her, you'll never stop wondering, *and* you won't feel safe. If you don't know the source of the danger, you'll be paranoid around people you should trust, and trust people you shouldn't."

"Even if the FBI promised to look for her?"

Joey glanced at me, then back at the road. "Wollie, I don't know any Feds besides my cousin Stewart in New York, but I've known my share of cops. They don't have a high opinion of informants. That's you. They pretend to care, if that's what it takes, because what works for them is surveillance, torture, and informants, and torture's frowned upon. I'm just saying a promise from them is not the same as a promise from you. If Annika's vital to their case, they'll find her. If she's not . . ." She changed lanes. "The good news is, cousin Stewart's heard of Simon Alexander. At least your guy's the real deal."

"You had him checked out?"

"Yeah, and the Bentley he drives was seized in a case last month. It's his bu-car, in Fed-speak." She looked at me. "Of course I checked, I was worried. It's weird, someone recruiting you. You're not ratlike enough."

"Thanks," I said, not liking anything about this conversation. "So what about tonight? Are we sure the agency's even open?"

"Fredreeq checked. She has ways of getting calls returned you can't imagine. They're open the Friday after Thanksgiving because of their international business. Till five."

"And we'll be back for *Biological Clock*? I'm spying tonight."

"Bing couldn't get the location till midnight, so it's a late start. You and I'll be done long before that. In and out. A drive-through burglary. Sorry, did I say burglary? Borrowing."

I rode to Au Pairs par Excellence with trepidation. Joey's casual about things I care about, like physical safety and staying within the law. But Marie-Thérèse, Annika's confidante, was still the most direct means of finding Annika. One phone number, an address, that's all we needed, and we could be home free. Instinctively, I checked the rear window to see if we were being followed. We were. Half of California was on the 405 South.

"Relax, Wollie," Joey said. "Even your mom approved this operation. By the way, who was she in a past life?"

"Everybody. She's a very old soul."

"Anyone I'd know?"

"Beethoven. Winston Churchill. Cleopatra's stillborn child."

Joey nodded. "It could be worse. She could be in the state pen and you'd feel compelled to go visit her every week. Or she could be dead. Of breast cancer, something you'd worry about inheriting and passing on to your daughters."

"I'm not having any daughters. Or sons. Even if I'm still physically capable, I'm not mother material. I'm broke, uneducated, bad at long-term relationships, really bad at math, and I recently let a three-year-old eat six cupcakes in four minutes. Fredreeq's still in shock."

"Well, nobody's perfect. You may not be the best judge of your maternal instincts; ask Ruby if you'd make a good mother."

I couldn't ask Ruby. She was in Asia. And I missed her.

"What my shrink would say," Joey continued, "is that you're childless because you fear turning into your mom. That's what he tells me."

I hadn't realized Joey had baby issues. "What does he say to do about it?"

"Since I can't change her, I have to take a stab at appreciating her so that turning into her doesn't depress me. Realize I'd like her just fine if she weren't my mom. Admit she loves me, however imperfectly. Acknowledge she's not truly bad, she's just off-beat—bad mothers leave their children alone in locked cars on hot summer days with the windows rolled up."

"This is good, therapy by proxy," I said. "Anything else you found out about me?"

"Yes. Your desire to find Annika is a way of wishing someone had rescued you at that age. When you were on your own in a big city, falling for bad men. This wish is unconscious. Consciously, you thought you were having a good time."

I didn't know what to say. Didn't everyone live like that at nineteen?

The rest of the way to San Pedro we talked about Lauren Rodriguez. And Britta and the pill that connected her to Annika, pills Rico was apparently handing out right and left.

"Sounds like he was exporting this to Germany," Joey said. "But the international drug trade—there are syndicates to go through. You don't just hang out a shingle and take orders."

No. You signed on with Vladimir Tcheiko and went global. Little Fish must've recruited Rico when he visited the set. Maybe Rico was eager to show some initiative, putting together his own team in preparation for the big merger.

"Joey," I said, "if someone on the show is into drugs, would you know?"

Joey glanced in the rearview mirror. "Depends on what you mean by 'into.' I've done everything that doesn't involve needles or aerosol cans, but I've never sold, even when I needed money.

Little kink in my moral code. Other people deal them but don't use. On *B.C.* I don't know; I'm the producer, people don't let their hair down around me. Production sucks."

Joey circled the block so Fredreeq could precede us into the Au Pairs par Excellence lot. We parked too, and went into the Laundromat next to the agency, positioning ourselves near the window. If any coin-op customers found it odd that we'd come in to enjoy the view, they didn't mention it.

Fredreeq got out of her Volvo, looked around, then approached a boxy orange vehicle next to her and slowly walked the length of it, touching it. "What's she doing?" I whispered.

"Drawing a line with Wite-Out," Joey whispered.

Fredreeq returned the Wite-Out to her purse and hurried into the agency, emerging seconds later with the secretary-receptionist we'd met the previous week. Joey and I slipped out of the Laundromat and into the empty agency.

File boxes were everywhere, as they'd been the week before. If anything, they'd reproduced. I checked under Marty Otis's metal desk. Even there, boxes. "Joey?" I said.

"Go for it."

"What about you?"

Before she could respond, we heard Fredreeq's voice outside, unnaturally loud. I crawled under the desk, amid boxes, and pulled the desk chair in after me. I was as cramped as I've ever been, but I was hidden. I heard the door swing open and Fredreeq's voice amplify.

"—didn't want you thinking it was me. People so damn irresponsible, no accountability— Where's the phone?" She made a call to her husband, Francis, asking about stores that carried car paint. I wondered where Joey was hiding and told myself not to worry, that she was a toothpick, that her hair took up more space than her body.

Fredreeq sounded prepared to talk indefinitely, but the receptionist eventually told her she had to close up. Thank God. Fredreeq said good-bye, drawers opened and closed, a window cranked shut, a phone machine message changed, and, finally, a key turned in a door.

Uh-oh.

I waited for Joey's faint "Wollie?" before I crawled out from under the desk. It took me a full minute to stand. Was this what arthritis felt like? I looked around and said, "Joey?"

A muffled sound came from a file cabinet. It was a vertical job not much more than four feet tall, moved out from the wall about fifteen inches, due to a fortuitously placed pipe. It rattled and from the back Joey emerged, looking like I felt, hair disheveled and body parts unfolding with difficulty.

"How did you fit back there?" I asked.

"Squatting and bent over. I may have to spend the night at a chiropractor's."

"We may have to spend the night here." I went to the glass front door for a closer look. "What if we need a key to get out? I didn't think about that. Did you?"

"It crossed my mind, but that's not what worries me. It'll be Christmas before we get through these boxes. This is insane. I can't believe I'm asking, but is it worth it?"

"It's worth it. I'm telling you, Marie-Thérèse knows about Annika. If I had a problem, who would I tell? You. This girl is the Joey Rafferty of Annika's life, and in one of these boxes is her address and a phone number."

There were over a hundred boxes. Had these people been in business since World War II? The au pair program hadn't been around nearly that long. I picked one at random, and looked at my watch. In less than seven hours we had to be in Beverly Hills for *B.C.* "Do we leave things tidy?" I asked. "Are we trying to cover our tracks?"

"We could turn a leaf blower loose in here and no one would notice. I say we just start in. Maybe put a check mark on the boxes we've looked at."

It was 5:22 P.M. At 6:49 we turned on the radio to liven things up, and listened to the latest report of volcanic activity on the Big

Island of Hawaii. At 8:03 we stopped the au pair search and began a food search. "Protein bars. Oyster crackers. That's what normal people keep in an office," Joey said. "I bet this place is a front for something."

"I found Sweet 'n Low," I said, rummaging through the receptionist's desk.

"Is that the edible stuff?"

"No, the blue's edible," I said. "This is the pink, cheaper but toxic tasting."

"It's my first breaking and entering. Next time I'll bring snacks."

By eight-thirty, in addition to countless au pair applications, we'd found tax receipts for Marty Otis, yearbooks from Millard High in Wisconsin, and old issues of *Playboy* and *Hustler*.

At nine-fifteen, Joey said, "Eureka."

"You found her?"

"No, I found Polaroids."

I crawled across the icky tan carpet to her. She passed me pictures. People smiled—or not—into the camera, dressed in swimsuits, leotards, or skimpy loungewear. One man in knee socks and boxer shorts wore some sort of harness that reminded me of Margaret, a ferret I'd once known. Not quite pornographic, but not au pair photo collages. The subjects ranged in age from teens to seniors, all body types, races, and genders, and were rated with one, two, or three stars, drawn in the upper corner with a felt pen. Each photo was numbered. "Look at this three-star guy in the Speedo. I think he's worth another half star. You know—" Joey crawled across the carpet. "I bet these numbers correspond to files—I saw a box of files somewhere—"

I didn't stop her. This wasn't getting us closer to Marie-Thérèse, but she was happier now than she'd been in three hours.

"Aha!" she said, moments later. "Quite the entrepreneur. Let's check out this Web site." She seated herself at Marty Otis's desk. "Good. Bills. His address. We'll keep that."

"What's the story?" I asked.

"Wait a second. Let me figure out how this computer—please, God, don't let there be a password—" She logged on to the Internet, still mumbling to herself. "I bet he charges a huge fee on that end and pays chicken feed on this end. Yes! Speedo, on the home page. Hello, Speedo. Mind-boggling what people will do for a few thousand bucks."

"No kidding," I said, thinking about *Biological Clock*. I was glad not to be on camera tonight. Espionage is less stressful than trying to look beautiful, act charming, and keep viewers from changing channels. Of course, if we got stuck in San Pedro and missed the shoot, that would be more stressful. The FBI probably frowned on calling in sick, and calling Simon at all would entail telling him some form of the truth, which—

And then, there it was. The name I'd been seeking so long that once I found it I almost missed it. Small, rounded printing. Marie-Thérèse. Last name DuCroq. Twenty years old. Staying with a family called the Johannessens in Minnesota. Arrived early January.

Elated, I showed the application to Joey, then used the copy machine to reproduce the contact information. We worked quickly now. I got the office back to the approximate state we'd found it in, and Joey tore herself from the computer to deal with the lock on the door.

"This doesn't look so bad," she said. "I mean, you do need a key to open it, but let's try a credit card. Oh. I didn't bring a purse in. Did you?"

I had my backpack. Joey said not to use a card I really needed, so I handed over my Blockbuster Video card, then my Costco membership, and, finally, reluctantly, my library card. When all three were mutilated, I started searching drawers for a spare key.

"You know, Gun Girl never had this hard a time," Joey said, still working the lock. "I realize that was TV, but . . ." She stood back and surveyed the glass. "I suppose it's a bad idea to smash the whole thing."

"Yes. Bad. Try it, though."

"Looks pretty flimsy. I bet I could just—"

For such a skinny thing, Joey was strong. She gave the double doors a shake that simulated a mild earthquake.

It didn't open them, but it did set off the alarm.

34

In my next life, if I'm a woman again, I'm going to be petite. I realize it's a drawback when you're at a rock concert or a parade and trying to see over the person in front of you, but for getting through bathroom windows, it's indispensable. Also, shoes look better in size five than they do in size eleven.

In the bathroom we found the plunger, which we broke while trying to smash the front door. Then we found the window. Joey squeezed through first, barely making it, which should have alerted us, but it's her nature to jump first, ask questions later, and I was distracted, watching our back. I expected armed security personnel to come bursting in—Secret Service, for all I knew, since au pair agencies are regulated by the State Department. When I heard Joey's "All clear" I threw my backpack through the window and followed it, arms first, then head, with my feet balanced on the toilet tank. My head made it. My rib cage didn't. Okay, my breasts.

"Joey, I'm stuck."

"You're not stuck." She grasped my upper arms to pull me into the alley. "Just inhale. No, exhale. On the count of three. One, two—"

"Stop."

"Just try it. Come on. Big breath, then let it all out. Flatten yourself."

I exhaled. It worked. Joey was able to get another six inches of me out into the night air. The downside was that I was stuck tighter. It was an old double window in a half-open position, big enough horizontally for my shoulders, too small vertically for my chest.

"Again," Joey said.

"I can't. This is not physically possible."

"It is."

"It's not."

"It has to be," Joey said. "I did it and you can too."

"You did it because you're Olive Oyl. I'm Betty Boop."

"You're not stuck. You can't be stuck. I won't let you be."

I now saw the kind of toddler Joey had been, forcing the round peg through the square hole with the plastic hammer, breaking the toy. "Joey, I like your can-do attitude, but without a breast reduction, this is it for me. I'm having a little trouble breathing and I might panic."

"No panicking. Okay, we'll put you in reverse. Here we go."

"Ow! Ow! Stop. Don't push. Major pain."

"Sorry." Joey raised her hands and stepped back. She was just a touch below my eye level, in the alley. She looked up and smiled. "Go at your own speed. Plenty of time."

I struggled to get myself back into the bathroom, but all I could do was wiggle the bottom half of me like a mermaid. The windowsill dug into my sweatshirt, bruising my armpits, and random bits of hardware scraped my back. "It's like when you try on a ring that's a little tight and then your knuckle swells up and you can't get it off."

"Canola oil. That's what we need. Or—uh-oh." Joey turned to look down the alleyway. "Is that a car door? Do you see head-lights?"

"I can't see anything from here, I— Okay, go. Run."

Her head whipped around so fast I was hit in the face with a wave of red hair. "Are you nuts? I'm not leaving you here."

"No, listen," I said. "There's no point in both of us getting arrested—"

"We won't. I'll talk our way out of it."

"What if you can't? Someone should be on the outside, arranging bail or whatever."

"I'll be a decoy," she said. "I'll run out front, head them off, they won't know—"

"Great," I said. "I'll be stuck here for the weekend while you're in jail. Sssh. Listen."

We listened. Silence. The alarm had stopped. Did I hear voices in the office behind me? "Joey," I whispered. "Don't argue. Take my backpack and go. No, leave the backpack, but take the stuff on Marie-Thérèse, the folded page—do it. Don't get sentimental on me."

Joey, torn between the unthinkable—abandoning me—and the illogical—sacrificing us both—hesitated. Then she grabbed my backpack, tucked the photocopied page into her jeans pocket, and looked me in the eye. "Tell them you work here, you were working late, you forgot your key. Tell them Marty Otis will confirm it. But stall. I need half an hour." She gave me a fast kiss on the forehead. "Don't worry. I won't leave San Pedro without you."

She slipped down the alley as a voice behind me in the bathroom said, "Hold it right there. Don't move."

"Don't worry," I said.

The voices in the bathroom turned out to be two people, from the security company. I assured them that I wasn't a dangerous criminal and that I was, incidentally, female, something the bottom half of me apparently didn't make clear. One of them actually informed me that my feet, standing on the toilet tank in sneakers, were men's feet. I suggested they reach under my heavy sweatshirt and check out my breasts, straining to get through the window. They declined. I told them to come around to the alley and meet the rest of me. One did. The other stayed behind to guard my legs.

A flashlight appeared first, then a uniformed woman, her hair in a tight ponytail that meant business. She shone the light in my face. "Bernie, she's right! She's female! You stuck?" I nodded. "Bernie, she's stuck!" She pointed the flashlight at the window. "You armed?"

"Heavens, no, I don't like guns. I was here working, going through that mountain of boxes you waded through." This was true enough. "And the receptionist locked me in, not knowing I was here, and I couldn't find the key and I accidentally set off the alarm. Um, Ms.—"

"Sims. Wait a second. You sound like—" The light blinded me, and I heard an gasp. "Criminy. It's you. Bernie! It's the woman from that show—that late show—what's it called?"

"Biological Clock," I said.

"Biological Clock! It's her. The blond one."

"What?" Bernie's voice, muffled, came back.

"That reality show, where we pick which ones should have a baby!"

"What about it?"

"It's her, the blonde!" The light hit my face again. "You work here? You're a TV star."

"We all have day jobs," I said. "We get paid for the show, but not a huge amount."

A second flashlight came around the corner. Another uniform, this one a guy with close-shaved hair. Another light in my face. Then: "Who's she supposed to be?"

"The one on that TV show, *Biological Clock*. The blond contestant."

"Who, her? You're nuts. She doesn't look anything like her."

I said, "We wear a lot of makeup. Everyone on TV does."

"No kidding," Ms. Sims said. "I saw Courtney Thorne-Smith one time in Century City and you couldn't even tell it was her."

Bernie was not convinced. Nor was he willing to accept at face value my story about working late. And neither of them seemed to understand how a person who turned up on television could also turn up in San Pedro.

"My backpack's on the ground there," I said. "You're welcome to check out my ID, but first could you help me out of this window, because I actually have to get to the set—"

"No," Bernie said.

"Why not?"

"Liability. We're not trained for that sort of thing."

"It doesn't take much training," I said. "If you go around inside and grab my legs—"

"No. If something happened, you could sue."

"I won't. I promise."

Bernie shook his head. "You might."

I closed my eyes, then opened them. "Bernie, people die of asphyxiation when their bodies are stuck in positions that interfere with their breathing. I'm not saying that will happen here, but I'm not feeling well. I could pass out, and then it will be tough getting me out of here because I'll be unconscious and unable to assist in my own rescue."

The woman spoke up. "She's right, Bernie. That's how Jesus Christ died. He was hanging on the cross so long he couldn't get air to his lungs."

"We're not authorized to physically engage with—"

"Bernie," I said, "never mind that I have a show to do. Have you heard of Good Samaritan laws? You can't ignore someone whose life is in danger, you have to help if you're able, or you're criminally responsible. Body parts might have to be amputated if I hang here much longer." I was straying from the truth, but my feet did happen to be asleep.

"Bernie," Ms. Sims said, "for gosh sakes, let's get her out. Call it in and give me a hand."

"Call it in?" I asked. "To whom? Who are you calling?" But Bernie was already on the phone and his partner was on her way inside.

Good Samaritan Sims lacked the upper-body strength to pull me through the window, and Bernie, impervious to pleas, wouldn't help. So we settled in to wait for the Harbor Division police. I felt like a West African goliath frog, whose throat swells to five times its size in order to croak. I felt like a circus woman, preparing to be shot out of a cannon. I felt like an idiot. My only comfort was that Simon was not witnessing this.

There's a psychotherapeutic technique called rebirthing that was big in the 1980s or '90s, where a therapist hypnotizes you so that you can reexperience the trip down the birth canal in order to work through the trauma of it all. I had never done this technique. Now, thanks to two San Pedro law enforcement officers pulling with all their strength, I would never have to.

Eventually, I was sitting at the receptionist's desk of Au Pairs par Excellence, rubbing under my arms and repeating the story I'd told the security response team, this time implying without actually saying "I work here."

The cops listened with no indication of whether they believed me. They were mildly interested to learn I was a contestant on a reality TV show, which I needed to get to—fast. They were somewhat more interested in how far I was from West Hollywood, my home address. Their attitude was as polite and respectful as one could ask of two men who had intimate knowledge of my waist and thighs and size eleven feet.

"Do you have any proof that you work here?" the younger of the two asked. He had a curly-haired cherubic look; I pictured him sitting for Leonardo da Vinci, the model for the archangel who tells the Virgin Mary the good news about her pregnancy.

"Like a paycheck or a time sheet?" I said. "Gosh, I don't. You can call Marty Otis. He runs the show. Here's his home number—" I pointed to the speed-dial list on the telephone, where "Marty—home" was listed as No. 4, right between FedEx and Gianni's Pizza. I was pleased with myself for having noticed it and hoped I gave the impression of familiarity with the office.

"Is that the 9032 number?" Bernie, of the security company, asked. "That's what we got on file. Already tried it. Got a machine."

The older cop, Asian, tired-looking, and a little crabby, nodded.

He tried the number, left a message for Marty Otis, then turned to Bernie. "All right, we're headed back to the station. You people got keys, right? You can lock up after us."

"So you're all finished with me?" I asked.

"No, you'll come with us."

I didn't ask if I was under arrest. It's the kind of thing Joey or Fredreeq would get clear on right away, but I'd function better pretending we were buddies driving to the station to sort out details. I'd hate for them to go into good cop, bad cop mode, when we were doing okay with good cop, crabby cop.

There were two cars in the seedy parking lot, neither of which was Joey's husband's BMW. No one asked me which car was mine, which was good, because I had no idea how to explain being without wheels so far from home.

In the back seat of the squad car, I hugged my backpack. It was the middle of the night. I was in San Pedro being transported to God knows where, some distance from the last place my friends had seen me, by police officers who probably did not consider me one of the good guys, in a vehicle that did not smell particularly . . . fresh. At least I was an American citizen and spoke English without an accent. Annika, in a similar situation, might have been a lot more scared than I was, and I was, frankly, scared.

Simon. Many hours ago, he'd told me to call him. I'd wanted to, but I'd been too busy trespassing, burgling, and misleading the police to find the right moment. Maybe after my sentencing hearing I'd get back to him.

LAPD Harbor Division had an actual building, more substantial than the LAPD West Valley trailers, although for a potential suspect, "substantial" isn't a big selling point. But Curly and Crabby walked me past the building to a trailer, a detectives' office much like Detective Cziemanski's. Few of the desks were manned or womanned at this hour. I was shown to a hard wooden chair and told to wait, while my captors did paperwork and checked voice mail. I brought up again the necessity of getting back to Los Angeles and *Biological Clock* as fast as possible, but no one got too excited about it.

I studied the carpet, not the teal blue I'd come to expect, but a nice dirt gray. I thought of Prana, what her reaction would be if she were awakened with the news that her daughter was in jail in San Pedro. She might be proud. She'd probably have some Zen-like take on it, that this was karmically necessary for my personal growth, that there are no accidents, that—

"That was your boss," the older office said, hanging up the phone. "Says you were authorized to be there. Next time take your key, save some trouble. Stay out of windows."

I stood. "I'm free to go? Really? That's . . . great."

"Wait around, we'll get you a ride back to your car."

Uh-oh.

Officer Crabby left. I called Joey's cell phone and got voice mail. This was not surprising, since Joey's cell phone often lies around forgotten on her kitchen table. I wondered how I'd explain a missing car, and if I'd have to fill out a stolen car report, and whether that would be perjury, and then, since Joey would be long gone, having given up hope of ever finding me, if there was anyone else who'd come from L.A. to give me a ride, since it was cheaper to charter a yacht from San Pedro than to take a cab. What was I doing in this godforsaken place?

I looked over at the next desk, at Good Cop Curly, diligently filling out reports, and had a moment of divine inspiration.

"Officer?" I said. Curly looked up. He had an approachable face. I prayed for the ability to lie to it. "The reason I was working late is there's been an accusation about one of our au pairs, and if it's true, I'm worried about her taking care of kids."

The face continued to look open for business. I explained the au pair program, and then—here's the sort of thing I appreciate myself for sometimes—I pulled out of my backpack the *Führungszeugnis* I'd been carrying around for days. "We know she has a police record, but for what? If it's littering, that can wait till Monday. If it's child molestation, I have to know, because then every day she's with children is on my conscience."

Curly took the document and looked at his watch. "Germany's nine hours ahead," I said. He nodded. Crabby stuck his head in the doorway and told me I had a ride. Curly told me to wait in the lobby. Well, I'd bought myself a few minutes in which to concoct a car story.

I didn't need them. In the lobby, a familiar voice and a mass of red hair was chatting up the officer at the front desk. I went weak with relief, and waited for the officer to pause for breath. ". . . want to remember," he was saying, "is a drug case, that goes to a detective, but if it turns into murder, that could get it bumped to Robbery-Homicide. Now those guys, they just want to close their case. If they're tracking a murder suspect, they don't stop to arrest jaywalkers, see what I'm saying, unless the jaywalker's useful to them."

"Joey?" I said.

"Gee whiz, Wollie," she said, turning. "I drove over to your work to pick you up, and the security guys said you were here. What's up?"

"Gee whiz yourself," I said, pulling her aside. "What did you do, break into Marty Otis's house and murder him so you could answer his phone?"

"What a good idea. No, I went and banged on his door and said I had his box of photos and if he did us one small favor, I wouldn't deliver them to the INS or the IRS."

Before she could explain further, Officer Curly appeared. "Got lucky," he said. "I faxed a request to Germany and someone in the office there spoke English, took pity on me. It helps my last name is Kubertschak. Here's the deal. This girl doesn't have what we'd consider a record. She had a boyfriend—" He checked his notepad. "Klaus Reichert, who was a member of a political group in Berlin suspected of ties to arms dealers in Saudi Arabia."

I swallowed. "But she's not an arms dealer herself, right? Or part of this group?"

He shook his head. "I'm not clear if the boyfriend even got charged with anything. But someone filed a report, and that's why her name's in the computer. Up to you whether that makes her nanny material."

I thanked him. Joey said good-bye to the officer at the desk, and we hurried out to the parking area, indicated by a fence, where Elliot's BMW sat.

"Wollie!"

A man stepped out from behind a van next to the BMW. A light went on, and I heard a whirring noise, subliminally familiar. A video camera. I experienced confusion, the instinct to hide warring with my recent training to smile and be interesting.

"How was jail, Wollie?" the voice behind the camera asked. "What's the charge?"

Joey stepped in front of me. "No arrest, no story," she said. "No paparazzi. Okay?"

With his free hand, the camera guy reached to move Joey aside, grabbing her arm. Hard. Joey knocked his hand away, then turned and elbowed him in the side. Harder.

He fell against her car and lost his balance. But he held on to the camera, even as it bashed into the BMW on its way to the ground. Joey had her hands up, ready for him to stand and charge. He lay on the ground, blinking. Then he brought the camera to his face and continued filming.

To my right, something flashed. I turned to see a woman in the van, taking pictures.

I grabbed Joey's arm. "Let's go."

Joey didn't resist. She pointed her keys at the BMW. The man hauled himself up and away from the car as we got in, still filming. The woman in the van snapped pictures.

On the van's side, I saw the words "P's Plumbers."

35

"**S**orry," Joey said. "It just came out of me. I've been taking double classes at Krav Maga." She didn't look sorry. She looked revved up on adrenaline and danger, red hair all over the place, driving onto the 405 like a maniac. "Body shots," she said. "We worked on them Wednesday, I took a level-two class by mistake. I think I got his liver. Or maybe he had a preexisting condition, to topple over like that. He didn't even fight back. I could've taken him."

"Joey, he didn't want to 'take' us. He wanted to take pictures of us. Film us." I thought about the plumbing van. Could my plumbers and stalkers be—paparazzi?

"Okay, I know. But I reacted, Wollie, I didn't freeze. It's one thing to practice, but to react when it really happens—I always think I'm gonna be the deer caught in the headlights."

I'd never thought of Joey as the deer caught in the headlights. But I noticed the white scar on her cheek and remembered that once in her life, she hadn't reacted. "Thanks for rescuing me," I said. "From him. From getting arrested. Sorry you had to resort to blackmail and assault to do it. And I'm extremely sorry about the damage to Elliot's car."

"He'll get over it. Eventually. Okay, so Marty Otis? He's running an agency within an agency. Green-card marriages.

Americans willing to get married and have sex and live with strangers from foreign countries for a year or two for lots of money. Or some money. There's a sliding scale, based on physical attractiveness."

I said, "Could this be something Annika stumbled onto and—"

"No." Joey shook her head. "He never met Annika. He got anonymous phone calls about drug use and some police problem in Germany and he blew them off because he didn't want to call the host family, file reports, attract attention. Same with her disappearance. This guy's all about staying under the radar. The agency gives him cover for overseas phone calls and operating expenses, but the au pairs aren't part of the green-card scam."

"He just told you all this? And do you believe him?"

"Yes. It's what I was talking to that cop about. There's a hierarchy to crime. Homicide detectives don't go after shoplifters, and on the other side of the fence, Marty isn't going to get all sweaty over his little green cards if he's just kidnapped someone. And he was sweaty. So I told him I only cared about Annika and keeping you out of jail, and he relaxed. I was nice. With a little encouragement, people love to talk about their work. Even sleazos."

I closed my eyes and melted into the heated leather seat. One short night's work resulting in violence, deception, destruction of property—albeit a plunger—all for a phone number. A doubt assailed me. What if Annika truly didn't want to be found? What if it wasn't just a case of her being noble, worrying about me? "At least we know Annika's not a criminal," I said. "She's a bad judge of boyfriends, but that's it. Well, and she lied on her au pair application."

"She's a bad judge of girlfriends too," Joey said. "She told Britta her dark secret. And Britta told the agency, which left Annika open to blackmail. Deportation. Except that Marty Otis wasn't blackmailing her. So who was?"

Little Fish, I thought. I had another thought, then, one far less palatable. The FBI.

Biological Clock had found, for once, a restaurant with class. Etude in Beverly Hills, tiny and chic, was willing to accommodate the show after hours. We got there a half hour late, before things had got under way. I'd never been on the set when not actually working, and I was nervous about my appearance. The disguise Fredreeq had put together for me, glasses and a cloche hat, was in the trunk of Fredreeq's car, an oversight on everyone's part. The best I could do at this point was my sweatshirt with the hood pulled up.

The shoot was outside, a garden warmed by standing heat lamps, yet cold enough to justify my hooded head. Still, my appearance was odd. I could tell by the way Etude's owner turned us away, until Joey identified herself as the show's producer and asked that I be seated at an out-of-the-way table. There were only nine tables, so out-of-the-way was relative, but to my great relief, no one paid attention to me. The other diners were "fillers," friends of the owner, and the cast and crew were too preoccupied to notice background players. I might be wiggy from a night in San Pedro, but I could still, apparently, spy.

I turned on my phone and listened to three voice-mail messages from Simon, each one more peremptory than the one before, the third one telling me to follow standard operating procedure tonight and all of them telling me to call him. I turned off my phone. The last thing I needed was to explain the last seven hours to the Feds. I was alone now, Joey having gone to deal with production details, so I began standard operating procedure, checking around for Beverly Hills shopping bags and listening for European accents. Etude did not have a working pay phone, according to my waiter, so I didn't have to deal with that. Meanwhile, the evening's couple and expert took their places at a table Paul had lit with a cliplight attached to a tree. A bottle of Takei Sake awaited them.

The contestants tonight were Vaclav and Savannah.

Savannah was a knockout. I'd seen her on television, on the Web site, in *TV Guide,* and twice in person, but I'd never seen

her like this. She looked Old Hollywood, fine-featured and radiant, perfectly made up. Her dress was forties, her red hair swept
over one eye à la Veronica Lake. She would have beautiful children. On visuals alone, she had my vote.

Vaclav seemed improved by his close proximity to her. I'd worried that he was too foreign for the TV audience to warm up to,
but tonight he seemed dashing and urbane. A lovely, sophisticated couple. I imagined that Savannah had the same improving
effect on Henry and Carlito. Not only would viewers want her to
reproduce, they'd want her to be their mom.

Across from them sat a generously proportioned woman in a
tweed suit and red turtleneck that suggested Wisconsin. I tried,
without success, to imagine her manufacturing drugs. Cheese,
maybe. When the camera went on, she smiled into it. "Hello, I'm
Ursula Fitzgerald-Camacho, a personal educational consultant,
here to shed light on a topic that many pre-parents do not find
stimulating."

"As long as *you're* stimulating, Ursula," Vaclav said, giving a
throaty laugh.

Savannah said something to Vaclav that sounded like Russian,
which produced another laugh from him, and an invitation to
Ursula to continue.

Ursula's smile faltered. "Education in California is one of the
most complex issues our elected officials grapple with. Sacramento,
like every state capital, must draft a budget that accommodates un-
funded federal mandates, demanding fiscal sacrifice—"

"Cut!" Bing yelled. "Sweetie. Words that bore us: 'Fiscal.'
'Budget.' 'Elected officials.' The only sacrifice we want to hear
about is human sacrifice, virgins in the rain forest, that kind of
thing. Start again. Action!"

Ursula's smile died, but she launched into a dissertation on
public versus private schools. I was distracted from this important topic by a woman one table over, shifting in her seat.
Revealing, under her chair, a shopping bag.

". . . study elementary school test scores to determine which
neighborhood suits you," Ursula was saying.

"We have to move to have a child?" Savannah asked. Good question, I thought.

"No, dear, only to educate the child. Think Harvard, then work backward. California ranks poorly in pupil-per-teacher ratio nationwide, and L.A. Unified is—"

"Cut," Bing yelled. "Sweetheart: ratios, nationwide, nobody cares. Make it sexy. Also, you got something green on the corner of your mouth."

I leaned down to get a better look at the shopping bag. Fendi, Hugo Boss, Ermenegildo Zegna: any of these would indicate a dead drop. And the people at the table, a nice middle-aged couple, would they be Little Fish's customers or employees? If I could just see the shopping bag's logo—

"—difference between public schools is considerable," Ursula was saying.

"So's the difference in rent between neighborhoods," Savannah said. "For what it costs to move to Beverly Hills, you could afford private school."

Another good point, I thought, and slid out of my chair. Ursula agreed, noting that rent saved by living in a less desirable neighborhood could add up to an annual twelve grand, which bought a year of preschool, five half days per week, with snacks.

What kind of snacks? I thought. Caviar? Dom Pérignon? I crouched between tables, straining to see Bing's camera. I didn't want to show up in the background of his shot. But Bing was on the move, so I waited, pretending to tie my shoe. I thought of Mrs. Rodriguez and Mrs. Glück, two women who'd helped with homework, packed lunches, gone to track meets, band practices, dance rehearsals, day after day for years. Now, having signed off on the last algebra assignment, term paper, college application, these soccer and *fussball* moms found themselves filling out police reports.

"The young brain," Vaclav said loudly, "is a sponge. Languages must be learned before nerve endings myelinate—"

"Vaclav!" Bing yelled. "No nerve endings, no sponges, no science words no one knows. Jesus Christ, it's like *Face the Nation* tonight."

Bing stopped moving, so I approached my quarry in a crouch reminiscent of a runner coming out of the starting blocks. It was hell on my back. I neared the table. The woman uncrossed her legs and the tablecloth shifted, obscuring the shopping bag.

A waiter with a large tray weaved around tables, delivering soup to one and all, intoning, "Lobster bisque" in hushed tones. I hoped he couldn't see me.

". . . overwhelming for pre-parents," Ursula said. "But look at the top ten best-paying jobs: physician, lawyer, pilot, pharmacist, marketing exec, architect, and the four engineers: aerospace, chemical, electrical, mechanical. Isn't that what we want for our kids?"

My God, was it? I hadn't given this any thought at all. I had no career goals for my preconceived child. The realization coincided with a severe leg cramp. I gasped, then straightened up to relieve it, and bumped into the waiter.

Soup bowls slid off the tray, sending eddies of lobster bisque into the air and onto the shopping-bag table, the waiter, and me. The bowls and tray made a lot of noise hitting the ground.

"Cut!"

All eyes turned our way. I flexed my foot, working out my leg cramp, and lowered my head, pulling the sweatshirt hood tighter around my face. The shopping-bag woman was making little whimpering noises. Her companion was swearing. The waiter was on his knees picking up soup bowls. My leg cramp eased, and I crouched to help him. The shopping bag under his companion's chair revealed its logo: Macy's. Fine. These people weren't drug dealers.

"Wollie?" Bing yelled. "What the hell are you doing here?"

I looked up. Bing Wooster and his broken fingers and his Betacam loomed above me. He was joined by Vaclav and Savannah, and then Paul. So much for my disguise. I smiled at them. Bing told everyone to take five, and walked off in disgust. Vaclav held out a hand to help me up.

I found myself face to face with Savannah Brook. Or chest to face, considering her lack of height. She smiled and held out her hand, as if meeting me for the first time. I wiped my hand on my sweatshirt, cleansing it of lobster bisque, and shook hers.

She didn't let go. She pulled me in close and said softly, "You better back off, bitch. I'm going to take you down."

I pulled my hand out of hers and backed up. She was smiling again. She said something to Vaclav in the eastern European language, and he said something back and they both laughed. What did she think I was doing here? I turned, apologized to the shopping-bag people, and started back to my own table, feeling sick, embarrassed, tall, and soup-drenched. And stupid. In a nice restaurant, a hooded sweatshirt is as inconspicuous as a nun's habit. What was I—

"Hi, Wollie."

Isaac was sitting at my table. Our huge sound guy, his trademark headset covering his ears as if he expected airplanes to land. I sat, shocked. In two months, Isaac had barely uttered my name, let alone initiated conversation. "Hi, Isaac," I said.

He took off his headset. "Whatcha doing?"

"Just . . . hanging out." I stared, wondering what had prompted this overture. Maybe it was my civilian clothes, my lack of circus makeup, the complete spectacle I'd just made of myself. Something occurred to me. "Isaac, I never asked you: do you have any thoughts on what happened to Annika? Our Annika, Annika Glück?"

"I always figured she found out about her boyfriend."

"Her boyfriend? Rico? What about him?"

"Catting around. Getting it on with Savannah."

My mouth dropped open. "R-really? You know this for a fact?"

"Heard Savannah talking to Venus while they were doing her roots." Isaac nodded toward an orange-and-purple-haired woman across the garden, sitting alone with a makeup kit. Venus,

Fredreeq's archrival. "Savannah said, Don't knock it till you try it. He's fifteen years younger than her. She made him wear a rubber, though, because he was getting it all over town."

Well, yuck. I started to ask Isaac if he'd recorded this incriminating conversation, but Bing yelled, "Let's go!" and Isaac lumbered off.

Savannah and Rico. I remembered how she'd raced into the Krav Maga studio, turning on the TV the day his disappearance hit the news. What did this mean in terms of Annika?

I wondered about several things over the next few hours, including what I was doing on the set, now that my cover was blown. Or was it blown? Did anyone know why I was here? Paul dropped by to say hi, as did Vaclav. Vaclav was the only one with a European accent; there were no more shopping bags, no pay phones. Either it was a slow night on the drug circuit or Little Fish wasn't there. Or Little Fish was there but had canceled all dead drops.

By three A.M. it was a wrap. The work nights were getting shorter, as if Bing's shooting style was losing steam along with the show's ratings. I felt both frustration and relief. I'd learned zip for the FBI, I was no closer to Annika, but I could at least get some sleep.

"If only Savannah had been Rico's last date," I said to Joey, on the way home, "that would interest the cops. And then I'd point out that Annika had introduced them, which would make it a love triangle, with two of the three sides disappearing within a week of each other—"

"How do you know she wasn't his last date?" Joey asked.

"Rico told his mom he was seeing a blonde."

Joey looked at me, her eyes wide. "Savannah's blond."

"What?"

"She's blond." Joey looked back to the road. "Bing wanted a blonde, a brunette, and a redhead so the audience could keep you guys straight. They decided your hair was too thin, it wouldn't survive coloring, so they made Savannah go red."

"My God," I said.

Savannah was beautiful. She knew three languages: English, French, and whatever it was she'd spoken to Vaclav in.

And she was blond. She was the bad blonde, the mystery girl-friend of Rico Rodriguez, the last known person to see him alive.

36

I **wanted to** drive straight to the cops, but Joey dissuaded me.

"We stumble in at three A.M., saying Rico Rodriguez slept with a redhead who dyes her hair, according to some sound guy on some TV show, and some desk cop writes this on a Post-it, and that's the end of it. We need a hard-core theory that makes sense of things, and hard-core evidence to back it up. But I agree, it's the cops we have to go to, if whatever happened to Annika happened to Rico. I don't think the Feds are interested in Rico, or we'd have heard it on the news. They're always doing press conferences. I'll drop you at home, then head to the production office and check out Savannah's *B.C.* application for clues. I'm too wired to sleep."

There was no one lurking on my block. I was sure now that the previous lurkers were the plumber paparazzi, that my street, at least, was safe from whatever danger Annika had hinted at in her e-mail. That I could sleep tonight.

Except that my mother was waiting up for me.

"Green tea," she said. "I had a bit too much, so I'm awake. You're out of champagne."

"It's not a staple item in my life, Prana. No sign of plumbers, I take it?"

"No, but the mailman came to the door, as it was too much

mail for the box. All those holiday catalogs. Such a waste of trees. How did it go in San Pedro, dear?"

I looked up in surprise, but she seemed interested, not like she was about to criticize my hair but like she really wanted to know. So I joined her in the living room. I told her about my night. Breaking and entering, near arrest, Joey's assault on the photographer.

Prana nodded placidly. "I practiced civil disobedience with you in utero. Not with P.B., he gave me morning sickness, but you were a cooperative fetus. They put me on the front lines. The media loved it, the pregnant woman and the military industrial complex. Theo has clippings. Did I spot a Cabernet in the kitchen? I prefer white, but I'm having sleep issues . . ."

I left June Cleaver to her memories and went in search of wine and pajamas. My body ached, from being pilloried in a bathroom window, frozen at an outdoor restaurant, tortured at Krav Maga days before. If I were a tadpole, I could regenerate limbs. Four new ones would do.

I brought the Cabernet and wineglasses into the living room to find my mother surrounded by her Tarot cards in a pattern I'd seen all my life, a circle within a circle within a circle. "Whose fate are you reading now?" I asked, sitting opposite her.

"Your German friend."

"Annika? Really? She doesn't have to be here for it to work?"

"No, I'm good at remote readings. I often lay out cards for you and your brother."

I felt strangely pleased. Sandalwood incense and the tuneless bell-like music on the CD player filled the room, calming me. My mother had been New Age before the phrase had been coined. It was a language I'd turned a deaf ear to, wanting to fit in with my friends whose mothers read *Reader's Digest*, not Tarot cards. "What do they say?" I asked.

My mother stared at her layout, then with one arm movement swept it aside. "The answers are in her own backyard." She picked up her wineglass, took a sniff, and made a face.

"Meaning?"

"Your friend must return home or what she left unfinished will haunt her forever. The lessons we choose not to learn recur, again and again, until we surrender to them."

Like math, I thought.

"You, however, must stay out of it, Wollstonecraft. Her back-yard is not yours. There is Evil present. My guides are clear on this matter."

The dreaded guides. There was, I knew from experience, no way to win an argument with my mother's guides. Arguing with almost anyone in the spirit world is fruitless. My eyes started to glaze over, drifting across the Tarot cards. Then an image jumped out at me.

♑

I popped up out of my chair and shrieked.

"Mom—Prana—what is this?"

"The Devil."

"This little squiggle down here at the bottom? That's the Devil?"

She put on her reading glasses and took the card. "No, that's the symbol for Capricorn. The Devil, the card you're holding, is asso-ciated with the Egyptian sun deity, Ra, and with Pan, half man and half goat, which in turn connects to Capricorn, the goat. A very sexual card."

"I'm sorry, you're losing me. Capricorn's astrology, isn't it?"

My mother took off her reading glasses and sighed. "Of course. Tarot embraces astrology, numerology, mythology—"

"So if someone uses that symbol, does it mean they're into Tarot cards?"

"Not at all. Astrology is everywhere—dinnerware, stationery, toothbrushes. Well, look at what you're wearing."

My flannel pajamas. There it was, the stylized little squiggle against the black background, alongside a goat. ♑ On my left sleeve, knee, chest, the cuff of my pants. I'd seen it hundreds of times. "When is Capricorn?" I asked. "What month?"

"My God, you're ignorant. Next month. It follows Sagittarius. Winter solstice through mid-January. Christmas. Jesus was a Capricorn, didn't you ever hear that?"

I sat, trying to process information. "What if you saw this used as a logo, on a pill, something like Ecstasy? The drug, not the state of bliss."

"Thank you, I live in an ashram, not a rest home. It could signify the insight and revelry of Pan and Dionysus, or it could be the sun sign of the pill manufacturer."

"Wouldn't that be a little risky, for a drug dealer? A signature of sorts?"

"Drug dealers, in my experience, are not particularly risk-averse. And they tend toward large egos. Speaking of ego, Wollie, this television enterprise—"

"Forget that for a minute—"

"Is the City of Angels so bereft of men you need to seek one on television? It wasn't that way for me, I assure you."

"You don't need to assure me. I was there, Mom. I grew up with you."

"Then perhaps you should have taken notes."

"For the record," I snapped, "I was engaged. Recently. To a married man. Who has a child, so there was going to be a custody issue, and he was a convicted felon, so he was going to lose her, so instead, he left me. Happy?"

My mother's face brightened. "Intriguing. This isn't the man who came to brunch?"

"No. That was Simon."

"*He's* not one of these reality people, is he? By the way, he left messages on your machine. I'd watch myself with him, if I were you. Those intense, testosterone-driven men, even one in the Peace Corps—"

"Simon's not in the Peace Corps. He's an FBI agent."

I'd done it. I'd rendered my mother speechless. But not motionless. She rose from the sofa, like a goddess out of the sea. Aphrodite, I think. She found her voice. "You're dating—*Feds?*"

"One date. One Fed."

She spat out the words. "My father—your grandfather— smoked a cigar with Fidel Castro. I followed Carlos Castaneda into the rain forest. This is your bloodline. For you to desecrate it by— Why not join the Marines and be done with it?" She turned and swept out of the room in the manner of Isadora Duncan, caftan swirling.

I sat on the sofa and closed my eyes. I opened them. I looked at my watch. Still too early to call Marie-Thérèse, even with the time difference. But not by much. I closed my eyes again.

The next thing I knew, the sun had found its way onto my face through the curtainless living room window, waking me. I was on my second cup of coffee before I realized my mother had packed up and gone.

37

At seven A.M. I left a message on the machine of the Johannessen family in Minnesota, asking that their au pair, Marie-Thérèse, call me anytime, collect, concerning our mutual friend, Annika, about whom I was worried.

I turned on my computer and looked for a new e-mail from Annika. Nothing. I looked again at the old one. "It will be over soon." Three days old, those words. Was it over already? Time was running out. Biological clocks, ticking clocks, the sun moving from Sagittarius to Capricorn, the sun approaching its eclipse, twenty-eight shopping days till Christmas, missing persons not found in the first forty-eight hours not getting found at all.

I called Joey to ask if Savannah's work application showed her birthday, to see if she was a Capricorn. Joey didn't answer. Sleeping, probably. I should've been sleeping too, but thoughts leaped in my head like frogs. Frogs. Rex Stetson and Tricia, his bride, would return—I looked at a calendar. My God. Impossible. Tomorrow.

The phone rang. "Had breakfast?" Simon asked.

"I barely—"

"Don't. I'll pick you up in ten minutes."

"Yeah, but—"

Simon was not big on chatter. In fact, he hung up on me. Maybe it was his seven calls I'd neglected to return, or maybe he wasn't a morning person. Or maybe, as we had a contract, as I was a cooperating witness, this was a business breakfast. One I didn't have time for. I'd suggest debriefing each other or whatever in the car, over doughnuts, so I could get to work.

Eleven minutes later I was outside my building in my best paint clothes, wearing makeup. Not a lot of makeup, because I didn't want to look like I cared. I did care. My nerve endings buzzed. The Bentley pulled up, and Simon reached across and opened the passenger door for me from the inside. Aha. We were progressing. The last time he'd gotten out of the car to open my door. The next time I'd open my own door.

If there was a next time.

The car was heated, a good contrast to the nippy November morning air. I got in, said hello, went for my seat belt, and Simon went for me.

The thing about morning kissing is that people tend to taste more like toothpaste than, for instance, red wine, which lends it a certain reality. You can't say, "I was carried away by the spearmint." But I was. That, the smell of shaving cream, whatever he used to starch his shirts had aphrodisiacal properties. The smells were cool, his body was warm, his mouth was cool, the car was warm. Even with the discomfort of the console between us, it was heaven. If one were considering making out in a Bentley, I'd recommend it.

As suddenly as it began, it ended. He pulled back to study me, his face unreadable. He said, "What are you hungry for?"

I didn't say anything.

That made him laugh. "I'm talking breakfast," he said.

"I'm not a breakfast eater."

"That's gotta change," he said, starting up the car. "Breakfast is key."

"To what? Anyhow, I don't have time to eat. I have to get to work, my day job."

"Tell me about this mural," he said.

"There's nothing to tell. It's visual. Frogs. I'm serious, I don't have time to eat; can't we discuss things in the car?"

"Start talking," he said, but he pulled away from the curb.

"Okay. Savannah Brook is Rico's blond girlfriend, the one he had a date with on Saturday night. Either she's working for Little Fish, or she is Little Fish—you know which. I think she's Little Fish. Here's my theory: Savannah met Annika and Rico on the set and offered them jobs. Annika was going back to Germany soon, she'd be a natural courier, and both she and Rico were students and Euphoria, this big-deal drug, this miracle, it's big on campuses. Rico said yes, but Annika said no. Savannah threatened Annika with deportation, and threatened her mother. That's where you guys came in. And when Annika disappeared. Maybe Savannah turned her in to Immigration, got her deported, and maybe you don't know this because maybe their guys didn't tell your guys. Or maybe Annika ran away and Savannah freaked out and sent people to Germany to kidnap Annika's mother, to ensure that Annika would keep her mouth shut. Or maybe Savannah kidnapped Annika *and* her mother, but three days ago Annika got ahold of a computer, for five minutes, and she wrote to me, because . . . all right, as theories go, it's got some holes, it's a little sloppy, but some of it must be right."

He drove in silence, his face impassive behind his sunglasses.

"Well, damn it. Tell me I'm right about something."

"You're right about a lot." He came to a light and shifted gears. Traffic was heavy on Santa Monica. "Tonight, *Biological Clock* shoots in the back room of a restaurant called Fini, in Culver City. This is where the big meeting gets set up. You'll be wearing a wire. Shooting starts at seven. I want you there at five."

"Five o'clock? Impossible. I'll be knee-deep in frogs at five."

"Extricate yourself," he said. "I want you on the set at five."

"No."

His head turned so fast I thought he'd hurt himself. If his dictatorial manner surprised me, my response surprised him more.

He must be high up in the food chain, I decided, to be so shocked at the word no.

"I quit," I said. "I'm terrible at this. Everyone on the set last night recognized me, I haven't helped you, I haven't told you anything you didn't already know. And you haven't told me anything, period. I don't believe you're any closer to finding Annika than I am on my own, and I have to take it on faith that you're looking at all. You know all about me, but I know nothing about you, what's going on with you, because you get to lie and shut down and clam up, and I've been dating men like you for years, I don't need to work for one of you."

Simon did a fast right. Horns blared as the Bentley cut off a car in the next lane and came to a screeching halt in front of a fire hydrant. He turned off the ignition, got his seat belt off in one snap, and threw his sunglasses on the dashboard. His blue eyes turned on me.

"There's nothing I wouldn't tell you if I didn't have ethical considerations. I do have them. I'm not apologizing. I like what I do. I believe in it. But I have a big conflict of interest here, and what's going on with me is I'm doing every goddamn thing I can think of to make this work, I'm bending rules on both sides, and I still don't know if I can pull off what I need to pull off, and I have no idea if you'll want to know me when it's over."

"Why will you want to know me?" I asked.

By way of answering, he reached over and pulled me to him. We didn't kiss. I could barely breathe. My face was mashed into his tie, my rib cage was getting crushed right where I'd been stuck in a bathroom window, and there was that console thing between us and a gun attached to his waist where one of my hands held on to him, but love is a strange thing.

Love. That word he was whispering in my ear. It covers a multitude of sins and a lot of other things. Pain. Awkwardness. Doubt.

Half an hour later he pulled into a parking lot near Hugo's and smiled at the attendant, who stared at us like a monk greeting the pope, nearly weeping over the Bentley. It's only the cheap Bentley, I could've told him, but why spoil his day?

The "L" word, once said, changes things. There are people who throw it around like salt on popcorn. Others are more comfortable with profanity than endearments. I'd have bet Simon was in the latter camp, that I'd heard it wrong, that he must've said, "dove" or "glove." But I couldn't come up with a good reason for someone to whisper "glove" with such heat.

I felt myself undergoing metamorphosis.

Simon told our waiter to bring us two spinach-and-mushroom egg-white omelets with sides of fruit, and that brought me back to earth. It's one thing to hear someone say "love" and another to let them order your breakfast.

"And pancakes for me," I said, snapping my menu shut. Simon smiled, but he didn't say anything until the waiter had gone. We were back in business. I was a CW, a cooperating witness for the FBI. He was my handler. For one last day.

"At three P.M." he said, "a man named Esterbud will drive you to the set, get you wired, and go over your instructions. You'll sign a waiver, acknowledging your consent to wear recording equipment and have your voice recorded. If you have problems, he'll be able to reach me. You won't. Anything you need in the next twenty-four hours, go through Esterbud."

My stomach clenched up at the news that he was going to disappear. Even for a day. I don't like people disappearing.

"Tonight's shoot will use all six contestants, to deflect attention you might attract for being on the set. Don't ask how I arranged it. The show will use a boom microphone, so the only body mike you'll wear is ours. You'll activate it at ten P.M. At that point an Indian woman and a companion will enter the restaurant and sit in a booth near you."

"American Indian or Indian Indian?"

"Calcutta. Heavy accent. One of ours." He paused while a waiter refilled our coffee cups, waiting for him to leave. "The woman will have a conversation with her companion. This is what you're picking up. When you hear her say, 'The best part of Thanksgiving is the leftovers,' stop talking, clanking silverware, all extraneous noise. When she says, 'It's not the heat, it's the humidity,' it's over. She'll go to the restroom. Notice who in the cast or crew her companion makes contact with. Esterbud will go over all this again."

I nodded, wondering who in the FBI made up the code sentences and whether they took courses in that sort of thing at Quantico. Wondering if anything would be more hazardous than Fredreeq, Venus, Savannah, Kim, and me in the same room at the same time. "Why can't Miss Calcutta wear the wire?" I asked. "Or just memorize the information?"

"Big Fish's people will frisk her. And we need the conversation on tape, later, to elicit . . . cooperation."

Cooperation. A nice word in other contexts. In this context, code for blackmail.

"Not to sound petty," I said, "but again, what about the quid pro quo? Annika."

"In twenty-four hours I'll contact you. I'll explain things I'm not able to talk about now. Anything you need before then, Esterbud will be nearby."

"Simon, what about Annika?"

"Twenty-four hours, Wollie."

I saw in his face the stress I'd been feeling myself, the lack of sleep, the proximity to danger. I thought about what it was he wasn't telling me, the thing so big I might not want to see him after tomorrow. Something in me went cold. "Simon," I said softly, "I just have to know she's not already dead, that you haven't found Annika in the last day or two, and you're not telling me, because——"

"Because?"

"You need me to keep working for you."

He stared. "You think I'd do that?"

"I think that you——" I couldn't say *love me*. Yet. Even though he'd as much as said that. Even though I believed him. I said, "I think for you, the end justifies the means."

"That depends on the end."

I focused on my napkin. "That's the wrong answer. It should depend on the means. There are lines you don't cross, even to serve a greater good."

"But whose lines? Drawn where? Good people cross lines all the time. On your behalf."

I shook my head. "I don't want them to."

"Yes, you do. You just don't want to know about it."

Was he right? I raised my eyes to his. A waiter came and plunked down two small bowls of sliced fruit on the table between us. Neither of us looked at him. "But if I don't want to know about it," I said, "what am I doing with you?"

He picked up his fork. "That's the question, isn't it?"

Leaving Hugo's, Simon drove east, toward Laurel Canyon.

"Where are we going?" I asked, alarmed.

"I'm driving you to work. We're carpooling."

"Carpooling? Nobody carpools. I need my car. How am I going to get home?"

"Esterbud."

"No." I could feel my temperature rise. "I'm not kidding. *No.* My God, this is L.A., you don't leave people stranded without a car. What happened to civil liberties?"

"I'm not taking chances. I want you on the set tonight, not in jail in San Pedro." He glanced at me. "I guess you don't watch the morning news. I hope Joey's got a lawyer. She's getting slapped with a lawsuit."

I closed my eyes. This was turning into a very long day, and it wasn't even noon.

"Want to tell me what you were doing there?" Simon asked.

"No."

"All right. We should have a talk one of these days about which laws you obey and which ones you ignore when it suits you."

"We should," I said. "You can explain the nuances of crime,

like how driving people to the Valley against their will doesn't constitute kidnapping. Seriously. What if I need to go to the store while I'm working, what if I need paints? How do you know I have keys with me?"

"I imagine your whole apartment's in that backpack. Whatever you need, send Esterbud."

"So nice seeing our tax dollars at work."

"Wollie, you'd make my job easier if you kept your cell phone on. And returned your calls occasionally."

When we got to Sherman Oaks, to the Mansion, which he found without asking directions, I did not say good-bye. I did not kiss him good-bye. I got out of the car with as much grace as possible and slammed the door behind me. I did not look back.

The way he gunned the engine and took off down the street, they could hear his cheap Bentley in San Pedro.

I looked out the window of the Mansion. There he was, not even bothering to hide. Esterbud. Parked in some kind of big Chevy with tinted windows. Drinking out of a liter bottle of Coke. That must be lunch. He'd be knocking on the door in an hour to introduce himself and use the bathroom.

I turned my back on Esterbud and his liter bottle and looked into the yellow eyes of my West African goliath, *Conraua (Gigantorana) goliath.*

He was monumental.

I'd avoided him for days, so the effect was stupefying. Either he'd grown recently, or the wall had shrunk. It was a poster for some low-rent sci-fi horror movie, it was an amphibian the size of a bear, a bald green grizzly holding the kitchen hostage. It was impossible that something that big existed, I don't care what the book said, maybe it was a printing error, that ninety centimeters, no frog could be that long—

I opened up my favorite frog book, and found it. No, there it was. Ninety centimeters. I had it right.

Uh-oh.

The measurement was not SNV, snout to vent, the standard

frog measurement. My favorite frog book was illustrating a point, measuring the length from nose to . . . toe. Ninety centimeters stretched out.

I opened up a second book. The snout-to-vent measurement of a West African goliath is thirty centimeters.

No. No, no, no. I'd given the West African goliath the torso of a normal-sized human. No wonder he looked like a freak. He was a freak. A mutant. Ninety centimeters is three feet. Three times the size of any frog inhabiting the earth.

My hand went to my mouth, stopping my exclamation. Technical accuracy, my last defense for this monstrosity, was no longer on my side. It never had been. I'd made a large math error. Science error. Whatever.

The phone rang. I answered. It was my brother.

P.B. started right in talking about his halfway house, and I stood, thinking about paint. White paint. Somewhere in this house were extra cans of Blush White paint. I'd find a paint roller and put the West African goliath out of its misery. No bridal couple wanted to walk into their new home and face a frog the size of a Saint Bernard. Three to five coats of paint ought to do it. If I started immediately, if the pain was quick-drying—

Except—the goliath wasn't alone.

Alongside him was another frog, so tiny as to be nearly insignificant. I'd forgotten he was here, having avoided the wall recently. He was a blue poison-arrow frog, *Dendrobates azureus*, brilliant blue with black spots, his arms and legs a deeper shade of blue, sitting on a leaf, preparing to hop off in search of something to eat. A happy guy. Poisonous, dangerous, but happy. Beautiful.

"—to Santa Barbara," my brother was saying. "But she won't come."

"Um, what? Your . . . girlfriend?" I asked, distracted. "With the body dysmorphic disorder? P.B., if she's a patient, she can't come. Maybe when she's healthier."

"No. She's out of the hospital, but she still won't come. She says her upper lip is too big. She says everyone in Santa Barbara will stare at her when she eats, so then she'll stop eating and they'll hospitalize her again. She says in her own neighborhood they're used to her, but she can't start over in a new town, she's too old."

I closed my eyes, awash with guilt. P.B. had never had a girlfriend before. This was a big moment in his life. I should be celebrating. I should be taking the time to discuss the mental problems of a woman I'd never met, whose name I didn't know, instead of wishing he'd get off the phone. If you can't take time for the people you love, what's the point? If I'd taken time for Annika, ten minutes one fateful night, everything might've turned out differently.

I told P.B. I'd happily pick up this girl every Thursday from wherever she lived and drive her up to visit him at his halfway house in Santa Barbara, every single week, and anything else he could think up for me to do. Anything except encourage him to stay at the hospital, because I didn't believe it was the right place for him anymore, and staying wouldn't help his girlfriend's upper-lip problem in any case. He told me I sounded subnormal.

"I am subnormal," I said. "People's lives are at stake, and I'm stuck in Sherman Oaks with a blue poison-arrow and a West African goliath that I need to drown in white paint." *If I can send the FBI out for paint rollers.*

"You can't paint over them," he said. "That's murder-suicide."

"What do you mean?"

"You're the frog."

Here we go. "The blue?" I asked, wondering why I'd even brought it up.

"No, the other one. The goliath. Female frogs are bigger than the males, you told me that. She's big, she's a girl; you're big, you're a girl. If you paint over her, you erase yourself. Suicide's one thing, if you're sad enough, but taking someone with you is murder. You don't murder things, you save things. You put the blue next to the goliath as a talisman. You're blackmailing yourself into staying alive."

"P.B.," I said, "I love you, but I don't understand a word you just said."

"I'm in a mental hospital," he said. "Do the math."

"Wise guy." I hung up and started for the basement in search of paint, but my cell phone, now that it was on, had other ideas. It practically leaped out of my hand, frantic with unplayed messages.

"Hi, it's Joey. Listen, something's bothering me. Since Rico spent time around *B.C.*, why is it the cops haven't shown up there to question anyone? You think the Feds told them to back off? And check this out: Elliot's at a meeting with Bing and Larry at Bad Seed Productions and he just called to say they need the whole cast and crew working tonight. How weird is that? And oh—we made the news this morning. That guy in San Pedro ran his videocam the whole time. Our housekeeper screamed and woke me up."

"Wollie: Fredreeq. What in the name of Jesus Christ on the cross were you two doing? I swear, I leave you alone to rob one little office, and— There's my other line. This is very bad for the show. Very, very bad. And we might be working tonight, did you hear that? Call."

"Wollstonecraft, it's Uncle Theo. Dear, I saw you and your friend Joey on the television this morning. Congratulations. It's always so wonderful to see you."

"Yeah, uh ... hold on. Okay. Wollie? It's Cziemanski. I saw that thing on the news and I'm a little—okay, I guess you're okay. Call if you need anything. Well, I mean, not *anything*, but—okay. I gotta go."

"Joey again. I forgot to say I didn't find anything incriminating on Savannah, except that you're right, she lies about her age. I have a photocopy of her driver's license. She was born New Year's Eve, the same year as you."

I gasped. Savannah Brook was a Capricorn.

She'd put her astrological symbol on the drug she'd developed. Euphoria.

She was Little Fish.

One pill connected her, Rico, and Annika. And Simon knew this. But then why didn't he know where Rico was? Or Annika?

Because he wasn't looking for them. He wasn't concerned with Little Fish's victims; to him, Little Fish was bait. For Big Fish.

And when it was over? When the big meeting took place, tonight's meeting, when Simon got what he needed, surely then he'd turn her over to the Sheriff's Department—

Or not. I thought of Sammy "the Bull" Gravano, a confessed killer, living in the witness protection program, having ratted out the mob. If Sammy could do it, why not Savannah?

The Feds could make a deal to get her to testify against Tcheiko, offer immunity, and turn a blind eye to the plight of one little German girl. Who wasn't a citizen anyway, so who cared? Maybe to the FBI, it was the cost of doing business, a small price to pay for a guy everyone wanted. Savannah would get witness protection, but Annika and her mother—would they stay missing? Afraid of what Tcheiko or his compatriots would do if they surfaced? Assuming they weren't already dead.

Simon's conflict of interest. The thing that would so appall me I wouldn't want to know him after tonight: that Rico, despite his prominent father, would never be found, or his case solved. That Annika would not be looked for, ever. Or her mother.

And everything I'd found was of no use to anyone because the Feds didn't care and the cops didn't know, and without evidence—

But I had evidence. I'd had it since yesterday. In my dirty, malfunctioning Integra.

And now I knew what to do with it.

I walked out of the Mansion, introduced myself to Esterbud, and asked him to buy me some paint rollers. He wouldn't take the twenty-dollar bill I offered. Special Agent Alexander, he said, had told him he might have to do a paint run.

But the cab driver was happy to take my money, forty dollars of it, to get me home.

Only the pill wasn't there. Not in the Integra's front seat, not in the back. I found the Williams-Sonoma shopping bag that had been rattling around in the car for ages, I found coins, paper clips, a valet-parking receipt, but I couldn't find the evidence Britta had so kindly donated to the cause. I tried sitting in the driver's seat to re-create the circumstances of the flying pill, and I still couldn't find it. It was here somewhere, someplace I couldn't see without dismantling the car.

Great. So now I was in permanent possession of an illicit drug.

There was only one thing left to do. I fastened my seat belt and started up the car. My pill had a twin, and if I was lucky Maizie Quinn had not yet flushed it down the toilet. I was betting she hadn't. She was a lot like me. A woman who saved things.

38

The entire block of Moon Canyon where the Quinns lived was cordoned off for the film shoot, overflowing with cars and trucks and equipment and people. I hailed a sunburned man in a muscle shirt and the leather back-support belt of a weight lifter or furniture mover, who advised me to park on Moon Crater, two streets ahead, and walk back. From somewhere on Moon Canyon, the sound of a megaphoned voice intoned, "Background . . . and . . . action!"

I did as advised, wedging my car between an Explorer and a Lexus in front of an Italianate castle, and approached the Quinns from the opposite direction. The houses here were set close to the street. Presumably they had yards in the back, a place for the pool, but from the front they were like multimillion-dollar tract houses. Through windows I saw wallpaper, books . . . children. Maybe someday when I grew up I would live in a real house, rather than a succession of cramped apartments. Maybe not. Uncle Theo lived in a converted hotel. My mother lived in an ashram. P.B., in two days, would be living in a house, but it was a halfway house, which wasn't the same thing. We probably weren't house people.

I carried the Williams-Sonoma shopping bag. Since I was never going to return the utensils I'd bought there, I'd offer them to Maizie. If ever there was a person for kitchen gadgets, it was

Maizie Quinn. Not that she was needy, with her fleet of cars and exquisite house, but I was always showing up unannounced and asking for things, so this felt right. A hostess gift. Even very wealthy people, in my experience, loved free stuff.

I reached the back of the Quinn property and a gate set in a wood fence displaying a Guard Dog on Duty sign. Packages were stacked up against the gate, FedEx and UPS, from Banana Republic, Martha by Mail, and Sur la Table. I noticed a doorbell on the fence. I rang it, then tried the gate. It was open.

I tried to pick up the packages, but there were too many. I took the Williams-Sonoma gadgets out of their shopping bag, stuffed them in the pockets of my jacket, forced the Martha by Mail box into the shopping bag, picked up the other two packages, and squeezed through the gate.

I followed a path through a profusion of fauna that must've taken some tending, to be blooming in late November. It was quiet here, the foliage seeming to mute the sounds of the film shooting out front. The door of the artist's studio was open. I knocked and stuck my head in.

"You look like Santa Claus," Maizie said, welcoming me. "Is all that mine?"

"Left at the back gate." I handed her the shopping bag and the packages and moved past her into the room. A fire blazed in the fireplace, making me want to stay forever.

"That damn film." Maizie headed to the kitchen area. "My across-the-street neighbors rented out their house. On and off for weeks. Just when we think we've seen the last of it, they're back. So inconvenient. Some workers don't even try to get through. Service people just take the day off. Garbage trucks. I've actually faxed the UPS people maps to the backyard. I can't live without my deliveries. Hot cocoa?"

"Yes. Great." I sneezed. "What are you making?" Wood in interesting shapes covered the studio floor, getting a coat of primer. The sawhorse and circular saw I'd seen a week earlier had been replaced by a professional sander. Maizie wore a denim apron over her white shirt.

"Lawn ornaments. I've never found a really satisfactory Santa and reindeer, so I'm making some. It shocks me, how people have gorgeous homes and landscaping, then stick a plastic— Cat, move." She made a pass at the yellow cat, who leaped out of the way, something in his mouth. She stood, hands on hips, then turned to me. "What's up?"

"I'm wondering if you still have the pill you found under Annika's bed."

"Well, I'm not . . . sure. Why?"

I told her about the logo on Rico's bedroom wall, and the pill Britta had given me. "Rico tried to recruit Annika and Britta as couriers, but this woman on my show, Savannah Brook, is the kingpin. Queenpin. Whatever. She's the woman Rico told his mom about, the woman he was dating when he vanished." I sneezed again. The cat was rubbing against my leg.

"God, that's wild." Maizie shooed the animal away. "And the police don't know this?"

"No, but they will tonight. If I can pull it off." If I had the pill, I told Maizie, I'd show it to Savannah, I'd tell her Rico had given it to me, that I was interested in a deal, in doing what Britta and Annika would not, because I needed the money. Savannah liked deals.

I did not, of course, tell Maizie I'd be wearing an FBI wire. I'd do what I had to for Simon, then get Savannah alone. She'd say something incriminating. If I had the pill. The pill would give me credibility with her, and then with Yellin, at the Sheriff's Department. The pill in my hand, the logo on Rico's wall, Savannah's natural blond hair, her Capricorn birthday, her affair with Rico, an incriminating conversation caught on an FBI tape—whether or not the FBI acknowledged its existence—if all this wasn't enough for the cops to investigate, it would be enough for the TV news. Especially when I, an FBI cooperating witness and incidental celebrity, was willing to give interviews. And explain that Annika Glück and Rico Rodriguez, two people who could tie Savannah to Vladimir Tcheiko, were now missing. What news station wouldn't be interested? Three out of four of those people were celebrities.

Maizie replaced the top on a can of primer and wiped her hands on a towel. "I think I know where it might be—I'll just run up to the house. Stay here, it's freezing outside."

I moved closer to the fire, and discovered the cat. He rolled around on a rag rug, as though doing spinal exercises. I said hello to him and he rolled away. He was still playing with his toy, batting it around gleefully. As long as it wasn't a frog.

I used my cell phone to check my machine. One message. Rex Stetson, reporting about Kona winds and the Big Island volcano. The Honolulu airport crew was working to get the ash under control, but when they did, he'd be home, carrying his bride over the threshold.

My heart stopped. I looked at the cat. He was a big cat, but my African goliath frog could eat him for breakfast. An *amuse-bouche*. How could I call myself a professional? The Stetsons' kitchen was a fright, and it was irresponsible of me to be here. I should be in Sherman Oaks painting the wall white, committing murder-suicide. Maybe there was still time. If Maizie found the pill fast, I'd drive back there, throw on the first coat of paint, and—

My cell phone rang. I answered. This was a mistake.

"Where the hell are you?" It was Simon, as angry as I'd ever heard him.

"I—took a cab home." I couldn't believe how feeble my voice sounded.

"Stay there. Don't even think of moving. Don't drive, don't walk. Stay. In. Your. Apartment. The next time I call I want to hear you're sitting in Esterbud's car. Jesus Christ, he's a federal agent, he's there to protect you, not play hide-and-seek. You got that?"

My heart was racing, angry at him for yelling at me, angry at myself for reacting. What kind of whistle-blower would I make, going weak in the knees in the face of someone's anger? I focused on the yellow cat, with its sudden energy, and reined in my emotions.

"Simon," I said calmly, "tell Esterbud I'll meet him at Fini at six. I think I'm capable of driving my own goddamn car to my own goddamn job. But thank you for caring."

I pushed the end button on my cell phone, cutting him off mid-word. It wasn't a nice word.

The yellow cat toyed with its little object, tossing it my way, chasing it, reclaiming it with the glee of a kitten. The first sign of real life I'd seen from him.

Why was Simon so flipped out, I wondered, turning off my phone. Was Savannah really so dangerous? Was she on to me? Or did he just not like having his plans messed with?

I went to the window. The light was fading. It was almost the shortest day of the year. In the distance I heard a high-pitched voice. Emma, skipping toward the Range Rover.

The outdoor lights popped on, the little ones that illuminated the footpath. The late afternoon was coming to life now: the singing of the child, the playfulness of the cat. He flopped onto his back, showing me his stomach as he played with his toy. I thought of the Oriental fire-bellied toad, *Bombina orientalis*, his body green for everyday life. When push comes to shove, he flips over, arching his back and exposing his red belly, threatening predators with poison.

How angry Simon had been. You never really knew someone until you pissed them off. People's styles of rage were so personal. As individual as sex.

I felt like someone had kicked me. What was I thinking? My God, if I pulled it off tonight, my own evidence-gathering mission, we would never have sex. I would never kiss Simon Alexander again.

I had to sit to absorb this. There would be no going back. He would never kiss a whistle-blower, someone who'd gone behind his back, to the cops, to the press. But how could I want to kiss someone willing to sacrifice my friend Annika?

But I did want to.

The room grew cold.

Emma's singing was stopped by the slam of a car door and the sound of an engine starting. I moved to the fire, thinking of the

song still going on inside the Range Rover. What was it about being three that made you sing the same song over and over?

Not three, though. Two and three-quarters. Fractions. Math. It
was everywhere.

It's strange how a mind works, how you can puzzle over something, a riddle, a song lyric, a poem . . . and then you relax and
look away for a moment and things slide into place like thread
across a loom, revealing the pattern you hadn't seen before.
Maybe that's all math is, a design. Maybe if I'd done the math . . .

I thought of Emma saying, "Two and three-quarters," and her
mother saying, "Two and eleven-twelfths. Santa brought you to
me," and my own mother saying, "Christmas. Jesus was a
Capricorn, didn't you ever hear that?"

My breathing changed. The coldness in the pit of my stomach
spread to my intestines and down my legs.

The yellow cat threw his toy in the air, the paws tossing it like
a volleyball. It landed at my feet. I looked at it. It was a strange-
looking thing, no bigger than a thumbnail, but thick. I'd been
watching it for minutes, ever since I walked in, seeing something
flash bright in the firelight. I reached down to touch it with my
fingertip.

It was hard and dry and gray.

I drew my hand back.

It was an earlobe. The small, once soft end of an ear. In it was
a gold stud earring. Embedded with a red gem. A ruby.

A gold stud earring I'd seen once before, worn by Rico
Rodriguez.

I felt a burning in my eyes. The coldness inside me turned to
nausea.

I heard the crunch of leaves outside. I saw the doorknob turn.
I watched the door open and Maizie Quinn come into the studio.

39

"**N**o luck," Maizie said, locking the door behind her. "But I thought of one more place the pill might be. I'm sure I didn't toss it, and it's not like I mailed it to Annika's mother."

I snapped out of my paralysis and pushed the earlobe aside with my foot. The yellow cat, thinking it was a game, bunched himself up, swaying, ready to pounce. I stepped lightly on the earlobe, covering it with my sneaker.

"Check this out." Maizie bent down to a braided area rug and moved it aside. "I designed it and, I have to admit, I'm pretty proud of it."

She knelt on the white floor and counted tiles. She found the one she wanted, pushed on one end with her thumb, then lifted it out to reveal an aluminum-like surface underneath. A metal ring rested in the aluminum. She hooked her finger through it and pulled. A section of floor lifted up and became a trapdoor.

She stood and smiled, gesturing to the open door. "After you," she said.

I thought of Seth, the Krav Maga instructor, and something he'd said in class: "Don't get in their car." I hadn't understood it then, but now it was obvious, which was funny because this wasn't a car but an underground room Maizie was inviting me into. I knew that going down there was a bad idea. Bad, bad, bad.

"Wollie?" She seemed not to notice that I hadn't said a word since she'd walked in.

I stepped forward and looked down. A light had gone on automatically, revealing a spiral staircase of polished oak. Spiral staircases, Fredreeq said, were bad feng shui.

The yellow cat nuzzled my foot.

Maizie was waiting. Smiling.

"I'd rather not," I said. "I get . . . claustrophobic." It wasn't a lie. I'd never been before, but now I had a profound need to be outside and far away.

"Wollie, it's incredible. I have something so similar, with airplane cabins. Severe. I can't fly, not for all the tea in China—it's not flight itself, it's the closed cabin. Believe me, you'll like this." Maizie put a hand on my arm, guiding me toward the trapdoor.

I kicked the earlob aside, talking loudly to mask the sound of its journey across the tile. "It's not claustrophobia, technically, it's—" I searched through what was available of my brain. "Spelunkophobia. Fear of caves. Basements, subways. Rec rooms."

"Try it. If you hate it, we'll come back up. Cat! Leave that alone, the primer isn't dry."

I turned to see the cat batting at the torso of a wooden reindeer leaning against a counter. The earlobe must've landed behind it.

I should run for it. Maizie stood between the door and me, but I could just barrel over her. We were probably in the same weight class, although I had two inches on her, even given her high heels. But she looked solid whereas I was a jellyfish. And there'd be no going back. There's no alternative scenario, no polite reason for bashing into someone. Once you do it, from then on it's all about who's stronger, who's meaner, who's been to the gym more. And that wouldn't be me.

But I couldn't go down that staircase. Only an idiot would go down there.

Unless she had a gun.

She did have a gun.

It was in her apron pocket, not even hiding. Part of the outfit. Had it always been there, or had she gone to the house for it?

Okay, once a gun shows up, the rules change. Don't they? Wasn't it better for the gun to stay in her pocket than get pointed at me?

She was looking at me. Her hand went to her pocket.

"Maizie!" My voice was shrill. "I'll do it. Before I lose my nerve. Feel the fear and do it anyway. I think that was the name of a book. Anyway, I love to see how other people do their houses. Did you design all this yourself? I think your husband mentioned that you did."

"That's right, you met Gene." The cat knocked over the reindeer torso. Freaked out, he raced across the room. Maizie grabbed him. She walked toward me, the cat wiggling and mewing, wanting to get back to the earlobe. Rico's earlobe. The earlobe of Rico Rodriguez.

The cat was no match for Maizie Quinn. Nor was I. She held him in one hand, the other hand in easy reach of her gun. The three of us were going down.

The staircase was a long one. The underground room had a high ceiling—or a low floor, depending on your perspective. And Maizie was right; it wasn't cramped. You could have ballroom dancing down here or, more likely, a cooking class. Half the room was a test kitchen, with extra sinks and stovetops, all of it well lit and aggressively clean. Walls, floors, and counters were white, with copper hardware. And it smelled of perfume, something spicy. That scent again. Annika's.

"What did I tell you?" Maizie said. "Does it feel like you're underground?"

"No. It's wonderful. Is this where you make your aromatherapy products?"

She smiled and stroked the cat, who purred so loudly I could hear him across the room. "That's right. Shampoo, conditioner, body lotion, and methylenedioxymethamphetamine. Ecstasy. With a little something extra. Fentanyl. X plus F: I call it Euphoria."

Another interesting thing about the human brain, at least my brain, is that while I expect it to work in an orderly fashion, one discovery leading to another, building to an inevitable conclusion, in fact it's one big shopping bag I throw things into: tax receipts, toenail clippers, half a banana, nothing connecting to anything else until it all comes together in one big Aha! moment. That's what Joey calls it, the Aha! moment, but in this case it was more of an Uh-oh! moment, followed by an I Can't Believe How Stupid I've Been moment.

Everything I'd surmised about Savannah Brook actually applied to Maizie Quinn. Maizie, with whom I'd spent time on a practically-every-other-day basis, Maizie, dropping clues right and left, except I was too busy admiring her quilts and flowers and homemade lawn ornaments to notice. Maizie, who made her own sausage and bread, now standing between me and the staircase that was my only way out of here.

I found my voice. "Wow. For . . . how long?"

"Down here? Less than a year. Oh, you mean when did I get into the business? I cut my teeth on Ecstasy back in college. I was the sorority supplier."

"But, Maizie—" I heard my voice squeak. "You act like it's nothing, but you invented a *drug*. That's historical. You're the Madame Curie of Encino. How did it happen?"

Maizie laughed delightedly. "I just love you, Wollie. Thank you. It *is* a big deal, it's huge, but you know, I was sitting around one night thinking about analgesics and hallucinogens, and voilà! Exactly like cooking. You know how that is?"

I said, "I don't cook."

"Well, but you paint. Cooking, painting, organic chemistry— same thing. The experimental spirit. If you're willing to make mistakes, you can achieve anything."

I nodded, thinking of my freehand mural. My West African goliath. My mistakes. *Just stay connected to her*, I thought. "But to go from an idea to an actual product—?"

She nodded too. "I derivatized some fentanyl, combined it

with MDMA, and started test-marketing. People loved it. So then I had to talk Gene into a regular supply of fentanyl—he's such a stick-in-the-mud, but once he saw the profit potential—" She guided me farther into the room, away from the staircase.

"That's right, Gene's a doctor, isn't he?"

"Not the most inspired, but he's found his niche now, running this pharmacy scam; he gets me all the fentanyl I need, in the form of pain patches. A man has to thrive professionally or he feels like a big fat loser. Remember that when you get m—. Oops. Sorry."

"No, what about?" I said brightly.

"I was going to say 'when you get married,' but obviously you won't. Now."

Something inside me started to tighten up, in my throat, but I waved off the implication as if it were nothing: a party I wasn't invited to, a bad haircut. I just waved it away, my hands doing air ballet. "Okay, but listen—Vladimir Tcheiko, it's him, right? That you're going into business with? Because I actually read about him in *International Celeb*—"

"My God, Wollie, I'm giddy." Maizie laughed. "Did I tell you it's tonight?"

"Tell me everything!"

Maizie nearly squealed. "We're meeting here. It's like the president coming for dinner. No, better, it's like the Rolling Stones. I mean, the arrangements—endless. They didn't want Gene here, no one but me, they did background checks on the family, Lupe, the gardeners, people in the neighborhood, the goddamn film across the street—"

"Why do this at all, if they're so paranoid?"

"Because Vladimir's bringing me into his organization, and he won't take on anyone he can't see face to face; he goes with his gut. And since I *cannot* get on a plane and you can't drive to Africa, the mountain, so to speak, is coming to me."

"Jeez, Maizie, it must be a big deal, it's like you invented Velcro or something."

"Yeah. It's my year to be prom queen. I could've had Forio, or the Asians. . . . That's a big reason Tcheiko's interested, because his competition is. And the timing's good; he's bored with hiding out, wants to show he's still in the game and expanding."

"But—what happened with Annika?"

Maizie rolled her eyes. "She brought Rico around. That's what happened to Annika."

"And he liked U4? He wanted in on it?"

"Loved it. He and his friends were my first distributors. But eventually he told Annika. And she might've gotten used to the idea, but she caught him kissing me one day and that was it. She was such a child about that, I wasn't comfortable around her anymore. But by then I couldn't send her home—Tcheiko doesn't like changes in domestic staff close to a meeting like this—so I had to threaten her mother's life, all sorts of nonsense. What a big, unnecessary mess." Maizie sat on the staircase. "Rico should've seen she had a streak of puritanism."

So what happened to her? I wanted to ask again but couldn't. If the answer was bad, I wouldn't be able to keep this up. I cleared my throat. "Rico was not, I take it, puritanical?"

She gave me a sidelong glance. "Not in any way you can think of." I don't know what my face was doing, but she laughed. The cat squirmed. She set him down. "Shocked that I slept with him?"

"Not at all. You're beautiful, Maizie." If we could just go on like this, I thought. Like friends. Chatting. Gossiping. "You have the skin of a twenty-year-old." And the earlobe of a twenty-one-year-old. Upstairs. Under the lawn ornaments. I was losing it.

"Elizabeth Arden day spa. And I got my eyes done last year." She patted her hip under her denim apron. Where the gun was. "Being ten pounds overweight minimizes wrinkles. Not that I wouldn't like to be skinny, but I am one damn good cook, and I'm not making foie gras for my three-year-old. Oh, my goodness, did I ever offer you some?"

"Foie gras? No." What was foie gras? Liver?

She looked at her watch. "Well, too late now, but you saw it in progress, so I thought you'd like to taste the result."

"I saw it?"

"Saturday night. The bird. Oh, there's so much to talk about. Such a shame. I always felt an affinity for you, Wollie. You know Emma thinks we're cousins? And you're Grammy Quinn's favorite, on that show of yours . . ." She stood, reached into her apron pocket—not the gun one, but the middle one—and pulled out a piece of Tupperware. It was the size of a hockey puck. "Lucky you. Fentanyl, far better than morphine. Nap time."

"And then what?"

"Hey." She winked. "Let's not get into that, okay?"

"No, really," I said, my voice shrill. "What will you do with my body? It's not easy to lug around—my feet alone—. Believe me, this is something I know about." Perhaps I was going into shock, talking about my body as though it were a suitcase.

"Honestly, you don't want to know. People get so squeamish. A guy in my charcuterie class Sunday had to leave the room when I pulled out Goosie's liver."

"That was Goosie?" I gasped. "I thought it was a turkey."

She laughed. "It was a pain in the ass, frankly. It took seconds to wring her neck, and forever to turn her into foie gras. But that's life: moments of drama, hours of cleanup. No time for that tonight, I've got dinner cooking. And you're right, I can't carry you anywhere; I could barely drag Rico across the room."

A murder confession. That was awfully easy. I swallowed. "This room?"

She shook her head. "Upstairs. I dropped him through the trapdoor."

"Then what?" I whispered.

"If you must know, I had to get his limbs off. I tried a Skilsaw, but tissue splattered everywhere, so I went with a hacksaw, fit the torso and head in one Hefty bag, ground up arms and legs in the meat grinder, the small parts, and got the large bones out to the car in a second trip. Not bad."

My mouth was very dry. "You're losing me. Wh—why the meat grinder?"

"I had to limit trips to the car. Not so important on this end, but in Antelope Valley that kind of thing attracts attention."

320 Harley Jane Kozak

"Why Antelope Valley?" I asked, keeping my voice conversational.

"Good distance. Nice Dumpsters."

"But wasn't there a lot of . . . blood?"

"Oh, at first, just spewing out, and his body thrashing around, but not so bad once his heart stopped pumping. I used an aluminum tub for his parts, the kind we use at picnics to store ice and drinks, and a six-mil plastic sheet to contain things. . . . Thank God for custom ventilation. Gene made a big fuss over the expense last year, but you don't do aromatherapy, let alone drug production with a ceiling fan."

What to do? She had to be a little mad. Maybe a lot mad. These were not words I used lightly, considering my brother's history with schizophrenia, but it helped me. I don't know much about real evil, but mental illness is a world I've lived in. It could work to my advantage. Since she was armed, it was perhaps my only advantage.

"What a week for you," I said. "You're not just creative, Maizie, you're brave."

Maizie shrugged but looked pleased. "It's no different from a surgeon or butcher. Once you get past the smell of blood and cutting through bones, it's a series of tasks. Killing him was harder in one sense. It comes down to a moment. You can't hesitate or you lose your nerve."

"Was it because he wanted to be a partner?"

"Oh, please. Fifty percent of my gross? For what, his people skills? Not in this lifetime. The problem was, he threatened to turn me in. Think about that. I'm arrested, Gene's arrested. Forget losing the house, the cars, Emma growing up in Palm Springs with Grammy Quinn. Prison would be the least of it, because by then I'd met Yosip and Frito——"

"Frito?"

"Tcheiko's lieutenants. I could identify them. I know some organizational details the Feds would be interested in. And Tcheiko would lose face among his peers, because of my error in judgment, and he's very unforgiving about that sort of thing, that was made very clear to me. I don't think federal custody is really the place for me, do you?"

"Then it was . . . self-defense. Killing Rico."

She smiled. "I'm not sure a jury would see it that way, since he was naked at the time. In front of the fire. Unarmed, except for prosciutto and olives, and a loaf of sourdough."

"What'd you kill him with?"

"The Wüstof."

"Excuse me?"

"Bread knife. Using what's at hand, that's a core homemaker philosophy. I went down on him, he fell asleep, I slit his throat. I always have my knives sharpened for the holidays, a little cutlery store in Beverly Hills. Ear to ear is what you always hear, so that's what I focused on, one good incision. And from there it was just a step at a time. You can do anything in the world if you break it into small, manageable parts. Oh, please." She was looking at me now, eyes narrowed. "Don't waste your sympathy on him. Do you know he came over on Saturday to ask if I'd killed Annika? You told him she was looking for a gun, so he thought I'd killed her. Thought he could squeeze me for a bigger percentage. Do you need a Kleenex?"

My nose was running, the way it does when I try not to cry. I thought of Lauren Rodriguez, the look in her eyes that would never go away now. She'd never get over losing her son. I couldn't stop my nose. I felt as though my face were leaking. "His mom," I whispered.

Maizie stood. "She shouldn't have raised such a selfish kid. I'm sorry for her, I truly am, but everyone's got a mother—you can't let that stop you. I have a child." She glanced at her watch. She was like Bing, ready to yell "Cut!" the minute the conversation palled.

"Capricorn," I said breathlessly. "Emma's the Capricorn. The logo on your pills."

Maizie smiled. "Yes. Emma." There was a counter between us, a white counter, sparkling clean, no trace of the blood that must have spattered here from Rico Rodriguez going through a saw.

"Because you know what real euphoria is? An epidural, after fourteen hours of labor. And then the prize. My Emma. Giving birth to my baby was the best day of my life."

"Maizie," I said. "She's so wonderful."

"Thank you. You'd have been a good mom, too, Wollie. I'm sorry, I had no idea you'd keep at this the way you did. And you figured out a lot. Surprisingly. Not to be offensive, but you just don't look that smart. I think it's your hair."

"I suppose——" I cleared my throat. "If I didn't want to take this——fen——"

"Fentanyl," she said, and her hand once more reached into her denim apron pocket. She drew out the gun. It was small. Black. "It's a twenty-two. It's all I could find; Gene's always walking off with the keys to the gun cabinet. It'll do the job, I just can't guarantee how fast, and you could be conscious the whole way out. And consider the mess. I don't have time to clean and even if Lupe were here, I couldn't ask her, she's Catholic. And it's loud. The room's insulated, assuming the trapdoor worked. It should close automatically——" Maizie walked over to the spiral staircase, heels clicking across the white tile floor. I looked around frantically, but there was no place to run, hide, no door, nothing. A weapon, then, something, anything. I tried a kitchen cabinet. Locked. Each cabinet had little locks.

How had she pulled this off, how could no one know about this, the police, the FBI——

They did know. She hadn't pulled it off. For the second time in an hour I felt like the stupidest person alive. Simon had tried in every way he could to prevent this. There was no crime going on at *Biological Clock* except bad TV; he'd "recruited" me to distract me. He'd done everything but glue my feet to Santa Monica Boulevard to keep me away from here.

But here I was.

Where was he?

The house must be under surveillance, bugged, the phones tapped——that's how it worked, right? Agents must be in a van on the street, listening to everything we'd been saying, getting it all on tape, maybe waiting for the right moment to come rushing in—

Now would be a good time! I wanted to yell.

Maizie climbed back down the spiral staircase with a smile. "Okay, all insulated. Wollie, don't be difficult. It's like Emma's pink medicine. She always thinks it will taste bad, but it doesn't. This could be so easy."

Simon wasn't coming. Not that my opinion of men is low, but in my experience, the cavalry doesn't show up just because you need them. If Simon was listening, he wouldn't be listening, he'd be in here already, he'd be in here at the first mention of guns and whatever Maizie kept yapping about in that Tupperware. He wouldn't use me for bait or for evidence gathering. He wouldn't use me, period.

Simon! I wanted to scream. I wanted to scream, period.

He wasn't here because he wasn't listening, because this was a soundproof room, with no telephone, and a secret entrance that no one, not even a state-of-the-art good guy knew about. And they didn't know I was here because my car was parked blocks away and I'd used the back-gate entrance that UPS knew about, but the FBI maybe didn't, since my hostess had neglected to fax the FBI a map and, most of all, they didn't know I was here because they all thought I was heading to *Biological Clock.*

"Shouldn't we do this in your car, Maizie? Or mine? If you're going to use my car to dump my body, wouldn't it be easier if I'm already in it?"

"No," she said, growing exasperated, "because then when I dump you, I'd have to drag you in one piece and it would attract attention. We went over that. Also, you'd be easy to ID, they could determine time of death—no. Trust me, it creates more problems than it solves."

"I see." I seemed to be both shivering and sweating now, and then I sneezed; it was as though my body were running through its repertoire of involuntary activities, sensing the end. My memory was running through its own repertoire, saying I love you to P.B., Joey, Fredreeq, Uncle Theo. Mom. Simon. Doc.

I loved you too, Doc said back. *I just loved my kid more.*

"One last thing," I said. "Where's Annika?"

"Wollie, it's so ironic. She killed herself. She left me a suicide note the day she left. I just couldn't show anyone; it was too incriminating."

That's not true, I thought, wrapping my arms around myself to fend off hysteria. Annika e-mailed me. Just days ago. I had to believe it came from her, because otherwise, what was all this for? If she'd been dead all along . . .

I held myself tighter and felt something in my jean jacket, in the pocket. Hard.

I slipped my hand in my pocket. Cold. One of the things I'd bought at Williams-Sonoma. The meat mallet. I could feel the tiny string on it, attached to the small rectangular price tag.

Words began to run through my head like voice-mail messages.

Crotch, neck, soft parts of the face. Seth, from Krav Maga.

I couldn't do that. I don't even do sit-ups.

You do what you have to do to stay alive. Ruta, my childhood babysitter.

Annika would never kill herself. Not over a guy. She was smarter than that.

If you're not dead, you're not done. Seth.

"Can I look at it?" I said, my voice squeaky and high, like little Emma. "The fentanyl?"

Maizie took a seat and pushed the small Tupperware container toward me.

My left hand worked the lid, my right hand staying in my pocket. I couldn't believe she didn't notice, but she didn't. I was shaking so badly that when I pushed the Tupperware back across the counter, it wouldn't go in a straight path. "I'm sorry," I said. "I can't get it open."

Of course she tried to open it for me. She was a mom. The Tupperware lid was tough, though. She needed both hands to pry it off. She held on to the gun but, still, she used both hands, and so then she wasn't looking at me, she was looking at the Tupperware.

This was it. Now or never. A last voice played in my head. *A moment. You can't hesitate or you lose your nerve.* The voice was Maizie's.

Some force reached into my pocket and pulled out the silver meat mallet with my hand attached to it. I don't know what you'd call it, some phenomenon of physics or biology stretching across a white Formica counter to bring the full weight of an arm onto someone's neck, head, shoulder, ear, cheekbone, not once, not even twice, but enough times to make her fall from the stool she sat on, onto the white tile floor. When that happened, I stopped.

The blows stopped, but the cries didn't, the raw sounds a throat can make, somewhere between a scream and a sob that I finally recognized as coming from my own body, not hers.

40

I ran up the spiral staircase. At the top, waiting for me, was the yellow cat, wanting out.

I wanted out too.

There was no handle, though, or door knob, so I pressed and pushed and banged the side of my fist against the trapdoor. It wouldn't open. There was a keypad but I couldn't begin to guess a code, so I punched numbers. The cat meowed at me. I thought about panicking and then remembered I had a cell phone. In my pocket. My other pocket.

I got reception. I called Simon. I didn't think twice. When his voice mail answered, I said, "It's Wollie, I'm in her house, the studio behind the house, underground, in an underground—and I can't get out and I've maybe—killed her. And she said Annika's dead but she can't be dead because she e-mailed me." My voice cracked and I hung up and clutched the banister of the spiral staircase, where I sat, my body knotted like a pretzel. The cat purred and rubbed itself against my shoulder.

I dialed 911. They asked me questions. I answered them. I hung up.

I sneezed. Then I waited.

Life is short. That's one of those things that occurs to you when you glimpse death, yours or anybody's. You think, "I'll remember this, this will remind me not to waste time," but you forget. You carry on like you have several hundred years to live and like it matters if some guy now living in Taiwan who once loved you still does, or if you pass a math test or win a reality TV show or finish the frogs or get your car washed before the end of the year.

When all that really matters is that you're not dead. The rest of it, like what that means in the long run or what I was feeling right at the moment, I couldn't sort out. I didn't know if Maizie Quinn was or wasn't dead, and I knew that this distinction would make a big difference in the lives of many people, me among them, but for the moment I didn't care. I had her gun on the top step, away from the cat, and I had the meat mallet. There were no sounds below me, the sounds of a human being rallying. If I were a different sort of person, a brave one, for instance, I might have gone down to see if I could do something about her, like revive her or tie her up, but I was the person I was, so I stayed where I was, crouched and tense and concentrating on steady shallow breaths, thinking about being alive. Sneezing.

I don't know how long it was just the yellow cat and me, but after a time there were voices, so muffled I might have been hallucinating. I screamed and pounded and then the door opened upward and people moved past me down the spiral staircase. Someone—he told me he was FBI, they were all FBI—helped me up, took from me the meat mallet, with blood drying on its silver surface, and, after I directed his attention to it, the gun. He led me to a chair near the fireplace and gestured to a woman, who came and stayed close to me. At some point someone from below called up, "She's alive," and for a moment I thought they were talking about me. And then I slid out of the chair onto the floor, I'm not sure why, except that I wanted something more solid underneath me. I stayed there across the room from the reindeer pieces with their primer drying until paramedic types brought Maizie up from below on a stretcher. I didn't see her face, only her healthy-looking blond hair, matted with the darkness of drying blood. I began to shake all over again. That's when Simon walked in.

When I saw his face, grim and tense and pale, I had to work not to cry. He scanned the room and saw me.

Came toward me with long strides. Stopped when someone grabbed his arm to whisper something in his ear. Nodded to him, spoke a few words, came over and looked down. Then he knelt on the floor next to me, very close.

"You all right?" he said.

I nodded, not able to speak.

"Hurt?"

I shook my head.

"Don't move." He gestured to the woman with me, then stood and walked away.

A minute later another medical type with a first-aid kit came over and checked out my vital signs and asked me some questions. My answers seemed to satisfy him. I started to tell him to check on the cat, but the words came out funny. He covered me with a blanket, let me stay on the floor, walked away to say a few words to Simon, and left.

Simon seemed to be the Bing Wooster of this operation. I wondered why the area wasn't being roped off as a crime scene, then thought that maybe no one but me knew a crime had been committed here, except the crime of me hitting Maizie with a meat mallet. I turned to the woman at my side. "There's an earlobe here," I said.

"A what?"

"An earlobe." I stood. She touched my arm and started to ask me something, but I wrapped my blanket around myself and walked over to Simon, standing in the kitchen. He must've had eyes on the side of his head. He turned immediately.

"Yes? What is it?"

"There's an earlobe around here somewhere. On the floor."

"A what?"

"An earlobe. It belonged to Rico Rodriguez. The cat was playing with it. The rest of Rico is in Antelope Valley."

Simon took a long look at me, then nodded. The news didn't seem to surprise him, but I figured they train them not to look surprised. He put a hand around my upper arm, gently, but his hand was so big it surrounded my bicep like a bandage. "Wollie," he said. "You need to—"

"Where's Annika?"

"Not now." As if to reinforce this, his cell phone rang. He listened, frowning, then addressed the room at large. "All right, we've got company. They're early. Exiting the 405 at Valley Vista, taking surface streets. Let's move." He addressed the woman who'd been hovering and asked where her car was. Base camp, she told him. "Put her in mine," he said, and fished keys out of his jacket. "Windows up."

"We've got a problem." It was a new agent, coming in from outside, leaving the door open. He came over to Simon, the urgency in his voice unrestrained. His manner was not deferential. "We picked up Dr. Kildare and Hazel at the Sportsman's Lodge. He's falling over himself to cooperate, but all he knows is she's to stand outside the house, meet them at the gate. Car one is Lenin. He verifies it's her, drives through, radios car two, that's Stalin. He comes through, she closes the gate, walks them here to the lab. If she's not at the gate, the deal's off. She's not alone, the deal's off. Lenin doesn't ID her, Stalin stays away, we shoot it out with him on the freeway all the way to Tijuana or Death Valley or wherever the hell he parked the getaway jet."

Simon nodded. "That's more than one problem. Hazel?"

"Nothing. Knows company's coming. Betty Crocker's been cooking all day."

Simon nodded. "Female agents?"

"Dahl, San Diego, stuck on the 405 and she's short. We're working on a wig for Ellis."

"Won't make it in time. Passwords?"

"Husband doesn't know. Surveillance says no, but we're reviewing transcripts. It's not something we were listening for. Right now I need you to look at the geography out front. If we can get him onto the block, Potemkin may have a shot from across the street."

Simon looked toward the door, shaking his head. "Not unless

we get them to roll down a window. Even then, it's going to be a bad night in the neighborhood."

"I don't need a wig," I said.

Both men turned to me. The room went quiet.

"No." Simon didn't even think about it.

But the agent with him thought about it. He looked at me with interest, then turned to Simon and said something I didn't catch.

"I can do this," I said to them. "I can. I'm like her."

Simon shook his head. "Not enough. They've met her."

"Tcheiko hasn't."

"No."

"What are you going to do?" I said. "I knocked out Little Fish. There's nobody else. I can get them to roll down the car window. I can be Betty Crocker for ten goddamn minutes."

Simon looked at his watch. "You didn't sign on for this."

The other agent said, "Actually, she did sign on for this. This is Kermit, right? Use her."

Simon's cell phone rang. He spoke into it, held up a finger to us, then walked outside.

The other agent kept looking at me. "Think you can do this?" he said.

I felt the room around me holding its breath. "Yes," I said.

He nodded. "Let's go."

The room came to life. Two women agents led me to a corner, helping me into clothes they must've found in the house, jeans that had to be Maizie's and a white sweater. They talked calmly and encouragingly. Nothing fit exactly right; the jeans were too short, and the sweater sleeves, but it was all close enough. I smelled like her now, subtle and spicy. It was Annika's scent too, the aromatherapy products. Sassafras oil, maybe.

One of the agents apologized, asked me to hold still, and then I heard scissors and saw my hair fall to the floor. Another put foundation on my face and handed me a lipstick and a mirror. Maizie's makeup. Maizie's haircut. On my way outside, I grabbed an apron from a peg.

Agents flanked me and we hurried down the path toward the house, the butter-yellow traditional American with white trim. The porch was lit up with the tiny icicle lights. We passed other people, one wearing a headset, others on cell phones, the agents on either side of me protective, as if I were the most important person in the world, which in their world, at this moment, I was. We walked faster and faster, toward the security gate, and it began to sink in, what I was doing. I pushed the thought aside. A man ahead of us opened the electronic gate.

The film was still shooting on Moon Canyon, a generator powering big lights that illuminated the street. Equipment trucks, trailers, and cars were everywhere, street, pavement, and grass, blocking one another. The crew milled around, a small army of cell phones and headsets. I had an impression of sailors on a ship, battening down hatches in preparation for a storm at sea. "Crossing Valley Vista," an agent said into a radio. "Kermit in place."

Simon stood by a tree, near the koi pond. He wore a headset too, head bowed in concentration, listening. He looked up and stared at me, his face hard. As when we'd first met.

"No," he said to his headset. "If there's a password and you can't come up with it, we pull her out." He signaled to an agent near me. "Kill half the lights."

I heard glass break. The yard went darker.

Footlights lined the driveway. I glanced at my sneakers, nearly the only things left on me that were mine. Maizie would spot the shoes immediately. Fredreeq too. But slouching in sneakers, I was close to Maizie's height, a detail more important than fashion consistency.

A black car turned the corner from Moon Rock Road.

I could see it, being near the gate. Across the street, the film crew could see it. Because of the fence around the Quinn property, none of the agents near the house could see it.

"Damn," I heard Simon's voice say. "Not enough."

Activity across the street had quieted but not stopped. A burly guy in a tool belt ambled past the generator, carrying a cable. Another balanced coffee cups in a cardboard take-out tray.

The black car pulled up closer and a window began to descend. The windows on the cars were tinted.

I was alone. The agents seemed to have melted into the darkness around me.

The car came closer. So quiet.

"Wollie, don't turn around." A woman was squeezed into a crevice made by the gate joining the fence. Very close to me. "I'm Agent Shepphird. I'll talk you through this. Approach the car. Say hello and shake hands. Say something friendly; Maizie Quinn's met this guy. His name is Fritz Benito. Tell him to pull ahead and park anywhere he likes. Then come back."

I stepped forward. I slouched. The car made the turn into the drive, the driver's window all the way down. A man in a suit, very dark, round-faced, rough-skinned, looked at me. He didn't look happy.

I told my face to smile and held out my hand. There was a man in the passenger seat and maybe more in the back. "Hello," I said. "Pull ahead and park anywhere you like."

It wasn't relaxed. I sounded like a computer. The man was staring. I swallowed. "Nice to see you again, Frito." The minute I said the name, I froze. I'd got it wrong. Bad call.

But he smiled, a brief showing of teeth. The window went up. The car went forward.

I stepped back, into the shadows, breathing hard.

Agent Shepphird's voice was in my ear. "Wollie. Good job. We're in. The next one's our guy. He's got his first lieutenant with him. Yosip Kasnoff. You've met Yosip, but only once. But you've talked to Karl Marx—sorry, Tcheiko—three or four times on the phone. He likes you. Hold on, Wollie, I'm getting instructions on my headset. Okay. You're cooking tonight. They found the transcripts of your last conversation. You promised him fusion cooking: applying California spa techniques to French recipes using African ingredients. And that's the password. What you're cooking for him."

"Okay. What is it?"

There was a pause. Agent Shepphird said, "We don't know."

My heart stopped.

"Make up something," she said. "He's not going to be eating it."

"I don't cook."

"Hold on. Dinner suggestions, anyone? Kermit doesn't cook." She paused, perhaps listening to her headset. "Meanwhile, Wollie, here's the goal: get Tcheiko inside the compound and out of his car. We have SWAT guys on the roof, MP5s pointing at both front windows in the limo. They just need to see what they're shooting at. But if it goes wrong, you panic, you see a gun, hear one, hit the ground. Agents will be on top of you like a football. We'll take care of you. Hit the ground, Kermit—Wollie. You'll be fine. Here he comes. Wing it."

Wing it?

My mother has always talked about out-of-body experiences. I'd never known what she meant. What an interesting time to understand something about my mother. Tcheiko's car pulled up just as the first had done. I stepped out of the shadows and approached. The driver's window went down, the tinted window, and I was looking into the face of a man, extraordinarily handsome, much more than Simon, more even than Doc, with a black-and-silver beard and a nearly shaved head and salacious brown eyes. "Hello," he said.

"Hello," I said. "I'm glad you're here. I hope you're hungry."

He regarded me calmly, not smiling but not with the fierce look of the man in the first car. I thought of the guns aimed at us. In the dark. I could feel the sweat form under my skin. Now what? Whose turn to speak? What were my instructions? Why didn't he speak?

"On a fait une réservation pour huit personnes à neuf heures, je crois," he said.

My heart was pounding. I was in the wrong movie; I needed the one with subtitles. My face quivered so badly I nearly—

"Et le menu?" he said. "What have you for us?"

I've never been to Africa. I know nothing about Africa. Except—

"Frog," I said.

"*Les cuisses de grenouille?*" he said, frowning. "This is not typically local."

"*Au contraire,*" I said. "The West African goliath, *Conraua goliath,* is native to Cameroon. And happens to be the largest frog on earth. Which I am honored to have in my kitchen. As I am honored to have you in my kitchen."

"How will you prepare it?"

"I had considered an *amuse-bouche* in puff pastry, but as the goliath is thirty centimeters, snout to vent, his legs are the size of . . . forearms. He's now a main course. *À la maison Maizie.* A little garlic, a bit of flavored oil. Voilà!"

He nodded. He smiled. His window went up. He drove forward.

A movement from across the street caught my eye. The film crew had moved out of sight of the black cars, but I was close enough to the gate to see them run silently across the street, to our side, a hundred feet north of the gate. Dozens of them. Every one with guns drawn.

Car One's doors opened and men got out, five of them, and walked back to Car Two. They opened the doors of Car Two, driver's side and passenger's side. Frito called to me, his accent heavy. "Mrs. Quinn," he said, with a gesture. "The gate, please. Close."

There was a movement, and a sound like a crack, like a tree limb breaking.

I hit the ground.

People piled on top of me like I was a football.

41

It was three days later.

I pulled into a parking lot in Woodland Hills, the north end of a dog park. I rolled down the windows and checked my watch. Almost noon. Twenty-four and a half shopping days till Christmas.

"We're early," Joey said. "By six minutes. Even with you driving."

I'd picked up Joey at a car dealer's in Oxnard, on my way home from Santa Barbara. Joey had sold the BMW. The paparazzo-plumber's dent had shown Elliot the wisdom of unloading his car before his wife could add more miles or damage. We'd been listening to a news update of planes grounded in Honolulu, damaged by volcanic ash. I turned off the radio.

"I'm nervous, Joey," I said. "Why would I be this nervous?"

We waited.

Four minutes later a Range Rover pulled into the lot, drove past us, and parked six or seven empty spaces away. Nobody got out.

One minute after that, another car showed up and parked near the entrance. Joey whistled. "Nice wheels."

"It's the cheap Bentley," I said.

"Ready?" Joey said.

"No," I said.

The passenger door of the Bentley opened. Annika Glück

stepped out. She was slight, not twenty years old, brown-haired, apple-cheeked. She was pretty, but what you noticed first was the radiance of her expression.

I opened my door and started to call to her, but she was already running to meet me, and as small as she was, the force of her nearly knocked me over when she arrived. *"Ich kann nicht glauben dass ich hier——"*

I hugged her back, smiling so hard my face felt stretched. How tiny she was, hardly bigger than Ruby, my almost-stepdaughter. I could feel her ribs shaking through her leather jacket and I was about to tell her I didn't understand German, but then I realized she was crying and that whatever she was saying wouldn't be any more coherent in English.

A door of the Range Rover opened, then slammed shut.

Annika looked up, and went silent. Her clutching relaxed; then she let go of me.

Grammy Quinn climbed out of the Range Rover on the driver's side. Lupe was already out of the car, reaching into the back seat, speaking Spanish. Emma Quinn jumped to the ground, holding Lupe's hand. Then she turned and saw us.

Annika gave my arm a squeeze and walked toward the little girl. Emma looked back at Lupe, who said something in Spanish. Then Emma turned to Annika again, and stared.

Annika reached her and dropped to one knee. "Hello, *Mausi.* Shall we go to the swings?" Her accent was slight. Emma nodded and turned away, arms folded, legs marching toward the playground. Annika followed.

How had I ever believed this girl to be a depressed, drug-abusing teen? It had been so easy for Maizie to plant the evidence and to plant the story in my head. She'd have done the same for anyone who came looking for Annika, but she got lucky. She got me. Ms. Gullible.

I looked back at the Bentley. Simon Alexander was leaning against it, watching me. The last time I'd seen him was three nights ago, outside the Quinn house. When the shooting had stopped, he'd picked me up off the ground, found me a blanket, plied me with brandy, and told Agent Shepphird to drive me home. Then he'd left town.

"He's really tall, isn't he?" Joey said, from inside the car. "Good luck."

I glanced back at Lupe and Grammy Quinn waiting by the Range Rover, then walked across the parking lot to the Bentley, gravel crunching under my sneakers. I stopped before I reached him, leaving four or five feet between us. "Hello, Simon."

"Hello, Wollie."

I nodded toward the playground. "So she's okay? Annika?"

"She's fine. Excited to be here. Thawing out from two weeks in Minnesota."

"And her mother?"

"Touring Beverly Hills at the moment, with Esterbud. So far, the mother likes Minnesota better. I don't share her enthusiasm."

I watched the progression to the playground halt, while Emma and Annika made the acquaintance of someone's dog. I glanced at Simon. He was watching me. I looked away.

"Annika hitchhiked to Santa Fe," he said, "where an au pair named Dagmar lent her bus fare to Minneapolis. Where Marie-Thérèse and the Johannessens, her host parents, not only took her in and believed her story but brought her mother over from Germany and kept it to themselves until they saw on the news that Maizie Quinn had been indicted. Trusting people, Minnesotans."

"Congratulations on Big Fish," I said. It had made the front page of the *Los Angeles Times*, Vladimir Tcheiko, drug lord, recaptured. A shining example of cooperation among several branches of federal and local law enforcement agencies.

"Condolences on *Biological Clock*," he said.

The show, to no one's surprise, had gone under.

I nodded. "I think I was really only in it for the health-care coverage. Now I have to go find a real job." I looked at my feet. "Would you have voted for me? In the contest?"

"No."

I looked up. "That's awfully . . . unequivocal."

"Think I want to see you pregnant with another man's child?"

"Oh. Well, put like that..." I didn't mention the show's disclaimer, how none of the contestants were required to have sex.

My brush with celebrity, in any case, would never have rivaled Maizie Quinn's. Even recovering from head wounds, Maizie was telegenic, especially against a backdrop of adultery, drugs, and murder. The Los Angeles Sheriff's Department expressed confidence in getting a conviction for murder one, but Maizie's defense team hinted at extensive pretrial motions, ensuring her airplay well into the next TV season.

"You're not getting any better at returning calls, are you?" he said. "Three days, Wollie?"

"I was catching up on sleep. I don't suppose it ever occurred to you to say 'Stay away from Maizie Quinn'?"

"No. You don't discuss an operation with a civilian."

"See, that's what I love about the federal government. That spirit of openness."

Simon turned suddenly, looking at my car. "That's Joey, isn't it? Wait here." He walked to it and talked to Joey through the passenger window. They shook hands. Then he reached into his pocket and handed her a set of car keys.

My heart started to pound. I thought I'd been doing well, but now I saw I'd overestimated my composure. Simon came back to me, his long stride slow and relaxed. My heart beat faster. "What was that all about?" I said.

"Joey's going to drive my car to her house. I'll pick it up later. Come on, let's walk."

"How will you get to Joey's house? To pick it up?"

"I have an agent standing by, for Annika, when she's finished."

"Oh." My heart rate returned to normal.

"This creates an interesting problem, though," he said. "I'm in violation of FBI regulations prohibiting a nonagent from driving an agency car. I've never done this. No agent does this. It's like giving up your gun."

I stared at him.

"Now," he said, "if I catch a ride with Agent Beggs in her

Chevy Monte Carlo, Agent Beggs is going to wonder why. I can't lie. I can't ask her to lie. This violation could come to light. I could even be unemployed by the end of the day."

"Unless?" I said.

"You give me a ride. It's all in your hands."

My heart rate sped up again.

Twenty yards ahead of us, Emma and Annika reached a grassy area, just outside the playground fence. They'd been walking with space between them, but now Emma reached up for Annika's hand. Annika caught her around the waist and lifted her off her feet and swung the little girl around, then turned her upside down. Emma screamed with joy.

I don't understand why a loss of equilibrium should make someone happy. I don't like dizziness. But maybe if your world is changing beyond recognition, seeing it upside down helps. Maybe being upside down does something beneficial to your heart. I asked Simon.

"Not really," he said. "The baroreceptor system notes changes in arterial blood pressure and tells the brain to adapt, compensating for forces exerted outside the body. But I don't want to bore you with physiology. Or physics."

The mention of physiology and physics made me think of herpetology, the science of amphibians and reptiles, which made me think of metamorphosis, of little tadpoles changing into frogs, learning to live upon the earth, which led to birds chirping in my head, and bunnies cavorting in meadows, signs that I'd reached the border of my brain's tolerance for math and science and philosophy and all things cerebral. "Well, anyway," I said. "You know what Feynman said."

Simon looked at me, hands in his pockets. He smiled. "What did he say?"

I wrapped my arms around his waist. His eyes, blue enough to swim in, widened in surprise.

I stood on tiptoe to tell him. "Kiss her, you fool."

acknowledgments

So many people shared with me their time, imagination, kindness, and expertise. Among them: Dr. Barry Fisher and his staff at the Sheriff's Department Crime Lab; Gary P. Chasteen and Lori N. Schumann at the Scientific Services Bureau of LASD; the Lost Hills Sheriff Station; Tony Hernandez and Craig Harvey at the Department of Coroner; Special Agent Jose Martinez of the DEA; and the LAPD, West Valley Division and Harbor Division. You are the good guys. Thanks to Jay Renfroe, David Garfinkle, Greg Normart, and the *Blind Date* Green Team—Joel, Lance, Ron, Sean, and Greg—guerrilla shooting at its finest; to Steve "no relation" Shelley; to Dan Rifkin; to EurAuPair, which, unlike its fictitious counterpart, always answers its phone; to Natasha Gervorkyan, for the ducks, the drums, and the horses; to Janalee P. Caldwell; to Sebastien Baumann, for giving up your lunch hour to a total stranger; to Dr. Joel Batzofin and Dr. Victoria Paterno and the pharmacist at Gelson's; to Fabrice at LaCachette; to Mike Milligan, tree person, Sarah Priest, plant person, Heike Knorz, party girl, and the Meano Man; to Karen Joy Fowler and Carolyn Clark Shoemaker; to Patty and Robert Flournoy, for friendship and love of math; to Dan Reinehr; to Judi Sadowsky; to Stefanie Pinneo, Catrina Boca, Julie Renick, Earlene Fowler, Nelly Valladares, Chuck Lascheid, and Arie Kapteyn; to Shent Nee; to Michael States; to Juli Gottlieb-Juteau;

to AJ Draven, Alan Predolin, Brent Wilkening, Jesse Shelley, Dave Famili, John Whitman, Kevin Bass, Marcus Kowal, Marni Levine, Romeo Portillo, Wade Allen, Sam Sade, and especially Vivian Cannon, the nicest bunch of people you'd never want to meet in a dark alley; to Carol Topping, Webgirl extraordinaire; to Cousin Beth; to Claire Carmichael and Gregg Hurwitz, who know everything and never tire of explaining it to me; to the Wednesday Night Group: Bob Shayne, Roger Angle, Linda Burrows, John Shepphird, Jonathan Beggs, and Nick Gillott, who shared my concern over each comma and every dead body; to Agatha and Rugi, Leah, Alessandra, Lisa and Batt, Rob and Jenny, Aunt Sandy and Uncle Jim; to Wendy and Gary Tigerman; to my sisters, Mary, Ann, Dory, and Joanie, and my brothers, Andrew, Joe, and Pete. Some year, huh? To Malibu Dan, and to Mrs. Malibu, for those hours he spent reading when he could have been rubbing your feet; to Joy Johannessen: *No livnar det i lundar;* to Stacy Creamer and Tracy Zupancis, my editors, and Rachel Pace and Meredith McGinnis, who go the extra ten miles, and to Joe Blades; to Amy Schiffman; to Renee Zuckerbrot, my amazing agent; to Uli Buchta and Anja Kubertschak, *alle meine Entchen,* who spent a year in our house and will spend a lifetime in our hearts; and to Greg, Audrey, Louie, and Gia, my ongoing happy ending.